ANOTHER WAY OVER

ALSO BY
JOHN J. MICHALIK

*The Extraordinary Managing Partner: Reaching
The Pinnacle of Law Firm Management*

*The Harriman Alaska Expedition of 1899: Scientists,
Naturalists and Others Document America's Last Frontier*

ANOTHER WAY OVER:
A NOVEL OF
Immigration
TO *America*

JOHN J. MICHALIK

outskirts
press

For Diane

AUTHOR'S NOTE

While *Another Way Over* is a novel, the story it tells is inspired by the travels of my paternal grandfather in immigrating to the United States in the early 1900s.

He was one of many in the peasant populations of Central Europe who, in the late nineteenth and early twentieth centuries, sought a new life in America. For those people, "the way over" typically involved a journey of more than three thousand miles that began with making their way — by various routes, depending on the location of their home villages — across parts of Bohemia, Austria, the Polish homeland, and Germany to one of the great embarkation ports of Hamburg and Bremen. From there, the usual sea voyage — two to three weeks, depending on the weather — was by steamship through the North Sea and across the vast expanses of the Atlantic Ocean to any one of a number of American harbors, but principally New York City, where immigrants were received.

As a young man, my grandfather exhibited courage and determination in pursuing his dream of a better life. In common with many others who set out from the Old World to the New — most of whom spoke little or no English and were unsure of exactly what they would do and what life would be like at their destination — he persevered and overcame uncertainties, unexpected obstacles, and what had in every case to be ever-changing fears and anxieties that were unknown in the life that he left behind. As with few other such immigrants, his way over was quite different: while enroute, he faced dramatic and wrenching changes in his plans that took him to places he had never heard of, threatened his cherished dreams, and surely tested his resolve and commitment.

The story follows, in large part, the route and the timeline of his journey. And, to the very limited extent to which an often reticent man cared to share them, the bare bones of some of his experiences along the way provide the seeds for parts of the story in the pages that follow.

That said, this is a work of fiction. Names, characters, dialogue, and correspondence, as well as the events that appear in this novel, are either products of my imagination or are used and presented fictitiously: any resemblance to actual persons, living or dead, as well as the circumstances of their lives and their experiences, is entirely coincidental. A partial exception to the previous statement relates to the main character: Jan was the given name of my paternal grandfather, and I have used that name in the story because his journey is the inspiration for this book. Still, though the fictional Jan Brozek you will meet in the following pages has much in common with my grandfather, those shared characteristics do not in any way imply that the story of the fictional Jan is in all respects and details the story of his real namesake. And as is often the case with a work of this sort, the telling of the story at times involves references to historical figures, settings, locales, and events — some well-known, some far less so. Those are accurately presented, though they are all passing in nature and in any case do not change the fictional character of this book.

John J. Michalik
September 2021

PART ONE
Across Europe

Chapter 1

The late-afternoon sun at Jan's back cast his long shadow on the hard, gray dirt of the cart path. He followed the shadow as it led him home and envied it just a bit, for while it roughly shared his shape and form, the shadow was free of the churning he felt in his stomach. Despite not having eaten since early morning, he knew that his discomfort was far less a sign of hunger than of the mixed feelings and the nervousness that came from being only a few hours away from leaving his family, and the only home he had ever known, forever. If everything went according to plan in the coming weeks, he would never again walk this path or spend another day in the familiar and — if only because of its familiarity — safe world in which generations of his family had grown up and lived out their lives. In the normal course of life in those earlier generations, such a leaving would have seemed almost incomprehensible, more wrong than right, and far more perilous than safe.

In the distance, the tall steeple of the evangelical church provided the first sign of the village of Važec. He was walking east from the neighboring village of Východná, where he had spent the better part of the day in the last of many visits with the transplanted German shopkeeper and tobacconist Johan Schmidt. They had met and formed a fast friendship some years before, near the end of

Jan's military service. German was the language of command in the Imperial and Royal Army of the Habsburg Empire, but Jan had not been comfortable with his fluency in that language, and his friendship with Schmidt had grown to include the twice-weekly lessons and drills that had progressed to the point that, as they had parted this afternoon, Schmidt had clapped him on the back and declared him "proficient." He himself wasn't sure of his proficiency, but he believed that his German would, with his native Slovak and his easy grasp of the related Polish language, be good enough to get him through Central Europe on the journey he would begin the next day.

Važec, Východná, and other rural Slovak villages were strung along the valley below the High Tatra Mountains, which formed a rugged frontier with the Polish homeland to the north. Walking was the usual local method of travel, and distances were measured by how long it took to get from one place to another. Východná was not much more than an hour from Važec, though today Jan's pace was slower than it had been on all those other days when, his lessons over, he had walked this way in the fading light of early evening. On those occasions, he had made better time, hurrying through the growing darkness to get home after a long day of hard work that began at sunrise.

Today was also different in that, not long after sighting the church steeple, he saw his father off to the side of the path just ahead. He was sitting on some large rocks, smoking his pipe in the meager shade of a small cluster of budding trees. The occasions were rare and far between when his father didn't work at something right up until dinnertime; much less be found taking his ease under a tree.

Michal Brozek was shorter and stockier than his oldest son, but apart from the disparity in height and build, they were very much alike. Father and son had the warm, weathered complexion and appearance of men who spent most of their lives doing hard outdoor work; Michal's tanned face also had begun to show the lines and furrows of a man well into middle age. Their hair was a distinguishing feature: both had—and had had, since each was a small boy—thick, predominantly dark hair that was prematurely streaked with gray. That coloring extended to the father's broad mustache and also became evident in the son's facial hair on those occasions when he didn't shave for a day or two. They shared penetrating deep-brown eyes under heavy eyebrows, and serious, determined expressions that could easily give way to broad smiles and laughter. And the son had inherited not only much of his father's appearance and considerable physical strength, but also his stoic outlook, calm disposition, and tenacious will.

As Jan approached, Michal reached into his vest pocket and extricated a second pipe, which he held out to his son.

"You left this behind this morning, and I thought you'd need it by now," he said, apparently in explanation of his presence under the trees.

"I do," Jan replied, taking the pipe. "But that is not why you are out here."

"I suppose it's not. And how is our friend Herr Schmidt?"

"He is fine and sends his regards. He also sends you this, with his compliments." From his rucksack, Jan retrieved a thick pouch of tobacco.

Michal took the pouch and carefully opened it to feel and smell its contents. "Very nice. Such fresh tobacco is hard to come by. Please thank him for me, though I guess that now I will have to do that myself. Did he have any news?"

"Very little—only that what is called 'nationalistic energy' is spreading throughout Europe. Leaders are posturing, armies are maneuvering, and his friends in Germany say the production and stockpiling of weapons in every country is proceeding without any

check. It seems that many fear that the presence of all that firepow-
er is a huge temptation and that widespread war is inevitable — and
is seen by some in power as highly desirable."

"Soon?"

Jan shrugged his shoulders. "According to Johan, no one knows,
and it is anyone's guess. He thinks it will someday reach a point
where something silly or meaningless will wound some important
person's pride and start a chain reaction that no one will be able, or
perhaps even want, to stop."

"It is, then, well that you are going now," Michal observed,
though Jan could sense the tinge of resignation in his father's voice.
"If war develops, whether sooner or later, traveling anywhere may
become impossible unless one is marching as part of an army.
Hopefully, you will be settled in America before that happens."

Jan watched as his father knocked the spent tobacco from his
pipe onto one of the rocks at his feet and prepared to refill it with
some of Herr Schmidt's finest. Both of his parents understood and
supported his decision to emigrate. At the same time, they knew
that if their oldest son was successful in making a new life in
America, they would almost assuredly never see each other again.
And as parents, they might then also have to face the prospect of
one or more of his brothers following his lead, though, at least to
this point, none of them had voiced any thoughts of that sort.

They both packed their pipes and fussed with lighting them
from the embers of the recently discarded tobacco. Jan shifted his
position and studied his father. As he had so many times before,
he wondered whether his desire to find a better life for himself and
his future family by emigrating created internal conflicts for his father — either because he had not taken such a step when he was
younger, or from feeling that Jan's decision might be based on not
wanting to be like his father and not being satisfied with following
in his footsteps. Michal had never expressed those sorts of feelings

and was unwavering in his spoken support of his son's plans. While Jan knew that if those conflicting feelings existed they would never be revealed, he still hoped that his father did not in any way take his departure personally. In truth, he hoped the children he might one day have would respect and admire him as much as he did his father.

"Though we have talked about this often and knew the day would come, this will be a difficult evening and night for your mother," Michal said after a long silence. "And tomorrow and the next day and many, many next days will be much the same for her.... and also for me. Not because we do not wish you well, but because a large part of our lives and our hearts will be leaving us. It is a very different thing than was the loss of your brother, and then your sister, when they were small and not even ready to crawl. That is a part of life almost every family has to bear. It is different when you have such a fine son for so many years and then you must say goodbye, even though you know that the times have changed and that the son is only doing what he feels he must do, and which his parents are proud of him doing, just as they are proud of why he is doing it. Parents are not good parents if they do not wish the best for their children, even if it carries some pain for them, as it also does for your brothers and your sisters. I also know how painful it is for you to leave us, and I suppose I came out here to have this last talk to be sure you understand that we know you feel the pain as well."

"I could wait another day or two," Jan said, his voice low and faltering. "It wouldn't matter that much, and—"

"A fine thought, but no," his father interrupted. "It is inevitable, and it will be no different, perhaps even worse, to delay. And you know that is true." Using his boot to grind out any remaining life in the spent embers on the rock, he stood and pulled his son to his feet. "Come. Your mother has been cooking, means to feed you well and to spend a late evening in the close company of her first-born child. I am nearly starved myself, and the sun will soon be setting."

As they set off on the cart path with the sun lowering in the west behind them and reflecting on the church steeple ahead, they could see Jan's younger brothers, Michal and Ondrej, coming out from the village to meet them.

In the Brozeks' Slovak homeland, the impetus for immigration to America in the late 1800s and the early years of the twentieth century was set in the circumstances of peasant life. As part of the Hungarian Kingdom within the Habsburg Empire, Slovaks and other minorities suffered under the repressive policies of the Hungarian government. However, emigration was driven less by a desire to escape what had become accustomed oppression than it was by a combination of demographic and economic circumstances.

The Emperor Joseph freed the Slovak peasants from the bondage of serfdom in the 1780s. Until that time, they were considered chattel: fixtures or a part of the land on which they lived and toiled. When one noble sold an estate or some other parcel of land to another, the serfs were simply a part of the transaction. They tilled the land, maintained the nobles' roads and estates, and were permitted to build their own humble homes and provide for their basic needs within the limits of their particular master's generosity. Formal education was minimal, and the people knew little of politics, economics, and the workings of government. In the country villages, there were no newspapers in the Slovak language. The people were parochially self-centered; oblivious to, and generally ignorant of, the world beyond.

Things changed and evolved slowly in the decades after emancipation. One of the biggest changes involved the implementation of a new pattern of land ownership. The owners of the landed estates were required to assign to the freed peasants modest tracts of land from among those which the peasants had previously tilled for their masters. Since each former serf might have raised potatoes in one location as part of a larger potato field, and grain or cabbage in other locations, the new peasant landowners often found themselves with several small parcels situated in different directions and at varying distances from the village where they lived.

The distribution of land accompanying the end of serfdom was a one-time affair. There was no provision for any additional allocations to keep pace with what had become an explosive growth in population: in the century following emancipation, the Slovak population grew by nearly 20 percent, to three million. When a Slovak peasant landowner died, it had become customary to divide his lands equally among his male heirs, who were becoming more numerous with each generation. As the greater number of sons in succeeding generations inherited the land, it became increasingly partitioned: smaller and smaller holdings strained to support larger families.

Additional land could be acquired from only two sources. One was other peasant landowners who became discouraged and were willing to sell their small parcels to others; though the new owner would frequently find that the added value of the property acquired was more than offset by the total tax burden he now carried. The other potential source of additional land was by purchase from the nobility – who had little interest in selling off small parcels at the prices that peasants could afford.

With little new land available, the partitioned landholdings became incapable of supporting even subsistence farming, and it became necessary for people to find other employment. A very few found it permanently in not-too-distant cities where the industrial age was beginning to have an impact. Others returned to working on the landed estates: men as temporary farm laborers during the fall harvests and young girls as household servants. And for those in the long valley below the High Tatras, some seasonal employment could be found in the mountains at the great health resort of Štrbské Pleso, which was frequented by the wealthy and the titled, including Germany's Kaiser Wilhelm II.

It was easy to recognize the progressively worsening conditions brought about, in an agrarian economy, by the limited amount of productive farmland and the expanding population. Nor was it difficult to perceive that things could be better, and that "better" could be found outside the Habsburg Empire. In spite of their generally isolated existence, the peasants in the small villages heard wonderful stories of America, and it began to enter the dreams of those who were seeking a better future.

<center>~~~≈≈≈~~~</center>

Dinner featuring potato dumplings, cabbage, and fermented sheep cheese had gone well. They had lingered long, reminiscing about family history and past events, and talking about Matej, the next-oldest of the four boys and now in his second year of military service in the same unit and with the same commanding officer Jan had served under. During dinner, his mother had laughed often, though occasionally casting a sad sidelong glance at Jan, especially when the conversation touched again on being careful about what they told others of his absence—they would say only what was, at least for the time being, the truth: that, as in years past, he had once again gone to Štrbské Pleso to work in preparing the resort for the summer season.

Later, with the village in growing darkness, he and his mother sat alone on the worn log bench outside the door. A low lantern burned in the quiet house behind them, and dim lights shown in a few of the other houses in sight. Važec was a poor village that went to sleep early, reflecting a community that arose with the sun, worked hard, and, not incidentally, had little that could be done by the meager lantern, candle, and firelight available when the sun was down. They said little; he knew that what mattered to his mother was just being at his side.

Like virtually all of those in the village, the home behind them was of fieldstone construction, with a heavily thatched roof built upon ancient central timbers. With three sleeping rooms, it was perhaps half again as large as most others. It had an adjoining structure and a small yard housing the family's livestock: currently two oxen, three milk cows, three hogs, a few sheep, and a number of chickens. Though large, the family was better off than many others in the village. That was in part due to the fact that over time, and for the most part by trading similar-size plots for others, all of the family's land, with the exception of one distant field, was in adjoining plots that could be worked more efficiently than scattered parcels. Just as importantly, there had been no partitioning of the land for two generations. Having five sisters and no brothers, Jan's father had inherited all the land from his father, who previously also had inherited all of it from his father when both of his brothers died in their youth. With four healthy boys in the current household, a potentially disastrous partition loomed ahead. A four-way split of the land that now sufficed to support the parents, four sons, and two daughters would yield four farms, each barely sufficient to support one of the sons and his future wife, much less the children they would have.

Thus, in addition to their genuine desire that he pursue the life he dreamed of, it was in part for practical reasons affecting their entire family that Jan's parents accepted and supported his emigration. They also were not opposed to the possibility that Matej, or "Matty," as his mother called him, might have the opportunity afforded few Slovak soldiers of becoming an officer in the emperor's army and making a career out of military service—though the discussion at dinner of Herr Schmidt's views on the possibilities of widespread war had been unsettling to her.

"Janko," his mother was the only person who ever referred to him in the diminutive, "Maria sat and visited with me a while this afternoon. She is anxious to see you before you leave. She is so brave...." The sentence and the thought hung in the air for a moment. "She said to remind you that you should come by this evening. No matter how late, she and her father will wait for you."

"I haven't forgotten. You see the dim light there at the Kresiaks'? I suspect that burns for me."

"She herself has a bright flame that burns for you, Janko. Though it will only be a few months, it will be hard for her to wait to hear you are in America and that she can join you. You know that she is *not* to be disappointed!"

"I know," Jan said, laughing. "I will not disappoint her, and I dare not disappoint you by disappointing her."

"You could not have made a better choice, nor could we have made a better one for you. She is very smart, is a hard worker, speaks and cooks well, has great compassion, and will be a wonderful mother. And she comes from a family where the women have strong wills and live long lives!"

Maria, Jan knew, was all of those things. In addition to the responsibility he felt as the eldest son to take the initiative and alleviate the potential family land issues and create better prospects for his brothers, it was Maria, and the chance for them to have a better life together despite the looming initial separation, that was the major reason for his emigrating. They had talked often about that, and about what Jan saw as the opportunity to also provide better prospects for their children and for the following generations than they could possibly create for them in Važec or anywhere nearby. When he had first talked that way, she had laughed at the idea of thinking of the futures of those in generations yet to be born, particularly distant generations she herself would never know, but that passion had also grown in her. And in this they differed in their dreams from many of their countrymen who had already journeyed to America by the thousands.

Many of those who emigrated—single men and married men traveling alone—did so without any intention of settling in America permanently. They were not immigrants, but migrants who lived cheaply, worked hard to accumulate sufficient funds, and then returned home to buy land and use their relative wealth in other ways to raise the living standards of their families. For Jan, and then Maria, this seemed a temporary solution to the overarching contemporary problems of Slovak life—and no solution at all to the inevitable problems in the years ahead and in the lives of the children they would raise, much less those in succeeding generations.

"I am sure, Mother, that you and she will *both* live a very long time," he said, holding her hand. "And I am also sure I should go over there. Her father will not appreciate me keeping him up too late."

"If he complains, you tell Michal Kresiak that I will twist his ears like I did when we were children!" She smiled at the memory and squeezed his hand. "You will leave with the herders in the morning?"

"I will," he said, standing and helping her up. With a quick hug, she gently pushed him away and turned to go inside. He watched her disappear into her bedroom with the lantern, closed the door to the house, and stepped off the low porch.

He could have found his way in pitch blackness, but a nearly full moon in a clear sky lit the path. The village was still, with the silence only occasionally broken by the muted sounds of people and farm animals bedding down for the night. In a space between two darkened buildings, he saw a raccoon skittering on a narrow path: probably in search of eggs in some neighbor's chicken shed.

He was still two houses away from the Kresiaks' home when he made out the forms of father and daughter on the front bench, backlit by a lantern hanging from the porch roof. They were talking in hushed tones, the conversation punctuated by her distinctive soft laughter. In the dim light, he could make out her familiar form, the long dark hair hanging down her back tied in a horse's tail with a length of brightly colored ribbon, and the movement of her hands, which were as much a part of her speech as the words she spoke.

As he reached the house, the father arose, extinguishing the pipe he had been smoking.

"Unless you have need of me, which I doubt," he said, "I myself am in need of sleep. But remember, I sleep lightly, and I know the ways of young men. I'll leave the lantern — Maria, put it out and bring it in when Brozek here has gone home." He pushed the pipe into his pocket and began to turn toward the door, but stopped and extended his hand to Jan. They shook hands with matching strong grips, and then he disappeared into the house.

They sat and talked quietly for long hours, once again going over their plans and dreams. Their goal in America was settling in Minneapolis, which had become the destination — originally for reasons no one could remember, but now because of the numbers who had settled there — for many of those who had permanently left the northern Slovak villages for the New World. Over the past two years, they had somehow managed to accumulate sufficient funds, at least from what they had learned from the travels of others, to pay for the costs of Jan's trip, plus a smaller amount to be used toward the similar expenses that Maria would incur in following him. Once in America, Jan would have to earn the remaining funds necessary for her travel and then send that money back to her. It seemed reasonable to believe that Jan would arrive in

Minneapolis sometime in July and that, with just the smallest bit of luck, she would be able to begin her journey perhaps six or seven months later. Maria's younger brother Daniel would emigrate with her, and he was also now well along to having earned and saved the money to cover his costs.

As he watched and listened to Maria talk, Jan thought of how difficult it was for each of them to leave their families. In Maria's case, her family was known to be especially close, even more so than his own. She was very devoted to her parents. He knew that for her to leave them and start a new life halfway around the world was not an easy task. That she would do this was an incredible measure of her devotion and her trust in him. She was not, as his mother had said, to be disappointed..

After a while, their conversation faded, and they sat silently watching as, one by one, the lights in Važec, save for the one behind them, went out. Off to their left, the measured hooting of an owl rolled across the village. Well after midnight, they embraced for a long time before he helped her take down the lantern. His hand rested on hers for a moment, and she looked up and silently met his gaze. While there were no tears, he sensed a sadness that burrowed deep within her eyes and, somehow, seemed to reflect more — what, he could not tell — than sorrow at his leaving. After Maria had gone inside, he took a deep breath, examined the night sky for some minutes, and haunted by the look in her eyes, slowly retraced his steps home.

⸻

At 6:00 a.m. the following morning, he was standing in the doorway; drinking a cup of hot tea and watching his mother stuff cloth-wrapped packages of rolled-up potato pancakes, sausages, and other foods in the nooks and spaces of his rucksacks. Though the rising sun was visible, the early-morning air was cold, and his frosty breath mingled with the steam from the tea. Looking up the path that wound through the village, he could see the herders and the livestock approaching.

Most of the herders were descendants of those who had become discouraged by the constant subdivision of property among numerous heirs, and had ultimately sold or bartered their remaining lands to others. After the proceeds were gone, they found themselves more or less destitute and were known, not derisively but only as a matter of fact, as "have nothings." Having only their village huts and no tillable acreage, they became the miscellaneous workforce of the village. The herders filled an important role. With most households having only a very few head of livestock, it made little sense for a member of each family to spend the entire day driving the family cows and sheep to the public pastures in the mountains and to then sit idly by for hours while they grazed. Instead, each provided the herders with potatoes, cabbage, or other produce, and sometimes a few coins, to collect and manage the combined herd of the livestock of many families.

He heard his father opening the wooden gate next to the house and turned to watch their cows and sheep as they crowded out and stood, as they did every morning, waiting to fall in with the moving herd as it passed by. The gate of their yard and others in the village would be reopened in the late afternoon as the herd returned, and — well trained by habit — each family's animals would unfailingly break off and turn into the proper yard.

To the north, the snow on the mountains, particularly on the high slopes of towering Mount Kriváň, was blinding white in the early sunlight. Spring had come late, preceded by a very hard winter, and that had changed some of his plans. The high mountain passes could be difficult to negotiate for as much as another month, if not two. It would only be when he got to Štrbské Pleso that he would be able to determine whether he would be able to cross those passes or whether he would have to travel farther east to lower country in order to reach his initial goal: the villages of the Brozek relatives on the Polish side of the High Tatras.

The jostling of the animals to his right as they moved to join the herd, and his mother's touch on his arm, brought him back to the task at hand. He waved to Samuel, one of the herders, and called out, "I'll walk with you a ways toward Strba this morning!"

His father lifted the two heavy rucksacks to his back, helped tighten and secure them, and handed Jan a hefty walking stick. His brothers and sisters had come out of the house, and he hugged each in turn, clasped his father's hands for a moment, and held his mother tightly for a long time, aware of her tears and holding back his own as she whispered, "I will love you, forever, wherever you are." He let her go only when Samuel's shrill voice called back, "Come along, then—the herd waits for no one!"

He started off after the animals, slapping a lagging cow on the rump to get her to catch up, and taking a quick look at the clock on the church steeple. After walking some distance, he stopped, looked back, and waved to his parents, who had moved out to the center of the broad cart path. As they all both feared and accepted, they would never see each other again.

Chapter 2

Štrbské Pleso

Jan was just starting to make his way up the hill from the railroad junction station at the village of Strba when he heard the woman's long, terrified scream; which was instantly drowned out by the even louder, squealing sound of hard iron sliding on hard iron. Like the few others with him on the path, he began to run.

The small crowd ahead at the rack railway terminus was frozen in place. Lying face down on the track between the rails, with the very end of the last car looming above her, was a young woman. She had tripped and fallen while running across the tracks ahead of the train as it completed its backward descent from Štrbské Pleso. In falling, her long skirts had become entangled with the center rack rail and with a stationary auxiliary gear that, once engaged, assisted in slowing the train to a stop. The exposed teeth of the gear had grabbed and twisted the mass of skirts, drawing the girl toward it while pulling the fabric into a noose around her midsection, leaving her nearly naked from the waist down. When she had fallen, her left arm had been thrown across the outside rail, and before she could pull it back, the billowing loose sleeve of her blouse and strands of her long blonde hair had been caught and pinned under the car's wheel as it ground to a halt. The fabric of the blouse made it hard to see, but the wheel looked to be just touching her arm. She was lying on the right side of her face, her nose and forehead inches from the wheel, trying through her tears to comply with the pleadings of a young man who was kneeling beside her, imploring her not to move.

The train's engineer had just come running up, and the young man cried out, "Is the train completely stopped and braked?"

"It is! I stopped as quickly as I could!" the engineer responded in an agitated voice. "The engine is secure and will not move, but there is some slack in the connection between the car ahead and this one, so it is not at the end of the rack! You can see by the worn surface of the rails that the wheels are still twenty-five or thirty centimeters from their normal stop and lock position. It is not much, but I don't know whether the car will hold or if it will release and roll that remaining distance."

It was obvious that if the wheels moved any farther the girl's arm would be amputated.

When no one moved, Jan began releasing the rucksacks on his back. As he twisted to drop the sacks to the ground, he caught sight of a burly man just joining the crowd and wearing the coat and armbands of the Emperor's Foresters.

"Woodsman!" he called, "I'll need your help! We're going to lift that car!"

For a moment, the forester didn't comprehend, but then he grasped the situation. Quickly, he set down the axe, a long branch-cutting knife, and the other tools he was carrying and began removing his heavy coat.

Turning to the young man, Jan said, "Whoever you are, take the woodsman's knife and cut away the girl's skirts so she is separated from the gear—but you must be sure she remains motionless and doesn't move her arm or try to get out!"

The young man nodded, retrieved the knife, and, getting down on his knees between the rails, began to cut the knotted fabric away from the gear.

"It would help to know your name, brave woodsman."

"Josef."

"Josef, I am Jan. The only way to save this girl before the train decides to complete its journey is to lift or at least push back the end of this car! I think we can do that if we carefully put our backs against the car so as not to disturb it, bend down enough to be able to grasp that low bar on the car, and then lift together with our legs and arms while pushing against the car with our backs. A position like this." And he demonstrated what he had in mind.

"I agree," Josef quickly replied, "but I doubt if we can raise it very high or hold it very long."

"A couple of centimeters should be enough. There is slack in the connection with the next car, so we do not have to push the whole train. Even just pushing this car back and holding it from moving down the track for a few seconds may be all we need," Jan said. Turning back to the young man, who was tossing the cut skirts aside, he continued, "When we two lift and push this, you must immediately pull her out, just a little farther down the tracks! There will be no time to be gentle. You will have to pull hard and fast, and if she is cut or scratched in the process, well, so be it."

"I understand. She is my sister. I will pull her out! It will only take ten seconds."

"That, and provided we can even lift this," said Josef, stretching his broad back, "may be nine seconds more than we have."

The two men positioned themselves with their backs barely touching the car, Jan on one rail above the girl's pinned arm and Josef on the opposite rail. Digging their boots into the gravel and squatting low enough to grasp the bar, they waited while the young man, continuing to calm his sister and reminding her to be still, got in position over her legs, ready to pull her back.

All three men exchanged looks and nods. "Now!" Jan cried.

The strain was enormous; something in Jan's lower back seemed to stretch and snap, and Josef cried out in pain. The car moved back behind them and seemed to rise fractionally, and they heard more than saw the girl as she was dragged back, before they both gave way and jumped to the side. The car settled and, as the engineer had predicted, rolled nearly thirty centimeters farther on the rails to its final locked position.

Jan sat on the ground, his forearms resting on his knees and his head resting on his forearms, totally spent from the few seconds of exertion. After a moment he opened his eyes and looked up. The girl was struggling to her feet: her knees and thighs, her left arm, and the side of her face were scratched and cut. She stood for only a moment, tugging to pull the remnants of her skirts down over her legs, before fainting into the arms of two men in the crowd.

Jan stood, with some difficulty, to approving murmurs and pats on the back from those nearby. He stepped across the track to Josef, whose right hand was bleeding profusely from deep cuts in the palm.

"The bar," Josef said, "it had a sharp edge. But it will heal."

"There was a doctor back in the station, waiting for a train," said a woman who had stepped out of the crowd and began to wrap Josef's hand in a long piece of fabric from the rescued girl's discarded skirts. "Come along with me."

As they started to move away, Jan clasped Josef's left hand, and the young man, whose sister was beginning to stir again, offered his thanks and the thanks of his family. He also asked the forester for his full name and his unit information. He then turned to Jan.

"And my sister's hero, are you going to Štrbské Pleso?" While he spoke Slovak, he seemed to be choosing and weighing each word, and his speech betrayed a definite Hungarian accent.

"I am," Jan nodded.

"Good!" the young man said, extending his hand. "I will talk to you further there. But right now I must tend to the woman who runs in front of trains."

Jan spoke briefly to some of those in the crowd, before catching the eye of the engineer and asking how long the train to Štrbské Pleso would be delayed.

"Not at all!" the engineer replied. "It is not damaged! And I am always on schedule!"

Jan nodded and walked slowly back to the station, mindful of his back and that it was probably best to keep moving and not allow whatever injury he had suffered to tighten up.

<hr />

An hour later, Jan was back, taking a seat in the car — the first coming downhill and the last going up — that he and the big forester had somehow lifted. There were only three other people in this last car, and none of them had been around at the time of the previous excitement, so he was able to find a seat alone and unbothered.

He had been seated for only a few minutes when the car lurched, accompanied by a loud hiss as the steam locomotive ahead began its climb. Although the total distance to be traveled was little more than five kilometers, the steep uphill grade, the weight of the locomotive and cars, and the need to move at a careful rate to ensure that each cog fell into place smoothly with the rack, meant the journey would take almost an hour.

The time gave him an opportunity to open his rucksacks and eat some of the food his mother had packed that morning. As he ate, he checked the oilskin-wrapped package that contained the money saved for food, train fares, and ships passage, and a second package that contained various papers, including his military Service Completion documents and an old but undated posting letter from his former commanding officer, Major Chara, transferring him to the command of Chara's brother in Krakow. That posting had been canceled, but Jan had saved the letter and thought to take it with him for possible use if his presence at some point in the early stages of his journey was ever questioned.

For peasants, questions involving travel and freedom of movement in Europe were most likely to arise on leaving the Habsburg Empire. On the one hand, immigration to America, or anywhere else, was one answer to the government's quest for solutions to the problems of Slovak overpopulation. Where the elderly, women, and children were concerned, leaving the country was a relatively easy proposition, provided standard forms were properly filled out. However, in the case of young men the situation was more complicated. Technically, if one had completed his required military service, fairly free and largely unquestioned movement was possible. In practice, ensuring the largest supply of able-bodied men under arms in the event of war was a priority. Guards at the frontier outposts were under orders to detain any man of an age of potential military usefulness. Jan had himself served at such an outpost: he knew from that experience that possession of Service Completion documents might or might not suffice.

Because of that situation and uncertainty, it had become a safer and more standard practice for a young man to start his journey to America illegally by first smuggling himself into the Russian provinces of Poland and traveling from there to Germany. The Russians, continually in these times at odds with their Austro-Hungarian neighbors, viewed each potential soldier leaving Habsburg lands as one less future enemy for them to face and they were known to facilitate defectors by assisting them in entering Germany, often accompanied by unofficial representation of these young men as Russian nationals. The Germans, for their part, were pleased by the sight of men of military age apparently fleeing Russia, with whom relations were often of the tinderbox variety, and presented no obstacle to them either settling in Germany or passing through on their way to Bremen or Hamburg.

Aware of all of these things, and bearing in mind the stories of their journeys that filtered back from America from those who had gone before, including those who had returned after making their "fortunes" in the United States, Jan felt he had planned reasonably well and was flexible enough to adjust his approach and route, depending on what he encountered along the way. An initial such adjustment might, depending on the conditions in the mountain passes, involve which route he would take to the villages of the Brozek families on the Polish side of the High Tatras.

While for the next three or four weeks he would work in preparing the resort for the summer season, and in doing so add a little more to the money in the oilskin package, he would also be gauging the snowpack, watching the passes, and looking for travelers who might be coming through them from the north.

He was lost in those thoughts when familiar sights in the deep woods along the tracks alerted him that they were approaching the lakeside station at Štrbské Pleso, and soon the train came to a shuddering halt. It took him some time to gather up his things and to test and stretch his back, which, though sore, was apparently none the worse for wear.

He was one of the last to leave the cars. As he stepped down from the train and moved forward along the track, Jan caught sight of the young man whose sister had been the subject of his recent exertions. He was talking excitedly to a tall man who had a neatly-trimmed dark beard and was wearing a buff-blue military uniform decorated with gold braid and a half-dozen medals and ribbons. The uniform was complemented by spotless high black boots and an enormous sword hanging from a thick black leather belt around his waist. Two other men in less resplendent uniforms, obviously aides to the tall man, stood off to one side.

The young man's report must have included a reference to Jan because the tall man turned his head to look in his direction, listened for another few seconds, and then, placing a calming hand on the young man's arm, stepped away toward the path Jan was taking. As he approached, Jan stopped and bowed from the waist.

"That," said the tall man, waving-off the bow, "is unnecessary. I do not yet have the full story, but I understand that I am in your undoubted debt for saving the life of my only daughter." His Slovak was impeccable, with but the slightest trace of the Hungarian accent that was so evident in his son's speech.

"Excellency, there is no debt involved when a man does what any man would do to assist someone in distress. In any event, I am not sure that her life itself was in mortal danger."

"In her life, as well as for her future prospects, the loss of an arm would be its own sure form of death. Your name and your home?"

"Jan Brozek. I am of Važec."

"And why are you here at Štrbské Pleso?"

"I am one of those who helps prepare the resort and the lodges for the summer. It is something I have done for the last two years."

"Wonderful!" the tall man smiled. Beginning to turn away and nodding toward the young man, he added, "We will both be here for a while and will have a chance to talk further; my son here will arrange it."

"I am honored to be at your service," Jan replied. He watched as, with his two aides in tow, the tall man moved to talk to the train engineer. He turned to the son and said: "You know my name, but I do not know yours or your father's."

"My apologies; I am Anatoly Ihnacak. My father is Baron Anton Ihnacak. He is," Anatoly said matter-of-factly, "of the Royal Court and temporary commandant of the garrison in the town of Poprad. We are here to supervise some additions to the lodge. It is not public knowledge," he added, lowering his voice, "and I should not mention this, but the additions are for the comfort of the Archduke Franz Ferdinand, and his wife, the Duchess Sophie, who are expected here in late June. Actually, of course, it is my father who is doing the supervising. Anna and I have come on holiday and to keep him company — though, with the accident today, the holiday has not started well."

"I will, of course, keep the news of the Archduke to myself. And how is your sister?"

"She is scratched and cut a bit. She is very thankful, but I think too embarrassed to tell you so herself. It is bad enough to have fallen like a child, but exposing her bare legs in front of her little brother and dozens of strangers has mortified her. She fears she has also embarrassed father and says she will not go out in public here."

"There were really only a handful of people, and very few of those came up on the train with us. Of those that did, I would wager that all but two or three have come up only for the afternoon and will be on board when the train returns to Strba this evening. What matters is her well-being. Please give her my regards for her health and healing."

"I will do so immediately, and I'm sure she will be pleased," Anatoly said. "Also, I will talk with father at dinner as to when he will see you as he suggested. It may be a few days, but it appears we will all be here for some weeks, so I am sure there will be a number of opportunities. I must go. Have a good evening."

"You as well," Jan replied. He turned to continue on the path and saw that Karol Bohus was standing off to the side, waiting patiently. Karol was a distant relative of the man who had built the original hunting lodge and some of its many later additions. When the government had acquired the lodge and surrounding lands, it had retained Karol to manage its maintenance and expansion.

"I've been anxious for your arrival!" said Karol, clapping Jan on the back. "We have some busy days ahead of us and more than the usual spring work to do, including some new construction. Will you stay as long as three weeks or a month? We need to get you settled in, and then let's find some tea and we can look at the plans. I have started some things with the workers I have, but they are all new, some brought from Poprad, and this year, since you know things here so well, I will need you to be a supervisor when I am not around. Come, we must hurry."

Jan was used to Karol's chatter, and "We must hurry" was a phrase that ended many of Karol's spoken thoughts. He returned the clap on the back and followed along dutifully.

⟨~⟩

The last few days of May soon gave way to June, with generally clear skies occasionally yielding to a day of rain or mist that seemed to linger and hang in the trees long after the sun broke through. Although spring was in the air, the nights were cold, and the first light of most mornings struck a quiet, frost-covered world.

The glacial lake from which the resort settlement took its name had cleared of ice, except for accumulations visible at the far distant northwest shore. The water remained very cold, which had slowed the work of Jan and a crew of two others in getting the new and much larger docks settled into the shore and anchored out in the lake. That work was done; much of the needed repair of ice and frost damage to the long sloping lawns was completed; and the excursion boats had been refitted and set out on the shore, waiting to be painted before being floated and secured to the docks. A crew of carpenters was hard at work, often into the evening hours, on the addition of a modest wing to one of the lodge buildings. And painting and refurbishing had begun on the rack railway cars, as well as in all building common areas that Archduke Franz Ferdinand and his party might see or pass through later in the month.

Jan had seen little of the Ihnacak family. The meeting with the Baron had yet to occur, though Anatoly had twice sought him out to assure him it would be arranged "soon." One early morning, while working on the docks, he had noticed Anna leaning against the railing of a balcony on the second floor of the main lodge, watching the project; and later, toward mid-day he had seen her in a lower first floor window, again apparently following the work closely.

He had been doing his own watching: looking for travelers and hikers coming around the lake from the north, signifying the mountain passes might be open. No one had appeared, and from the south shore of the lake it was clear that the snow-line on the heights to the north was still low, receding slowly, and likely still too deep for passage.

In the pre-dawn hours of a Friday morning Jan donned his boots, stuffed an extra shirt and a heavy wool sweater into a rucksack, and made his way to the lodge. In the already busy kitchen, crowded with cooks preparing for breakfast, he reopened the sack to add sausages, a dozen hot biscuits, and a canteen of water. With a long-handled axe over his shoulder, and a saw and a shovel strapped securely to his back, he headed out to begin the task of clearing the lodge's many kilometers of riding and hiking trails of the winter's accumulation of downed trees and broken branches.

He enjoyed the hiking and the solitary work, which he would do alone at first but, if the winter damage was widespread, would require the help of other men if it were to be completed by the opening of the lodges in another ten days. This day, he worked the heavily wooded west side of the lake. The damage was minor, with the exception of one large, downed tree that it took him over two hours to clear. He worked continuously throughout the day, with short breaks to eat and drink, and a few pauses to look out over the cold, still lake. He also took care, mid-afternoon, to begin taking branching trails that would ultimately wind back to the lodge so that he could work as he returned and not waste time on a return route over trails he had already traveled and cleared.

Coming over a small rise where the trail cut through a grassy meadow before climbing a short hill to the lodge area perhaps half a kilometer farther on, he slowed to a silent stop when he caught sight of Anna Ihnacak in the meadow. Barefoot and with her skirts tied up above her knees, she was feeding a deer, with two other deer approaching her warily. He watched for a few minutes, and then moved far enough off the trail to not only get downwind from the deer but to also come into Anna's line of sight. She saw him and started, but then smiled and continued coaxing the deer.

Now that she had seen him, he retraced his steps and looped around so as to come up behind her, clearly in the field of vision of the deer. They all straightened-up with their ears alert and legs stiff, but apparently satisfied with his slow pace and the girl's lack of alarm, and very much interested in the food she held out, they soon relaxed.

He stopped some distance behind her, carefully set down his load and tools, picked the last of the biscuits and crumbs out of his pack, and sat down in the long grass. When Anna's food was gone, she looked over her shoulder to see what he was doing, then walked back and sat down next to him. He gave her some of the biscuits, and after a few moments the deer came slowly forward to sample the new treats. Perhaps ten quiet minutes passed before the biscuits were gone and then, as the deer looked at them inquisitively, a delighted laugh from Anna sent them scampering off.

"Oh, such fun!" she exclaimed and then, aware of her skirts, began untying them and pulling them down over her knees. "I seem to be in some unacceptable state of dress, or perhaps undress, whenever we meet!" she wailed softly, and then blushed as she thought of their first encounter on the railroad track. Her command of the Slovak language matched her father's.

Jan leaned back in the grass with his hands behind his head and, changing the subject, asked "How are you feeling? Are the scratches healed?"

"Are they? Are there any left?" she asked as she turned to lean over and look down at him.

He looked up at her flushed face, the deep-blue eyes, and the sunlit blonde hair. He realized he had stopped breathing. "I . . .. I can't see any," he stammered.

"There are a few left .... but you aren't allowed to see *those*!" she laughed and, as she straightened up, exclaimed, "Why, you're blushing!"

"Men don't blush," he growled, quickly deciding that purposefully staring at the clouds was a wise course of action.

"Really? There is nearby evidence that that's not true." She paused and looked away for a moment. When she spoke again, her voice was almost a whisper. "I am sorry I have not been able to thank you for saving me. I was very frightened and had no idea what I was going to do or how I would get out from under that railroad car. And no one seemed to be ready to help. You were very thoughtful and brave. And I am embarrassed that I have been too embarrassed to speak to you and thank you."

"You have now, so let's let that be in the past," he replied, continuing to study the clouds. "And what are you doing out here? These trails are not open for hiking yet."

She ignored the scolding. "I was tired of being inside, and warm sun was what I needed. And then I followed the deer, and when I got to this meadow they seemed more comfortable and waited for me. Isn't it wonderful here?"

"It is," he said, sitting up, "but perhaps we should go to the lodge. The sun is getting low. And it would probably not be a good thing for a Princess — are you a Princess? — to be found lying in the grass in the woods with a peasant."

She pushed him back down and laughed. "Perhaps, but it is you who is lying in the grass, not me. And I am not a Princess. I am just a young woman out in a meadow thanking a man who saved her life and who also seems to enjoy things like feeding these precious deer."

He sat up again, stood, and extended his hand. Her soft hand was lost in his as he pulled her to her feet. "And where, Not-A-Princess, are your shoes?"

"I have a new nickname!" she giggled. "And my shoes are, well, they are somewhere in this grass."

After a few minutes of searching, the wayward shoes were back on her feet and they moved down the path, with Anna telling him of her life in Vienna and Poprad as they walked slowly through the meadow and soon crossed the broad lawn toward the lodge buildings. He left her at the lakeside entrance to the main lodge, walked around the corner, and was heading toward the stables to return the tools when he ran into Anatoly.

"My father would like to see you before dinner; can you meet him on the lakeside porch at six o'clock?"

"Certainly. What time is it now?"

Anatoly consulted his large pocket watch. "Half after five."

"Then six o'clock will be fine, but I have no fit clothes for a meeting with a baron."

"He said you should come as you are. Wash up a bit, I suppose. And have someone brush the grass off your back."

———※※※———

As cleaned up as he could possibly be, freshly shaved, and with his hair combed, Jan waited until his own pocket watch told him it was almost six. He walked around the lodge building until he saw Baron Ihnacak seated in a long, hazy beam of early-evening sunlight at the lone round table at the far northwest corner of the porch. As he climbed the stairs, the Baron smiled and motioned to both the chair opposite him and the teapots and cups on the table.

"I am honored to join you, sir," Jan said, standing by the table, "though I am not certain of the proper manners and protocol when one is about to have tea with a baron."

"The first thing is to sit down. And we are not at Court, so I suspect that if you behave as I am sure your fine Slovak parents have taught you, we'll both be comfortable. The tea is excellent and hot; please help yourself. It will take off the early chill, though if you would rather have something colder to drink, I can arrange that as well."

"The tea will be fine," Jan replied, while somehow simultaneously sitting and pouring.

"I have been thinking about how it is that I can somehow satisfy my debt to you for saving my daughter. As for the forester, Josef, I have arranged his promotion. That was easy. Your case is harder."

"I truly have, sir, all the thanks I need in just your expressions of gratitude and in knowing that your daughter is well and unharmed. I did not assist her with the thought of any reward."

"Of course not, but that's not the point. Tell me a little about yourself; if you don't mind."

Jan wasn't exactly sure if a peasant could "mind" when asked such a question by a baron, but in any event, he felt comfortable with Ihnacak and proceeded, somewhat to his own surprise, to speak of Važec, his family, his military service and that of his brother, as well as the work at Štrbské Pleso and his planned trip across the High Tatra Mountains to see the Brozek families in southern Poland. When he mentioned Major Chara, the Baron interrupted to say: "I know him well. A very fine officer."

"He is also the commanding officer of my brother Matej, and I believe will recommend and sponsor him to be an officer."

"Few Slovaks have become officers or even been admitted to the officer's school," the Baron observed. "Chara himself is one and a great example. And of those two colonels, my aides, you see walking down the lawn below, one is Slovak and the other Czech, and they are outstanding men. Sometimes our army needs a push to provide opportunity to those who it would otherwise ignore."

The Baron looked closely for a long moment at the young man across the table from him. "Perhaps I can repay you in part by influencing the process for your brother. Mind you, he cannot get the appointment if he does not completely deserve it. But I will speak to Chara when I next see him, likely in Pressburg in August. If Major Chara is willing to sponsor and recommend him, I will see that he is fully considered on his merits and not eliminated because of peasant and Slovak origin. If he is at all like you seem to be, I would consider him far superior to some of the Austrian and Hungarian dolts we are afflicted with in the officer corps simply because of where they were born or who their parents may be."

"That is most gracious of you, sir. It is far in excess of any repayment I am due."

"It is a trifle. You have told me much about yourself; let me tell a little of my family and of Anna. We were four at one time. My wife, Caroline, who I had known since we were toddlers and even before we had learned to speak, died of a massive stroke three years ago. I was in Krakow at the time, and she was at our home in Vienna with Anna, who was then seventeen, and Anatoly, who had just turned fifteen. Caroline was the center of all of our lives, especially Anna's. They were inseparable, and Anna was, and still is, developing into her mother's twin in beauty, grace, curiosity, and intelligence. Like Caroline, she is remarkably fluent in Hungarian, German, and Slovak. And now she is learning Polish! I think that she wants to prove that she can master as many languages as her father!"

The Baron smiled and paused for a moment, but the smile slowly faded. "Caroline's death was devastating to us all, but particularly to Anna. She was inconsolable, reclusive, and silent for many months, and I feared for her and her future. Also, Vienna had too many memories of Caroline for Anna to handle. So we returned to our true home and our roots, Budapest, for some months. Then we traveled rather extensively, and as we passed through, we all, especially Anna, were taken by the High Tatras and this country. When the temporary post at Poprad opened, I maneuvered to secure it, though some at Court considered it menial, and we have flourished there as a family. But Anna, I know, remains fragile. Anatoly says that the situation she was in when you found her was highly likely to cost her that arm. For a beautiful but presently still-fragile young woman, the loss of an arm would be its own form of death in terms of her self-confidence, future marriage prospects, and many other things. And for a devoted father, a hard thing to help her with and a sure form, if you will, of 'death' for him as well as for her."

He sipped his tea and looked out across the lake. "So, you see, she and I are both in your debt. Helping your brother achieve what it seems he deserves is a small thing. But it is a start. What will you do after your visit to the Polish Brozeks?"

Jan liked this man and instinctively trusted him, but he was Hungarian and an officer in an army whose border guards were a potential future obstacle, and he had no way of knowing the Baron's personal views of young men seeking to leave for America or anywhere else. He quickly determined to be vague.

"Return to Važec, I imagine. I am the oldest son, and there are responsibilities there."

"You should think bigger, my young friend. With due respect to your honored father, you seem, in my brief observation, to have more in you than being a peasant farmer or working at this resort. There is a bigger world, and, despite these times, it has opportunities beyond farming." Glancing again for a long moment at the darkening lake, he continued, "I do not know what your wages for working here these few weeks are, other than being undoubtedly inadequate. I will see that when paid those wages are doubled, no, tripled..."

"Sir," Jan interrupted, "I cannot thank you enough for that, but it is truly not necessary."

"Necessary, no, but deserved, yes," the Baron smiled, as he looked at his pocket watch and began to push his chair back from the table. "I must get ready for dinner. If, young Brozek, you find that with your newly found 'wealth' you would like to extend your time in our Polish territory, consider traveling to Krakow. I will be there by no later than the early days of July, once I have the Archduke and the Duchess settled-in here for their vacation. I will have Anatoly provide you with instructions as to how you can contact me there."

Jan stood also, unsure of how to adequately say "thank you" and also unsure of how to end the conversation. The Baron provided the answer by firmly clasping his hand, patting his shoulder, and turning toward the two aides, who had quietly appeared at the edge of the porch.

Watching them walk into the lodge, Jan glanced up at the second floor, where his gaze was drawn to a single illuminated window—just in time to see Anna pull back out of view behind the curtain.

The work clearing the trails consumed Jan's time and that of three other men for the next two weeks. He worked alone on the west side of the lake, dispatching the others to work the longer trails that looped into the mountains on the east side. Often, when he returned at day's end, he found Anna waiting for him in the sunlit meadow, where they would sit and talk before slowly walking back to the lodge together. On the last day of his trail work, at the far end of the lake, she hiked out alone with a basket of bread, containers of soup, and large blocks of chocolate to meet him and share a long mid-day meal on the shore. She stayed with him throughout the afternoon; following along, enjoying the sun, reading, and watching him work before they made their way back to the lodge as twilight set in.

Anna to him was a beautiful mystery. In a short time they had formed an easy, surprisingly close friendship, marked by laughter and honesty, and hampered only by their different stations in life. She had clearly been disappointed, though only briefly, when he spoke once of Maria; after that, and though it troubled him, he found himself taking care not to mention Maria in their conversations.

With the trail work done, only a long morning was needed to finish his business, draw his wages, arrange and pack his things, and write a letter to his family. He left the letter with Bohus, who promised to see that it was carried to Važec the next day. Later in the afternoon, as he set out to ride the railway down to Strba, he found Anatoly and Anna waiting to walk with him to the station. Anatoly was talkative and excited about the pending arrival of the Archduke. Anna walked slowly, spoke softly, and said very little. She watched him intently as he said his goodbyes. At length, standing in line to board the train, he turned to look back and their eyes met in a long, unblinking look that ended only when he felt a nudge from the man behind him.

It began to rain as the cars moved down the hill, and a downpour was in progress when the train ground to a halt. He jumped off and ran to the junction station building. There was only a short wait before the train east to Poprad was ready for boarding. As he settled into a crowded half-passenger, half-freight car, and the train began pulling away, the sound of the locomotive engine was drowned out by tremendous crashes of thunder.

Chapter 3

Poronin

In Poprad, Jan waited in the station until the rain had slackened to a drizzle and then made his way through the town to the Poprad River, which ran north into the Polish homeland region of the Habsburg Empire. He hoped to find passage on any sort of boat headed downstream toward Stary Sącz, a Polish city and railway junction located near the confluence of the Poprad and Dunajec Rivers.

A few questions of those working on and around the wooden boats at the riverfront led him to one Michal Slimitz, the grizzled owner of a small, shallow-draft barge that was destined first for the Slovak town of Stará Ľubovňa and then on to Stary Sącz. Slimitz was willing to exchange passage for the help of a strong deckhand, and Jan was soon at work in loading farm implements, a few small tables, a consignment of oil lamps packed and wrapped in rags, and a large number of loosely tied bales of coarse woolen cloth made of homespun yarn. The last of their cargo arrived late and was secured on board as the twilight deepened: it was too late to begin traveling.

Jan walked through the still-wet streets to the town square, where he bought a simple dinner of soup and bread at a bakery. It was well after dark when he returned to the riverfront, which was dotted with the single lanterns that glowed on the bow of each barge and small boat lying at anchor. The river was still, and the dock area was quiet. Here and there, small groups of men squatted on the ground or sat on overturned crates, smoking and talking in low voices. Slimitz was asleep in the small cabin at the stern of his barge. Jan settled in for the night among the bales he had loaded that afternoon.

The two-day journey to Stará Ľubovňa was uneventful. They stopped there for only a few hours, found no one looking to ship any goods north, and were soon pushing off and working their way back into the current. The river north of the town was high and running fast with the winter runoff from the mountains to the west, helping them to make good time until on their second day out they encountered a jam of broken trees and debris. It took some hours of strenuous work to clear their way around the jam while taking care not to swamp the barge. Though the last traces of daylight remained, they were both exhausted from the exertion and tied up onshore for the night.

Despite the helping current, their further progress was slow as the result of more obstructions in the river. At one point, they maneuvered to shore to meet two farmers who, with their wagons, waited at a well-used clearing on the river's low banks. Jan soon learned that these same farmers had been consigning produce to Slimitz for years. He would transport it to the market at Stary Sącz, sell it to the stall keepers there, and on his return trip to Poprad meet the farmers at the riverbank to turn the sale proceeds over to them.

It was not until late on the afternoon of the fifth day that they arrived in Stary Sącz. When unloading was completed, Jan found his way to the railroad station, bought a ticket on the morning westbound train to Krakow, and, as the evening wore on, joined a half dozen others curled up for the night on the station's wooden benches.

The early-morning Krakow train, belching stinging, black, cindery smoke that was regularly blown back into the open windows of the cars and the faces of the passengers, departed more or less on time. The cars were crowded. Despite the smoke, the close quarters, and the hard wooden benches, most of the passengers immediately settled in and began drifting off to sleep. The trip would take many hours, with frequent stops at towns and villages along the way. In Krakow, Jan would transfer to a train headed south for Poronin. The morning light revealed a green and varied countryside, and between naps he watched it roll by, while thinking ahead to his relatives in Poronin and the first critical stages of his journey to America.

〰〰〰〰〰

The Polish Brozeks were concentrated in two villages. Furthest south, the village of Zakopane was situated on the flank of the High Tatra Mountains and was overshadowed by the towering north face of Kriváň, the same peak whose opposite face looked down at Važec. Poronin, a larger village, was eight kilometers north of Zakopane and seventy-five kilometers south of Krakow.

Both villages were located in Western Galicia, whose rural areas comprised one of the least economically developed precincts of the Habsburg Empire. The region also served as a buffer zone against that part of the partitioned Polish homeland, farther to the north and northeast, that was Russian territory.

Jan's interest in his distant Polish relatives was less familial than it was practical. Rural poverty in Galicia was widespread and historically even more severe than in the Slovak lands to the south. Beginning in the 1880s, the economic conditions precipitated a mass migration involving several hundred thousand Polish peasants, most of whom traveled to the United States or Canada. Poronin was in the center of that dislocation, and Jan was anxious to learn from the Brozeks and other Poles in the region what they knew and might share of the experiences of their sons, daughters, and other relatives and acquaintances in traversing northern Europe to ports such as Bremen and upon arriving in America and its great port of New York. The idea that he was "visiting relatives" who could be identified and whose location could be verified also provided him with some justification for being in Galicia, should that question be raised by any of the authorities.

———————

He quickly became used to the train's stops in various ramshackle villages, slept through many of those as the day wore on into dusk, and was in the midst of a dream involving some pigs and two exceptionally vicious mountain trolls, when the sudden and pig-like squealing of the train's brakes startled him awake — just in time to brace himself from being pitched into the back of the seat in front of him. Looking out the window and through the twilight, he could see orange flames that seemed to be engulfing a small woodland village some distance from the tracks.

Two soldiers had flagged the train down. They scrambled aboard as it rolled to a stop, and were soon coming through the cars, shouting as they passed: "All able-bodied men off the train! You are needed to fight this fire! No exceptions! Get off! Now! The train has been ordered to stand here and wait for you! Run! Follow us!"

He rose, realizing he had no choice, and that he would either have to leave his rucksacks on the train or set them down in some exposed and unguarded place when he reached the scene of the fire. Ahead, he saw a man leaving the place where he had been seated with two women and a small, sleeping child. He quickly decided that entrusting the rucksacks to the women was a safer risk than leaving them on his seat or taking them with him. The women readily agreed to watch the rucksacks, and also agreed that, if the train should leave before he returned, they would drop them out the window on the opposite side of the tracks from the fire.

It took only a few minutes to reach the chaotic scene of the blaze—it involved two or three large buildings, including a granary, that seemed far gone, and at least three other smaller structures that had only recently caught fire and might yet be saved. There was little nearby water; a double line had been formed to pass buckets drawn from the only available well. Those men and women not in the line were using shovels to throw dirt on the fires, and many were also attempting to beat the flames out with blankets. Others were working to clear a firebreak of sorts to prevent the blaze from spreading to a nearby stand of pine trees, which sheltered many low huts. The heat was intense, and the crackling of the flames mingled with the cries and shouts of the villagers and the swirling smoke to create an eerie, urgent, and frightening atmosphere. To the side, out of harm's way, Jan could see a small herd of cows looking on and nonchalantly munching grass as their stable burned down.

A shovel was thrust into his hands, and he joined six others throwing dirt on the fire that was attempting to catch hold and establish itself in the crumbling wooden walls and thatched roof of a peasant's small home. With his head down, and pitching shovels full of dirt as fast as he could, he was aware only of the fire in front of him, which after a half hour of hard work was under control, with its remaining embers capable of being stomped out by the heavy boots of willing villagers.

When he turned away, he saw that similar progress had been made on two other buildings and that the firebreak seemed to be effective, but that attempts at controlling the fires on the main structures had ceased and they were being mournfully allowed to consume all and burn themselves out. He also saw people gathered around a man and woman who were lying on the ground in silent but obvious pain from burns they had received. The man had been severely burned on his hands and arms. The women's right hand was a charred, deformed mess; her face was blistered; and much of her hair had been burned off, leaving a blackened, puffy scalp. The thick, sickening smell of burned flesh was in the air. A priest kneeled near the woman to administer last rites but was roughly pushed away by two shouting and distraught men, both of whom berated the priest for, it seemed, having urged the woman to enter one of the burning buildings to save some of his property.

After some initial ministrations, it was decided that, with no medical help available in the tiny village, the two burn victims should be put on the train to Krakow. Jan helped carry the woman to the first car behind the locomotive, where she was gently lowered to lie on blankets that had been placed on the floor in the aisle, with her head resting in the lap of one of the men who had driven off the priest. She seemed to have passed out. As the burned man was brought in and placed in the aisle near the woman's feet, the engineer could be heard outside, announcing that the train would leave in five minutes and would go straight through in the night to Krakow, skipping all intervening stops.

Leaving that car, Jan trotted down the track to the third car, where he had been seated, and swung on board. It was empty. With long strides, he reached the place where the two women and the child had been seated, and on his hands and knees felt and searched for the rucksacks under the wooden seats. Standing up, he leaned out the window and concluded that, though the light was poor, the rucksacks were not on the ground next to the tracks. Running to the back of the car, he crossed over to the fourth and last car but saw no sign of the two women and the child – while at the same time realizing he wasn't at all sure of exactly what the women looked like.

From the fourth car, he jumped to the ground and moved

forward. The passengers were rapidly getting back on board. Ahead, the sound of steam building and hissing in the locomotive was growing louder. Running down the track and peering into the windows of the second car, he saw a woman standing at the front with a child and wondered whether this was part of his missing group—but there was no second woman. He felt a rising panic until, farther back in the car, he saw another woman motioning to him. He climbed on board and moved down the aisle to where she was seated.

"I was afraid you might miss the train," she said, raising her skirts and pulling out the two rucksacks. "When my sister and her daughter got off temporarily, I thought I should move up to this car and that, being alone, I should hide these better."

He took the rucksacks, smiled his thanks, and, with a relieved sigh, sat down across the aisle. The woman smoothed her skirts, looked at him for a moment, and then pulled out a cloth, which she spit on a number of times before standing and, as she leaned over him, saying, "You have soot all over your face! Now hold still and I'll clean you up." And she did.

〰〰〰〰

It was well after midnight, in the midst of a fine sleeting rain, when they pulled into the city of Krakow. The dimly lit and deserted station was not prepared for the arrival of any train, much less one that was not expected to travel at night and was seven hours ahead of schedule. Hurried arrangements were made to transport the burned to the hospital. Those whose final destination was Krakow moved off through the rain into the city. Those who had connecting trains in the morning or who would need to travel back to reach the skipped stops, were allowed to remain overnight in the station.

When things quieted down, Jan slipped outside. In the darkness behind the station, under the shelter of a small water tower, he removed his smoke-smelling clothes and stuffed them into the bottom of a rucksack. As he put on a clean pair of trousers and a shirt, he made a mental note to find a place to do his laundry in Poronin.

At 7:00 a.m. he was out walking about the city. The rain had given way to broken, scudding clouds. After purchasing tea, biscuits, and berry jam from a street vendor, he found a bench in a quiet square and sat in the warm sunlight, eating his breakfast, tossing crumbs to pigeons, and watching the neighborhood wake up. After a time, he worked his way back to the station, purchased a ticket to Poronin, and wandered about the square outside the station until his train was ready for boarding.

He stepped off the train in Poronin in mid-afternoon, under a cloudy sky. The lone employee in the station sent him to the town hall, where a sleepy clerk directed him to the Stanislaw and Pawel Brozek homes farther down the same street that fronted the train station he had just left. As he moved down that street, questions of a few residents eventually pinpointed the rough-sawn wood and fieldstone homes of Stanislaw, the father, and Pawel, the son, which were on the same side of the narrow dirt street, though separated by two other small dwellings and their side yards. He stopped at the first house, which proved to be that belonging to the son — who, after no more than twenty seconds of introductions, welcomed the Slovak "cousin" he had never previously met, or even heard of, as if he were a long-lost prodigal son returned home. He was similarly enveloped by Pawel's wife Katrina, a short, buxom, dark-haired woman who Jan could not come close to getting his arms around; an experience that was repeated with each of the couple's two healthy teenage daughters. One of the daughters was immediately dispatched to get "the old man," and more hugs ensued when Stanislaw (who, it turned out, was a widower) burst into the house as if shot from a cannon.

Pawel subsequently took his visitor in tow to introduce him to neighbors up and down the street, accompanied by more hugs and seemingly genuine delight on the part of all at the rare occurrence of an out-of-town visitor. When they returned to Pawel's home they were greeted by a headless chicken escaping from the side yard, with one of the daughters in hot pursuit. The chicken turned out to be one of two birds the daughters beheaded and which within a few hours were the featured course of a meal that also included enormous quantities of potatoes and slices of hard, dark bread slathered with sweet fat.

After dinner, they sat by lantern light, sharing family stories. Later, Jan revealed the purpose of his trip and asked what they might add to his knowledge of traversing Europe and traveling to America.

"That," Stanislaw said, "is something we can help you with! As I mentioned before, I have worked for the railroad for thirty years and know all the systems quite well. Pawel, perhaps we should also have Kubica speak with Jan?"

"Yes, that would be good. And we should see if Stachnik will come, perhaps tomorrow? Kubica," Pawel explained to Jan, "has had two sons immigrate to America. Stachnik and his wife went to America for two or three years, but he returned last winter after the wife died. A sad story there. I will speak to both tomorrow and see if they can join us here in the evening."

"For now," Stanislaw said, getting up, "it is getting late and I have the early shift tomorrow. Jan, you will spend the night at my house."

As they were leaving, Katrina touched Jan's arm. "Father will leave very early, before it is light. So when you rise, come back here for some breakfast."

"I will, and perhaps then someone can direct me to where I can wash some clothes. I need to do that tomorrow."

"You can come with us," said Katrina. "The girls and I will be doing laundry tomorrow and can do yours as well. You can keep us company."

Jan nodded and followed Stanislaw down the street.

———≈∿∿∿∿∿≈———

The next morning when he awakened, and though it was still dark, he found that Stanislaw was long gone. He gathered his things and went back to Pawel's. After breakfast, he set out with Katrina and her oldest daughter, Sophie, both barefoot, on a twenty-minute hike that took them into a stand of woods through which a shallow but swift creek ran between banks lined with large rocks. Three women were already there, standing knee deep in the cold water, washing clothes and arranging them on the rocks to dry in the sun.

"If you wish to bathe," Katrina offered as she took the clothes Jan pulled from his rucksack, "Sophie can show you a place a little distance upstream where there is a small pool."

He followed Sophie, and after perhaps a hundred meters they came to a wide, deep pool in the creek. After she left, he entered the icy water, scrubbing himself with a cloth Sophie had brought along, and then climbed out to dry in the sun. By the time he had dressed and returned to the creek-side laundry, all the clothes were spread out to dry. After an hour, they made their way back to the village, where the still-damp clothes were draped over a rope that Sophie and her sister strung between two scraggly trees behind the house. Taking a large slab of the hard bread with him, Jan spent much of the rest of the day wandering about Poronin.

That evening, shortly after dinner, Marek Kubica and Lech Stachnik arrived. The five men sat around the table and talked, with Katrina and her daughters in a corner sewing quietly and listening in on the conversation, which went on until almost eleven o'clock.

As he lay in bed in Stanislaw's house later that night, Jan went over in his mind some of the things he had learned or which confirmed what he had previously learned or heard.

One related to the matter of crossing the border and the advisability of first entering the Russian-occupied portion of the Polish homeland, proceeding from there into the Prussian-controlled portion, and then into the heart of Germany. While there were two borders to cross, Kubica and Stachnik agreed that the only real border guards to contend with would be those of their own country, Austria-Hungary, in entering Russian territory. They recommended crossing the border somewhere well east of Krakow, perhaps even back beyond Stary Sącz, where Jan had begun his westward train trip.

Another important consideration was that of booking passage and the differences between steamship lines. Kubica's two sons and Stachnik himself had crossed to America from Bremen on relatively new ships of the Norddeutscher-Lloyd Line. Though a less-crowded third class had replaced steerage as the lowest class of travel on most steamship lines, it still had its issues, according to Stachnik. However, he said he had heard far worse stories about conditions on the ships of other companies and positive or at least acceptable stories from others who had also traveled on Norddeutscher-Lloyd ships.

"We went to America in 1906," Stachnik had said, "and I did not find third-class accommodations to be so bad, though my wife, as was always her way, had expected better. It was certainly better than the stories we had heard of crossing in steerage on ships twenty years before. If you travel third class, you will be on the lowest decks of the ship, just above the cargo hold. On our ship, third class involved very small cabins, really closets, with bunk or stacked beds for four or six people. Those for six people had two stacks of bunks, one stack on each side of a very narrow cabin. Each stack had three beds, and getting to the third one, on top, could be difficult and awkward, especially since there was very little room between that bed and the ceiling. It would be hard for all six people to be in such a room at the same time, unless all were in their beds. They were usually used for six single women or six single men. We shared a cabin for four with another husband and wife. It was all right, but privacy was difficult—we men left the cabin when the women dressed or undressed. Then when they were in bed, we would return, and they would turn to face the wall when we undressed. We reversed that process in the morning."

"On the whole," Stachnik reflected, "the situation was not too different from second class, though we were much more crowded in the common areas, where you almost had to spend the day in order to get some exercise and some air. And the food, while cheaper in third class, was not as good as in second class. It was not enjoyable, and second class or, I am sure, first class, was a better experience. But it was tolerable—and first class or second class or third class, you get to New York at the same time!"

It seemed, Jan thought, as it had from the time he had committed to emigrate, both simple and difficult. But it would be no more so for him than for the uncounted numbers who had gone before. If anything was troubling, it was the bitterness or disappointment, clearly not all related to his wife's death, that Stachnik seemed to feel about his experience in America.

"It was not as I expected," Stachnik said quietly. "It was more difficult than I imagined and was told it would be, and it was a struggle—to work, to live, to be happy—all the time I was there. Perhaps my dreams were unrealistic. Perhaps I thought we could become a part of our new country and be prosperous right away. I guess I don't really know, even now, what I thought or expected. I believed it would be better and finally convinced my wife to go. Instead, life was hard, and we were still poor peasants of sorts; misfits, to me, in a strange society, living with many other people, in what in New York they call a 'tenement' — a tall building of many floors and crowded, dirty, and noisy conditions. My dreams did not come true. When I lost my wife, I felt guilty about having talked her into leaving this place. Even after having been in New York for more than two years, I was left empty and alone. I suppose I am happier now that I am back here, the same as I was before I left. At least, though I miss my wife, I am not as alone. I suppose that for me, going to America was a mistake, though I know that for others — such as Kubica's sons — it has not been so bad."

As Jan eventually and fitfully drifted off to sleep, he thought of Stachnik's words about having "convinced" his wife to go. That seemed to weigh heavily on Stachnik. And he thought of the better life he himself had painted for Maria.

Chapter 4

Krakow

The train rolled into the long trainshed at Krakow's Główny Station. It had begun losing speed when it first entered the city, but as it approached the station the train slowed to an almost imperceptible crawl, as if it had a mind of its own and was reluctant to end its journey. Their progress was so slow and prolonged that those on board seemed to fall into a trance and were startled to discover that the train had finally come to a complete stop.

Stepping down to the platform, Jan fell in with the line of passengers making their way, through the dissipating clouds of steam drifting back from the idling locomotive, toward the entrance to the station building.

Inside the station, he stopped at a bench to dig through his rucksacks until he found the slip of paper on which Anatoly had written the address of Baron Ihnacak's lodgings. He had no great desire to linger in Krakow but did not feel that he could ignore an invitation from a Baron, especially one who had been so kind to him. He worried that Ihnacak would not yet have traveled to the city and, in that case, whether and for how long he should wait for his arrival. The address was on Krzyza Street, which the clerk in the waiting room kiosk told him, while drawing a rough map on the back of Anatoly's note, was walking distance from the station and not far from the city's great Planty Park and the main Market Square.

It was an old neighborhood, marked by mature trees, shaded streets, and the strong, pleasant smell of lilacs in bloom. Krzyza Street was lined with imposing houses: none more so than the one he was seeking. A heavy, ornate iron street gate opened into a garden courtyard, which was dominated by a tall fountain and featured stone walkways and meticulously tended flower beds. He circled around the fountain to the building and pulled the bell cord hanging near the carved wooden door. After a moment, a middle-aged Polish maid opened a small window in the door and, looking him up and down, asked, "Who are you, and what are you selling?"

"I'm not selling," Jan laughed. "I'm looking for Baron Anton Ihnacak, who told me I would find him here. I am known as Jan Brozek."

"Aha!" the maid exclaimed, swinging the door open. "The Baron arrived just a few days ago. He told me he was expecting you. He is, at the moment, out in the city on business of some sort, but instructed me that if you should arrive I am to welcome you and to have you wait here until he returns. He has ample room in his quarters and desires you to stay with him here unless, of course, you would prefer to stay elsewhere."

"I am happy to wait for his return, but I do not wish to impose on the Baron's hospitality."

"He has invited you, so there is no imposition, and you will not find a better place to stay," the maid assured him. "Follow me, then."

The house contained four apartments, two on each floor. The Baron's was on the south side of the second floor and, like its companion apartment on the north side, extended the entire length of the building. Each apartment was reached from the foyer on the main floor by its own spiral staircase. At the top of the stairs they entered a large parlor and sitting area, with windows facing east and south. The east windows overlooked the courtyard and fountain. The parlor was filled with heavy, opulent furnishings of a style Jan had never seen.

"The Baron would like you to have the third bedroom," the maid said, "so we should take your things back there. I think you'll find it most comfortable."

The third bedroom was near the end of a hallway that extended back from the parlor, with the hallway's long north wall separating the two apartments. They passed the doors to two other bedrooms before reaching the open door of the third bedroom, which to Jan seemed nearly as large as the room that served as living room, dining room, and kitchen in his parents' home in Važec. The bedroom had an enormous elevated bed, a large washstand, a writing desk, and other furnishings. Broad open windows looked out to wooded parklands to the south.

Feeling a bit overwhelmed, Jan carefully set his rucksacks on the floor and gingerly tested the bed.

"You will sleep like a baby here," the maid said, laughing, "and you will get used to it. You should know that the other apartment on this floor will be empty this week; its owner is in Budapest. But both of the apartments downstairs—they are much smaller than this—are occupied year-round by lesser officials. So realize who they are, and act appropriately if you should see them."

"Thank you, that's good to know. Is there a place I can wash up?"

"Of course," she said, leading the way to the final room at the end of the long hallway. This room had a wash basin and a large tub. Pointing to two huge pails of water on a low shelf, she said: "You have time to bathe before the Baron returns. Pour those into the tub while I go get hot water from downstairs."

With that, she was gone. He paused for a moment before pouring the water into the tub, then stood waiting until she returned carrying two steaming pails, which she quickly emptied into the tub, followed by a handful of granular soap that she scooped out of a nearby bowl.

"It will work better if you take your clothes off and get in," the maid observed. "You can use those towels, and when you're done pull that leather plug at the bottom. It drains the water into a pipe that runs through the wall and empties into the vegetable garden in the back."

She looked at him for a long moment, laughed, and left the room. After a moment's hesitation, he undressed and climbed in.

⚒⚒⚒

Baron Ihnacak returned home in the early evening and invited Jan to join him in the front parlor for supper, which was served by the maid, whose name turned out to be Helena. They talked briefly about the Archduke's grand arrival at Štrbské Pleso, and Jan described the stop his train to Krakow had made to fight the fire in the small village and his subsequent visit to Poronin.

"Will you," the Baron asked, "return to Važec from here?"

Jan hesitated a moment before saying, "Perhaps not directly, though I don't plan to stay in Krakow very long." And then, in an effort to change the subject, he asked, "Have Anatoly and Anna returned to Poprad?"

"Yes, but while Anatoly must stay there, Anna is due here tomorrow. You must come with me to meet her train! It will be such a great surprise for her! You are welcome to stay here for at least a few more days as my guest. With Anatoly in Poprad, the room you have now can be yours for as long as you like until Anna and I leave."

Jan sipped his tea slowly, again thinking how kind this noble had been to him and how he did not want to offend or disappoint

him. A day or two longer in Krakow would not affect his plans
greatly. He also wanted to see Anna, and in fact had hoped that
when he got to Krakow she would be there with her father.

"I would, sir, be honored to accompany you to the station and
to see Anna again. And the offer to stay in these elegant quarters is
very much appreciated. This room, this apartment, and the room
I am using are grander than any I have ever experienced. I cannot
refuse your offer to stay here with you, but I must travel on in a few
days."

"Well," the Baron replied, "where those travels may take you is
none of my business; though I was a young man once myself, and I
know the urge to explore and to see places other than home. I wish
you Godspeed and good fortune wherever you travel. As for me, I
must travel off to bed; it has been a long day. Helena will have tea,
breads, and other things for us in this room at nine o'clock in the
morning, and then, after a bit, we will fetch our Anna."

<hr>

They were joined at breakfast by Ihnacak's Slovak aide, Colonel
Michal Zakof. The older aide, the Czech Colonel Tomas Strzala,
had been assigned to accompany Anna as she followed her father
from Poprad. Both the Baron and Colonel Zakof were dressed in
plain gray field uniforms, with very visible revolvers at their belts.

After breakfast, a carriage drawn by two matched black horses
was waiting for them on the street. "We could walk," Zakof observed dryly as he and Jan followed the Baron out through the
courtyard, "but Miss Anna travels with, shall we say, a certain
amount of luggage."

Główny Station was less crowded than it had been the previous day when Jan had arrived. They walked through the station
and reached the train shed just as the train, running a little behind schedule, pulled in. Passengers soon began disembarking,

crowding past the three men who stood waiting on the platform. It took only a few minutes for all but a couple of stragglers to pass by and make their way into the waiting room. There was no sign of Anna or Colonel Strzala.

"Jan," the Baron said with a worried frown, "would you please walk back through all the cars and look for them. If you do not find them, check the baggage car at the end for their luggage—Anna will have had five trunks of matching colors: two large and three small. I believe Strzala would have had one, standard-issue military trunk. Colonel Zakof, please find the conductor and bring him here."

Jan walked back through the length of the train, which was now empty. At the baggage car, he found that their carriage driver had made a stack of Anna's trunks and the one belonging to Colonel Strzala. He hurried back up the track to where the Baron was standing.

"Sir, they are not on the train. Their baggage is and has been unloaded, and the driver is putting the trunks in your carriage."

As he spoke, Colonel Zakof arrived with the conductor trotting along some distance behind.

"The conductor," the Colonel reported, "says he spoke with Anna as the train was leaving Nowy Sącz and saw Colonel Strzala sometime later that morning, but does not recall seeing them after that, either on the train or getting off at any of the stops."

"How many stations between Nowy Sącz and this place?" the Baron asked as the conductor joined them.

"This is an express, your Excellency, so only three and we made them all, including one stop during the night, just after midnight. Your Colonel here asked when the next train from Nowy Sącz would arrive, and that should be at approximately two o'clock this afternoon."

"And that train makes the same stops?"

"Yes, at the stations, though not being an express, it has four or five additional stops, and hopefully, it won't have an emergency stop as we did near dawn this morning. There was a dead ox on the track, and it took us some time to push it aside."

"And where was that? And did people leave the train?"

"Less, I would say, than three kilometers before the village station at Wieliczka. I was occupied with the ox, as was the entire crew, but a few passengers — the curious, you know — did get off to see the animal, and some helped in its removal. Some others may have gotten off to stretch their legs. It was actually not a very long stop, and it was a desolate sort of place."

"Other than the ox," Colonel Zakof inquired, "did anything else unusual happen on the train after leaving Nowy Sącz or on the journey?"

"Nothing, sir. It was a quiet trip, except for the ox."

After a few more questions, the Baron thanked the conductor and then pulled Jan and Zakof aside.

"We will await the two o'clock train. It is possible they got off at one of the stations or at the ox stop and somehow failed to get back on in time. I checked the schedules, and this train," the Baron continued, gesturing at the one the conductor was now reboarding, "begins a return trip to Nowy Sącz at two-forty p.m. If they are not on the two o'clock, then, Colonel, you and I will be on the two-forty train to retrace the route. Jan, we could also use your help, if you choose to join us."

"Of course," Jan quickly responded.

"Good. Go with the carriage driver and take the luggage to my quarters. Tell Helena what has happened and have her pack food for the three of us for two days in case we do travel on the afternoon train. Be sure you are back here by two o'clock. Colonel, please find the engineer of this train; I want to get a better idea of the circum- stances and exact location of the ox incident. And if he is the one taking this train back this afternoon, I need to discuss with him some of the out-of-the-ordinary procedures we may follow on that trip."

By 2:00 p.m., they were all gathered back at the station, Jan bringing one of his rucksacks with the food Helena had packed. And by half past two, they were boarding the eastbound train for Nowy Sącz.

≈≈≈≋≋≈≈

They sat in the rear of the last car, which was otherwise empty except for two men and two women seated near the front. Those four were traveling together; the women occasionally glanced over their shoulders at the three men in the back. Jan imagined they were probably gossiping about two armed men in military uniform traveling with a peasant who was likely a prisoner of some sort.

As they left the station, the Baron explained that, from his conversation with the engineer, he believed that Anna and Colonel Strzala had become separated from the train at the time it stopped for the dead ox or at the succeeding stop in the nearby town of Wieliczka. The ox, according to the engineer, had been lying on the track in the midst of a long straightaway, where it was easily visible. Despite its great weight, the engineer said that the ox had been relatively easy to drag from the tracks because its joints and limbs seemed stiff; after enough men had gotten off the train and been put to the task, it had been fairly simple to move the weight by grabbing the stiff limbs. The most time had actually been consumed, before and after the ox was moved, in talking about the ox and the stoppage. The engineer had looked at his pocket watch once the train was completely stopped and later shortly after again getting underway, and could confidently say they were delayed there, and later in Wieliczka, a total of forty minutes; time which he had made up as the journey continued.

When the Baron asked about the delay in Wieliczka, the engineer shrugged and said someone had come out of the station and asked him to wait for a late-arriving passenger, who was just then fording a creek a short distance away on the other side of the station building. A few minutes later, a man had run out of the building and entered one of the cars, and the engineer had then brought up steam and pulled out of the station.

After talking to the engineer, the Baron continued, he had reinterviewed the conductor, who had little to add to the story of the ox, but who said that the person who ran out of the station was not a new passenger. According to the conductor, that man was definitely someone who had been on the train since Nowy Sącz and had simply been late in reboarding in Wieliczka. In fact, the only other odd thing the conductor could recall was that, despite the absence of both Anna and Colonel Strzala, his final count of people disembarking in Krakow was twenty-two instead of the twenty-three it would have been if all those who should have been on board to the final stop in Krakow had in fact been on the train.

"Sir, I may not be following you," Colonel Zakof interjected with a puzzled look, "but if there were supposed to be twenty-three people disembarking at Krakow, including your daughter and Strzala, and if it was not a new passenger who got on in Wieliczka, which was the last stop the train made before Krakow, and if, as we know, your daughter and Strzala did not get off in Krakow, then I believe there should have been twenty-one passengers, not twenty-two."

"Correct," the Baron replied, "and I cannot explain that. I do believe that those things that occurred at the stop for the dead ox and at the Wieliczka station are related, though I am not sure how. I also believe that Anna and Strzala left the train—or were perhaps taken off the train—at one or another of those stops and were not able to get back on, or were not allowed to get back on."

"If they got off, at whichever point, of their own choice, and simply did not get back on before the train left," Jan said slowly, "they could easily have boarded the later train. Even if they were left behind with the ox carcass, they had more than three hours to walk perhaps three kilometers to the Wieliczka station to catch the next train, the one that arrived in Krakow shortly after two o'clock."

"Also correct," the Baron answered. Looking out the train window for a moment, he added, "I think we can eliminate the idea that they left the train or failed to return to the train because they *chose* to do so."

"Who would detain them? And why?" Jan asked.

The Baron shook his head slowly from side to side, and the Colonel shrugged his shoulders.

After a moment, the Baron said, "We will work backwards and not leave the train at Wieliczka. In fact, out of perhaps an excess of caution, I believe we must not be seen on the train by anyone who might be on the platform there or even on the other side of the tracks. We will disembark in the vicinity of where this train encountered the ox. The engineer will not stop at that point, but will slow down enough that we can jump off with safety. We will see what we can discover there and take our next steps based on that, including walking back to Wieliczka if our answers are not where the ox was."

They agreed that when the train stopped in Wieliczka, Jan, whom no one in this part of the country would know, would leave them and walk through the train, disembarking through one of the front cars. Once outside, he would casually wander down the platform and through the station building, all the while watching for anything unusual. He would return, retracing his steps, as the train prepared to leave, making note of any new passengers who might have boarded.

The stop at Wieliczka was uneventful. As the train stopped and

Jan began moving forward, the two couples at the front of the car gathered up their bags and, with worried glances at Jan, got off. When the train started up some minutes later, Jan worked his way back to the last car, with nothing to report to his two companions.

After traveling for less than a half hour, the train began slowing and they exited the car at the rear, standing on the small platform between it and the baggage car. As they rolled slowly on, Colonel Zakof suddenly pointed at something on the north side of the tracks and jumped out from the platform, disappearing from their view. The Baron followed immediately; and with a deep breath, and as he felt the train beginning to regain speed, Jan followed suit. In the air, he was hit full in the face with the eye-stinging smoke and cinder bits from the accelerating locomotive. He hit the ground on his left hip and rolled forward into a thistle bush, enveloped by clouds of fine dust stirred-up by the passing train. He sat up coughing and trying to clear his eyes and feeling gingerly for any injuries.

After a few moments, and through the mingled dust and tears in his eyes, he made out the form of Baron Ihnacak, silently waving to Jan to join him back down the track. He walked unsteadily to the Baron, who, while dusty, seemed none the worse for wear. With a clean handkerchief, the Baron helped him clear the grit from his eyes. They turned and headed for Colonel Zakof, who was kneeling by the track some distance away. The Colonel had broken two fingers on his left hand and had also suffered minor cuts to his forehead.

As the Baron tore two small strips from the handkerchief and used those to tie Zakof's broken fingers together and to the neighboring uninjured index finger, the Colonel pointed back down the track with his right hand, saying, "The ox is there, less than one hundred meters distant."

"We need to proceed carefully and quietly," the Baron said softly, "until we are sure of this territory and who may be here."

The ox, whose limbs were now very stiff and sticking straight out into the air, lay by the tracks, apparently where he been deposited earlier in the day by the train crew and passengers.

"This ox has been dead for some time," said the Colonel, kicking one of the animal's front legs. "I'd guess maybe two days; though, if that were the case, he would have impeded other trains using this track."

Jan was still picking dust and tiny cinders from his eyes as he walked around the carcass. He stopped, bent down, and studied the head for a moment.

"We need to lift and turn his head so we can see his neck," he said, while himself starting to pull the head up.

With some effort by all three, they twisted the head around.

"There," said Jan, pointing, "his throat was cut and then, as you can see, the cut was sewn up with rough thread after he died. I would say he was killed nearby and then dragged here to block this track."

They were silent for a moment until the Baron said, "We need to examine the area on both sides of the track to see what else we can find. There may be tracks or other signs that will be of use in making sense of this. Be quiet and alert. It is not likely, but whoever was responsible for all of this, and it would need to be a number of people to kill and move this dead ox, may still be nearby."

It took only a few minutes to discover signs of the ox being dragged and, no more than thirty meters from the carcass, to find an open area behind some low bushes where large amounts of dark dried blood were mingled in with dirt that had been swept about in some attempt to absorb the blood and cover it up.

"Obviously, the ox was killed here, I would say yesterday or the day before," the Colonel said as he kicked at the dirt.

"And," Jan added, "dragged onto the track early this morning with a purpose to stop some train ... or perhaps a particular train."

"It would appear that the purpose was to stop the train my daughter was on, though I do not know if it was *because* she was on that train. Nor do I know how anyone would have known she and Strzala were on that particular train—or why anyone would want to abduct her." The Baron paused for a moment and then added, "I believe they left the train here. We have a few hours before darkness and need to see if we can find any signs of them or tracks or whatever that may help us follow them. Zakof, you and I will search this side of the tracks in all directions. Jan, please do the same on the other side. Be vigilant."

With that, they split up. In his search, Zakof soon found multiple sets of poorly-covered boot tracks both coming and going from the place where they had found the dried blood. He followed them to a point near a large dead tree and then went to collect Jan and the Baron.

They examined the tracks, which had been made by at least six people, possibly more. Some of the tracks were made by the heavy boots of men, though there were smaller imprints, likely made by women's shoes, and occasionally the footprints of small bare feet. They followed these tracks for some time through a dense thicket before the growing darkness of a cloudy, starless evening made further progress and tracking impossible. Despite his concern for his daughter, the Baron realized how difficult it would be to follow the trail and move safely through the thicket in the dark and decided to stop for the night. They found a small, sheltered clearing where they opened and shared some of the food Helena had packed. It was agreed that the first to awaken with the day's light should rouse the others.

＝＞＜＝

They slept fitfully until the Baron, detecting enough light to see for at least nine or ten meters, awakened the others, and they picked up the trail. Within an hour they reached a point where the group they were tracking had split, with a larger group continuing to the north while a smaller party of three or four broke off on a course bearing generally to the west. Both sets of tracks were scuffed, and it was no longer possible to discern the smaller imprints or the tracks left by bare feet.

Watching as the Colonel began to slowly explore the trail of the larger group, the Baron turned to Jan and said "we must split up as well. We cannot ignore either group. Zakof and I will follow the trail he is on, and you should follow the other, smaller party. If you catch up to them and Anna is part of that group, be careful and do not lose them. It is hard to tell how this will work out, and these groups may never rejoin. If the trail runs out, or if more than two days, counting today, pass and you have not found anything, go back and wait for us at the Wieliczka station."

At that point, they were interrupted by Colonel Zakof, who was running back from his reconnaissance of the northward trail. He was carrying an army uniform jacket.

"This belongs to Strzala!" he exclaimed. "I recognize this small red stain on the left elbow, and the jacket smells of his tobacco. I found it perhaps fifty meters up that trail."

"That makes that trail of even higher interest to us, but there is no certain guarantee that both Strzala and Anna are in that group," the Baron reasoned. "Jan, you still need to follow this other trail. If it continues westward, you will, I would judge, be some fair distance north of Wieliczka in a few hours. Do your best, but if you turn up nothing or you lose the trail, go on to Wieliczka by tomorrow night and wait for us as planned."

After they split up the remainder of the food from Jan's rucksack, the Baron and the Colonel moved off after the larger group while Jan continued west by northwest. The trail of the smaller group became clearer after about an hour when he reached a long stretch of damp ground, and from time to time he could clearly make out the smaller, shallower footprints made by a woman's shoes.

He, the Baron, and the Colonel had started out very early, and it was only a little past midmorning, with the day already growing warm, when he thought he heard voices. Almost at the same time, he glimpsed brightly-colored cloth waving in the sunlight some distance ahead. He moved forward cautiously and stopped dead in his tracks as a grassy clearing opened before him; after a quick glance, he moved silently to his right and dropped down on one knee behind the cover of a tangle of bushes.

Two roughly-dressed men were standing in the clearing near a small shed. Anna was sitting in the grass a bit farther from the shed wearing a thin chemise and little else — her colorful skirts and other clothes had been thrown over the branches of a tree near the edge of the clearing and were hanging in the breeze perhaps three meters off the ground. Jan could see that her hands were tied behind her to some sort of low post or stake. She was watching the two men, who were packing rucksacks.

Neither man was very large, but their small size was balanced off by the fact that one had a rifle. Being unarmed, Jan was considering his next step when he realized that the men were preparing to leave. The man with the rifle walked over and spoke briefly to Anna while resting the butt end of the rifle on her bare leg. She sat stiffly and said nothing. After a few minutes, the rifleman laughed and waved to his companion. They lifted the rucksacks to their backs and, after a brief discussion and a last look back at Anna, disappeared into the trees and brush.

Jan waited for nearly ten minutes. Anna did not move, and that made him wonder if perhaps there wasn't someone in the shed. He retreated silently and carefully circled well around the clearing to come up behind the shed. There was an opening in the back wall, and through it he could see that it was empty. Silently he moved past the shed into Anna's line of vision, signaling her with his index finger pressed to his lips to be silent. Coming around behind her, he untied the rope and pulled her to her feet as she collapsed into his arms.

"Quickly," he whispered, "we must get your clothes and leave before they return."

"They will not return," she said, mostly into his shirt. "They have a long way to go and I am not important to them. I think they believe that by the time I could work the rope loose, find a way to get my clothes down, and make my way out of here, they will be many kilometers away."

Anna paused for a moment, looked up, and touched his face with a dusty hand. "I prayed that somehow you would rescue me, and you have miraculously come out of thin air to save me again, Jan. And I am dirty and once more not at all in the presentable condition a lady should be in for her hero."

He realized she had started sobbing, and he held her tight until she recovered. With a cloth from his rucksack, he dusted off her face, arms, and feet as best as he could. Then, after gauging the height of the branches, he got down on his hands and knees while she stood on his back and pulled her clothes down from the tree. As she gathered and arranged the clothes, he followed her instructions and went to retrieve her traveling boots from the shed, where she had spent the night while the men slept and stood guard outside. From the shed, he saw her pull the soiled chemise over her head and throw it aside as she reached for a petticoat. He started to look away and then stopped. She was standing sideways to him, naked in the sunlight as she brushed and straightened her clothes for some minutes before beginning to put them on. When she was reasonably dressed, he left the shed, boots in hand.

While he waited for her to finish dressing, Jan mentally

calculated how far, west and north, he had come since leaving the ox carcass and how far north they might be of the railroad tracks.

"I believe, Not-A-Princess, that if we travel to the southwest we can't avoid stumbling on the railroad track, probably east of Wieliczka. If so, once we find the tracks we can simply follow those west to the village. I am not at all sure of how far we will have to travel."

"Her Highness the Not-A-Princess is tired and must walk slowly," she smiled, "but she can make it if she's with you."

As they walked, she told him how, when the train stopped for the ox on the track, Colonel Strzala had left the train to help in the removal of the ox, but then, apparently with no one but her looking, had turned, headed toward the rear of the train, and then slipped into the woods. Curious, she got off the train and followed him. She had caught up with him, and he was in the process of urging her to return to the train when four men appeared, hailed Strzala as "Tomas," and, catching sight of Anna, quickly determined – over Strzala's objection – that she must be detained until the train had left. As they were tying her hands behind her back and stuffing a rag in her mouth, she had noticed two horses tied to a tree some distance away. She had watched as Strzala quickly stripped off his uniform in favor of a peasant blouse and coarse trousers that one of the men handed to him.

"It made no sense," Anna noted, "but I thought I heard them talking about needing to ride hard to get to Wieliczka to board the train. In any event, the Colonel and one of the men ran to the horses and rode away at a gallop."

At that point, Anna went on, three more men and a woman had joined the group, and after some discussion, and as the train was starting to leave, decided they would have to keep her with them. The whole group had set out together but after some time had split into two groups, and the two men had taken her along with them.

It was after dark when they arrived at the area of the shed, built a low fire, and ate what she thought were "stale pancakes that tasted like tobacco," after which they pushed her into the shed to sleep. She had slept very little and knew that the men had taken turns sleeping and looking in on her. Just before dawn, she had crept to the door of the shed and listened to the men talking as they rebuilt the fire and boiled tea.

"They were talking about what they were going to do with me; they talked of stripping me, taking my clothes, and leaving me there. I was very afraid when I heard that, imaging what else they might do before leaving, though," she quickly added, "they didn't. They also talked about Colonel Strzala and how he would book passage for America! They argued about how long that journey would take."

Later, and not long before Jan arrived, the men had pulled her out of the shed and told her she could either disrobe herself or they would do it for her. They had then spent some time discussing what to do with her clothes before deciding to throw them up in the tree.

"And then," she concluded simply, "after a while they left, and you arrived."

The afternoon passed as they slowly made their way through dense woods along a faint trail. Jan told her about the things that had occurred since he, the Baron, and Colonel Zakof had gone to meet her train the day before, including that her father and the Colonel were, at that moment, pursuing the trail of the larger group.

They continued on, with Anna clearly concerned about her father and Jan keeping an eye out for signs of the railroad track. It was past sunset when they came upon the rail line. They started walking west along the track, but after twenty minutes he became convinced that they had actually come upon the tracks to the west, not the east, of the Wieliczka station, and they turned around.

After an hour, the light was completely gone, and in the darkness they were tripping and stumbling as much as walking when they caught sight of the dim lights of the station ahead. They were soon sitting on a bench on the platform, discussing how they would have to wait until the following evening for the Baron and Zakof to arrive, as had been planned when the men had split up early that morning. They were also aware that they were drawing long looks from the half-dozen people waiting on the platform, and who were obviously curious about the dusty peasant and the young woman who was so well dressed, though herself dusty, sweaty, and sporting tangled blonde hair. From time to time, Anna dabbed at his red and irritated eyes with a cloth she wetted at the pump in front of the station.

It was nearing midnight, long after the last train of the day had passed through, with the station dark and empty and Anna falling asleep in his arms, when they heard the men's voices. They moved quickly into the shadows of the station and watched as two men approached. As their voices became clearer, Anna jumped up to run into the arms of her father as he hurried across the platform to her.

———❧———

The next morning, after spending the night in the station, where Anna went over her story again for her father and Colonel Zakof, and they in turn told of how they had completely lost the trail of the group they had followed after discovering Colonel Strzala's jacket, they all boarded the first morning train for Krakow.

Back at the Baron's apartment, and after Zakof had left for his quarters, Helena took charge, simultaneously making a late breakfast, asking questions, boiling water, and organizing an order of bathing, with Anna getting first call.

The two men were left alone in the parlor. As he refilled their cups with tea, the Baron said, "I guess I shouldn't be surprised by Strzala's actions. His mother and wife have both died within the last year, and his only brother and his brother's wife left for America three or four years ago. He is alone, growing older, and also, I suppose, growing tired of the army. Perhaps he intends to join them. But deserting is a serious thing. I will need to report that, and that will lead to a search for him, with dire consequences if he is caught."

He was silent for a while and then continued, "If Anna had not left the train, what had become of Strzala would be a greater mystery and would have led to an investigation and ultimately a different sort of search, though not for some days, and who knows where he might be by then."

"Was Colonel Strzala the man who boarded the train in Wieliczka?" Jan asked.

"I have been thinking about that, but do not know. If he was, it might explain why the conductor, with but a quick glance and with Strzala no longer in uniform, would have identified him as someone who had been on the train since Nowy Sącz and was just late in reboarding, even though he did not recognize him as being the Colonel. However, it is hard to reason why he would have hurried so to reboard that same train and go on to Krakow, which was already his destination and which he would have arrived at in due course."

"The only difference," Jan offered, "would be that if Anna had not left the train, he would simply have been mysteriously missing and, not being in uniform when he got off, might not have been recognized by anyone. As it was, he might, if he was on the train when it arrived in Krakow, have even somehow walked right by us as we waited."

"True," the Baron mused. "We were certainly looking for him in uniform and for the two of them to be getting off the train together.

In any event, I will have to honestly report that he appears to have deserted. But perhaps, would you agree, I should wait a day or two to see if he doesn't come back of his own accord with some reasonable explanation?"

Jan studied the Baron for a moment and realized he was thinking of delaying in order to give Colonel Strzala time to either turn up in Krakow, or to reach Russian territory, or Prussia, whichever route he was following if indeed he was going to America. He slowly nodded an affirmative reply to the question.

"I cannot, of course, wish Colonel Strzala good luck," the Baron continued, "but I can extend that to a young Slovak who I believe has plans for a long journey of his own. Your destination, Jan, I have guessed, but I assure you that secret is safe with me. That is so even though I am not sure you should share it with the young lady you seem to have a penchant for rescuing."

"She is quite remarkable, sir, and...." Jan's voice trailed off as he grappled with what to say.

"It will be hard for her when you leave; but I believe she knows that you will and that you must, despite how much, unless I am very wrong, her young heart has become yours. And now," the Baron said, standing, "I hear rustling in the hall and believe it is my turn to wash the dust and dirt of our adventures down the drain."

Jan sat alone, sipping his tea and trying to make order out of his confused thoughts ... most of which centered on where his own heart was. He had only partially succeeded when Helena came by to announce his turn at the bath was imminent and that she was going for more hot water. Fifteen minutes later, he headed down the hall. As he passed by the partially open door of Anna's room, he saw that she was napping peacefully on her bed, wrapped in blankets and towels. He suddenly realized how very tired he was and how inviting his own bed would be after his bath.

The next morning, Anna appeared at breakfast in simple peasant dress. She was accompanying Helena to the market, and hinted strongly that heavy purchases of various sorts were planned and that an extra set of hands and arms to carry packages would be "most helpful." Jan took the hint.

The huge cobblestone Market Square was festooned with bright flags and banners waving in the light breeze and was crowded with people, the stalls of florists and farmers, food and clothing carts, street musicians, and a large population of pesky Rock Pigeons, with carriages wending their way through it all.

"The Market Square," Helena explained sourly, "is famous for these cute, filthy, diseased pigeons."

The Square was surrounded by old brick buildings and dominated, as identified by Helena, on the one side by the Sukiennice, or the Drapers' Hall, while the other sides featured the Town Hall, the ornate Church of Saint Wojciech, and, at the far end, the towering façade of Saint Mary's Basilica. They wandered the Square and the adjacent streets and shops for some hours, rapidly filling the baskets they had brought with them with flowers and produce. At one stall, Jan stopped to admire some flat-topped woolen Fisherman's Caps, and Anna insisted on buying him a gray one with a brim made of leather that, she said, gave him a "mysterious" look.

After returning to the Baron's quarters with their purchases, Jan and Anna set out on their own, returning to the Square and passing through it until after some distance they came to the banks of the Vistula River. They spent much of the sunny afternoon walking along the banks, feeding breadcrumbs to pigeons and gulls, and eventually sitting for some time in a grassy area watching the boats and river traffic. As they sat shoulder to shoulder, Jan slowly and hesitatingly told Anna of his plans and that he would need to leave soon, perhaps the next day.

"I know," she said when he had finished. "I wish it were otherwise and that we could sit here forever together, the Not-A-Princess and her shining hero. I could not wish for more, but it is a wish that it is hard for life to grant to two such as us." She linked her arm through his and leaned her head on his shoulder. As they sat in the sun, she smiled as she felt his tears on her forehead, running down slowly to mingle with hers.

After a time, a rowboat pulled up to the bank below them, and its "captain" offered them a ride at a reasonable price. The sun was warm, the river was calm, and time passed by quickly. Hours later, they returned to shore with the sun growing low in the sky, climbed up the grassy bank, and walked slowly back through the streets and a now much quieter Market Square to the house on Krzyza Street.

When dinner that evening was over, they sat in the courtyard with the Baron—listening to the soft sounds of the fountain and enjoying the night air and the stars overhead. Anna was the first to turn in, kissing her father and, as she leaned over to kiss Jan, whispering "Goodbye, safe travels—I will think of you, always and forever" in his ear.

After fifteen minutes, the Baron followed his daughter into the house. Jan sat alone, smoking his pipe and reliving the events of the last few days. In another half hour, he too went inside. As he walked down the hall past Anna's bedroom, he could see the light under the closed door and thought he heard her singing softly to herself.

<hr />

The next morning, Anna did not come to breakfast. Jan ate, packed, and, on his way out, stopped in the parlor to thank the Baron and say goodbye.

"It would be too hard for Anna to see you leave," the Baron said. "But", he smiled, pointing to a side table, "she asked me to be sure you took those."

His new gray Fisherman's Cap and two others, one brown and one black, were lying on the table next to a folded note. He opened the note, which read, "So you will always remember and never, ever forget me." On the inside flap of each cap she had carefully sewn "*Anna*" in gold thread.

Chapter 5

Russian Territory

The morning was unseasonably cold following a night of steady drizzling rain that, in the wakening predawn hours, gave way to clearing skies. The first rays of sunlight began to work on the lingering ground fog and brought the promise of warmer temperatures. Jan sat at the long, heavy wood table in the candle-lit monastery outside the village of Siewierz, carefully sipped the boiling hot tea, and returned the nods of the monks who had shared their breakfast with him and were now, one by one, heading out to tend their fields. He was well to the north of Krakow.

―――≈≈≈≈≈≈≈――――

Before leaving Baron Ihnacak's, Jan had checked the delicate compass he kept wrapped in soft cloth in his rucksack and also consulted his rough map of Central Europe. The map showed many rivers, villages, and towns, but gave little guidance as to the location of roads and railroads in those areas outside the Habsburg Empire. In unpacking the map and compass, he had also run across the undated reposting notice signed by Major Chara. He decided that, because he was now moving away from Krakow, that document could be more of a problem than a help if he were stopped, since it might appear to any border guards searching his bags that he was ignoring the reposting and, instead, deserting. He tore the letter into small pieces and dropped it into Helena's kitchen fire.

He set out toward Główny Station; though not for the purpose of boarding a train. Despite the advice those in Poronin had given him about crossing into Russian territory far to the east, he had decided to move on foot and take a shorter route to the north and northwest. That route, though perhaps involving a riskier border crossing, was a more direct way of reaching the city of Łódź where he planned to catch one of the few trains that ran into Germany.

The area of the Grand Duchy of Krakow formed the extreme northwestern part of Western Galicia, lands of the Austrian Emperor that had been acquired in the partitions of Poland. East of Krakow, and at some distance north, the Galician border with Russian territory ran along the Vistula River, a border that was easily and regularly patrolled. As it approached Krakow, and at a point where its course began to bend south into the city, the Vistula ceased to be the border; from that point, the border continued westward across open fields and rolling low hills. Northwest of the city and the river, still within the Grand Duchy, the roads from Krakow ran for some distance through various small towns and on to the border precincts.

Jan passed by the Station, crossed the river bridge, and moved northwest toward the village of Krzeszowice. Just before the village, and taking care not to be seen, he left the road where it curved briefly through an area of thick woods. He set a course through the trees headed slightly northeast, hoping to avoid any guarded border crossing and to strike the frontier at some isolated point when a patrol was not passing.

It was broad daylight on a Sunday morning, not what most would consider the optimum time for smuggling oneself across a border; but from his own experience on border patrol, he knew it was a time when vigilance was not at its highest state. The actual border here, he soon discovered, consisted of a broken rock wall, in most places a little less than two meters high, extending far off in both directions — to the east it merged into the Vistula where the river became the border. When he first caught sight of the wall, he stopped and concealed himself in a small grove of trees and low bushes where he could watch and listen.

After almost twenty minutes, he noticed thin wisps of smoke rising from behind the wall at a point a short distance to the east. A few minutes later, first one head and then three others popped up on the far side of the wall: the four members of a uniformed Austrian border patrol. They soon began clambering over the wall from the Russian side where they had been sitting, backs against the wall, assumedly watching for anyone who might climb over within their range of vision. Once over the wall, they stood smoking and talking for some time before two of them headed off down the wall to the east. The other two began walking slowly toward where Jan was hidden, though after just a few steps, they veered to the west and disappeared on a trail into the woods.

He waited for half an hour and then cautiously worked his way to the wall, where he scanned the countryside in all directions. He saw nothing and concluded he was alone. Climbing halfway up the wall, he looked over to be sure no other soldiers were lying in wait, then swung over the wall and dropped to the ground on the other side. After another quick look around, he broke into a dead run across a broad open strip of land and into the woods beyond.

Walking at an unhurried pace in wooded country, encountering a few open fields and an occasional low rock fence, he traveled for some hours before coming upon a small, muddy village of eight or nine huts. Smoke curled up from the crumbling chimney of one of the huts, but apart from some chickens scratching in the dust there were few signs of life. Most of the villagers, men and women, were apparently at work in the fields to the east — except for an ancient man sitting in the sunlight near the village gate.

Tipping his cap, Jan asked, "What village is this?"

"The village is Krap," the old man responded.

"The name of the village is Krap?"

"Yes!" the old man said with some annoyance, "Didn't you hear me? You *speak* Polish, but apparently you don't *hear* Polish so well. This is the village of Krap. It is named for what it is."

Jan pulled out his map and, looking at it intently, said, "I don't have any Krap on my map."

"I would think you would be happy about that. Here, let me see that." The old man peered at the map. Pointing with a shaking finger at a blank area north of a line that marked the border, he said: "If it were worth having Krap on the map, this is where it would be. Your map not only doesn't show Krap, but I suppose you've noticed it doesn't show railroads or many roads either. This map is crap."

"I am traveling to Częstochowa," Jan said, pointing to that town on the map. "I don't suppose you would know where the roads run that would take me there."

The old man sighed heavily. "I am old, but my brain has not deserted me. I have lived here forever, and I know everything. When you leave Krap behind, just over there to the left you will see a foot path. Walk on that, and after a few kilometers it will veer into a road of sorts that goes to the village of Siewierz, which is bigger than Krap and which, as you can see on this crap map of yours, is south of Częstochowa. Ask in Siewierz, and I suspect any of the dimwits there can tell you how to get to Częstochowa. Do you have any bread or biscuits?"

Taking off his rucksacks gave Jan a chance to turn away from the old man and hide his laughter. Reaching into one of the sacks, he extracted three biscuits, handed them over, and bent to pick up the rucksacks. When he turned back to the old man, he saw that the biscuits had disappeared. Instinctively, he looked around on the ground.

"What!?" the old man growled. "Do you think I would throw the biscuits on the ground? They were all right, though shamefully small."

Jan tipped his cap and moved on.

The footpath the old man had instructed him to follow led to the road, which, last night, brought him to the monastery and the hospitality of its small cadre of monks. The monks had not only supplied a bed and breakfast but directions to Częstochowa, which they estimated to be another thirty-five kilometers distant.

〰〰〰

As the last of the monks left the table, Jan set his tea mug down and followed them outside. He again turned north. The dirt road wound over low hills and through untended grassy meadows. After walking for almost an hour, he calculated that by maintaining a consistent pace, and provided the monks' estimate of the distance was correct, he could easily reach Częstochowa on Wednesday.

He was still of that opinion and was making good time when, coming over a rise in early afternoon, he saw a number of brightly colored, slow-moving wagons also heading north, less than a kilometer ahead of him on the road. He recognized them as the wagons of gypsies, and he slowed to stay out of sight.

Although there were many exceptions to the rule, in Jan's experience gypsies could be troublesome—and perhaps especially so, he thought, in the case of a lone traveler on a sparsely traveled road. It was best to give them a wide berth. He considered his options. They were moving slowly, so merely following along at a distance would waste hours, perhaps a day, depending on their destination. Going well around them through the woods ahead would be difficult, and he could lose the road. Catching up with them and simply going by without getting entangled was unlikely: he could well acquire their noisy company for the rest of the way to Częstochowa. Waiting for them to camp and slipping by them on the road in the night was possible, but traveling in dark, unfamiliar forestlands would be slow, difficult, and potentially dangerous in terms of unseen obstacles and topography.

While he mulled these choices over, he continued to follow, staying at a distance that strained his ability to keep the wagons in view without himself being seen. Up ahead, the road paralleled a wide stream to the right, and he watched as the wagons began to turn off the road to ford the stream at a point where it was quite shallow. As the wagons crossed the stream, they veered away to a partially concealed clearing, where they stopped; it quickly became apparent that, though hours of daylight remained, the wagons were being unloaded and camp was being set up. Jan considered for a moment, and then determined that passing them in the early evening while some light remained and they were less likely to be watching the road closely might be possible. He moved some distance off the road and climbed a low hill to a point where, sitting with his back against a tree and screened by some low thorn bushes, he could watch the gypsy camp.

The afternoon faded into twilight, and campfires became visible in the clearing just past the wagons. He could see women beginning to cook and men squatting in small groups to smoke their pipes and, almost absentmindedly, watch over small children playing in the dirt nearby. After another half hour, he began moving through the tree line on the left side of the road, slowly closing the distance between himself and a point across from the campsite. By the time he had covered that distance there was little light left, but ahead he could see a small bridge where he would be out of sight of the camp and could return to the road. From there, another half kilometer or so along the road would provide enough distance to begin looking for a place to spend the night; and an early start the next morning would allow him to continue his journey before the gypsies could break camp.

He reached the bridge and returned to the road as the last light failed. With his head down watching the ground, it was some time before he noticed the fires to the side of the road a short distance ahead. He strained to see as he approached, and then quickly stopped in his tracks and moved carefully off the opposite side of the road as the scene ahead became clear. Around the fires and, in fact, putting them out after lighting a number of torches, was a group of perhaps twenty dragoons: by all appearances, and though somewhat out of their normal territory, Cossacks. Their restless horses were tethered in the nearby trees. While the Cossacks posed no particular threat to him, it was probably best to avoid any encounter since they would undoubtedly be curious about a lone traveler on the road at night. He moved as quietly as he could back into the trees and lay flat on the ground facing the road.

Within a few minutes the Cossacks had extinguished the campfires and, many with torches in hand, collected their horses and led them to the road, where they mounted and gathered in a group. He could hear their voices, though he was too far away to make out what they were saying. After a while, they moved off slowly down the road in the direction from which he had come. As the torches faded around a bend, he returned to the road and set out to put some distance between himself and the Cossack campsite.

A half hour later, by what moonlight there was, he made out a small clearing some few meters beyond the trees where he could spend the night. He glanced back down the road and saw the glow of flames in the dark sky. His first thought was that embers had started a forest fire at the Cossack campsite. Then he realized the flames were farther away. He thought of the Cossack torches and the gypsy camp by the side of the little stream, and hoped they were not related.

———≈≈≈≈———

Jan was on the road again early Tuesday morning and traveled overland for two days, reaching Częstochowa early Wednesday evening. He managed to find a café and bakery where he ate dinner and purchased bread, cold boiled pork slices, and three apples, all of which he packed away in his rucksacks. He returned to the road as twilight deepened and soon fell in walking with the vicar of an Orthodox church located on the edge of town, who offered him a bed for the night.

The next three days were spent moving farther north toward Łódź, where he arrived late on Saturday afternoon. He was tired from a long day on the roads, and for the last two hours he had walked in a steady drizzle that left him soaked. The sun had now broken through, and his wet clothes were heavy and steaming as he found his way to the railway station. The schedule on the wall advised him that the "international" train to Poznań—or Posen, as the Germans called it—left on Mondays and Thursdays. He purchased a ticket for Monday's train. The ticket seller advised him that if he was continuing on in Germany he would need to buy tickets in Posen and offered to exchange currency for him. The rate seemed fair and, as they were completing the transaction, Jan asked where he might find a place to dry off and stay for two nights.

"That large old house with the faded-green trim down the street," the ticket seller said, pointing through the window, "is the Pensione Panas. It is a boardinghouse that serves rail travelers at a modest rate that will get you a room, a place to bathe, and two meals a day. The Panas family is trustworthy, and it is the only place nearby that I would recommend. The proprietors of the other places are neighbors of mine, but I'm sad to say they will take advantage of travelers who are strangers. In any event, the Pensione Panas is the closest to the station."

Jan followed his advice and soon found himself in a small room on the second floor facing away from the tracks: "So the trains won't disturb your sleep," according to Mother Panas, who had greeted him at the front door. She also showed him a communal room just down the hall that was equipped with a washstand, bathing tub, soaps, and towels. She noted that water for bathing was available downstairs but that carrying it up was his responsibility. The tub drained much the same way as the one he had used at Baron Ihnacak's quarters.

"I serve a large breakfast for guests promptly at six thirty in the morning and a large dinner at four o'clock in the afternoon," she said as she left him in the room, "and, when you leave, I will pack you food for the train. Also, I will wait in the hall, and if you will turn those wet clothes over to me, I'll wash and rinse them and hang them outside to dry."

Five minutes later, he opened the door a crack and handed his wet trousers and shirt to her. Donning dry clothes, he made three trips downstairs for buckets of cold and hot water and enjoyed a needed bath. The communal bathing room had a small mirror that he used to shave. He also inspected his eyes. Ever since he had followed Baron Ihnacak in jumping off the train near Wieliczka, and despite repeated rinsing whenever he had access to water, his eyes often felt irritated. And most mornings, when he awoke, they were held shut by an accumulated dried crust. This afternoon he noticed the left one was quite red. He had not noticed any change in his vision and assumed that, as with most things, time would heal all.

Later, he sat on the porch at the front of the house, smoked his pipe, and watched darkness settle in before going upstairs for a night of sound sleep.

He spent Sunday wandering about the city with its many Christian churches and its towering Great Synagogue. As the afternoon wore on, he began retracing his steps toward Pensione Panas. He arrived almost exactly at four o'clock and hurried into the dining room, where six other guests were already seated and filling their plates. He settled into an open seat, thought to remove his cap, and was surprised to look up into the eyes of Colonel Tomas Strzala, seated directly across from him. Strzala started, then shook his head slightly from side to side. They said nothing to each other during the meal, though both joined in the occasional discussion among the diners. Strzala was the first to finish eating; he declined tea and left the room.

After dinner, Jan again retired to the porch with his pipe. He knew that Colonel Strzala was unlikely to have any way of knowing whether Jan had knowledge of the events along the railway east of Wieliczka, including the temporary kidnapping or detaining of Anna Ihnacak. On the other hand, he would know that Jan could cause him some serious problems since he could identify him as a colonel in the Austrian army who clearly had no business being deep in Russian territory dressed as a civilian.

After a time, the door opened and Strzala walked out onto the porch. Jan determined he would not be the one to start a conversation. He smoked his pipe and studied the wooden floor.

"I am surprised," Strzala said at length, "to see you here."

"Perhaps not as surprised as I am to see you, Colonel. A secret mission, perhaps?"

"Let's not talk in such terms," Strzala said as he sat down next to Jan. "I am sure we each have our own reasons."

"Undoubtedly." Jan smiled. "And how is Baron Ihnacak... and Anna?"

Strzala looked at the buildings across the street for a long moment before replying. "I am sure they are fine, though I am no longer in his service and have not seen them in some weeks. How did you come to Łódź?"

"On foot from Krakow. I had been visiting relatives south of there and then had some other people to see in Krakow. And you?"

"By train," Strzala said vaguely. "I am not staying here long. How did you make it across the border?"

"Let's just say that I did. Might I ask where you are going from here — or perhaps this is your final destination?"

"No, no, I am not staying in Łódź. I will go to Gdańsk tomorrow and then on from there."

Jan stood, knocked the ashes from his pipe out on to the ground next to the porch, and began moving toward the door. A step past Colonel Strzala he turned and, glaring at the older man, said quietly, "In Krakow, I went with the Baron to meet Anna's train. I also went with him and Colonel Zakof to look for her... and you. Fortunately for her — and for you — we found her. She is fine, despite how you abandoned her to whoever those men were that we found her with. I know you meant her no harm, but if any harm, *any harm whatever*, had befallen her, your life would be worth less than the ashes from my pipe."

"She shouldn't have followed me from the train. And I know that when she did, I should have secured her safety … but there was so little time. Those people had risked much to help me, and I assumed they would put her back on the train."

"You also assumed to risk her safety, if not her life! A bit of advice, *Colonel*, and that is to be sure you are on your way to Gdańsk tomorrow. I may not be feeling as charitable toward you if we meet again."

Jan left Strzala on the porch and, feeling his pulse racing, walked out into the town to calm down. When he returned some hours later, it was almost dark, and he found Mother Panas sitting alone on the porch steps. She patted the step next to her, and he sat down.

"The older gentleman you sat across from at dinner took his things and left, oh, perhaps thirty minutes ago. He asked me to tell you he was sorry, though," she said, turning to look at him, "he didn't say what he was sorry about. Was it something that happened here, or do you two know each other from before?"

"It is from before. I am not sure that an apology corrects the wrong, but it is, I suppose, good that he recognizes an apology is needed, though it is really owed to someone who will never know of it."

Mother Panas sighed heavily and looked out across the street. "There are, you know, two parts to being sorry for what one has done. One part is to understand and feel the sorrow for the wrong you have committed. The other is to be able to tell the person you have wronged that you are sorry and to know, whether they forgive you or not, that they at least understand how you feel. That understanding will be missing here, and the gentleman you spoke with will know that and either have to live with it—for he will think of it all again and again—or find some way to deliver the apology to the person to whom it is owed."

They sat silently for a while until she spoke again. "It is not too late for an old woman to get a little exercise if she has a young man to walk with her and hold her arm."

They stepped off the porch, she put her arm through his, and they walked off down the street.

—⁓⁓⁓⁓⁓—

The Monday train to Posen—an aged locomotive, a coal tender, and three well-worn passenger cars with hard, splintered wooden seats and dusty windows—was making steam as he boarded. It was a German train, though at this point it had a Russian crew. There were no stops before the border, and at the border the Russian crew would be replaced by a German engineer and crew.

Before they pulled out of the station, a Russian official accompanied by three bored soldiers entered the train and proceeded
through the cars, checking documentation and asking questions. At
the front of the car Jan was in, the official spent some time talking to
two young men traveling together. After perhaps ten minutes, two
of the soldiers escorted one of the men off the train and took him
into the station.

At length, the official came to Jan's seat and took his papers. He
paged through them carefully, pausing at the Service Completion
document and staring at Jan for a moment.

The official spoke Polish. "And what is your final destination
after Posen? Would it be Bremen?"

"Ultimately, yes," Jan responded, having long ago decided to
answer any questions from border guards or other officials quickly
and honestly.

The official looked at all the papers again. After studying them
for a third time, with occasional glances at Jan, he handed them
back and, using a balky fountain pen, began to fill out a yellow
card.

"When the German border officials ask for your papers, give
them this card and all of the papers you have shown me, except
for the Austrian Service Completion document. On the card, I have
indicated that to my knowledge you have been a resident of Łódź
for more than a year and are a Russian citizen. Once you have entered Germany, the documents you have will not allow you to re-
enter Russia, so if you have ideas of coming back here, legally, you
shouldn't leave but should get off the train now. Is that clear?"

Jan nodded and took the yellow card, and the official moved
on. A half hour later, as the train whistle sounded, Jan saw the official and the soldiers, with another, sullen-looking passenger in
tow, go into the station.

The route to Posen covered some one hundred and eighty

kilometers, with the single stop at a desolate point at the border. As the train crew changed, a German army officer and a lower-ranking soldier came through the cars. While he looked at the documentation most people offered, he seemed most interested in the yellow cards, which he studied and then handed to the soldier, who stamped each card in two places, cut it in half, and handed one half back to the passenger. As he handed Jan's documents back to him and gave the yellow card to the soldier to stamp, the officer forced a smile and said, "The Russians are idiots for letting their young men, or Austria's young men, leave the country, but we are happy to welcome such to Prussia."

The soldier handed Jan the yellow card and trailed after the officer, who was already questioning passengers seated in the back of the car. After perhaps twenty minutes, the train began to move slowly forward and they entered Prussian Germany.

<hr />

The train rolled on through the German countryside. While to other passengers he appeared to be watching the passing fields and woods, Jan was oblivious to the scenery. His mind was focused on the things he had been thinking about before the train reached the border stop and which, in fact, had preoccupied him in the long solitary hours as he had walked northward from Krakow to Łódź.

A set of those recurring thoughts dealt on the one hand with the family he had left behind and, on the other hand, with the journey and the life ahead. He imagined that every emigrant had concerns or fears about both, including whether the decision was the right one. He had no doubts on that score, and he expected to outgrow some strong longings for the familiar comfort of Važec. But his heart ached for the family which had been so supportive, and he thought often of them all, especially of his mother — undoubtedly lying awake at night thinking of him, wondering where he was and whether he was safe. He hoped those worries, though not her memories of him, would pass in time. He couldn't imagine that all those he had left behind would ever be out of his thoughts.

The journey and Maria were inextricably tied together, and she dominated his thoughts. Until that early morning in May when he had left with the drivers and the herd, there had not been a day in the last two years when he hadn't seen her. Many of those days, beginning almost a year ago, had been spent sharing and building their dreams, talking of this journey, and planning for when she would follow and join him. She was a unique person, perfectly suited for him, and he wondered at the fortune that had caused them to grow up together in the same small village. He admired her for many reasons and took seriously what he knew was her complete faith in him, though that faith carried its own heavy burden of living up to her dreams and her expectations. He knew the separation would grow more difficult as the months passed, but with luck they would be together in America by sometime next winter or spring.

The train moved through a long stretch of open, overgrown, and carelessly tended fields. He took off his cap to wipe his brow, and the name sewn on the inside flap caught his eye. Anna was also repeatedly and persistently in his thoughts. Those included memories of her coming out to meet him on the days he was clearing the trails at Štrbské Pleso; how worried and afraid he had felt when she turned up missing; how she had held on to him when rescued; the day they had spent together in Krakow, sitting on the bank of the Vistula and enjoying the long rowboat ride. All of those moments and others had occurred over just a handful of days, but something undeniable had grown between them. It troubled him to feel love for two women, though he knew there were subtle but important differences in those feelings and that Maria's place was unshakeable in his heart. He also knew, as he looked at the cap resting in his lap, that if there were no Maria he would have stayed in Krakow much longer.

Chapter 6

Germany

As the afternoon wore on, he dug into his rucksack for the packages Mother Panas had given him. One held a large cucumber, radishes, and boiled potatoes cut into round slices as thick as his finger. The other held two smaller packages, each of which contained thin pieces of baked chicken placed between two slices of soft dark bread. He halved the cucumber and cut it into slices, which he ate with some of the potatoes and one of the chicken-bread combinations. He finished as, in a light rain and growing darkness, the train pulled into Posen.

He had done well enough in his short conversation with the officer at the border, but knew that his lessons with Herr Schmidt, and his proficiency in German, would meet their first real test here at the station. Stepping down from the train, he joined the crowd of passengers making their way into the waiting room. A quick look around led him to a big chalkboard listing departures. From there, he joined a line at the ticket kiosk, rehearsing in his mind what he would say when his turn came.

"Is there space left on the night train — train number fourteen — to Berlin?" he asked as he stepped up to the cage.

"There is," the agent replied. "Light or dark coach?"

It was not the response he had expected. He tried to choose his words carefully, hoping he didn't sound like either a fool or a foreigner. "I'm sorry, I don't understand. Does the color of the coach matter? Is there a difference in the fare?"

The agent glanced up from under a heavy set of eyebrows and gave him an exasperated look. "I'm not talking about colors. This is the night train: so named because it travels at night. The light coach is lighted so, you know, you can see. The dark coach has no lights; in case you wish to sleep or whatever you do in the dark. The fare is the same."

"Oh, well, the dark coach, then." Jan counted out what seemed to be the fare and pushed it through the cage slot.

"The train leaves on track four in—let's see—just about two hours," the agent said, sliding the ticket and change back through the same slot. "The train has four cars. The dark coaches are cars three and four, take your choice. You may sit wherever you wish."

He walked about the station for a while until he located track four. A train waited, motionless and silent, on the rails; an occasional wisp of steam escaping with a muted "chuff" from under the idling locomotive. On the nearby platform, a half dozen people sat on luggage or boxes, apparently waiting to board.

The waiting room was dimly lit and cavernous, with few benches and a bare, oppressively cold feeling. It was largely peopled by heavily armed soldiers; most of whom were sitting on the stone floor in small groups, surrounded by piles of knapsacks and rifles, and wreathed in hanging clouds of pipe and cigarette smoke. A few glanced his way as he walked by, though he got the distinct impression that they barely noticed him or anyone else; their facial expressions were at best sullen and brooding, at worst hostile. He stepped outside and found not only fresher air but also a bench under a small overhang that provided shelter from the dripping rain.

He sat outside until the wind came up and the rain began to blow under the overhang. Back inside the station, he made his way to track four. The conductor confirmed that the train was bound for Berlin, with two intermediate stops. Cars three and four were not totally devoid of light, but they were considerably darker than the first two cars. He climbed aboard car number three, which was—though departure was still nearly an hour away—a third full, with some of the passengers already beginning to doze off.

The train pulled out promptly at 9:45 p.m. For a while he slouched against the window, watching as the train worked its way through the town and its outskirts, the locomotive occasionally emitting long, sorrowful-sounding blasts of its whistle.

—≈≈≈≈≈—

The whistles and the sudden, jarring sound of escaping steam woke him up at each of the two stops, but for the most part he slept through the night, waking stiffly as the train slowed coming into Berlin. Having been to Vienna and Prague, he was not unprepared for a large metropolis. But Berlin impressed him as apparently bigger and definitely drearier, though he concluded that perhaps that was due to the misting rain and fog that engulfed the still-dark city.

The train shed was long, and disembarking was slow. The station was vast, well lit, and very busy despite the early-morning hour. He had no great desire to spend much time there, and, after again studying the schedule boards, he stood in the queue and purchased a through ticket to Bremen via Hannover, where he would change trains. Checking the ticket, he saw that it showed the date to be August 1.

He stretched his legs by walking about the station, went outside for a while to catch some fresh air, purchased tea and biscuits from a cart in the waiting room, and sat down on a bench at a long, empty table. As he ate, he opened one of his rucksacks and surreptitiously counted his remaining money; he was reasonably satisfied that he had more than would be needed to pay for passage to New York, travel from there to Minneapolis by way of Chicago, and other expenses. He made a mental note that he needed paper if, as he had promised, he was going to write to Maria when he reached Bremen.

As he left his seat at the table and went off to board the train, he glanced again at the schedule boards and noted that the journey to Hannover, with a number of stops along the way, would take over seven hours. And at that point, it would still be roughly another one hundred kilometers to Bremen.

———⟨⟨⟨⟩⟩⟩———

The rain was everywhere, and the day passed slowly. The train was newer than the others he had ridden and considerably more comfortable, since the seats were padded, albeit thinly. However, the seats were closer together, with little leg room, and the seat back was set in such a way that within an hour he had developed a sore back, which he attempted to alleviate by getting off at a couple of the intermediate stops to walk on the platforms and stretch his back and legs.

Halfway to Hannover, the man across the aisle rolled up his Berlin newspaper and asked Jan if he was interested in reading it. He accepted the offer with thanks, glad at the opportunity to both fill time and to further test his language skills. The most interesting part of the paper was a story about an event that had occurred some months before, the visit to Berlin of former United States President Theodore Roosevelt, who had arrived on what was apparently a grand European tour following a hunting trip in Africa. The story purported to present some new information about Roosevelt's visit, including what the paper described as his "close" relationship with Kaiser Wilhelm II.

Hannover was reached in due course and on time, and in the interval between trains Jan was able to purchase writing paper and envelopes at a shop across from the station. The connecting train to Bremen was scheduled to make seven intermediate stops. However, because no passengers got off at some stations and no one boarded at others, it made good time and pulled into Bremen more than an hour ahead of schedule.

Getting off the train, he realized he had no definite idea of where he was going. A station clerk, who acted as if he had heard the same questions many times before, directed him to Bahnhof Street, then past the Town Hall and from there to the Weser River, where he would find government offices, the offices of various steamship companies, and the city docks.

The directions proved to be generally accurate, and Jan acquired important pieces of information. First, he found a small office of the Norddeutscher-Lloyd steamship company. There, he learned from its agent that the company's liner *Grosser Kurfurst* would leave for New York from the company's wharf in Bremerhaven in three days and that it had room for additional third-class passengers. However, the company would not book passage for anyone until they had been cleared by the German emigration officials. The agent directed him to the appropriate government office, which was closing for the day when he arrived, but he was able to confirm the documents he would need, which he had, and was told that processing in the morning would begin shortly before 8:00 a.m. He was also advised that if he expected to be on a ship sailing in three days' time, he needed to complete his processing the following day.

At the Norddeutscher-Lloyd office he also thought to inquire as to lodgings in the area and was directed to two small hotels. One of those, the Altstadt Pensione, proved to have a single room available. While it served only breakfast to its guests, Jan still had some of the food Mother Panas had packed for him in Łódź. After eating, he borrowed a pen and an inkwell from the proprietor, took out the paper he had purchased, and sat at the table in his room in the low light of a small oil lamp.

1ˢᵗ August
Dear Maria:

I have arrived in Bremen after my time at Štrbské Pleso and a journey much like that we had talked about those many late nights, the walking and long train rides made the easier by the kindness of many, including the Brozek families in Poland. I had no trouble at any of the borders and experienced very little along the way that could be called unusual. It was an easy trip, though I am glad you will not have to walk the many kilometers I did. I am in good health and in good spirits.

The Polish Brozeks and friends in their village of Poronin who know of these things recommended I travel if possible on Norddeutscher-Lloyd Lines, a steamship company that serves the great city of New York from Bremen. On arriving in Bremen today, I inquired at the company's office and discovered that their modern steamship the Grosser Kurfürst leaves on 4 August, in three days, for New York. I cannot purchase my ticket until I have seen the German emigration officials, which I will do tomorrow. By the time you receive this I will be well on my way and should arrive in America in no more than ten or twelve days' time from sailing. I will, of course, write you from New York and tell you of my plans for reaching Chicago and beyond, and also of those things I will recommend to you for your own journey, when that time comes.

I will write to my family separately today to also let them know that I am safe and well. I will also write to them about the Polish Brozeks, which I know will interest my father. I will ask them to share that letter with you as well.

It has been difficult to spend this time away from you but through that sorrow I see the vision of the better life in a new world that we will share together for more years than we can now count.

Jan

He completed a second, longer letter to his parents and sealed each letter in its envelope, on which he carefully printed the simple Važec addresses. As he set those aside, he looked at the remaining paper and envelopes, and thought of Anna. He had an address for her in Vienna and was sure that she and her father were on their way there even now. What would he say? How would he say it? Would she think him a fool ... or was she even now hoping such a letter would come? He started a letter, but after two lines scratched it out and crumpled the sheet. A second, longer try ended in the same way. The wick in the lamp on the table was growing low when he put the paper away and capped the inkwell. Perhaps, he mused, my thoughts will be clearer tomorrow night.

———⟫⟫⟫⟪⟪⟪———

After breakfast the next morning, he returned the pen and the inkwell to the proprietress of the Altstadt Pensione, who offered to post the letters for him when she went to the market later that morning. He thanked her, gave her what she thought would be needed for postage, and headed back toward the Weser River waterfront.

He reached the building housing the German emigration officials well before eight o'clock and joined a line that already included three or four dozen people. Some of the people ahead of him seemed to have spent the night on the sidewalk and the few nearby benches, waiting for the office to open. When the doors were at last unlocked, officials came out to organize the crowd into two processing lines. One line was for families and the other, to which he was directed, was for single travelers. Those in line spoke little, other than to complain about how slow the line moved. Most appeared to be Polish or Russian; many of them seemed very nervous. As he moved inside the building, he could see that those waiting in each line moved through a series of stations. It was almost 9:30

a.m., and the line of people behind him had grown long, stretching well down the street outside, when his turn came.

At the first stop, he was seated at a table across from a civilian official who took his documentation and, as he read through those papers, began to slowly fill in the blanks on a form that he took from a stack at the edge of the table. He worked silently for perhaps ten minutes, writing carefully and moving down the sheet.

"In order to complete this form," he said at last, looking up at Jan, "I have a few questions, the first of which is your date of birth. The church certificate says March 1886, but the date is unclear."

"Sir, the date should read March 3, 1886. I am twenty-four years of age."

"I see you entered Germany from Russia on the Łódź-to-Posen train and have only been in this country for a few days. I assume from that that your only reason for traveling to Germany has been for the purpose of emigration?"

"That is correct."

"And from here your destination is...?"

"America."

"On which ship, and have you ascertained whether passage is available on that ship?"

"On the *Grosser Kurfürst*; it leaves from Bremerhaven in two days. I visited their agency here yesterday. They have space in third class."

"I need to count the money you have with you, whether in German Marks or other currency. This is to be sure you are not a pauper and can pay your passage and other expenses that are usual for a trip to America."

Jan dug in his rucksack and pulled out the packet with the money he carried, adding to it that which he had in his pocket. The official counted it quickly.

"That, if it is of interest to you, is perhaps half again the minimum required amount we need to see in your possession. You can do as you wish, but I suggest you exchange the Austrian money for German Marks before you board your ship," the official said as he handed the money back. He then signed his name at the bottom of the form, gathered it and the documents Jan had presented together, and placed them all in a large folder.

"Please," he said as he handed the folder to Jan, "remove your cap." He studied Jan for a long moment and then said, "You now need to see the doctor. He is at the next table there, finishing up with that fellow. You can stand off to the side here until the doctor calls you over. Give him this folder, and keep your cap off."

Jan moved down the line, and in a few minutes the doctor dismissed the man he was talking to and motioned for Jan to come forward and be seated. Taking the folder, he removed the form the official had just filled out and scanned it for a moment.

"Do you speak German?" he asked. And to Jan's nod, the doctor continued, "Good; that makes it easier. Brozek — is that Czech? Polish?"

"No, it is Slovak."

"Ah yes, I see that now. And, Slovak Brozek, you desire to emigrate to America on the *Grosser Kurfürst*?"

"Yes, sir, I do."

"I hear it is a fine ship. I need to conduct a brief examination because the United States of America has certain health laws that apply to immigrants, and we must certify that travelers from Germany meet those requirements when leaving Bremen. That is necessary as a matter of law and because if we pass you through without meeting the requirements, you will be denied entry in New York. I need you to come around to the side here and stand on that mark on the floor."

The doctor stood and waited while Jan moved around the table. The examination was brief—the doctor grasped Jan's hands and turned his arms; had him do a half dozen deep knee bends; ran his fingers through Jan's hair and across his scalp; checked his teeth and mouth; looked into his ears; listened to him breathe and cough; and looked closely into his eyes. From a jar on the table he took a buttonhook, of the sort used to lace up high-buttoned boots, and used that hook to pull each eyelid back and turn it inside out so he could see the inside of the eyelid. He examined each eye with some care, then pulled a small white cloth from a little black bag on the table and used that to wipe the corners of first one eye, then the other. He gazed thoughtfully at the cloth for a moment before dropping it in a wastebasket and motioning Jan to be seated.

As the doctor again looked at him across the table, Jan felt a sudden dryness in his throat and a rising tightness in his chest.

"How long have your eyes been red like they are now?" the doctor asked, handing Jan a small mirror.

"About, perhaps, two weeks — or maybe a bit longer," Jan replied, looking in the mirror and thinking back to when it was he had jumped off the train with Baron Ihnacak near Wieliczka.

"And how long have your eyes been discharging? In other words, how long have they been tearing or making mucous?"

"About that same length of time — though it is much less than before."

The doctor sat thoughtfully for a moment before leaning forward, resting his forearms on the table and folding his hands.

"You have," he said quietly, "a rather significant eye inflammation that may or may not be permanent, and may or may not be a sign of disease. It could be early trachoma, which is a contagious and at times dangerous infection that can lead to blindness. Frankly, I think that it is unlikely to be permanent and is *probably* not trachoma; but at best, in my opinion, it will not clear up for some time, perhaps weeks or months. This eye condition will not be acceptable to the immigration officials and doctors in America.

It is required by the Bremen Senate that any emigrant not admitted by the American authorities must be transported back to Germany at the ship owner's expense. Obviously, we cannot expose the ship owners to this cost when we know a person has a condition that will or may prevent his admission in America. So," the doctor paused, "I cannot sign this form to authorize your emigration. I would advise you to return home until this condition has cleared up and then remake your plans for America."

"I-is th-th-there not," Jan stammered, "some ointment or lotion that you could prescribe that would clear this, this inflammation up quickly?"

The doctor slowly shook his head, and Jan could sense there was no point in pleading his cause. He felt his stomach turn over and the tightness in his chest increase. An initial, blank feeling of despair quickly gave way to a jumble of thoughts that seemed to trip over each other and crowd his mind in a matter of seconds. He could not stay in Germany, and any journey back to Važec would be difficult. If he did make his way back, a second parting from his family — at some unknown time in the future — would be even harder, especially for his mother. The difficulty of leaving Važec a second time and crossing the borders again would be magnified in every way.

And what would he do if the problem with his eyes cleared up on the way back to Važec? Or when he arrived there? Or even at some future time? How would he know for sure that it had cleared up permanently and that another trip across Europe and back to Bremen, at whatever time, would not end in the same result? In returning to Važec there would also be embarrassment in the jeers of the friends he had left behind, and who by now surely knew the reason for his absence.

Most importantly, if he went back, the plans he and Maria had made, and the confidence she had in him, would be jeopardized, with the prospect of not ever leaving Važec a possibility. In that case, their future and their dreams of a better life would be dashed in his personal failure, and they would have a lifetime of thinking about what might have been. Would she understand and could she still be happy, or would he lose her? He thought of the letters that were being posted that morning and the optimism and progress they expressed.

While the room was not warm, he realized that he was sweating, and he wondered if the doctor noticed. Almost instinctively, he began to fight the negative thoughts and the rising panic. He knew that he had to go on and deal with reality, and that he had to find a new plan.

He looked at the doctor, who sat quietly and expressionless across the table. After a few minutes that seemed like hours, he asked, "Are there any countries that have immigration laws that would tolerate this eye condition?"

The doctor thought for a minute, nodded, and, motioning Jan to stay where he was, walked over to talk with the doctor in the other processing line. After a short discussion, with both doctors glancing at Jan from time to time, he came back.

"There are some places in Europe, but I know that is not where you want to be, and in any event, you don't need my permission to go to those places. In the New World, Argentina isn't particularly interested in relatively minor health conditions or infirmities. They also welcome immigrants. My colleague and I agree that I can sign the documents authorizing your passage to Argentina."

"Where, exactly, is Argentina?"

"It is in the continent of South America, whereas the United States is in North America. Both are across the Atlantic Ocean. I would guess, though I have never been to either place, that it is probably as far from New York to Argentina as it is from Bremen to New York. I can sign the documents for you, but you will then have to find a ship that is bound for there, probably to its largest city, Buenos Aires. I have signed documents such as this for a few other Argentinean immigrants, and there are ships that sail from here to there, though I don't know what ships or when the next may be leaving. My impression is that there are not as many ships sailing that route as there are ships transporting people from Bremen to New York, so it could be weeks or months, I suppose."

Jan turned slightly away from the doctor and looked out across the room. He knew he needed to decide and do something: there were but seconds or minutes to make a change in plans that had developed over years. Without knowing exactly how he reached the decision, he said, "Thank you for your advice and information. At least for now, I think I will go to Argentina and find a way to America from there."

"Take this folder," the doctor said while crossing out "United States of America" and writing in "Argentina Only" and signing the form, "to the man at the last desk by the door. He will give you your documents back and issue your clearance and exit pass. You will need to report also to the emigration office on the docks in Bremerhaven to obtain a boarding pass, once, assuming there is some available ship, you have passage booked. And good luck to you."

Jan nodded his thanks, stopped at the last desk, and was soon outside on the street. He felt disoriented, almost lost, but somehow found his way to a small park on the river and sat on the grassy bank for a long time. Looking at the boat traffic, though seeing very little, he sought to control his emotions and collect not only his thoughts but his resolve. Slowly, he began to think in terms of an unplanned detour, not an end, and of taking that detour until it led him back to his road to America. Although he had made one decision, it was not final, and he still had time to think; nothing was really settled until a ship he was on, and that was bound for

Argentina, left the dock in Bremerhaven. His next task was to find out if there was such a ship.

It was well after noon when he gathered his things and set out for the office of the Norddeutscher-Lloyd line. They did not have any passenger ships leaving for South America. However, the man at the desk had a shipping list for the entire port for the remainder of the month and found that there was an English freighter docked at Bremerhaven and due to depart for Buenos Aires on the same day the *Grosser Kurfürst* left for America. He advised him that freighters sometimes carried a limited number of passengers and noted that the English ship's agent had his office three doors down the street.

That office appeared deserted when Jan walked through the door, but the agent soon appeared from a smoky back room. The freighter in question, the *Kastledale*, under an English captain, was indeed leaving in two days with scheduled ports of call in Cardiff, Lisbon, the Canary Islands, and Recife, Brazil, before arriving at its final destination in Buenos Aires. It carried up to twenty-six passengers, with all but eight of the places spoken for at this time. In addition, the ship was listed as being two crew members or general deckhands short, with the captain seeking to fill those positions in Bremerhaven. Passage to Buenos Aires as a passenger would cost one hundred and sixty-eight Marks, quite a bit more than Jan would have paid on the *Grosser Kurfürst*. The agent explained that was not only because the voyage was longer but because the owner, the Kastle Lines, was not in the business of being a carrier of thousands of passengers. That said, the agent added, the quarters on the *Kastledale* would be "far better" than third class on the Norddeutscher-Lloyd ship, and the fare included meals. "On the *Kastledale*," the agent assured him, "passengers eat what the crew eats, which is superior to the meager fare you would be able to buy in third class on any ship to America."

Jan hesitated for a moment: the added cost was another change in plans. Later, he could not recall what else, if anything, he had thought of in those few minutes while standing at the counter in the agent's office. Whatever those thoughts were, he soon found himself counting out the fare and booking passage. As he wrote the ticket and receipt, the agent suggested that Jan would be well-served to take the early-morning train to Bremerhaven. And if he was interested, he should find the ship at its wharf and speak to the captain or the dock agent about the deckhand positions.

"If," the agent advised, "you sign on as a deckhand, the dock agent will refund your fare, though you would then move to a crew bunk."

With his lips pressed tightly together, he retraced his steps to the Altstadt Pensione, thinking as he walked of the day's shattering events, and of whether he had made the right decision about going to Argentina; and of whether he wanted to be a deckhand on the *Kastledale*; and of finding out the time of the morning train to Bremerhaven; and of exchanging his remaining Korona for Marks; and of the need to once again spend the evening writing letters — and what he would say to Maria; and of when and how, in an unknown new world, he would somehow get from Argentina, wherever that was, to America.

PART TWO
At Sea

Chapter 7

Waking up early wasn't a problem for someone who had not been able to fall asleep. It was well before dawn when Jan doused the oil lamp, carefully closed the door of his room, and made his way as silently as possible down the creaking stairs. The pensione was quiet except for the kitchen, where he found the husband and wife owners: she working on the beginnings of breakfast, he sipping tea and tallying items in a heavy book of accounts. Jan paid his bill and also counted out the change necessary to cover the postage on the letters he had written the night before and which the proprietress once again agreed to mail for him that morning.

He set out through the wet, dimly lit streets for the early-morning train to Bremerhaven, carrying the large brown leather and blue canvas duffel bag he had bought the previous afternoon. One of the rucksacks was strapped on his back. The other—now empty and folded flat—fit into the duffel bag along with all his other personal belongings, including the lighter-weight boots he had also purchased as better for travel on a ship than the pair he was wearing, and which had brought him across Europe.

The train was full of sleepy seamen, early-shift dock workers, and anxious travelers. One of the last to board was the agent who had booked Jan's passage on the *Kastledale* the previous afternoon.

The agent was carrying a bulging case of papers. He slid into the seat next to Jan and, before falling asleep, explained that the papers were the final passenger lists and other documents for three ships, including the *Kastledale*, that were leaving port in the next twenty-four hours.

In Bremerhaven, signs provided directions to the emigration offices. Even though the offices would not open for another hour, long jumbled lines of people, and piles of their bags and luggage of all sorts and descriptions, had already formed outside the building. Some small groups were engaged in low conversation, but for the most part, those in line stood silently: faces anxious and serious, eyes scanning the crowd and the nearby street. The air was heavy with fog, tobacco smoke, and the watery smells of the harbor.

When the doors opened, the lines moved slowly, and it was midmorning before Jan emerged with a pass which, after 2:00 p.m., would allow him access to the wharf where the *Kastledale* was tied up. He wandered about the neighboring streets until he encountered two side-by-side shops, one a bookseller and the other boasting the sign "Uffsted—Famous Ships' Chandler and Seamen's Supply." At the bookstore, he searched in vain for anything about Argentina, but did buy a German translation of a novel by the Slovak writer Martin Kukučin. At the chandler's, he procured a dark-blue wool peacoat and a map that showed Europe, the Atlantic Ocean, and the Americas. Wending his way back to the waterfront, he found a seat on a low wall at a spot where he could see the clock on the tower of an old brewery building, as well as two nearby steamships.

Although he had seen a few pictures of ocean liners, the size of the ships amazed him. Studying them provided a diversion from the continuing turmoil and anxiety he felt over the expected fact that he was about to leave Europe and the unexpected fact that he was headed to a place that, until yesterday, he had never heard of before. While he was now committed to that journey, his mind still wrestled with doubts about whether that decision was the right one. Those doubts were sure to linger and, he imagined, would inevitably rise to the surface again and again.

He packed and lit his pipe, and watched the activity on the ships and on the nearby docks as the morning slowly passed into early afternoon. Shortly before 2:30 p.m., he slid down from the wall and headed for the wharf.

The guard at the gate examined his pass and directed him down the wharf. He found the *Kastledale* and, in a small white shed nearby, the dock agent. While the agent inspected his papers and ticket, Jan looked up at the ship. It had what appeared to be a recently painted hull: gray above the water line and dull crimson below. The center of the ship was completely taken up by a sprawling, white four-deck structure topped by two towering funnels, one of which was emitting a thin plume of black smoke. The lower half of each funnel, as well as the top quarter, was painted black. In between the black areas there were four stripes running around each funnel in alternating colors of bright blue and gold. The main deck featured four cranes, two located forward and two aft of the center structure. The long arms on the forward set of cranes were busy maneuvering large crates that had been lifted to the deck from the wharf. While Jan couldn't see the surface of the main deck, he assumed those crates were being loaded into the ship's hold through open hatches.

"The *Kastledale*," the agent said without looking up from his papers, "is a refrigerated cargo vessel, though only the aft cargo holds – those toward the back of the ship – are refrigerated. The forward holds, up front, carry nonrefrigerated cargo. Generally, the refrigerated holds are used only when she's bringing meat, mostly beef, from Argentina. Sometimes she makes the return trip, like this one, only partially loaded, since there isn't much that Germany has in the way of cargo for South America that needs refrigeration."

"So, what is the ship carrying on this trip?"

"Well, the refrigerated holds will actually be pretty full—frozen chickens and a lot of good German cheeses. In the forward holds, she'll carry a large shipment of light machinery, some chemicals of one kind or another, and about thirty big crates of fancy furniture. There will be a stop in Wales to load coal in one of the forward holds that is designed to carry cargo coal. Fully loaded, she can carry about four thousand tons of cargo. That's not counting the coal that's stored in the bunkers for the ship itself to burn."

"I've never been on such a vessel," Jan observed.

"I can tell," the agent remarked drily. "Your papers are in order, and you're clear to board. I have a note here about the open deck-hand spots, but those have been filled by experienced seamen."

Reaching into a box at his feet, the agent pulled out a wide red ribbon and handed it to Jan. "You need to wear this on your left arm at all times, starting now. It identifies you as a passenger. Anyone on the ship who doesn't have such an armband is a member of the crew. The ship will be loaded by this evening and will be leaving as soon as it is cleared by the harbormaster, which could even be late tonight. Most of the passengers are on board now. A few are still to come. Once everyone is here, Captain Cameron will have a meeting with the passengers in the ship's Mess, which is the room where you'll take your meals, to give you some of the rules and schedules for the voyage, where you can go and where you can't go on the ship, and some other information. A crew member will come around and call you to that meeting. Until that meeting has been held, don't wander around too much."

"Is a meal available this evening?"

"Eh, yes, and the food on the *Kastledale* is pretty damn good. It'll be set out in the Mess around seven o'clock. Take your papers here and go up that gangway. There should be a steward, German named Dietrich, at the top. Tell him you're in number five, and he'll show you where that is and also how to find the Mess. Number five is a two-bunk cabin, so you'll be sharing with somebody else; but you're the first, so you can choose which bed you want."

Dietrich was lounging on the rail watching Jan come up the gangway, and he immediately began a running commentary as they turned toward the midship structure.

"This that we're standing on here is called the weather deck, and it runs from bow to stern—from front to back. Inside here on this deck," he gestured as they entered the big midship structure, "are crews' quarters and storage. Some of the crew have quarters in the forecastle, which is in the bow, up front. And we got a few bunks right below this deck: for engineers, greasers, and stokers to use if they need to be near the engines for some reason. These stairs go all the way up to the bridge, and there's another set of stairs opposite on the starboard corner, aft. Starboard, if you don't know, is the right side of the ship facing forward. What we're on here is the port side…the left side."

They climbed to the second deck and looked in on the Mess, which had large, square windows facing forward overlooking the weather deck and tables and chairs that Jan guessed could seat about thirty people at a time.

"Between meals," Dietrich went on, "this is a smoking area, or you can read or just watch the sea and the air go by, I suppose. You can also smoke outside on deck, but no smoking in your cabin. That over there is the door to the galley where the cooks make the meals. There's also some food storage lockers there. The stewards—me and a kid named Ansel—serve passengers' meals and keep all four decks here shipshape and in order. Usually crew eats here at one time and passengers at another, but I haven't seen the schedule for this trip yet."

When they reached the third deck, Dietrich stopped and, pointing up the stairs, said, "We won't go up there right now, but the fourth deck is the bridge, where the captain steers the ship. Also up there, aft, are cabins and quarters for four officers. On top of the bridge is a compass platform. If you want to go up to the bridge someday to look around, ask one of the officers first."

As they entered the third deck, they came into an open area between the portside windows and the funnel housing that ran up through the middle of all the decks. This area had a few wooden benches, tables, and chairs. Ahead, Jan could see that there were cabins facing forward across the entire width of the deck and a smaller number—he counted five—facing aft between the two sets of stairs.

"This we're in here," Dietrich indicated with a sweep of his arm, "is a passenger sitting area. The fancy English name for that is "lounge," whatever that means. You got cabins one through six forward and seven through eleven aft."

"Up here," he continued as they walked ahead, "cabins one and six, in the corners, each have bunks for four people. Sometimes families are in those. The four in between are doubles, and yours is here, number five."

Cabin number five proved to be eight feet wide and ten feet long. To Jan's right as he entered were lower and upper bunks, each with a set of dark curtains. To the left and against the wall was a long padded bench. The wall above the bench had six clothes hooks, three on either side of an enclosed lamp that was centered above the bench. Straight ahead was a washstand with a large pitcher and two small basins. To the left of the washstand was a series of hooks holding three or four well-worn towels. Above the washstand was a square housing for a porthole that looked out over the weather deck to the ship's bow.

"You can open that porthole for air," said Dietrich, "and on the back of this door you'll find a mirror and a hook with two door keys. One of those keys is for you and one for your roommate, when he shows up. Like I said, no smokin' in here, and nobody but you is responsible for any valuables you leave in the room—which is a way of saying always lock the room when you're gone and don't trust your roommate until you're sure about him ... and I'll be telling him the same thing about you. Any questions about the cabin or anything?"

"The agent said the captain would have a meeting with passengers. Do you know when that will be?"

"Not yet: it depends on when everybody is on board. Ansel or me will come around and tell everybody as soon as Captain Cameron tells us. It might be at dinner, which for passengers tonight, at least, is at seven o'clock. I'll be at that meeting if you have other questions. Right now, I need to get my butt back to the gangway because that bell you hear means the agent's checking in another passenger."

As Dietrich closed the door behind him, Jan set his duffel bag and rucksack on the lower bunk, took out the peacoat and his three shirts, and hung those all on the hooks to the left of the lamp. He decided not to lay claim to the lower bunk until he met his roommate. Pulling out the map he had purchased at the chandler's, he spread it open on the bench and began to study the Atlantic Ocean he was about to cross.

The map showed a good part of Europe, including the port of Bremen. He traced the route he imagined a ship like the *Grosser Kurfürst* would sail—into the North Sea, south through the English Channel, and then across the Atlantic Ocean to New York. It wasn't exactly a straight line, but it was a very direct route. Chicago and his ultimate destination of Minneapolis both seemed to be due west of New York.

He then traced the route that the agent had indicated the *Kastledale* would follow from Bremen, down the English Channel to Cardiff in Wales, then to Lisbon, the Canary Islands, the port of

Recife, and finally to Buenos Aires. From Buenos Aires, he would somehow eventually have to travel north almost the entire length of South America; across the broad, island-dotted eastern opening of the Caribbean Sea; up the coast of the United States to New York; finally, west to the cities in the central part of the country.

Comparing the two routes he had traced on the map, it was clear that the first — his planned and long anticipated route — represented what was surely the shortest practical distance between the starting point of Bremen and his final destination of Minneapolis. On the other hand, it was hard to imagine how there could be any longer distance between those same two points than that involved in the journey he would undertake when the *Kastledale* weighed anchor.

———

The old man came through the door of cabin number five slowly but somehow still briskly, his hand resting lightly on Dietrich's arm. They were closely followed by what turned out to be Ansel — the latter weighed down with the man's three bags.

"Jan," Dietrich said, "let me introduce you to Mr. Gareth Willows, your cabinmate for the trip to Cardiff. He is a Welshman but has lived for some time in Germany, though now he is headed back home for the last time. I'll be back shortly to collect you for the captain's meeting."

As Dietrich and Ansel backed out the door, Willows leaned against the supports for the upper berth and, peering over the top of his wire-rimmed glasses, studied Jan with remarkably bright-blue eyes. Jan nodded, grabbed his bags from the lower bunk, and set them over on the bench.

"Thank you," said Willows in impeccable German. "My days of climbing to the upper berth are unfortunately long past. And in any event, my legs actually were never long enough for scaling such heights. I promise that I will try not to be a burden, but could I trouble you to slide those two larger bags of mine under this bunk?"

While Jan stowed the bags, Willows removed his light coat and hat and stepped across to hang them on one of the hooks. After a quick glance out the porthole, he sat down on the bench. A bit self-consciously, he pulled a tortoiseshell comb from his vest pocket and quickly but carefully combed his gray Napoleonic beard and mustache. Though he was past seventy years of age and had the bearing of a man whose career might have been spent in grand offices and behind ornate desks, he had the evenly weathered but unwrinkled skin that often denotes an active life spent in the outdoors and at the mercies of Mother Nature. He was much shorter than Jan and noticeably bowlegged.

Willows carefully put away the comb. "Dietrich says you are Slovak and are bound for Argentina. Those two things, Slovak and Argentina, do not go together."

"My plan was to come here to go to America on a ship such as the *Grosser Kurfürst*, which is docked farther down the wharf. However, I have an eye condition of a sort that would not allow me to pass through immigration in New York City. Argentina is apparently less concerned about such things, and, well, I have to go somewhere while the condition clears up."

"And what will you do in Argentina?"

"I do not know. I haven't had time to think about that—I only found out yesterday that I was going there. I will go to America from Argentina ... someday."

"If you do not mind sharing a story with an old man," Willows said kindly, "I would be interested in hearing how you came to Bremerhaven and also why you set out for America in the first place and why it is so important to you to go there, even if you have to go by way of Argentina."

"I do not mind at all," Jan replied. He sat down on the bed

across from Willows and for the next twenty-five minutes talked of Važec; the dreams he and Maria shared of life for themselves, and for the lives of their children and their children's children; and his journey from Štrbské Pleso to Bremerhaven. Willows leaned back against the wall, listening attentively and occasionally asking a question or offering a thought. When Jan finished, they sat silently for a few minutes.

"You have," Willows said at length, "a dream not unlike one I once had, though my destination and motivation were different. I also had a modest upbringing and much to overcome, but I never lost sight of my goal and my determination to reach it. You must not either. Many people give up on their dreams too easily. A worthwhile and meaningful life does not come to those who are not willing to adjust and to take the turns in the road that come along. We have some days together on this ship, and I would like to talk more of this. I may have a thought or two, or an experience in my life, which can be of some help to you. Old men, you know, fancy they have wisdom to impart."

"I would be eager to acquire such wisdom," Jan said with a smile. "If I may, Dietrich said you were headed home to Cardiff? And I think he said for the last time. Have you retired?"

"Yes, from business in Germany. I am taking my wife home."

"Is she on this ship!? In some other cabin? I would be happy to move elsewhere immediately so that the two of you can be together."

"That won't be necessary. She is in the refrigerated hold with the chickens and the cheese."

A knock on the door interrupted any response from Jan, and Dietrich's head popped in to announce that the captain's meeting would start in five minutes.

"You need to go to the meeting," said Willows. "I have been on this ship a number of times before and know every word Captain

Cameron will have to say. I would benefit more from a short nap. When the meeting is over, will you come back here to get me for dinner so that we can eat together?"

"Of course," Jan replied.

A bit shaken by the thought of a frozen Mrs. Willows, he joined the group following Dietrich down the hall and the stairs to the Mess.

Although there was space for twenty-six passengers on the *Kastledale*, there were only twenty-one spaces booked, and, with Willows absent, twenty people sat at the tables facing Captain Graham Cameron. The majority, by far, were men traveling alone. There was a couple with two children—they were in one of the four-berth cabins—and two other childless couples. In addition to Captain Cameron, also attending the meeting were the First Mate, Paul Townsend; the Navigator, Thomas Weedfield; and the Stewards, Dietrich and Ansel.

Captain Cameron appeared to be about sixty years old. He was tall, bewhiskered, weathered by the sea, solidly built, kindly in appearance, and somehow commanding in his presence. Townsend and Weedfield were perhaps twenty or twenty-five years younger than their captain, and each had occupied similar positions under Cameron, initially on other ships and now on the *Kastledale*, for over a decade. Weedfield seemed a mirror image of Cameron in countenance and personality, while Jan thought he saw a harder edge, and perhaps a lesser level of tolerance, in Townsend. Weedfield also served as the ship's doctor.

All of the passengers spoke either English or German, and the Captain deftly ran the meeting in both languages. Jan listened attentively to the portions that he delivered in English, but quickly realized that there were only minor similarities among the three languages he knew and the language of the country that would one day be his and Maria's new homeland.

The meeting lasted perhaps half an hour, covering areas of the ship, the cargo they were carrying, the ports they would stop at along the way, the time each day of passenger meals, where they could and couldn't go on the ship, other crew members they were likely to encounter and what their duties were, and other needed information about lifeboats and life vests. Walking about on the weather deck for exercise was permitted, Captain Cameron noted, but it was important to watch weather conditions, not get too close to the edge — and to understand that rescue of those who went overboard was not always possible. To a question about the crew, Cameron noted that for this trip, the ship carried a crew of twenty-four. That number — apart from officers, stewards, and cooks — was divided between those involved with stoking and maintaining the engines and the deck crew, which was responsible for the ship and the cargo.

Cameron also noted that while they were losing some passengers in Cardiff, they would undoubtedly take on others in Lisbon. And he smiled wryly when one of the women asked about bathing facilities. "If we get a moderate steady rain, you'll find members of the crew will strip on the aft weather deck to take advantage of Mother Nature. Passengers can certainly join them, but I recommend the ladies tend to bathing privately with the cloths and water provided in the water closets."

As the meeting broke up, the chief cook, introduced by the Captain only as "Tiptooth," opened the galley door to announce that dinner for passengers would be served in fifteen minutes.

<hr />

After dinner, Gareth Willows settled himself into the third-deck common sitting area to read and review documents he carried in two portfolios, while Jan went down to the weather deck to take in the warm evening air. He walked the perimeter of the deck, looking curiously at its features and noting that the hatches and hold covers, as well as the rigging of the cranes, were now all secured. As the evening light faded, he climbed the stairs to the sitting area, which was empty except for Willows.

"I did not have the chance at dinner," Jan said as he took a seat, "to express my sorrow about your wife. I am not sure what to say, except that I am truly sorry."

"Thank you. We were married for over forty years, and it is an immeasurable loss. Like you, we once had sought a better life than the poverty of our families in Wales. We had a wonderful life together here in Germany and, ultimately, as we became wealthier, back in Cardiff. We had homes there and in Hamburg. My business success enabled us to raise fine children and, despite the turmoil of the world, to enjoy life and each other. I have wonderful memories to sustain me."

"How," Jan asked, searching for something to say, "did she pass away?"

Willows was silent as he looked out the port windows to the harbor lights.

"Elizabeth," he said slowly after a few moments, "had been ill for some months, and we both knew our remaining time together was short ... but it was not the weakness of her heart that killed her, rather, it was suffocation in a fire. I was traveling, concluding some last-minute business in Frankfurt. She was in Hamburg, preparing the house for sale and packing our belongings to go to Wales; where she wished, when her time came, to die and be buried. Our son was there helping her, and when all was in order, he had, the day before I was to return, left for Bremen, where he lives.

"That night, there was a break-in at the house, a thief. The officials believe that Elizabeth awoke and surprised him and that he tied her to a chair in a small room, really a closet. Later, as he was taking what he wanted, he somehow started a fire in the house. *He knew! He knew of the fire!* And it burned while he finished his thievery, and then he fled, leaving her as she was. After a time, the flames broke through to the outside of the building and were seen by passersby. Two brave men ran into the house and somehow came upon Elizabeth before the fire found her — but not before the air had been sucked out of that closet, which was thick with almost impenetrable smoke. They somehow untied her and got her outside to the street — where she gasped her last few breaths."

"I should not," Jan said, "have asked you that. I did not mean to cause you new pain."

"The pain is not new. It has quickly become something very old and will be an eternal part of my remaining life. In that life, I really have but two final missions. One of those is to take Elizabeth home. Fortunately, the owners of this ship are old business partners, and Graham — Captain Cameron — and I are acquainted from many past journeys. It is one of the few ships that ply this route, and its refrigeration allows me to bring Elizabeth home in a decent state. It is also, under the circumstances, more comfortable than making such a trip on an opulent passenger steamer. And it suits my purposes for other reasons as well."

Jan hesitated for a moment, wondering what to say next. He thought of the theft. "Do you know what the thief wanted and whether he got it?"

"That," Willows said, "is hard to tell. I believe, though I cannot be at all sure, that while a large quantity of money was also missing, he was really after documents relating to the investigation of massive building projects in South America and evidence of official bribery there and in Europe. I was the custodian of those documents as an impartial stakeholder. Whether he got them, I cannot say with certainty; either he did or they were consumed in the fire.

In any event, they were not found in the ruins, and the evidence is gone. It will take many, many months for all of that evidence to be reconstructed, but I have lost my taste for that project, and the work has fallen to others."

As they sat in silence, Dietrich walked into the lounge carrying a tray with a steaming teapot, cups, sugar, and a few biscuits.

"Ah!" said Willows, "you have come. Here is the key. Will you put that in our room while we gather up these papers?"

Jan helped organize the papers and placed them in neat stacks, which Willows slid into their portfolios. In the few minutes it took to do that, Dietrich returned, announcing as he passed by that he had left the door to number five open, with the key on the tray.

"You mentioned," Jan remembered, as they reached the door, "that you had two remaining missions in life …."

"I do. One is to take Elizabeth home. The other involves her murderer and exacting an eye for her eye, a tooth for her tooth."

"How will you find him?"

"I know who he is," Willows said quietly as he closed the door behind them. "And he is on this ship."

Chapter 8

Gareth Willows did not volunteer more, either that evening or in the days that followed, about the identity of the man he believed had caused the death of his wife. As the *Kastledale* moved through the North Sea and the English Channel on its three-day journey to Cardiff, he was a comfortable roommate and amiable dinner companion, but was also at times withdrawn, clearly lost in his thoughts.

Jan also had other things on his mind—and his stomach. The seasickness began on the first afternoon out of Bremerhaven. It started with a dull headache and an odd sense of detachment and lightheadedness: it seemed to him as if everything inside his head was somehow loose and adrift. From there, it quickly progressed to weakness in his arms and legs; intense growling and a rolling feeling in his stomach, which quickly became severe nausea; and finally, inevitably, a need to bolt from cabin number five while struggling to keep his mouth closed as he rushed down the stairs to the weather deck. He couldn't help but notice that his hurried exit from the cabin was observed with poorly concealed amusement by Willows.

Moments later he stood at the deck railing, gasping for breath and watching much of what was left of his breakfast as it rose, fell, and drifted away on the surface of the waves. Steadying himself and slowly making his way back to the stairs, it crossed his mind that if his distress was cause for some light relief for Willows it might be worth it; however, while pleased with himself for having such a noble thought, he quickly dismissed it when it became clear that his troubles were not over. Clambering up the stairs, he prayed there was no one in the men's water closet. He became intimately familiar with both the railing and the WC on a number of occasions into the late evening, at times competing for space with some of his fellow passengers. Near midnight, in the darkened cabin and as he listened to Willows's deep, relaxed breathing, he managed to fall into a restless sleep — while dreading what he was sure would be a reprise of discomfort and illness the next day.

Much to his surprise, most of the symptoms had passed by the following morning. He not only ate a hearty breakfast but, after a couple of hours of waiting to see if the food would stay with him, felt confident enough to don his new peacoat against the light rain of a passing squall and venture outside on the third deck.

He found Weedfield on the narrow stair landing, leaning against the railing leading up to the bridge. The Navigator was chewing on an unlit pipe and watching a group of crewmen working, under the First Mate's supervision, on one of the aft cranes.

"Good morning," Weedfield smiled. "You look well enough, though Dietrich alerted me last night that you might be joining the line of heavers needing to see me in the infirmary."

"I'm actually feeling fine. The 'heavers' are …?"

"Those whose innards don't interact well with the swells of the sea — like the peaks and troughs of the waves, those innards tend to want to rise and heave-up perfectly good, partially digested food. I had a dozen in that group yesterday. Many of them are still in that elite club and in their beds this morning: ready, willing, and able to heave whatever they've got left inside if you so much as mention food. Most of them should be fine in another day, provided we don't hit rough weather."

Jan suddenly realized that it would be a good idea to change the subject, since he felt the power of suggestion beginning to take hold of his own innards. He gestured to the crew at the cranes and asked, "What are they doing?"

"Those? Those are deckhands, working under Mr. Townsend. We've got a worn cable there. I don't know why we didn't catch that while we were in port in Bremerhaven. In any event, that needs to be replaced before that crane does any unloading in Cardiff. Actually, we've only one or two things to unload there, but we'll be taking on coal forward."

As they watched, the Mate turned from the group he was supervising and gave a shout, directed to someone below them on the weather deck. Jan looked down to see another hand break away from a conversation with Willows and trot across the deck to join the group at the crane.

"You'd think," Weedfield said with a shake of his head, "that a new man like Clysters would be careful not to be late for a work party under Townsend. He'll get his ass chewed, just watch."

"You mean he's new to the crew?"

"Right. He just signed-on a couple of days ago in Bremerhaven. We had a couple of open spots in the deck crew and picked him up. An experienced seaman, I guess, and also a man of the cloth, a preacher. I'm not sure that we really needed two more men, but I don't make those decisions. I need to get up to the bridge. Have a good day. See me if you decide to be a heaver again."

As Weedfield clattered up the stairs, Jan watched as Clysters, having been lashed by a few choice words from Townsend, bent his back to the work of the cable repair crew.

The rain squalls continued with increasing intensity through-out the day. Those passengers still fighting seasickness stayed in their cabins, with some periodically running down to the weather deck to lean over the railing under the bemused gaze of those far above on the bridge. Jan sat at a table in a corner of the ship's Mess, which was quiet except for the occasional crew member passing through to the galley for hot tea or coffee.

A large mug of that coffee sat on the table in front of him. Until breakfast that morning, he had never tasted coffee, but had found that, with a spoonful of sugar, it suited his taste far better than most teas. Sipping the coffee, he looked out at the rain. His mind's eye, however, was miles away as he tried to look into a future that was clouded with a world of questions.

What would Buenos Aires be like? Where would he live? Since he would undoubtedly have to pay for lodging and food, what would he do to earn money, not just to live on but that he could save for his future travel to America? How much money would he need, how long would it take to save that amount, and how long would he have to stay in Argentina? He wondered how he would com-municate with people who spoke languages that were completely foreign to him—Willows had told him that while he believed there were some Germans in Buenos Aires, it was his understanding that most of the population spoke Spanish or Portuguese. Would he be able, from such a distance, to write to Maria? If he couldn't, or even if he could, would she despair? If it would be many months before he reached America and could send for her, would she wait and would she still come—or would the added uncertainties make her turn to someone else for security? The string of questions and un-certainties tumbled after and over each other, churning his mind and his stomach far more than yesterday's bout of seasickness.

A gust of wind slapped the rain against the window in front of him and brought his mind back to the ship. As he reached for the coffee mug, his eye caught the brown fisherman's cap lying on the table. The cap rested on the sheets of paper he had taken from his duffel bag. Willows had offered to post, in Cardiff, any letters he wished to write and had loaned him pen and ink. After a moment, he set the mug down, pulled the paper toward him, and opened the ink bottle.

5th August

Dear Anna:

I hope you will not think it out of place or be troubled by my writing to you. Nor, if by some chance you have been expecting such a letter, do I want you to be upset with me for being so tardy in writing.

My journey from Krakow to Bremen was completed safely, with no difficulty, attributable to much luck, in crossing the border into the Russian part of Poland. There were many days of walking and welcome breaks of riding trains, which brought me to Łódź and from there by uninterrupted train travel to Bremen.

I stayed for some nights at a pensione in Łódź where one evening I looked up at dinner to see Colonel Strzala seated across from me. He was, of course, not in uniform and was bound for Gdańsk. I confronted him, privately, about his conduct and the danger he had put you in, including abandoning you outside of Wieliczka. He expressed some remorse and later, through the pensione's proprietress, expressed his sorrow and apologies for the entire incident. I find an apology delivered by him to someone else to convey to me, inadequate for what he owes to you. It was fortunate that he went on to Gdańsk when he did. I think that, if I would have seen him again, confrontation by words would not have sufficed.

When I arrived at Bremen, the medical authorities denied me passage to America because of the redness and discharge of my eye that you will recall troubled me in Krakow. That, I believe, started before the train incident at Wieliczka, though that perhaps aggravated the condition. I could not stay in Bremen, nor could I return to Važec. The doctor who examined me told me the eye condition was not such as to prevent my booking passage for Argentina in South America. Argentina is more tolerant of immigrants and less concerned with such conditions. With very little time to decide what to do, I did so and am writing this at sea on a freighter ship bound for that country. We stop in a few days in Cardiff, which is an English port, and a kindly and refined gentleman who lives in that area and shares my cabin on this ship has offered to post this letter to you from there.

It will be some weeks before I arrive in Buenos Aires in Argentina. There is much uncertainty involved in that and in when I will reach America. I would admit this perhaps only to you, but I am anxious for many things and trying to set my mind clear and at ease on my course in life and whether this is merely a diversion or detour – or whether it is an unwanted permanent change in direction, and, if so, how I will control or deal with that.

I will be embarrassed if you are troubled by my saying this, but I think of you daily and am grateful for the brief time we were allowed with each other. It would not be right for me to express that otherwise, as much as in my heart I find that I would wish to do so.

Please forgive me if this letter is a burden, in which case, destroy it. I cannot know how you feel about my writing to you, but I may do so again when I arrive in Argentina, provided I can find a way to post such a letter to you.

One of the hats you bought for me in the Market Square with the inscription you sewed on its flap sits in front of me. It is truly a prized possession and a daily reminder of the Not-A-Princess.

Jan

After carefully addressing the envelope, he inserted the folded letter and sealed it for its journey.

He returned to watching the rain, which now seemed to be falling horizontally. He was alone in the Mess for some time until two men entered from the starboard stairway and walked noisily across the room toward the galley. They were both powerfully built, dressed completely in black, though it seemed that the color of their clothes was both natural and the result of staining and wear. Jan noticed the heavy pairs of gloves and the goggles they carried, and that the hands and faces of both men had a slight, peculiar grayish tinge. When they reached the galley door, they opened it, and one of the men said something to those inside. In short order, Dietrich appeared in the doorway holding two enormous mugs of steaming coffee. After a few words with him, the men made their way back across the room and headed down the stairs.

Dietrich reappeared in the galley door with a coffee pot, which he raised inquisitively and, on a nod from Jan, walked over to fill his mug.

"Who were those two?" Jan asked as he held the warm mug with both hands.

"Stokers. Engine room crew. Actually, the Jolly Rodgers. One's named Rodger Cousins and the other's Rodger DeGroza. Very much alike, but not identical. DeGroza is quiet and usually easygoing, but no question the strongest man on this or maybe any other ship, and no one to trifle with—even Cousins knows when to give him a wide berth, and Cousins himself fears no living man. Tough guy, Cousins. Don't know what he used to be before he became a stoker, but I'd say it wasn't what genteel-type people would call 'good.' The two Rodgers can almost always be found together."

"Do they shovel the coal?"

Dietrich nodded. "Hardest job on any ship. Here we got two big steam engines and three stoker crews. Two men in each crew, and they work eight-hour shifts straight through with no breaks and then get sixteen hours off. I think they sleep most of those sixteen hours, must spend about two hours washing up, and, for all I can tell, eat like horses the rest of the time. Dirty work and dangerous, especially since about every other shift they need to get back in the bunkers, climb around on the coal, and shovel it closer to the boilers. That also keeps the weight in the bunkers balanced."

"Doesn't," Jan reflected, "sound like a healthy job."

"No," Dietrich replied as he started back for the galley. "It's for younger men for a few years, and then they usually move on to other jobs in the engine room or off the ship. Except for Cousins and DeGroza—I'd guess they'll be stokers until they die."

Jan remained alone in the Mess for some time, finishing his coffee and watching the last of the squalls sweep away.

～～～～～

The evening meal was served for passengers at 6:00 p.m., and on this day consisted of roast mutton, cold ham, mashed potatoes, pickles, turnips, toast with jam and marmalade, tea, and coffee. Jan and Willows ate at a table with the Dischingers, Richard and Karin, who were also traveling to Argentina. They apparently had, fairly recently, come into some money, which the husband spoke of proudly but also guardedly. Mrs. Dischinger had been quite seasick and was attempting her first meal since leaving Bremerhaven; after eating, they quickly excused themselves to go to their cabin and see if her meal would "settle."

After the Dischingers left, Jan noticed Clysters cutting through the dining area to the galley and, pointing to the seaman, said, "I noticed you talking to Clysters this morning."

"Who?" said Willows, looking around. "Oh, him. I didn't know his name. I had stopped him since he seemed to be a deckhand, and I thought he would know something about the unloading of the coffin. He was of little help, and I ultimately had to consult with the First Mate, Townsend, about the coffin. By the way, I put the letter to your Miss Anna with some letters I will be posting back to Bremen as soon as we have docked in Cardiff. And no, don't reach for any money. I will handle the trifling cost of postage."

Jan nodded his thanks. They talked a bit about the Dischingers, other passengers, and the day's weather before Willows excused himself to rest a bit before doing some reading later in the evening, adding that if Jan would join him he would arrange for Dietrich to bring them coffee in the third-deck sitting area at 9:00 p.m.

After Willows left, Jan lingered to watch the setting sun, which was making a brief appearance low in the western sky through what were now broken clouds. As the time passed, he realized that the other passengers had all left the Mess and crew members were beginning to take seats for their evening meal. Most of the crew had breakfast early in the morning before the passengers, but ate dinner later in the evening, at 7:30, after the passengers had eaten. He gathered his things, stood, and almost bumped into Clysters, who was right next to him, carrying a plate of food in one hand and a mug of tea in the other.

"I am sorry, sir," said Clysters. "I was thinking of where to sit and just didn't see you."

"That's all right. It was my fault. Why don't you take this table? I am done here."

"Bless you, sir. It's a good table with a bit of a view. Thank you."

Jan started to leave and then, for a reason he couldn't articulate, said, "You look familiar. Perhaps it was you that I saw talking with my cabinmate Willows earlier today?"

"It could be, sir," Clysters said after a moment's hesitation. "I recognized Mr. Willows from when he sailed with us last year. We met then. We did speak a bit about the weather this morning."

"Ah, I see. I thought you might have been talking about the unloading of his wife's coffin when we reach Cardiff."

"Is her coffin on this ship?" Clysters asked with what Jan thought was a look of some surprise.

"Yes, he is taking her home to Cardiff for burial. Well, I'm delaying you from eating. Please go ahead. Enjoy your dinner."

Jan walked toward the starboard stairs, where he paused for a moment before deciding to go down to the weather deck and take in the early-evening air.

Chapter 9

Cardiff

It was nearing 5:00 a.m. Lying half awake, it took Jan a few minutes to realize that the engines were barely audible and the ship was motionless. As quietly as possible, he climbed down from the upper bunk and pulled on his trousers and boots. Through the porthole above the washstand, looking out over the forward weather deck below, he saw that the scattered clouds in the sky ahead were flecked with intermingled and changing shades of red and pink, signaling that, almost directly astern of the idling ship, the sun was rising above the eastern horizon. That sunrise was just far enough advanced to cast the faint elongated shadow of the ship's superstructure, topped by the bridge, across the deck to the very tip of the bow. Grabbing his coat and cap from the hooks, he glanced at the sleeping Willows and left the cabin, locking the door behind him.

On deck, he could see the lights of a large harbor and the city behind it.

"Cardiff," said Townsend coming up behind him. "We arrived here an hour ago and have been treading water waiting for a pilot. He'll be in that tug you see coming up off the starboard bow. He will take us in, and the tug will snuggle us up at the Queen Alexandra Dock. We should be tied up and secured by breakfast."

Townsend's German was precise and cultivated. And something in the way he spoke left no doubt about where a sentence ended: periods seemed to pop out and hang in the air, making each sentence a very distinct and separate expression.

"Will we be in Cardiff long?" Jan asked.

Townsend shrugged. "That is hard to tell. It depends on how long it takes to maneuver cargo. We have very little—just a few crates—to unload, and then I believe we're going to take on a load of iron. That is a God-send; otherwise we would be using the space to transport tons of cargo coal to the refueling station in Tenerife. Coal is messy cargo in a ship like this. It takes a lot of clean up afterward. After we load the iron, we will need to move down and take on coal in our own bunkers to replace what has been burned getting here. We may be able to recoal tonight; though more likely it will be early in the morning. With any luck, we will be back at sea sometime tomorrow, but you never know."

"Will we passengers be able to leave the ship here?"

"I would imagine so. You look like you can take care of yourself, but the area around these docks is not exactly a place for sipping tea or gawking about, if you know what I mean, and especially so after dark. It is rough enough for seamen, much less those who do not know their way around." Townsend studied the approaching tugboat for a moment. "I need to meet that pilot when they pull alongside. I wonder if you could keep an eye on the lady at the railing over there. She is one of Mr. Weedfield's prize patients this trip. I would rather not have her pitching over the side when we start moving."

Jan nodded and looked at the figure at the rail some distance aft. He recognized Karin Dischinger, holding on for dear life.

The tug pulled up alongside, and soon the pilot climbed aboard and went up to the bridge with Townsend. It took but a few minutes for the engines to begin throbbing and for the ship to get underway.

Jan eyed Mrs. Dischinger for a moment and then walked slowly in her direction, deciding to stop when he was still a few long strides from reaching her. She was of medium height, with long, flowing brown hair that whipped about her head in the wind. The cloak she was wearing was pitch black in color, which accentuated the white knuckles of the small hands that were squeezing the railing. Her face was drawn, her lips were pale, and she was clearly both ill and ill at ease, and very unhappy. He could see that she was shivering slightly, and he noticed that while she wore a slipper on one foot, the other foot was bare.

"Good morning," Jan said.

"Is it? I hadn't noticed. I've been hoping someone would come by, push me overboard, and end my misery — are you he?"

"I'm afraid not. You look like you've been out here for some time. Unless you really need to keep leaning over this rail, I think it might be better to go inside; it's much warmer there. Though first," Jan said as he pointed to her bare foot, "we should locate your shoe. Do you know where it is?"

"It was ill and jumped overboard," she giggled nervously, then quickly clapped her hand over her mouth and swallowed hard. For a moment, with only one hand on the rail, she swayed unsteadily, but with a determined effort regained her balance and resumed a two-handed grip. Her lips moved convulsively, as if first testing the safety or consequences of speaking. Apparently satisfied, she continued, "I guess I am cold, and it probably is time to go back inside. I can't imagine I have anything more to heave up out here. The slipper — well, actually, it felt strange, and I slid it off to adjust it, and then somehow kicked it and it went ... out there. I suppose it's lost forever."

"I would say that you are correct."

"Well, then this one will do me no good." And with a deft kick and another giggle, she sent the other slipper out into the waves.

"You sound to me like you're feeling better, but I think if you stand out here barefoot and in the wind and spray, you'll catch a chill." Jan put an arm around her shoulders and began to steer her toward the stairs. "Besides, I worry what you'll throw or kick out to sea next. Come along, I'll walk you back to your cabin."

Once back on the third deck, at the door to cabin number two, she turned to him and said quietly and simply, "Thank you. I am sorry for being sick and for troubling you. I needed fresh air. But even more I needed to laugh and have someone put an arm around my shoulder ... and care just a little."

She quietly closed the door behind her. As he turned to go back down to the weather deck, Jan couldn't help but wonder about Richard Dischinger.

<hr>

After the ship was secured to the wharf, Jan went back to his quarters, where he found that Willows had dressed in a dark three-piece suit, packed his bags, and was sitting on the bench, ready for breakfast.

As they sat eating in the Mess, they could see one of the forward hatches being opened, and soon the cranes were lifting the first of three wooden crates out of the hold. Willows identified two of them as his, containing everything salvageable from the fire.

"When they're done with those," he said as he pushed his plate away, "they'll get to the refrigerated hold. I would like, if you would, for you to be with me when they bring up the coffin."

"Of course," Jan nodded. "Will you be staying in Cardiff?"

"No, no. We will need to leave the city immediately. My youngest son will have a horse-drawn hearse waiting on the dock. He and I will take Elizabeth home to Llandaff."

"It is not my business," Jan said after a moment, "but in Bremerhaven, you said you knew who was responsible for the fire and that he was on this ship."

"Indeed, and he is still on the *Kastledale*, there having been no place for him to disembark since we left that German city," Willows said with a quiet smile. "I don't think, though I do not wish to be rude, that I should say any more about that. It is, my young friend, like a stage play, perhaps something by Shakespeare. The final act will play itself out. It may be that you'll see the final act. Or it may be that the curtain will fall, the mission will accomplish itself, and only an unanswered question will remain in the air. Sometimes in the theater, the audience is left in suspense."

"I am not familiar with the theater and plays, and not sure that I understand what you're saying."

"In time, I think you will," Willows responded. "Just as, in time, I am sure you will sort through the uncertainties that trouble you now, and you will find the way to accomplish *your* mission and reach the shores of America. I wish you luck in that, but I think you need less luck and just more faith in your own ability to overcome, as you surely will, the obstacles. In my view, they are but temporary."

They sat in silence for some minutes before, pointing out the window, Willows said heavily, "Now, come along, if you will; some of the deck crew are headed aft, ready to play undertaker."

They took the stairs down to the weather deck; stopped for a moment at the head of the gangway, where Willows spoke briefly to Weedfield; and then made their way down to the dock, where they were met by Willows's son and Captain Cameron. Although the outer harbor was busy with vessels coming and going, the only nearby ship seemed almost deserted. There were few other people dockside, and it was strangely quiet. In the distance, a lone bell tolled the hour. Unloading of a single crate from the *Kastledale*'s refrigerated hold proceeded slowly and without incident. Once carefully placed on the dock, the crate was opened and the coffin was lifted out, wiped spotlessly clean by two deckhands under

Cameron's supervision, and secured in the waiting hearse. The two crates containing Willows's household items were soon loaded on a second wagon, along with the three bags Dietrich brought down from cabin number five.

After quick words of goodbye to Jan and a longer, private conversation with the Captain, Willows climbed into the cabin of the hearse with his son, and the small procession headed off to Llandaff. Watching them move slowly away, Jan happened to glance up at the *Kastledale* and saw that Richard Dischinger was leaning on the weather deck rail, apparently staring after the hearse. Jan looked away for a moment to acknowledge the Captain as he passed by on his way back to the ship; when he looked back at the railing, Dischinger was gone.

He lingered on the dock as the loading of a quantity of iron bars, beams, and ingots began. It was a process that would continue through the morning and into the afternoon, and as it proceeded, he walked back to the gangway and returned to the ship.

<hr/>

The day wore on, a cold wind and a dreary, dripping sky rolled across the harbor. The damp, gray conditions seemed to drive most of the passengers to their cabins. Crew members not involved in the loading operation gathered in small groups in the Mess: talking quietly, drinking strong coffee, and occasionally watching the deck operations. Near dusk, the forward holds were closed, the decks secured, and the lines brought in. With assistance from two tugs, the *Kastledale* maneuvered laterally away from the wharf, turned slowly about, and made for the coaling dock on the other side of the broad harbor. Once tied up there, the members of the deck crew were granted shore leave for the remainder of the evening, while the engine crew, including the stokers, was held on board for the early-morning coaling.

Alone in cabin number five late that evening, Jan passed the time reading and studying his map of the Atlantic and the Western Hemisphere. Outside, the air grew thick with fog and, beginning at about 10:00 p.m., it was pierced from time to time by the sound of fog horns: some located on the wharf, others on ships sliding slowly through the murky harbor.

It was nearing midnight when he thought he heard sobbing sounds outside his door. They seemed to fade away but returned perhaps twenty minutes later. Slipping on his coat, he quietly opened the door and stepped into the hall. No one was in sight, but he heard the click of what he thought was the port stairwell door and strode quickly in that direction. Opening the door, he looked up and down the stairs but saw and heard nothing more. After standing outside for a few minutes, he returned to his cabin and turned in for the night. He lay awake for over an hour, but heard nothing more save for the fog horns and the normal shifting sounds of the ship as it lay at the dock.

〰〰〰

Sunday morning had a sullen feel to it. Coaling began in the misty and gray hours before dawn. Watching from the third-deck stairs with Dietrich, Jan could sense some tension between the ship's crew and the coalers on the dock, who were perhaps hungover from Saturday night and not at all pleased about working at such an early hour. At one point, Rodger Cousins, who was supervising on deck and was clearly disgusted, seemed to lose his temper with the pace of the loading and, throwing down his gloves, started for a ladder leading up from the deck to the coaling dock. Rodger DeGroza was close behind. Those working on the dock, the objects of Cousins's wrath, quickly began scattering. Townsend intercepted him at the ladder, and after the exchange of a few words between them, Cousins and DeGroza walked away. Townsend himself climbed up the ladder and had a short, pointed conversation with the coalers—after which the work of loading the coal resumed at a far more urgent pace.

"I would guess," Dietrich observed dryly, "that Mr. Townsend told—or, shall we say, counseled—those coalers to bend their backs into the morning's work, or else he'd look the other way if Cousins and DeGroza should again take it in mind to climb that ladder and create a bit of holy-day mayhem."

In time, the coaling was completed and the ship secured. Shortly after 9:00 a.m., Cousins signaled the bridge that the operation was complete and the ship was ready to make steam.

By midmorning, the *Kastledale* had cleared Cardiff harbor, left the fog behind, and was out in the open sea bound for Lisbon.

Chapter 10

Lisbon

The dark night sky had yet to lose its ancient and daily battle with the advancing forces of the sun. Although the *Kastledale*'s outlights were on to signal its presence to any passing ships, on the bridge the lights were dim to avoid interfering with the vision of the lookout, who, from alternating positions starboard and port, scanned the seas ahead and to either side. It was early, just past two bells, and Townsend was officer of the watch. He stood a bit behind the helmsman, his own newly-issued binoculars hanging heavily on the strap around his neck as he poured coffee from the large pot he had brought up from the galley when he had relieved Weedfield. He took a sip of the coffee and was thinking ahead to Lisbon when a sharp "Mr. Townsend!" interrupted his thoughts.

He turned to the right and caught the eye of the lookout, who nodded aft toward the starboard set of stairs. Through the glass at the top of the stairs and outside the door to the bridge, he could see Karin Dischinger. As he stepped toward the door, he motioned for her to come in.

"I'm so sorry to interrupt your work," she said, her voice shaking, "but I thought I should tell someone that my husband is ... well ... he seems ... I mean, he seems to be missing."

"Please, sit down right here." Townsend pulled a low wooden

stool out from under the counter at the rear of the bridge. "Why do you say he is missing?"

"Well, when I awoke some time ago, he was not in the cabin. And that is the way it was yesterday morning as well."

"Perhaps he could not sleep and is just out walking the deck. Did he tell you where he was yesterday morning when he was absent?"

"No, but then again, that is the point!" she said, dabbing with her fingers at the tears rolling slowly down her cheeks. "I did not talk to him yesterday because I did not see him *at all* yesterday, and I have looked throughout the first and second and third decks and also asked Mr. Cousins—I believe that's his name—if Richard was below decks. No one has seen him."

Townsend leaned back against the railing across from her. "Let's back up a step. When *exactly* did you last see your husband?"

"The day we left Cardiff! After dinner, as I was undressing for bed, he said he was going for some air. I was tired, but I waited up for him, and did not fall asleep until after he returned. When I awoke yesterday morning, he was not in the room, but since I had slept late I believed he had gone to breakfast. When I did not see him there, I thought he might have gone on deck or somewhere. I sat waiting in our cabin most of the day. I did leave at one point to use the washroom, and when I returned, things had been moved around and it looked like someone had been in the room, so I assumed it was Richard. But I did not see him."

She paused to take a breath and after a moment added, "When he didn't attend dinner last night, I became even more concerned and started asking around. Some thought they might have seen him yesterday, but they weren't sure. I didn't know what to do. I thought he would surely return in the evening, so I sat up and waited and waited, but he hasn't, and since no one else is up and about I came up here. I don't wish to be a bother, but I didn't know what else to do."

Townsend thought a moment and then motioned to the lookout. "Are we clear?"

"Yes, sir; I just swept one hundred and eighty degrees. And the light is coming on fast."

"Good—I need you to roust Andrews, Meganne, Clysters, and the steward Dietrich. They're to meet me in the Mess in twenty minutes. When you have them up and moving, you can return to your post here. Mrs. Dischinger," he said, turning to her, "I'm going to talk to Captain Cameron. Either he or Mr. Weedfield will sit with you while I lead a full search of the ship. Please stay here with the helmsman until I return."

Townsend poured Mrs. Dischinger a cup of coffee before waking the Captain and Weedfield. They both dressed quickly. Townsend stopped to reassure Mrs. Dischinger and then hurried to the Mess.

<hr>

It took only until the end of the passenger breakfast hour, and Dietrich coming around to check each cabin on the third deck, for everyone on the ship to know of Richard Dischinger's disappearance. An extended search, which the Captain called off shortly before 10:00 a.m. when some areas were being searched for the third and fourth times, had failed to turn up any sign of the missing husband, except for a handkerchief found in the Mess, which his wife thought might possibly be his.

While it seemed obvious that Richard Dischinger had been lost at sea, the gossip among the passengers was whether that was the result of an accident or something else. Some claimed to have witnessed "tension" between the Dischingers caused by financial issues and the husband's unwillingness to share anything about that state of affairs—which many surmised was "desperate"—with his wife. Others, to the contrary, felt Dischinger had been boastful about newly-found wealth, while also apparently keeping his wife in the dark about the exact reasons for what to her was a spur-of-the-moment journey to Argentina. For her part, Karin Dischinger said little to anyone after her early-morning interview with Townsend on the bridge and had retreated to her cabin, aided by a sleeping potion Weedfield had provided her. It seemed likely that she would stay there for some time, since it became known that the stewards had been instructed to serve her meals in her room until further notice.

———————

As the afternoon wore on, the wind and the seas increased, and the weather, combined with the day's events, seemed to drive the passengers to their cabins. Jan sat in the third-deck lounge, where he was deep into the final chapters of the Kukučín novel. He was quite pleased with his ability to comprehend written German, though he wondered how useful that knowledge would be to him when he reached Argentina. His reading was interrupted by the appearance of Townsend, who indicated that the Captain would like to speak with him.

On reaching the bridge, Townsend directed him to the small map room directly behind the helmsman's position, where he found Captain Cameron seated at a table strewn with charts.

"Close the door and, please, have a seat," the Captain said, motioning to the only other chair in the room. "Townsend tells me you provided some assistance to poor Mrs. Dischinger one morning early last week when she wandered on deck."

"Yes, sir, that was the morning we arrived in Cardiff, though we were actually still outside the harbor."

"As you can imagine, I must make some reports when we arrive in Lisbon about Mr. Dischinger and the possible or probable cause of his disappearance and loss. And I also feel some small responsibility for Mrs. Dischinger and what happens to her, at least as to what she does next when we arrive in Lisbon. And she herself is, as you might imagine, uncertain of her plans." He paused for a moment before continuing. "Few people on board had much contact with either of them, but I am trying to track down what information anyone may have. This gets us back to that morning outside of the harbor at Cardiff. Was there anything in your conversation with Mrs. Dischinger that involved her relationship with her husband? Or their financial situation or anything else that seemed unusual or that might relate to all of this, his disappearance?"

"I am probably not going to be of much help. It is the only time I have really talked to her, and it was very brief. I helped her back to her cabin and she thanked me for that, and, as I think about it, did in thanking me say something about needing someone who 'cared just a little' about her. I believe that is what she said. I thought that a bit—oh, I don't know. Perhaps awkward."

"Do you think she was referring to lack of attention from her husband or marital issues?"

"Probably, though I know little of marital issues."

"When you reached her cabin, did you see Mr. Dischinger or speak to him?"

"As Mrs. Dischinger opened the door, I could see he was in the lower bunk, apparently asleep."

"Did you hear anything from the cabin after she went inside and you were leaving?"

"No," Jan shook his head, "I don't recall hearing anything."

"The people in the neighboring cabin, number three, say that that morning they heard blows struck and Mrs. Dischinger crying while her husband told her to be still. You, I take it, heard nothing like that?"

"No. And I can't imagine why he would strike her."

"Neither can I, but such things do happen, even if they are hard to imagine," the Captain said.

"Do you have any idea how Mr. Dischinger died?"

"No—assuming, of course, that he did. Without a body or any-one seeing him go overboard, one can't be completely sure; though once out and left behind in these seas the ultimate result is inevi-table. I am, however, fairly certain that while she might possibly have had reason to do so, Mrs. Dischinger is unlikely to have had anything to do with her husband's disappearance. Beyond that, there are many possibilities." The Captain absently examined one of the charts for a moment and then pushed it aside. "If you think of anything else you may have noticed that morning or at any other time, please talk to me or Townsend. And don't forget your book. I see it's a Kukučín work. While he is not widely read, he is one of my favorite authors. I have a couple of his other works, in German, in my cabin if you'd like to borrow them."

Jan nodded and walked out to the bridge and from there to the weather deck. Looking about, he found himself wondering at what spot on the rail Richard Dischinger had found himself falling into the sea.

—⁓⁓⁓⁓—

Cabin number five seemed relatively spacious when serving as a temporary home for one person instead of two. Late in the eve-ning, downing the last of a mug of coffee and leaning back in an armchair he had pulled in from the sitting area, Jan was content to be alone with his thoughts. Those started with his last conver-sation with Gareth Willows, and the older man's confidence that Jan's own abilities and determination would be more than enough to overcome any "temporary" detours in his journey. He realized that he had subconsciously begun to view Buenos Aires differently and in much the same way as Krakow and Łódź—places to pass through, for whatever time proved necessary, on the way to reach-ing the shores of America. He could feel his dreams coming back into focus and that the disappointment, if not desperation, he had felt since the morning of his medical examination in Bremen was no longer as overpowering.

As those thoughts came together, he also felt a heaviness of heart that he recognized as the loneliness of someone far from home and family, combined with longing for a world where day-to-day life was predictable, even if not promising. He was not a philosopher, but he knew well that leaving the land that had been the home of generations of one's ancestors was not a normal thing to do. Despite wars, crop failures, poverty, and other factors, most people who thought of going to America ultimately chose to stay where they were and hope for a better future. That was true of many of his contemporaries, including men he had met in the course of his military service. Others found "hope" to be a poor strategy and were willing to risk the unknown. Few, he suspected, thought as he did, consciously and deliberately, about accepting that risk for not only his own sake but for that of offspring and descendants to whom he would not even be a memory—but somehow those as yet unborn generations fortified his resolve.

He stood and moved to look in the mirror on the back of the cabin door. While his right eye had improved substantially, the left one continued to feel irritated at times, was held closed by dried matter when he awoke in the morning, and was more often than not tinged with red. He had faith that time would heal this and, as he began to prepare for sleep, he preached a small sermon of patience to himself.

〰〰〰

It was the middle of a humid afternoon when they were secured wharf-side in Lisbon. For a small handful of passengers, this was their destination, and they disembarked. New passengers, bound for South America, would be taken on in the morning, along with additional cargo that would fill the forward holds, all with a plan to put back to sea as soon as all was battened down and tugs were available.

After dinner, Jan went ashore with Dietrich. Ansel was stationed at the gangway, making a log of those passengers and crew leaving the *Kastledale* and announcing to all that the gangway would close and the ship would be secured at midnight at the start of the middle watch. He also passed along the word that the Captain had heard of unrest and recent demonstrations against the Portuguese monarchy, which those going ashore should be mindful of while in the city.

The bar was "Cuellar's" and it was three narrow streets and one even narrower and dark alley over from the wharfs. Its distinguishing features were an almost total absence of chairs, acoustics that magnified the noise of the conversations of dozens of seamen and dock workers, a busy tattoo parlor in a far corner, and a small, elevated stage of sorts behind the long bar. The stage featured three marginally attractive women — who drew the attention of the shouting crowd by their willingness to remove clothing and assume different explicit positions in response to the wants of the crowd and the value of the coins thrown on the stage.

Dietrich procured two large mugs of ale and a bowl of hot sausages of an undetermined type of meat, and they worked their way through the crowd to stand at one of the small, round waist-high tables that peppered the room.

"That," Dietrich said excitedly, pointing to the stage where one of the women was, without the hindrance of much of any clothing, standing on her head with her back to the cheering crowd, "is what they call 'an 'Upside Down Arse'."

Jan raised an eyebrow. "I can understand that. Is there a name for what that other one is doing?"

"Yeah," Dietrich responded after a careful stare. "'Tits to the

Moon,' damn good effort too! Say, you should get a tattoo while we're here—your arms are big enough for a ship, though I suppose that would take more time than we've got tonight. Maybe a ship's anchor? Or a coiled sea snake? How about a girlfriend's name?"

Jan shook his head, dug into the sausages, and studied those in the room, especially a group off to his left who seemed to be engaged in the start of a shoving match that had the look of a fight in the making. He was surprised to see a couple of women here and there, soliciting drinks and vying for attention with those performing on the stage. Most of the men in the room seemed satisfied with drinking pitchers full of the watered-down ale, smoking pipes and cigars, watching the activity on the stage, and sharing stories and lies. Standing at the table, Jan noticed that the air in the upper half of the high-ceilinged room was an opaque bluish gray; that haze had the appearance of having been there, undisturbed, for days, if not weeks or months.

After about twenty minutes and Dietrich's enthralled identification of a "near perfect 'Split Leg Six'," they were getting ready to have another round when Dietrich was jostled and pushed by one of those whom Jan recognized as having been in the earlier shoving match. He was of medium height, with large hands, red hair protruding from under a flat seaman's cap, a rough and stubble-covered face, one eye that seemed sleepily half-closed, and nostrils that appeared to be filled with tangled hair.

"You little girls need to move on. This was our table," the intruder said roughly, waving a large mug of ale and gesturing to three others trailing him, "and we need it back. So, run along now."

"Go find a dark corner and play with yourself!" Dietrich responded.

"Whoa, Tommy!" said one of the intruder's companions. "The little man has a smart mouth on him!"

Tommy glanced at Jan briefly and then looked at the cap Dietrich had been wearing and which was lying on the table. Carefully, he poured half the contents of his mug of ale into the cap. Dietrich froze. Jan was taking a step around the table toward Tommy when he felt a restraining hand on his shoulder and a low, unhurried voice said, "Tommy, it appears you and your mouthy friends have a bit of a mess to clean up."

It was Rodger DeGroza, who Jan somehow had not noticed being in the room. Tommy's expression changed instantly at the sight of the big man, and he hesitated. However, a smirk quickly returned to his face; he was about to speak when the seaman who had made the "smart mouth" comment hissed through clenched teeth, "Tommy!"

He was standing, erect and unnaturally stiff, slightly off to Tommy's right. Looming behind him was Rodger Cousins. The stiff posture was dictated by the fact that Cousins had pulled the man's right arm up behind his back so far as to painfully twist the shoulder to which it was attached. His left arm was held firmly immobile by the grip of Cousins's left hand.

The smirk disappeared as Tommy looked first at Cousins, then Jan, and finally at DeGroza. He studied DeGroza for a few seconds, shrugged his shoulders, and began to turn away, but then suddenly wheeled around with the half-full mug of ale held high in his right hand.

Bad decisions, Jan recalled his father once saying, are made in seconds, and Tommy made one when he began to swing the heavy mug toward DeGroza's head. With a short, quick step forward, DeGroza caught the blow with his left arm and sent the mug flying toward the women onstage while his right fist, with all of his considerable weight moving forward behind it, delivered a powerful blow that snapped Tommy's head back and sent blood and teeth spraying across the room. As Tommy began to slump to the floor, two loud cracks and a scream signaled that, with a flick of his right arm, Cousins had dislocated the shoulder and probably broken the collarbone of the man he had been holding. As that man dropped to the floor, Cousins turned to Tommy's other companions, who were quickly sliding back into the crowd and making for the door.

It had taken all of a few seconds, and Cuellar's was deathly and tensely silent; even the action on the stage had stopped. Jan noticed Cousins scanning the room, alert for any other of Tommy's shipmates.

"Do you want this cap?" DeGroza inquired of Dietrich.

When Dietrich shook his head, DeGroza picked it up, poured the ale in it on Tommy's face, and then leaned over to grind the cap into the blood running from Tommy's mouth and his broken nose. Cousins pulled the other man across the floor and dropped him next to Tommy.

"Sorry for the mess, Cuellar," DeGroza said as he stepped over to the bar, took a towel from one of the bartenders, and carefully wiped the blood from his fist.

"It happens," Cuellar shrugged, "and usually to those who deserve it. Don't worry about the mess; my men will drag this trash out to the alley."

DeGroza nodded toward the door, and the crowd parted as he began to make his way out, followed by Dietrich and Jan, with Cousins bringing up the rear.

"Thanks," Dietrich said as they stepped outside.

"No need," DeGroza replied. "You and the Slovak here probably could have handled it but, as it happens, I had some unfinished business with Tommy from a late night in Dover a couple of years back, so ...."

They moved through the dark alleys and streets toward the wharf, passing a number of bars that seemed as loud and unruly as Cuellar's.

"Nice evening," Cousins observed as they approached the *Kastledale*.

"Yes, yes, it is," said DeGroza, looking thoughtfully up at the stars. "A little chill in the air, though, don't you think?"

Chapter 11

The Cape Verde Islands

Having provided the *Kastledale* with some marginal assistance in clearing the inner Lisbon harbor, the rusted and battered vessel that had begun life as a river ferry, but now passed for a tug, belched a final cloud of cinder-filled black smoke and broke away to meet an approaching inbound freighter. As he watched from the bridge, Captain Cameron was pleased that, despite the vexing events of the morning, they were putting out to sea reasonably near the time he had planned and anticipated.

When he came on deck that morning and relieved Weedfield, he had surveyed the overnight watch reports which, for a night in port, were normal, with two exceptions. Those were both reported by the steward Ansel when he secured the ship at midnight.

One was that the cargo that was to have been delivered late at night and stacked on the dock for loading early in the morning was nowhere to be seen. This was cargo that Cameron had been offered the previous afternoon and which was destined for the Portuguese archipelago of Madeira. It was an easy, profitable, and short-haul load that he was glad to take on; having escaped transporting coal from Cardiff to the refueling station in Tenerife, the *Kastledale* had no reason to stop in the Canary Islands, but a paying cargo along the same route to nearby Madeira was a bonus.

Cameron had read Ansel's entry in the watch report a few minutes after 8:00 a.m. and was ruing the delay when he had looked out to see a line of wagons, carrying the missing cargo, lazily maneuvering their way toward the ship. Townsend and the deck crew had the forward hatches open and the cranes at the ready, but loading was already more than two hours behind schedule. Given the slow movement of the wagons, he had guessed correctly that it would be another hour or more before anything in those wagons would find its way into the hold.

The second item in Ansel's report was the absence of the deckhand Andrew Clysters, who had left the ship at 6:50 p.m. the night before and had not returned by the time the gangway was pulled up at midnight. Weedfield had stationed Dietrich at the gangway when it was run out early that morning, with instructions to send Clysters directly to the bridge when he boarded. Just after nine o'clock, when Cameron was considering sending a couple of the stokers out to scour the bars and streets in the area for the still-absent seaman, Townsend reported that a search of the deckhand's berth and locker in the forecastle uncovered only a few odd items and that his clothes and personal effects were gone. Ansel subsequently confirmed that Clysters had been carrying a full duffel when he left the ship, though he had said nothing about that or when he would return.

At that point, and since Townsend now considered Clysters an unneeded extra hand, the Captain had decided against launching a search onshore. Freelance seamen sometimes left ships without a by-your-leave, though seldom without collecting what they were owed for the time they had served. The fact Clysters had taken everything he had of value with him indicated a planned departure, not an absence due to drunkenness, women, or some type of foul play ashore. It was unusual, Cameron thought, that an English seaman who had first joined the crew in Bremen would jump ship in a port that, at least according to the experience he had detailed when signing on, he had never before visited. As a precaution, and shortly before heading out to sea, Cameron dispatched Dietrich to the Harbormaster with a brief written report concerning Clysters and his "presumed voluntary" departure.

〰〰〰

Jan was watching the morning cargo loading operation when Dietrich returned from the Harbormaster's office and, passing Jan at the railing, told him of Clysters's "disappearance." Having spoken to Clysters only once, Jan did not know the man, but he was reminded of the curious and different stories Willows and Clysters had told about both the conversation he had observed and in response to his questions about whether the two had known each other before this trip.

The departure of Clysters was, to passengers and many crew members, far less of a surprise or matter of interest than was the continuing presence of Karin Dischinger. Almost everyone had assumed that she had disembarked in Lisbon. The Kastledale was leaving the harbor when Jan and others first saw her leaving her cabin wearing a flowery, long-sleeved blouse and a pair of her husband's corduroy trousers with the cuffs rolled up.

It later developed that after she and the Captain had observed the formality of reporting the disappearance and apparent loss at sea of Richard Dischinger to the Lisbon port authorities, she had determined that since the trip was paid for and because she understood that business associates of her husband were expecting to meet them when the ship arrived in Buenos Aires, she would complete the journey to Argentina. This would also give her time to consider her options, as opposed to immediately disembarking in Lisbon, where she might have to stay for some days while seeking transportation back to Bremen; a city that, in truth, she wasn't

at all sure that she wanted to return to. As she would also later explain over dinner one evening, she had the funds to book passage
on the *Kastledale* when the ship made its return trip to Bremen via
Southampton with a full load of Argentinean meat and hides. All
of this, she told her dinner companions, would give her more time
to plan her future without the need for rushed and possibly poor
decisions.

Having but a few weeks ago had his plans and life altered
dramatically by an unexpected event, with the need to make an
immediate decision about what new direction to take, Jan could
understand the young woman's approach. It seemed particularly wise since it appeared that her late husband had made all the
decisions, whether important or trivial, during their two years of
marriage, leaving her with much to learn about her own present
personal circumstances, much less how those circumstances would
impact her future.

<hr/>

When he saw Mrs. Dischinger leaving her cabin that morning
as the *Kastledale* began maneuvering out of the harbor, Jan was
standing outside cabin number five, where Dietrich had just introduced him to his new cabinmate: a middle-aged, prematurely bald-
ing, clean-shaven, German-speaking Portuguese named Gaspar
Chaves. Chaves was of medium height, moderately bowlegged,
and never at a loss for words. At the time, Jan was unfamiliar with
the terms *ebullient* and *exuberant* in any language; later in life, he
would come to define those words by mental pictures of Gaspar
Chaves.

Chaves was from the village of Peso da Régua in the Douro
Valley of northern Portugal. This area, he explained animatedly,
had the ideal climate for the cultivation of the grapes that made
superior dry red wines and Port; and never mind that Jan had no

familiarity with those wines, he would remedy that deficiency before they reached Buenos Aires.

"My family," Chaves declared proudly, "is among the leading wine merchants in Portugal and Spain, if not the entire world, or perhaps at least those parts of the world that are worth anything — excluding, of course, the heathen, the Slavic countries, and so on and on."

"I," Jan noted carefully, "am myself Slovak."

"I was, my friend, speaking only generally! Certainly, of course, *many* Slovaks, Bohemians, and others are the exception! In any event, I travel this route often, carrying choice wines to market in South America. You undoubtedly noticed the many crates that were loaded yesterday on this monstrous ship, which, by the way, I have traveled on many times before. Those crates are mine! Over one hundred cases of fine Port, plus a few cases of acceptable French wine, Bordeaux mostly. However, I am also transporting hundreds and hundreds of delicate cuttings that will be planted and used to further develop a *tremendous* vineyard in Mendoza, which as you know is northwest of Buenos Aires. I will *personally* take those cuttings by train from Buenos Aires to Mendoza!"

"It sounds like you are quite familiar with Argentina."

"I am! I have been there ten — no, wait — probably a dozen times. This will be perhaps my thirteenth trip ... or maybe fourteenth? Whatever. Buenos Aires is wonderful. Are you going to live there? There are a lot of Spanish, of course, but also an exemplary Portuguese community, some Germans, quite a few English, actually, and other groups, though I'm not sure about Slovaks."

"I don't plan on staying there long," Jan said, and then explained the nature of his journey, his eye condition, and the circumstances of his travel to Buenos Aires.

"Hmm," Chaves reflected after peering at Jan's eyes, "I am not a doctor, of course, but I would guess, from my wide, general knowledge of all things, that your eyes may dictate how long you have to remain in Argentina before going to America. The good news is that it is not a bad place to be. More good news is that I know *many, many* people there, especially in Buenos Aires, where I am almost famous, and I may be able to help you get settled there. Or you might travel with me to Mendoza! Of course! It will be an adventure!"

"I would naturally appreciate any help you can give, though I am not sure about going to this—this Mendoza."

"Of course you're not sure! We can decide that when we get to Argentina, and we have some days on this magnificent ship on the wild ocean to think about things. And," Chaves continued, reaching into one of the large duffel bags he had been unpacking, "a bottle of the fine Port I was talking about! I knew it was in one of these bags. We will share it at dinner!"

Chaves set the bottle of Port on the bench, slid his bags under it, and turned to pat the upper bunk. "I prefer the upper; unless you have already claimed it. For some reason, I sleep better when elevated. Fewer bugs, you know? Incidentally, do you know the beautiful young woman, the one in the rolled-up trousers, who was in the hall?"

Jan explained the saga of the Dischingers onboard the *Kastledale* and Karin's decision to go on to Buenos Aires.

"Sad," Chaves said sincerely. "Perhaps I can be of assistance to her there, though I suspect that at this time she mostly wishes to be alone. Getting on in the world is not an easy thing for a single woman, and she needs to take care not to be taken advantage of by those who prey on the lonely and the uninformed, to say nothing of the beautiful. There are those sorts of men everywhere, unfortunately."

After peering out the porthole for a moment, Chaves turned and said, "I should go on deck. Whenever I leave Portugal, I like to look back at my country, stare her directly in the eye, and assure her I will return! I suppose that is a silly superstition, but it has worked so far! And I have always returned! Will you come along?"

"Yes, of course, can you hand me that cap?" Jan said, standing and pointing to the black Fisherman's Cap on the peg behind Chaves.

"And who," Chaves asked as he handed over the cap, "is Anna?"

"I might tell you that at dinner over this Port of yours," Jan replied as they left the cabin and he locked the door behind them.

The Port went well with dinner, which featured three different chicken dishes. According to Ansel, that was the result of some of the frozen chickens in the aft holds "deciding" not to go to Recife or Buenos Aires. Chaves and Jan ate with Mr. and Mrs. Vargas, a couple from Lisbon who were going to visit relatives in Buenos Aires. They spoke only Portuguese, putting Chaves in the position of translator, though at times he gave his companions reason to question their reliance on his language skills. At one point, he advised Jan that Mrs. Vargas was interested in whether he was married. After Jan responded, Chaves offered a translation that seemed to shock her.

When Jan asked if everything was all right, Chaves looked thoughtful. "You know, I *may* have inadvertently told her that you have been married eight times, the first time when you were seven years old."

Later, he advised Jan that "Mr. Vargas wonders whether you can hear him passing gas." When Jan couldn't help but burst out laughing, Vargas looked very perturbed. "Actually," said Chaves, "as I think about it, it *may* be that he wanted to know whether you thought his wife handsome."

Eventually, and laboriously, Chaves corrected the confusions and put everything straight before they retired for the evening. Chaves had some documentation to complete concerning his cargo and immediately spread papers all about the cabin. Jan found a lighted corner in the third-deck sitting area, where he relaxed with a book he had borrowed from the Captain.

It was after 11:00 p.m. and, except for the familiar throb of the engines, extremely quiet when Jan heard the click of a door opening and Karin Dischinger walked into the lounge, surprised to see him sitting there.

"I thought I would go outside for some air," she declared, as if her presence required some explanation.

Jan nodded and with a smile cautioned her, "Be sure to keep your shoes on this time."

She laughed and asked, "Will you come with me?"

He thought a moment, nodded, put down his book, grabbed his coat and pipe, and followed her down the stairs to the weather deck.

They stood at the railing a long time, saying little. She looked out to sea; he smoked his pipe. After perhaps an hour, they walked back to the third deck and as she went to her room she touched his arm and whispered, "Thank you."

Jan returned to his chair and his reading. Sometime after 1:00 a.m. he fell asleep, and the book slid to the floor.

━━◆◆◆◆━━

Two days later, shortly before 6:00 p.m., they approached the island of Madeira and soon entered the sprawling harbor at the base of the hillside town of Funchal. The next day was warm and cloudless. The deck crew spent much of the day unloading the cargo that had been taken on in Lisbon and loading provisions, mostly fresh fish, to the galley, and in repairing deck rails and lines. The engineers, greasers, and stokers spent their time inspecting the ship's two funnels. With few exceptions, the passengers took advantage of the weather to stretch their legs on deck or on land in the town. Almost exactly thirty-six hours after arriving, the *Kastledale* was secured and headed back out to sea.

The ship's course from Funchal was generally due south, skirting west of the Canary Islands before heading slightly southeast to pass well off the African coast and between that coast and the Cape Verde Islands to the west. Once past the Cape Verdes, their course would run south by southwest across the South Atlantic to Recife.

The last of the Cape Verdes were coming into sight off the starboard bow the third morning out from Funchal. When the occupants of cabin number five awoke, it was immediately apparent that they were proceeding through rougher seas. Going down to breakfast, they encountered Weedfield on the starboard stairs outside the Mess. He pointed to an enormous, roiling buildup of clouds of multiple shades of gray in the sky south of their present position. The system was expanding while moving slowly to the west.

"Take a good look," Weedfield said. "That's probably a future hurricane in the making, and a big one at that. Neither the Captain, Townsend, nor I have ever seen one this well-developed this close to the African coast."

Jan stared at the clouds for a moment and asked, "What causes such a storm?"

"Well," Weedfield began, "they say that ocean storms that become hurricanes start off as big areas or waves of low air pressure that come off the hot African plains and deserts. When it gets out over water, low pressure usually creates bad weather. Under the right conditions out here, as I understand it, the trade winds start the low-pressure area to spinning, and that spinning increases slowly as it gets out farther over the ocean. By the time they get a good ways across the Atlantic and to the warmer tropics, they begin to pick up speed and pull up a lot of moisture. That process creates a hell of a lot of energy and wind, which sucks up more sea water, so the system becomes a tropical storm. And if it keeps on building, you get a big hurricane that smashes into the Caribbean Islands south of the United States with tremendous rain and winds that can get to one hundred and eighty kilometers per hour or more. If this one is going to be a big storm that becomes a hurricane, it's developing earlier than most: that thing we're looking at is already reaching the size of a tropical storm such as you'd normally only expect to find many hundreds of kilometers west of here."

"So," Chaves asked, "are we going through that?"

"We could and probably would ride it out fine, but we'd get banged around quite a bit. And with the sort of cargo we've got, like the furniture and all those cases of that bottled wine of yours, the Captain's going to slow us down, and we may zigzag some so that we let a lot of this system pass off to the west and don't go plowing right into the heart of it. Even at that, I bet we get very wet, and I think it's going to get a damn sight rougher before it gets better — which is why you see the deck crew being sure the cranes and such are secure. We're not really anywhere near it yet, but you can see how the waves and winds are building even here."

Weedfield continued up the stairs to the bridge, and they went in to breakfast, where Chaves — fairly accurately, as far as Jan could tell, though with some embellishment — began relaying Weedfield's comments to the other passengers. This had the unintended effect of causing a few to eye the food in front of them and consider, as the ship's roll increased perceptibly, whether sending anything down to the depths of their digestive systems was a wise course of action.

The navigator's predictions proved *generally* correct. Though the system seemed to be moving steadily westward and the *Kastledale*'s course was designed to keep it well to the east of the storm's center, by 10:00 a.m., they were being lashed by rain driven by fifty-knot winds and were experiencing waves that threw water well across the forward weather deck. Most of the passengers had reeled to their cabins, though Jan, with Townsend's permission, buttoned up his peacoat and ventured to the bridge to get a higher view. There he drew a nod from Captain Cameron, who moved about the bridge easily, apparently unaffected by the pitching and rolling of the ship that kept Jan constantly off balance unless he had a firm grasp on a railing or some other stationary object.

"Perhaps a bit rougher than I expected," the Captain observed, "but the pressure is stabilizing. Mr. Weedfield believes that the barometer will start rising later this afternoon, and things will be improving by this evening or, at worst, tonight. I hope he's right. We are getting a good washing, though."

Jan was willing to take Cameron at his word about improving weather later in the day. He stayed on the bridge for a quarter hour, fascinated by the churning waves, the constant action of the clouds, and the sheets of rain that at times completely obscured the pitching bow of the ship from view. He couldn't help but wonder what the lookout, binoculars pressed tightly against his eyes, could hope to see in the maelstrom around them or what action they could take if something, such as some other ship, came into view at close quarters.

After a glance at the map room, where Weedfield could be seen casually sipping tea and studying his maps, he turned toward the stairs to return to the third deck. As he went out, he held his cap on tightly with his left hand, but when a sudden gust pulled the door handle from his grasp and sent the door banging into the railing, he instinctively grabbed for the handle with both hands. That left the brown Fisherman's Cap in an unequal battle with the wind, and it went spinning off into the air, rising like an untethered kite until it disappeared into the rain, fog, and clouds astern. He secured the door and, momentarily unmindful of the storm, stared blankly into the fog where the cap had disappeared. A sharp gust threw him off balance; he cracked his knee painfully against a post, twisted his shoulder in trying to steady himself, and was almost pushed over the railing before he was able to clamber down the stairs.

Cabin number five was empty. After pausing to dry his head with a towel and hang his wet coat up to dry, Jan continued on to see if Chaves might be in the sitting area. It also proved to be empty except for Karin Dischinger, who was moving unsteadily toward her cabin.

"Are you all right?" he asked.

"No. But I am not as sick as I thought I might be. And I am better when I'm not alone and have someone to talk to, if perhaps you have the time."

Jan shrugged and, since it would have been very hard to say he didn't have the time or that he was busy, followed her to her cabin.

"Shall I leave the door open?" he thought to ask.

"Actually," she replied as she sat down on the lower bed, "I'd prefer the privacy of it being closed."

He took a seat on the bench, leaned back against the wall, and after a moment observed, "I see they've removed the upper berth."

"Yes, the Captain has been very kind. I found it difficult to be here alone with that upper bed creating a closed-in space. It seemed to be trapping me or something like that, and even made the room seem somehow lonelier. Without it, there is much more light when I'm in this bed."

"You seem to be holding up well," Jan said.

"Do you mean about the weather and seasickness or about Richard?"

"Well, I suppose both."

"I am surprised—and I wonder if I should even tell anyone this—that of the two, the sickness bothers me more, though it really is less of a problem in this storm than it was the first few days at sea when we left Bremerhaven. And I seem to have gotten past mourning for Richard, though I feel guilty about that. I hope you don't think me strange or heartless for not still being terribly grief-stricken."

Jan shook his head in what he hoped was a reassuring way.

"The truth is," she continued, "that Richard and I were not as close as I had always dreamed or thought people would be in marriage. He was kind enough in his way, but always preoccupied and never shared much of his business or ideas or whatever with me. He was, well … not forthcoming about many things. This trip to Argentina is an example. It came on all of a sudden. One day, there was nothing, and then the next, it was that we were going to Argentina, which he had said almost nothing about before, and that we were leaving in ten days. When I asked why and for how long, he waved his hand and said that it might be for a very long time. I didn't know what to say or do, but I was his wife …."

"Did you talk to anyone about this—perhaps your family?"

"My parents were quite old and both died some years back, and my only brother went to America two years ago just after my wedding. There was no time to consult with him or with anyone else. It was so sudden, like so much else with Richard."

"Have you decided what you will do after you reach Argentina?"

"I am still unsure, but I believe I will return on the *Kastledale* to Bremen. I have the money to pay for that, and I am sure there may be bank accounts of Richard's and perhaps some property. He seemed to have acquired some large funds just before we left, but I don't know from where. He mentioned that he had business associates who he thought would meet us when we arrived in Buenos Aires and perhaps they can give me some information, though I am somewhat nervous about them as people I do not know. However, I at least need to meet them, if they are there, to tell them of his death. It is so hard to sort through these things and to know the right thing to do."

As she talked, Jan studied the attractive young woman sitting across from him. He guessed she was near his age, perhaps three or four years older. Her world had taken a huge, dramatic, and unsettling turn, and she had many decisions to make and a new role to assume in her own life. Uncertainty about what to do was natural, but she spoke firmly and seemed to him to have a clear understanding of the problems or issues, if not yet the answers. She had, he thought, some fear of making poor choices, but that was due in large part to her lack of knowledge about her husband's doings and his situation, which would come to light in time.

"You have, of course, some time to sort all of these things through," he began, "and, at least in my opinion, the first decision you've made—to go on to Argentina—is the wise choice. It provides you with that thinking time. And you will have more of that on the return journey. If you like, I will be happy to go with you to meet your husband's business associates in Buenos Aires, and I believe Mr. Chaves would come as well. He could be the interpreter, and he is something I am not: an experienced businessman, or at least he appears to be."

"If you could go with me," she said, looking up with obvious relief, "I would feel so much better."

"You also, I believe, need to begin to think about business and perhaps legal advice when you return to Bremen. You remember my cabinmate, Mr. Willows? He has, of course, returned to Cardiff, but he may have further business in Bremen or perhaps could be convinced to return there. I believe he is trustworthy, and from his years in Germany, I am sure he has many business contacts there that might be of help to you in uncovering your husband's affairs and making decisions. I have his address in Cardiff and would be happy to write to him on your behalf."

"Those are wonderful ideas, and I am pleased you mentioned Mr. Willows. I was going to ask you of your opinion of him since you spent so much more time with him than I did while he was on this ship. He seemed to me to be experienced in the ways of the world, which I am not. It would be an answer to my prayers to have his advice in addition to yours. And you have already helped me a great deal today."

"I have done very little but listen."

"You listen, Jan, and you seem to care. For someone who is alone, that is very important. I have thought about speaking to you about these things for some days, and I am glad I finally had the courage to ask to talk to you. It is so important to have someone to trust and share your thoughts with."

They sat silently for a few moments. He saw the tears in her eyes and how she was blushing, both of which seemed to unsettle him in a strange way. He also felt that the ship was rocking less than before, though the rain continued to pelt against the porthole window. He stood and looked outside.

"The wind may have died down a little. The Captain, or rather Mr. Weedfield, has predicted things will settle down by this evening."

"I would like to talk again about these things and my ideas, if you don't mind," she said, wide-eyed and hopeful.

"Certainly, whenever you wish. And now, perhaps I should go, and you should rest."

"Wait a moment," she said. "Stand behind the door a little, and let me open it to see if anyone is outside. I am not at all ashamed to have you in my cabin—in fact, it is very comforting—but there are gossips everywhere, and you being seen coming out the door might start tongues wagging."

She opened the door, looked about, and then stepped aside as he left the room. He heard the door click closed and the key turn in the lock behind him.

Chapter 12

The Tropics

The storm proved fickle.

While for a time the winds had shown signs of abating, they regrouped and renewed their assault in the late hours of the afternoon. The rain intensified and was driven in billowing sheets, making the outdoor stairs and decks so treacherous that the Captain ordered the stairwell doors secured and barred. Inside, everyone, even those on the bridge, struggled to secure loose items and, with mixed success, to move about and avoid being thrown off balance. The tumult reached a crescendo shortly before the dinner hour — and then, almost without any transition, the wind suddenly dropped. At the same time, those gathered in the Mess caught sight of a few straggling rays of hopeful sunlight in breaks in the clouds far to the south.

As the ship began to steady and the stairwells were reopened, a towering, silver-blue waterspout slowly emerged astern of the *Kastledale*. It was far enough away that it presented no threat to the ship, while providing a spectacular sight for those who ventured on deck to watch as the waterspout drifted off into the dark to the northeast.

A relative calm after the storm, with a shift in wind direction, prevailed in the moonless hours before midnight. Weedfield made the rounds of the passenger cabins on the third deck, then worked his way up to the bridge to report that most of "the paying customers" had survived the storm well, in some cases because "they were obviously too frightened to think of being sick."

The high seas and the buffeting the *Kastledale* had taken did no apparent harm to the ship itself, but as he took the watch in the early-morning hours on the darkened bridge, Townsend was concerned whether the hatches had held water-tight and whether there had been any shifting of cargo, particularly in the forward holds with their crates of furniture and Gaspar Chaves's one hundred cases of wine. He also wanted to open the hatches on the aft, refrigerated holds to check for damage and so that the cranes could be used to sort that cargo and bring together the crates that would be unloaded in Recife.

However, while the dawn brought clear skies, the winds remained moderately high and the seas were still unsettled, with water occasionally spraying across the forward weather deck. Those conditions prevailed throughout the day, and Townsend was forced to delay his plans. He was able to check the forward hold from below decks, where a cursory inspection revealed some tipped crates and at least one that could be seen to have fallen off the top of a stack, with some visible damage to the crate and perhaps to its contents.

By the following morning, and though the skies were once again low and overcast, conditions had improved considerably. In the Mess, Jan and a few other early risers among the passengers were seated at breakfast which, as it did every other day, featured porridge and milk, smoked herring, fried tripe and onions, dry toast, marmalade, tea, and coffee. He had to reflect that, for the most part, he was eating as well on this ship as he had at any point in his life and certainly better than everything he had heard about the bill of fare he would have encountered as a passenger in third class on a trans-Atlantic liner such as the *Grosser Kurfürst*. He also was eating things he couldn't always identify, such as the tripe.

He had asked Chaves about the tripe one morning shortly after they left Lisbon, but Gaspar merely shook his head. "It is best that you do not know. But," he said, nodding to a nearby table where Mrs. Vargas was plowing through a large plate of fried tripe and onions, "I would not want to be spending the day in a small cabin with her."

As he was finishing his meal, Jan looked out to see the deck crew gathering around Townsend near the forward hatches. It wasn't long before some were at work unfastening the straps that held the arms of the cargo cranes secure, while others made ready to open the hatch covers. As he watched, Chaves sat down next to him with a full plate of food, conspicuously missing any of the fried tripe and onions.

"You know ..." Chaves began, though, looking up and out the window, he immediately discarded whatever train of thought he had intended to pursue and exclaimed "Sweet Jesus!" He jumped to his feet, stuffing his coat pockets with rolls, herring, and, perhaps injudiciously, marmalade.

"I must go on deck!" he cried. "Why would they open the holds if not for a problem? Are there rivers of Port running free below decks!? It is the devious work of Spaniards, I am sure!"

"Where," Jan observed, "would these Spaniards come from? I would think the men are more likely just checking for storm damage."

Chaves waved an arm and bolted for the stairs. Soon he could be seen trotting across the weather deck, aiming straight for Townsend.

An hour later he burst through the door of cabin number five, where Jan was washing some clothes in the sink before taking them on deck, where Dietrich and Ansel had strung some clotheslines for the passengers' use.

"To allay your concerns, the Port has survived intact!" Chaves reported. "Some of the crates of furniture were tipped or fell, and they are using the crane to get those back in place. One, as it fell, smashed the top of one of the crates of cuttings, but the crew has repaired that crate. Do you know — of course you wouldn't, and how could you? — that among the furniture there are crates with twenty fine grandfather clocks? Swiss or German, I suppose. What, I ask, is the market for such in Argentina!?"

Jan shrugged his shoulders. "I can't say, but I have seen those types of clocks in Vienna and would imagine there are wealthy families in Argentina who would purchase them. In any event, I am almost through washing here if you need to use the sink. Dietrich has strung ropes for drying on deck."

"No, no, I have plenty of clean things to last me until we reach Buenos Aires, where I can procure a full laundry." As he said that, Chaves thrust his right hand in his coat pocket, and a strange look flickered briefly across his face. "But, you know, perhaps maybe one or two things. I'll think about it. Please, don't wait for me."

The hand remained in the pocket, though Jan could see it moving slightly. He thought of the marmalade. After wringing out the last of his things, Jan gathered them up and headed for the door. As he closed it behind him, he glimpsed Chaves watching him — with his hand still in his pocket.

<hr/>

When he returned, Chaves was bent over the sink working on the coat. Three small, slimy-looking herring were arranged neatly on a towel at one end of the bench.

"While you are working on that," Jan said, settling as best he could on the other end of the bench, "I wonder if I might ask for your help on something."

"Of course. This washing requires little skill and far less concentration."

Jan outlined that part of his conversation with Karin Dischinger that related to the business associates of her husband who would apparently be waiting in Buenos Aires, and whether Chaves would be willing to be a part of such a meeting and to act as interpreter in the event those men spoke only Portuguese or Spanish.

Chaves straightened and almost saluted. "I would be honored! The lady deserves our help. That she trusts us is of course only natural, given the type of men we are! Will these associates of her late husband come to the ship? Or is she to meet them somewhere else?"

"She doesn't know. She also doesn't know their names or what they look like or their business. If they do not come to the ship, I do not see how she can do anything to find them, if indeed they are there to be found. Also, since the decision to go to Argentina was apparently made quickly, I am uncertain how her husband would have gotten word to these men as to what ship the Dischingers would be on. Of course, it is possible he had planned this trip for some time, made the arrangements with these men, and did not say anything to her until the last minute."

"Then we must do as the circumstances dictate and render what assistance we can. In honor, we can do no less. Will she stay in Argentina? Or will that depend on these men and their business?"

"Her plan now is to return to Bremen on the *Kastledale*, which I believe is her best course of action — without, of course, knowing what may come about or be learned in the meeting we are talking about."

"We three," Chaves said as he twisted the coat to ring out as much water as he could, "should talk about this shortly before we reach Buenos Aires and before this meeting comes about. For now, I need to go hang this on Dietrich's ropes to dry."

Once Chaves was gone, Jan moved to clean up the sink area. He decided the herring were best left where they were. Glancing out through the porthole, he could see the deck crew beginning to secure the forward hatches and cranes.

〜〜〜〜〜

The refrigerated holds were covered and insulated by four large hatches on the aft deck. The cargo that Townsend wanted to reposition for unloading in Recife was all to starboard. The cranes had lifted and set aside those hatches and, within an hour, the work of men and cranes in the hold had achieved the desired results. They had also righted three stacks of crates of frozen chickens that apparently had toppled over in the storm.

The work had gone so quickly that, mostly because of the discovery of the toppled crates of chickens, the First Mate decided to make a quick check for any similar damage on the port side. With the starboard hatches replaced, the cranes lifted those on the port side and swung them aside.

As he and the chief deckhand, Meganne, walked around the edge of the open hold, Townsend was pleased to see no further signs of toppled crates. They had almost completed their circuit of the hold, and he was looking across the deck with the thought of signaling the cranes to replace the hatches, when Meganne touched his arm and pointed … to the body of a man wedged down near the floor of the hold in the narrow space between the wall and the stacks of crates.

By the time the Captain arrived, Townsend had dispatched three men into the hold and they had, with considerable difficulty, extricated the body from its tightly-wedged position and were maneuvering it into a sling that had been lowered by one of the cranes.

They watched as the sling slowly came up, was swung around, and deposited on deck, where it was detached from the crane. The body was frozen by rigor mortis and the refrigeration into a stiff, grotesque position: one leg bent up against the chest, the other fully extended, and the arms bent at odd angles. It was covered with a light frost, though that didn't conceal the stiff, matted blood on the back of the head.

"Richard Dischinger?" Cameron asked.

Townsend nodded. "Yes, I would guess so, though we'll need a positive identification by Mrs. Dischinger."

"And how he died? And how he got there?"

"One would think," Townsend said as he kneeled by the body, "that the cause of death is this head wound. It is fairly deep and could have been made by a heavy instrument, though it certainly could be the result of a fall, and we did find him head down near the floor. I suppose it is also possible that the head wound, however received, didn't kill him, and he froze to death. Weedfield may be able to answer that after a look at the body, especially after it thaws out some."

Townsend stood, looked into the hold, and continued. "As to how he got there, certainly a fall is not out of the question. But I believe Mrs. Dischinger said that she last saw him sometime *after* we had left Cardiff and put to sea. The only time before today when the refrigerated holds have been open since we left Bremen was in Cardiff, when we unloaded the coffin containing Mrs. Willows. These hatches were once again secured before we left the dock. The only other access to the holds from the deck is that emergency escape hatch there, which is fairly close to being above where the body was found. If it was left open, it is probably wide enough for someone to have fallen through it, but then someone else would have had to secure it. I was not informed of that hatch having been found unsecured at any time, but I will check with all the men to see if any found it open and closed it."

"He also could have gotten in there from below decks," the Captain observed, "through the refrigeration control room. I can't see it from here, but it is just around that corner, not far from where the body was found. If he was in the control room, he could have gone through that into the hold, as you do when you verify the readings on the gauges by going into the hold and reading the temperature there. Perhaps once in there, for whatever reason, he was unable to reopen the door, climbed the ladder toward the escape hatch, and fell from there, bouncing off the crates to where he was found. Though how would he have gotten into the control room? Who besides you has the control-room duty and keys?"

"On this trip, just myself and Meganne—and Clysters, before he jumped ship. Actually, there is only one set of keys, which the three of us, or now just the two of us, pass to each other as the duty rotates."

"So there are two possible ways—from the deck through the emergency hatch or from below after coming through the control room—that he could have followed to wind-up where you found him."

"Yes," Townsend said slowly, "and in either case, he might have died from a fall. Though if he tumbled through the hatch, there is the question of it being open after he fell in. And if he came through the control room, the question is how he got in there." He paused for a moment. "If he didn't die from such a fall, then there is the distinct possibility he died from a blow to the head—with whoever delivered that blow pushing the body through the hatch or bringing it into the hold through the control room."

"We need to talk more of this later," the Captain said. "Have some of the crew take the body below decks. I'll send Weedfield to take a look and Dietrich to help get it in shape. I'd like it to be in more presentable, less frozen condition before Mrs. Dischinger has to view it. Once you have things underway here, and you might as well close and secure the hold, come to my cabin, I'd like to have you with me when I speak with her. Oh, and also, take a look around the refrigeration control room and the area inside the hold between that room and where this man was found."

Townsend nodded and began putting the deck crew in motion.

———

Karin Dischinger had positively and emotionlessly identified her husband's body. Ten minutes later, she sat calmly in the map room on the bridge as Cameron and Townsend explained the circumstances of the opening of the refrigerated hold, how the body had been discovered, and the conclusion, provided by Weedfield's examination, that the cause of death was a blow to the head. They advised her of the possibility of that blow being caused by a fall into the hold and how that might have happened. Townsend related how, in his questioning of the crew, the deckhand Winston Andrews had remembered finding the emergency hatch ajar and not fastened late one night after they had left Cardiff and before they reached Lisbon. He couldn't recall what night that was or whether it was before or after Richard Dischinger had been discovered missing. Andrews had secured the hatch and thought nothing more of it since it wasn't the first time he or another crew member had found that hatch unsecured.

Cameron also carefully explained the possibility that Richard might have been murdered and his body dropped into the hold from above, or that the body had been taken into the hold through the refrigeration control room. They questioned Mrs. Dischinger about anyone who might have had a motive for killing her husband, especially including anyone on the *Kastledale* that he might have known. She shook her head, noting that she wasn't completely aware of her husband's past before she met him or of all his current business dealings, but that she was sure that there was no one on the freighter that either he or she had been acquainted with before they boarded in Bremen.

"Gentlemen," she said after a moment of silence, "is there something I am supposed to do or that you expect of me at this time?"

"We certainly don't want to intrude on your grief," the Captain responded thoughtfully, "and there is no immediate need for decisions on these matters, but I believe there are two things where your direction and opinions will guide or influence our actions. One relates to how we treat the death. If it was an accident, then the book is, so to speak, closed, as it was when we thought he had fallen overboard."

"However, the possibility is there, as we have explained, that it was not an accident; though at this time we have no proof of that, no known motive among anyone who was on the *Kastledale* at the time of his disappearance and death, and no logical or even illogical suspect. If we had proof, a motive, or a suspect, we would have to report this to the authorities in Recife and perhaps elsewhere. And it may be that we should report it in any event, especially if you wish the circumstances of your husband's death to be investigated further, including detailed examination of the body by the authorities. It is, I should note, not unlikely that the authorities in Recife will have little interest in this since the event occurred far from their jurisdiction and your husband was not Portuguese. If, however, they wish to pursue such an investigation, we would naturally cooperate, and you would probably need to remain in Recife for some time."

"The second issue," the Captain continued, "relates to disposition, and by that I mean burial, of the body, and that may be affected by how the death is treated or characterized."

"As to that," Townsend added, "there are three or four options. One is to arrange for burial in Recife or Buenos Aires when we arrive there. The second would be to carry the body back to Bremen; the Captain has mentioned that you likely will book return passage with us, and I imagine we could have the body prepared in Recife and carry it back, much as we brought Mrs. Willows to Cardiff in the refrigerated hold. A third option is burial at sea, which is often done in the case of the accidental deaths of seamen and others. The choices might, of course, be affected or delayed if an investigation of the cause of death is done in Recife."

"I am not sure that it affects my answers to your questions, but what do you think or guess the result of an investigation, if there were one in Recife, would be?" Karin asked. "And are there any consequences or improprieties or whatever in not reporting this to the authorities there?"

"Mrs. Dischinger," the Captain responded, "I have to first note that I am obviously not a Brazilian official or police officer, and am not qualified to speak of their approaches or methods. That said, I believe the investigation would be less than exhaustive and the result inconclusive. As to the consequences of not reporting this, and especially since we have already filed a report in Lisbon about your husband's disappearance, I would say there are none *if* it is treated as an accidental death at sea. As far as official interest is concerned, I would think the book would be closed."

"Thank you, Captain," Karin said. She gazed out the window of the map room, looking past the helmsman to the ocean ahead. After a long moment, she turned back to the two men.

"To me, my husband has been dead and lost to me since he went missing after we left Cardiff. The discovery of his body does not change anything for me or my future. It merely confirms what I thought I already knew and believed. I am not sure of whether his death was accidental; though I tend to believe — and, I suppose, want to believe — that it was, and I would think the authorities in Recife would reach the same conclusion. It is unlikely that there is any answer to that which would be free of all doubt. If nothing else, the five hundred Marks you found in his coat, and which you've given to me, would seem to be money a murderer would certainly take. I also see no point in burying him in a strange land or shipping his body back to Bremen. His only living relatives are two brothers in America; who would likely never visit a grave in Germany. I think a dignified and simple burial at sea — which, after all, and until this morning, was assumed to be his final resting place — is the best choice. And that would be my wish, if you can grant that."

"We can and we will," the Captain said quietly. "Under all of the circumstances, I believe your wishes close the matter for us. Is there anything else Townsend or I can do for you now?"

"No, you have been most kind. I would like to be alone in my cabin for the rest of the day. Can we do the burial tomorrow?"

"Weather permitting, yes, at ten o'clock in the morning. Mr. Townsend, will you escort Mrs. Dischinger to her cabin? Also, be sure that Dietrich brings her evening meal to her there. When he brings the meal, Dietrich will have more information about the burial."

"Thank you," she responded as she rose. "You both have both been kind and understanding. I appreciate that very much."

Walking to her cabin, she could sense that word of the discovery of her husband's body had spread throughout the ship to the crew and passengers. Although she believed otherwise, a very small part of her couldn't help but wonder whether among that group was a murderer and, if so, whether she was in any danger.

———

The ship lay motionless in a calm sea. Aft on the sunlit weather deck, seamen and passengers stood silent and hatless, listening to Captain Cameron's final words.

"... into the depths and into the hands of Your gracious and final care, we commend the earthly body and the eternal spirit of Your humble servant, Richard Dischinger."

At the rail, DeGroza and Cousins lifted the end of the long

plank, and the heavily weighted canvas bag slid straight down, dropping with a small splash into the sea below.

The crowd on the deck, most of the crew and all of the passengers, walked slowly by Karin Dischinger, who, lifting the black veil she had borrowed from Mrs. Vargas, acknowledged their words of sorrow and thanked them for coming to the brief service. Weedfield happened to be last in line, and he escorted her back across the deck. The engines came to life, and the ship eased into motion.

Jan had, with Chaves, been among the first to express their condolences, and they had moved back midship, with Jan stopping on the second deck to get a cup of coffee from the galley. He wondered whether a person could become addicted to coffee. He dismissed that fleeting thought and paused to look out the windows. After a few minutes, he turned and went back down the stairs and out onto the forward weather deck. He was soon standing alone in the sun at the rail, watching the waves break away from the strong thrust of the bow as it pushed the water aside.

He had been there for almost ten minutes when Dietrich, also with a mug of coffee in hand, stopped for a moment on his way to the forecastle.

"It is nice that so many took time to come to the service," Dietrich said between sips, "though I suppose it was more for her than any memory of him. I doubt he spoke more than twenty words to anyone while he was alive and walked these decks."

Jan shifted his position on the rail. "It seems he had much on his mind. Mrs. Dischinger did well today, and I think she will, going forward."

"I expect so," Dietrich agreed. "She is an exceptionally attractive woman and seems to be handling this well. And for whatever else he may have been—and, of course, I mean no disrespect and God Almighty rest his eternal soul—I suspect he left her with sufficient means. We found over five hundred Marks in his coat pocket, which of course we turned over to her, and I would guess there is more money and property here and elsewhere."

"You are probably correct, though she may not be aware of it. He was apparently quite closemouthed about things, especially his business."

"Well, it may be that some of the papers he had in his pockets will help her figure things out."

"What sort of papers?" Jan asked idly, leaning on the rail and looking out at the passing clouds.

"Oh, hard to tell. I just bundled them up for her, except for some scraps and the one odd handwritten note that we found stuffed in his shirt pocket, which Weedfield and I figured were worthless."

"What was the odd note about?"

Dietrich shrugged his shoulders and said, "It wasn't really about anything. It … oh, there's Mr. Townsend. I need to catch up with him. The note was just a scrawled Bible verse, though I think it was not accurately quoted. It said, 'An eye for her eye. A tooth for her tooth.' Figure that."

Jan reached for the coffee cup as it slipped from his grasp and fell into the sea. He looked quickly around, but Dietrich had already turned his back and was hurrying to catch up with Townsend.

Chapter 13

Recife

Recife lay in the distance, the scattered lights of its harbor clear and bright in the late-evening darkness. The *Kastledale* rode at anchor outside the harbor, thin wisps of smoke rising from its funnels and drifting off to the west toward the city. They had arrived with the last fading light of day and were met by a small boat bringing the message that the harbor pilots, apparently as part of a pay dispute, were refusing to work between sunset and sunrise, and that they should drop anchor for the night. As the evening wore on, two smaller freighters, having encountered the same small boat, maneuvered to similar anchorage nearby.

The bench Jan was sitting on was actually a large tool chest bolted securely to the forward weather deck near the crane closest to the bow. Although the chest was not intended as a bench, it served as one: with a back rest of sorts in the form of the flat side of a nearby vertical steel shaft or duct that provided ventilation for the hold below. It was a quiet, good-place-to-think spot after dark, and it wasn't the first night that he had enjoyed the solitude it afforded. They were now just below the equator and the night was warm, though comfortable enough thanks to the trade winds blowing inland from the ocean.

Three days had passed since the burial at sea, and during that time Jan had thought often about the note Dietrich had found in Richard Dischinger's shirt pocket. The immediate question had been whether to say anything to Captain Cameron or, for that matter, anyone else. There was certainly something well beyond coincidence in the language of the note and in Gareth Willows's use of the exact same phrase in describing the punishment to be exacted on the man who caused the death of his wife and who Willows had unequivocally asserted was on the *Kastledale*.

On the other hand, apart from the note in his pocket and what that might infer, there was nothing to point to Richard Dischinger as that man. There was certainly no observable tie or acquaintance between Willows and Richard, and nothing that anyone, except perhaps for Willows, knew or might even be able to discover to tie Richard to the robbery and fire. Karin had talked of the sudden decision to leave Germany and go to Argentina, but that alone meant little. Since Willows had left the ship before Richard's disappearance, there was also the question of who would have killed Richard for him. There was little to point to anyone, with the possible exception of Andrew Clysters, and the only connection between Willows and Clysters was apparently Jan's observation of the two of them having a brief conversation that they later explained with conflicting, but hardly incriminating, stories. Apart from that, there was almost nothing else but the suspicion that might arise from the fact that Clysters had joined the crew at the last minute in Bremerhaven and then had left the ship at the first opportunity after Richard disappeared. And Clysters was, at least supposedly, a man of the cloth—could, Jan wondered, a servant of God be a killer?

In a way, apart from the inconclusive or circumstantial evidence concerning the identity of a murderer, the possibility that the death was the result of an accident was not out of the question. It was not inconceivable that, in the dark, Richard had stepped into the opening of the uncovered emergency hatch and fallen to his death.

That hatch had been found left open or at least unsecured on past occasions and certainly could have been an inadvertent, accidental death trap waiting for some unwary, perhaps preoccupied stroller on a dark, foggy night at sea.

Finally, Jan thought, if he were to speak with Captain Cameron, it would be to what point or to what end? Leaning back against the ventilation shaft, he thought again of how difficult, if not impossible, it would be to find other evidence. Clysters's present whereabouts was unknown and perhaps unknowable, and it was difficult to see who would be interested in tracking him down. Willows could be found in Wales but might easily deny having used the language in the note or referring to the killer of his wife as being on the ship, and in any event would affirm his conversation with Jan that he didn't know Clysters. And while Jan had developed great respect for Captain Cameron, was he likely to act on thin evidence with regard to Willows, someone he apparently had known for a long time and who was an old man in mourning for his wife?

Jan had also developed great sympathy and respect for Willows and, in fact, truly believed he would be the best person to advise and help Karin. He also believed that Willows would provide that advice to her in her best interests, even if she were the widow – the innocent widow – of the thief who had caused Elizabeth's death. He was positive that Willows would fill that role and never mention the connection, if indeed there actually was one, between Richard and Elizabeth. And as to Karin, he very much wanted the best for her, something that would come about with much more difficulty if he were to raise in her mind unprovable doubts about her husband's death and vague questions about Willows's role in that death. She seemed comfortable with the state of affairs as to Richard and was focused on her own difficult future, something Jan did not wish to disturb.

All of that and more had led him to the conclusion that the

question was both of what was "right" in the abstract and that of what was right for the people affected—to some extent Captain Cameron and his relationship with Willows, but more importantly Willows himself in his grief and the last years of his life, Karin in her present life and in her future, and perhaps even Clysters, if he were blameless. Sometimes in life, he was sure, the wisest thing to do was to do nothing, and despite the fact that a death, perhaps even a murder, was involved, this seemed to be one of those times. On balance, he felt comfortable with that course of action.

As he looked across to the lights of Recife and packed his pipe with some of the last of his tobacco, his thoughts lingered on Karin. Although she faced some questions with the business associates of her late husband, provided they existed and turned up in Buenos Aires, she had a plan in mind, including at least an initial return to Germany and the probability of advice and counsel from Willows. It also appeared she had sufficient financial resources to carry her for a reasonable time. And being attractive, personable, and young, he guessed that she had other possibilities in her future.

His and Karin's situations were clearly not perfectly parallel, but he too had a plan: he was going to Buenos Aires and was determined to make it to America. However, beyond that there were many uncertainties. He certainly did not have enough money to immediately buy passage to America. In any event, he could only undertake such a trip when his eye condition was completely cured; he could not afford, financially or otherwise, to undertake that journey until his eyes were not an issue. He had a cold fear, which returned every time he thought of it, of being turned away upon arrival in America. That would destroy every dream and had to be avoided at all costs.

In the meantime, he would need to eat and find a place to live, and those costs would gradually consume the money he had unless he quickly found work in Buenos Aires or, perhaps, as Chaves had suggested, in Mendoza. He did not know what sort of work might be available, how he would acquire such a job, and how he would communicate, at work and otherwise, with people who spoke only Spanish or Portuguese. Because of all of those factors, it would very likely be months, and perhaps many months, before he would be able to leave for the United States. All in all, it was a frustrating situation, made all the more so by the need to take things one at a time, step by step, as they developed.

It was, he saw with a quick glance at his pocket watch, nearing midnight. Stepping to the railing, he knocked the remaining embers from his pipe and watched them disappear in the water below. Walking across the deck, he waved at the lookout on the bridge and, reaching the stairs, started up to cabin number five.

———

The dock to which they were secured in Recife was wide, running fully seventy or eighty meters back from the ship to long, low wharf buildings and warehouses. Early in the morning, as they moved into the harbor, the word was passed that due to necessary work on one of the engines they would be in Recife for at least two full days, if not longer.

"I think, my friend," Chaves said, looking out the window of their cabin, "that we should escape this closet and get some exercise on this excellent dock, especially exercise that takes us to what the steward Ansel tells me is a superior tobacconist located well down the wharf in that building with all the flags flapping in the breeze. I would like to acquire some long, fat, and sweet-smelling cigars, and perhaps they will have acceptable tobacco for your pipe. The fresh air of the land will also be good for whatever ails us in body and spirit!"

The tobacconist's was large and crowded. Jan quickly found tobacco at a reasonable price. Chaves took an hour to settle on three dozen cigars of great size and great price that came elegantly boxed. Eventually, they left the shop and wandered down the wharf to a café of sorts, where they ordered huge cups of steaming aromatic Brazilian coffee served outside at little tables shaded by an enormous canvas awning.

"Do you think this coffee is safe to drink?" Chaves wondered, gazing at the thick clouds of steam rising from each cup.

"Not, I would say, in the immediate future," Jan said skeptically. "Perhaps when the steam has thinned out enough that we can see each other across this table."

"Then we have time to enjoy the sun that God has given us this morning and to talk! I spoke to Captain Cameron last night about these friends of the late Dischinger who may be expecting to meet him in Buenos Aires and of our plans to accompany the widow when she meets with them. I also explained all of the uncertainties around that, including such minor things as when they will come, if they will come, how many there will be, and so on. He agreed to alert the dock agent and the stewards who control the gangway to be on the lookout for anyone seeking Richard Dischinger."

Jan nodded his agreement. "That will be very helpful. I am concerned that if these men do not appear and a meeting does not happen on the day we arrive, we will have disembarked and will not be on board if they come at a later day."

"Ah! I have also taken care of that! Well, actually, the Captain has. The ship will be in port in Buenos Aires for at least five or six days, perhaps longer, unloading and loading and so on. Mrs. Dischinger will, of course, be able to stay on board throughout that time since she will go on the return voyage. The Captain has agreed that I may also stay on for three nights since my wine and cuttings will not be unloaded until our third day in port. And after I explained your situation to him and Mrs. Dischinger's need and desire for you to be with her, he agreed that you may also remain in cabin number five for that time, though of course we will both have to leave the ship prior to the boarding of any new passengers."

"You did not have to do that, but thank you; that eases my mind both as to Mrs. Dischinger and what it is that I will do upon arriving in Buenos Aires. It will give me some time to find a place to stay in the city and to look for work."

"Don't thank me; thank the Captain." Chaves absently poked his finger into the coffee. "As to you, let me suggest again that you go with me to Mendoza! I have two excellent reasons for that suggestion. One is that, although I do not *know* this to be true, there *could* be a job for you in the vineyards—outdoor field work such as that you may have been used to in your home country. Second, I have a friend there—well, actually not a close friend as such, but someone who I have met before, one Ronaldo Guterres, who is the brother of a man who is a brickmaker, apparently a large operation and business, in Buenos Aires. That might create a connection that you can use for employment there if you did not care to work in the salubrious vineyards in Mendoza. And, third, I could use the company on the train trip, and it will give you a chance to experience the country of Argentina outside of Buenos Aires."

"I thought you said there were two reasons?"

"I said there were two 'excellent' reasons! And there also just happens to be another, a third reason. You know, perhaps the sun will burn off the bank of fog this coffee is creating." As he spoke, Chaves began to carefully unwrap one of his thick, expensive cigars.

Jan couldn't think of a reason, excellent or otherwise, to say no. "What you suggest about this Mendoza may be something I should do. Can you allow me a few days, until we are at sea or perhaps even until we reach Buenos Aires, to make a decision? I have many things to think about and also wish to be sure I am able to keep my commitments to Karin—Mrs. Dischinger."

"Of course, and I would not want you to in any way feel you

have failed her." As he spoke, Chaves dipped the end of the cigar into his coffee for a few seconds, then put it in his mouth and loudly sucked the coffee from the tobacco before tossing the soaked cigar into a nearby barrel. Raising the cup, he pronounced, "It has cooled enough! A coffee toast to Mrs. D! Salute!"

Jan raised his cup and took a long sip as Chaves began an extended discourse on grapes and vineyard operations in Mendoza.

<hr />

Unloading of cargo proceeded throughout the day, including all of the chemicals and some of the crated furniture that had been in the forward holds, as well as nearly half of the frozen chickens from the refrigerated holds. A dozen or more passengers, including a number who had come aboard in Lisbon, disembarked in Recife, leaving another dozen who would go on to Buenos Aires. That group included the Tremolos, who with their two children had boarded in Bremen; Mr. and Mrs. Vargas; Karin Dischinger; Jan; Chaves; and three other single men who had come on board in Lisbon.

That afternoon, Jan talked with Weedfield about the letters he and Karin planned to write to Willows and whether he would post those in Southampton when the *Kastledale* made port there on its return trip. Weedfield readily agreed and also offered to post any other letters destined for Europe that Jan might wish to entrust to him.

Dinner was a quiet affair since some of the remaining passengers, including Chaves, and virtually all of the crew had gone ashore. The Tremolos family occupied one table, the Vargases another, and Jan joined Karin at a third table. She had forsaken her black mourning dress and veil in favor of a dark shirt with rolled-up sleeves and a pair of gray trousers, both items apparently having belonged to her husband.

Looking across the room, she whispered, "Mrs. Vargas keeps looking this way. I would guess she is taking me to task with her husband for not dressing in proper respect for Richard, and for dressing in an unladylike way, and probably for so scandalously and publicly eating alone with another man."

Jan stole a glance at the Vargases' table. "Perhaps; though it seems to me she is quite engrossed in her dinner, especially the tripe."

She giggled and whispered, "I notice her husband is not a tripe connoisseur." She poked at her food for a moment, finally saying, "I spent the afternoon looking through Richard's things: what he had in our cabin and what was in the crate in the hold. The crew was kind enough to pull that up on deck for me and to break open the top. I am not sure what to do with it all: shaving items, tobacco, men's toiletries, many writing instruments, some tools, books, and, of course, all of his clothes. It is too bad you are so much bigger than he was, or I would give you your choice of the clothes. I don't wish to carry all of those things around the ocean with me and back to Bremen—or wherever I go. What should I do with all that I have no use for?"

"You might ask the Captain. Some things might be of use to members of the crew. Or perhaps there is some charity in Buenos Aires that would accept the clothes; Mr. Chaves might know of such a place."

"I will. If I cannot dispose of them in such a way, would it be disrespectful of the dead, of Richard, for me to throw them away or have them destroyed?"

"That I do not know. It is an area of social rules or acceptability where a peasant from Važec, such as I, has no experience."

"I think you have much 'peasant wisdom,' Jan," she said earnestly, "and you are such a strong and determined person. Your advice, to me, is very important." After a moment, she continued.

"I also found some papers, letters really, in Richard's things. Some relating to long past business dealings that I do not understand and which seem to be unimportant. Some about schemes and plans he had for making money. Some from other women — including letters after we were married and which ...." Her voice caught, and she stared at her food.

Jan took a quiet deep breath. "I would think," he said softly, "that some of those are papers you should destroy. They seem to have no use or value. If you prefer, you can give them to me, and I will see that they are seen by no one else and are burned by the fires of the ship's engines. There is no use in keeping those."

"Thank you. Perhaps you — no, we — can do that tonight? So far, I have found nothing in any of Richard's papers that I have looked at that have anything to do with this trip to Argentina or the business associates who may be waiting there. I had hoped there would be something to cast some light on that, and perhaps there is in all the papers I have yet to look through. There are still quite a few of those. Do you think those men will be there? And what would this business be about? It would so help to know before meeting these men. I am, perhaps, just a little frightened of all of this."

"It may be that the men and the business they may have had with your husband will be a mystery to us until such a meeting, if there is one, takes place. And if it does, and once they discover that your husband is dead, there may be no business to pursue and they may take their leave and be gone. I cannot see how they would have any claim on you."

Karin was silent for a long moment. "While I have some fear, it is nothing to what I would feel if I had to deal with those men alone." With her fork, she rearranged the food on her plate. "I don't want to eat any more. Those papers I was talking of, could we destroy those this evening? Soon?"

"Would now be soon enough?"

He pushed back his chair, and they made their way to the bridge, where Townsend was the officer of the watch. After a short explanation, Townsend summoned Ansel and sent him scurrying to the engine room while Jan and Karin went to her cabin, gathered up the papers, and then headed below deck. Ansel had returned to the bridge but Pitkin, the Chief Engineer, was waiting. He took the papers and shoveled them into the low flames. They watched until there were only ashes.

〰〰〰〰〰

Those working on the starboard engine encountered some difficulties, but by the evening of the third day in Recife, all had been overcome, and it was announced that they would leave the harbor and begin their run down the coast to Buenos Aires some time the following morning.

Jan was up early, well before dawn. He reached the gangway just as Dietrich and two deckhands were maneuvering it out and down to the dock for the morning. He needed exercise and set out walking in the direction of the distant tobacconist's shop. From there, he worked his way around through some streets paralleling the wharf before beginning to circle back toward the *Kastledale*. As he walked, he pulled out his pocket watch from time to time to be sure he would be back at cabin number five by 6:15 a.m.

In their weeks of sharing a cabin, he had discovered certain inescapable facts about the sleeping habits and routines of Gaspar Chaves. One of those was that when Chaves went to bed he would very carefully lie on his left side with his arms and legs just so, in exactly the same position each evening, and would then almost instantly fall asleep. While the time of retiring might vary, the time of awakening never strayed a minute from 6:15 a.m. — as a cabinmate, he could set his watch by when Gaspar would open his eyes.

The awakening was, however, deeply affected by a third habit:

once asleep, Chaves never changed position or so much as twitched a finger until his internal alarm clock chimed at quarter past six. Because of this, when Chaves awoke, he could be essentially immobile. This condition was most likely to come about if he happened to sleep for more than six or seven hours. A certain "rigor sleeptis," as he called it, would set in; with muscles, ligaments, and joints seemingly frozen and rendered inoperable by the lengthy period of inactivity and deep sleep. He literally could not move and required the assistance of someone to at least knead and bend his arms, back, and neck into a working state, from which point he could, on his own, though not without some effort, get the rest of his body loosened up. On a good day, it was a ten-minute operation; on a bad day, it could take three times as long. Oddly enough, when limbered up, he would be loose and flexible with no aftereffects for the rest of the day.

At home, his wife was his therapist. When traveling, he relied on cabinmates and new friends such as Jan. As to what he did when staying alone in inns or lodges while traveling, he said, "I can usually pay the innkeeper or some housekeeper to look in on me and get me going at 6:15. Sometimes it is a young lady; which is often preferable since it takes them much longer to straighten things out."

When he finished his walk and returned to the ship, Jan encountered Townsend at the foot of the gangway and stopped to ask a few questions about the ship's departure. Once back on deck, he was also delayed in going up the stairs by a group of people coming down and then by crew members painting the railings. So it was that it was after 6:30 a.m. when he opened the door to cabin number five.

Chaves had somehow managed to roll forward, first onto his face and then a bit farther toward the wall in an attempt to get onto his right side. The wall was, however, closer than he had gauged, and he was now wedged against it, neither on his back nor on his right side. His arms and legs were still frozen in their sleeping positions, though now sticking out in the air at odd angles.

"Good to see you!" he gasped as Jan came through the door.

"I am sorry. I was delayed. How did you get over there?"

"I am not at all sure. But enough of the small talk! Perhaps we should figure out where to begin. I do not recall ever starting from this particular position."

"Well, let's see — perhaps we should start here with your left arm."

"That would be fine, though I should note that the left arm you have laid hold of is my right leg. Might I suggest that, provided it isn't too much trouble, you try pulling and rolling me back to my starting position? That will be familiar ground, and we likely can proceed as if it were any other day at 6:15 a.m."

Pulling Chaves back to his sleeping position proved relatively easy. From there, in another twenty minutes, and accompanied by various snaps and strains resembling an incessant cracking of knuckles, Chaves was standing on the floor bending, stretching, and progressively regaining freedom of movement.

As he watched, Jan asked, "Has there ever been a morning when whoever was to help you forgot for more than a few minutes?"

"Well, obviously never completely, or I wouldn't be here, would I? There was a time in an inn in Seville when the daughter of the proprietor dawdled in at close to eight o'clock. As you might imagine, it took considerably more time to loosen me up, though it was not a completely unpleasant experience since she was quite attractive, loosely dressed, and wound up climbing all over me to get what I thought would be better angles from which to manipulate my limbs. She worked up a mighty sweat, which was also quite becoming to her."

"Have you ever tried falling asleep on your right side or back?"

"Well, of course, but once asleep, some automatic action takes place, and I roll to my left side. My wife once used various ropes to strap and tie me securely into the bed on my right side. I slept in that position all night but, since I couldn't move, when I awoke at quarter past six I was, if anything, worse off since I was seriously frozen into an unfamiliar position." He paused for a moment and shrugged his shoulders. "The best thing is not to go to sleep too early. But the ocean air in particular seems to be sleep-inducing. I am looking forward to aging further since it seems the old do not need as much sleep!"

"Perhaps — though I hope this 'sleeptis' of yours is not a contagious disease."

"No, no!" Chavez assured him as he moved toward the door and breakfast. "Though," he said, pausing for a moment, "I encourage you, as I have my dear wife, to fight any urges or tendencies to wake up every day at 6:15 a.m. I believe it is the earliest symptom. But, of course, nothing that you should obsess over or lie awake at night thinking about! Come, the morning porridge waits!"

PART THREE
Argentina

Chapter 14

The route south from Recife to Buenos Aires covered some twenty-two hundred nautical miles. The *Kastledale* steamed through moderate seas off the South American coast, which remained in sight on the western horizon throughout the journey.

Settled in their routines, the few passengers kept largely to themselves. Karin Dischinger had resumed taking her meals with the other passengers, usually forming a group of three with the men from cabin number five. Those cabinmates often finished their morning coffee on deck; the two of them leaning against the railing for an hour or so while the waves slipped by and the seagulls, who now accompanied the ship throughout the day, wheeled overhead.

When they stepped outside with their coffee early on Friday, the seventh day out from Recife, they saw that the morning sun was no longer to port but was now almost directly behind the ship. It was evident that they had begun to bear west. They found Weedfield with his binoculars at the railing near the forward cranes.

"Aha! We are entering the Río de la Plata and that..." Chaves gestured to the distant land mass to starboard, "is Punta del Este. Uruguay. And there, the opposite shore is Argentina. Of course, you have to *imagine* Argentina since you cannot *see* the Argentinean shore because the river is almost two hundred kilometers wide here!"

Looking off into the distance, Jan observed, "On my map, this looks much less like a river than just a part of the ocean that intrudes into the land."

Handing his binoculars to Chavez, Weedfield said, "In some ways, it is both. The Río is what the English call an 'estuary': an arm of the sea that meets the mouth of a river, though in this case it is even more confusing since here the sea meets two rivers, the Paraná and the Uruguay, which have become one. Far to the north and west of here, well beyond Buenos Aires, though not at the same place, those two rivers empty their waters to form the Rio de la Plata. I understand that in that area, after both rivers have come in, the Río is already many kilometers across. It widens progressively, and at some point—though I don't know where that point is—the river waters mingle with and become part of the ocean waters. At that mysterious point, I suppose the waters are no longer really a river, but it is referred to as the Río de la Plata all the way to these opposing headlands and what people *say* is the mouth of the river. In any event, there are many cities and seaports on both sides of the Río de la Plata, including Montevideo in Uruguay and, to be sure, Buenos Aires."

"Will we reach Buenos Aires today?" Jan asked.

"Sometime this evening I believe, before dark. But I doubt if we will be secured for unloading before tomorrow, perhaps as late as tomorrow afternoon, and maybe not until the next day," Weedfield said a bit sourly. "The waterfront, they call it Puerto Madero, is not—even though the current docks and wharfs are only perhaps fifteen years old—constructed to handle very many large cargo ships such as this one. There are limited and narrow waterway approaches to the docks. So, we may have to wait our turn. They are constructing a huge new port area with many more staggered docks that open more directly onto the Río. However, the Captain says that, from what he heard last time we were here, even the first section of those is not due to be opened for another year."

"So," Chaves said from behind the binoculars, "will we still be in port for five days?"

"Oh yes, perhaps longer. Once we are there, we have some very definite schedules and commitments, including those for the unloading of your wine. As a refrigerated ship, we have some priority over many others. We may have to wait our turn before docking, but once tied up, the dock is ours."

"Good," Chaves said with relief. He handed the binoculars back to Weedfield. "That reminds me that I have a number of hours of paperwork to do concerning that wine and its sale, and I have put that off long enough. If you both will excuse me."

After Chaves had left, Jan picked at some loose paint on the railing. "I had never been on the ocean before this, and I must say that I have grown to love the sea. When I leave the *Kastledale*, I will miss it and the kindness of you and the Captain and others. It has not been what I had expected when I set out."

"The sea can do that to you, I suppose." Weedfield made a mental note of the loose paint. "And it may be that you have found some security on the ship, what with your forced change of plans. Have you decided what you will do next, in Buenos Aires?"

"I will need to stay and work in Argentina for a while. I may go with Chaves to the wine country since there may be work available there. He also has some contacts with people who do business in Buenos Aires, so that may develop into something. It is all more uncertain than I would like, but ..." His voice trailed off.

"It will work out, I am sure," Weedfield said with some conviction. "And I think if, as time passes over the next few days, you should decide not to stay and wish to return to Bremen, well, we will have an open deckhand position that Mr. Townsend and I have discussed, and which is yours if you want it. You seem to have developed your sea legs, and we are sure you could handle the deck work." He looked at his pocket watch. "I need to go to the bridge."

Jan nodded and smiled his thanks.

He stayed on deck most of the morning, watching a thin, dark line on the southern horizon. With their progress up the Río, and as they drew ever closer to Buenos Aires, that narrow line grew first into a distinct shoreline, then into a more definable set of brown hills rolling off into the distance. While Argentina had been on his mind every day since leaving Bremen, it had seemed detached and at times unreal; what he would do there and what he would have to face there had lacked immediacy in the many days at sea. Now, it was imminent, and he felt the nervousness returning as he wondered what Argentina would hold in store for him.

Weedfield was correct. In the last light of the day, they approached a large, rusted, and seemingly permanent raft anchored in the shipping channel. The raft carried a shack of sorts, and from that shack a man with a megaphone emerged to direct them ahead to buoy eleven, where they were to drop anchor and maintain position for the night.

They sat at the buoy until nearly 3:00 p.m. the next day, when a small boat from the raft came by with instructions to prepare to weigh anchor and make steam. Shortly thereafter they were passed by the outbound refrigerated ship *Queen of Spades*, closely followed by two tugboats which accompanied the *Kastledale* into the harbor, slowly maneuvering her through the approaches and to the dock. Her lines were not completely secured until half past eight.

At dawn on Sunday morning, the Captain and Townsend went down the gangway and crossed the broad dock to meet with the shipping agent, whose office was in a timbered wharf building directly across from the ship. Among other things, they advised the agent of the burial at sea and the possibility of visitors having business with the late Richard Dischinger, and that, when those men arrived, the steward at the gangway should be alerted. The agent indicated a small, unused room off the main office where the visitors could wait for the Dischinger party, and he agreed to say nothing to those visitors about Dischinger's death.

The gangway was officially opened at 8:00 a.m., and a team of immigration officials boarded the ship to check the documents of all those on board, including Jan, who were immigrating to Argentina. Medical examinations were also carried out on board the ship by a doctor — while the admission standards were perhaps not as high as America's, immigrants with highly contagious diseases or obvious mental health problems were not allowed to enter the country. All of those passengers on the *Kastledale* who were bent on staying in Argentina as immigrants were cleared for disembarkation and final processing, which was done through a new complex of buildings collectively and popularly known as the Hotel de Inmigrantes, situated not far from the northern docks at Puerto Madero. The complex provided immigration processing, some medical services, accommodations for those in need of temporary quarters, and help with finding employment. It took its name from the elongated four-story hotel that was its dominant building. The hotel was still under construction and only partially occupied; when completed, it was intended to feature four dormitories per floor, each of which could accommodate as many as two hundred and fifty people.

When the immigration officials completed their work, all of the *Kastledale*'s passengers, save three, disembarked for the Hotel de Inmigrantes. Much of the day's activity on board was devoted to unloading a few small crates of passenger possessions, particularly those of the Tremolos family, and with the careful unloading of the many crates of furniture from the forward holds. The furniture was destined for high government offices and, in addition to dock workers and drayage laborers, the dock was crowded with minor officials bent on not only inspecting the furniture for damage, but also on arguing over and securing the best pieces for the higher officials they each represented. It was late afternoon when the last of the furniture crates was eased down to the dock, and the holds and cranes had long been secured when the final wagons were loaded and moved slowly off into the city.

It was during the afternoon's furniture wars on the dock below that Dietrich, as he was giving the watch over to Ansel at the gangway, saw the two men leaving the agent's office across the way. A moment later, the agent stepped outside and, all the while watching the backs of the men as they walked away, waved and signaled to Dietrich, who scurried down the gangway and made his way across the dock. Ten minutes later he was headed back to the ship, and five minutes after that was reporting to Mrs. Dischinger in her cabin, with Jan and Chaves leaning in the doorway listening.

"There were two of them, and the agent wasn't sure which one he liked the looks of least. They asked if the agent had a list of passengers, and when he said he did, they asked about Richard Dischinger. The agent ran his finger down the manifest as if the name wasn't familiar, then told them that Mr. *and Mrs.* Richard Dischinger were listed as passengers. Seems they hadn't expected there to be a Mrs. Dischinger, but then said 'fine' and asked if *Mr.* Dischinger could be summoned to meet with them and that he would be expecting them. The agent told them that he was sure Mr. Dischinger wasn't available today — though, as he told me, he did not know what he would have said if they asked him why not. Luckily, they did not pursue that and merely said to get word to Dischinger that they wanted to meet with him at eight o'clock tomorrow morning. The agent said he would relay the message and asked where Dischinger was to meet them. They said, 'Right here,' and then they left. He said they spoke Spanish; though when they talked between themselves, he thinks they spoke in German."

Karin frowned. "Did they say anything about the business they had with Richard? And what did the agent mean when he said he didn't like their looks?"

Dietrich shook his head. "He didn't say anything about them mentioning what business they had with your late husband. As to their looks, well, he thought they were a little rough-cut. They didn't look like the usual business types you see in the city. They had worker's boots and calloused hands, and one had cuts and what looked to be dried blood on a couple of his knuckles. The agent also told me that he thought they looked like they were there to get something, not to talk about something."

Jan rubbed his chin for a moment and looked at Karin. "If you are not comfortable with this, we can skip the meeting and just have the agent tell them the truth; that your husband died and was buried at sea."

"I think that would be hard since he didn't tell them that to-day," Karin said. "They might believe otherwise and think Richard is alive but trying to avoid them, though I'm not sure what they could do about it. It would be nice not to have to do this, but the right thing to do is to be there at eight o'clock. I feel a need to know what 'business' my husband was about. And these two men have, you know, an interest here. It may be something simple, some-thing that I know that can help them. If not, at least they will know Richard was keeping his commitment and coming to meet them, and perhaps the knowledge of his death will somehow be of use to them. I hope you will still go with me."

They both nodded their heads. "Of course," said Chaves, "we are at your service."

It was later that evening, and Jan sat alone with paper, pen, and ink in the sitting area on the third deck. He had letters to write and felt it was better to write them now, rather than waiting until the last minute.

4th September

My Dear Maria:

I hope this letter finds you well. And I hope you received the letter I sent to you from Bremen after my plans were changed. If you did not receive that, the change in plans was because of an eye condition that the doctors at the emigration station discovered and which was unacceptable for travel to the United States. Instead, I have journeyed to Argentina, in South America, as a temporary destination and will as soon as possible go from here to America.

Our ship has arrived in Buenos Aires, the largest city in Argentina, after its long journey, which I have survived well. The weather throughout our time at sea was calm except for a very few days. I was ill only briefly when we first left Bremerhaven and adjusted well to the ocean and traveled very comfortably after those first few days. On the journey I have become more comfortable with the change in plans and am fully determined that that is all but a temporary thing which I will overcome. Our dreams of America are alive and will come true.

It pains me to think, much more to say, that I will need to be in Argentina for some weeks and, I would think, probably some months. I will need to find work to earn additional money for passage to America from Buenos Aires. As of yet, I do not know how or when that passage will be made. Also, the eye condition is still present and I cannot leave for America until that has cleared up.

In Lisbon in Portugal, the ship took on as a passenger a Portuguese wine merchant, Gaspar Chaves by name, who has become a friend during these travels. This is, I believe, very fortunate since he knows people here and may be able to help me in finding the work I need. I will be traveling with him to a wine-growing area known as Mendoza, which is some days distance from Buenos Aires. It is possible that I would stay there to work. If the work prospects are not good, I would return to Buenos Aires. In either case, I believe Mr. Chaves has contacts that can help me find employment. He will also be very helpful as an interpreter for me since it seems that the languages spoken here are mostly Spanish and Portuguese.

An officer on this ship, Mr. Weedfield, will be taking this letter with him on the return voyage to England and Bremen, and will post it to you. That means it will be some weeks from today before you receive it and much will, I am sure, have changed by then.

When my situation is more fixed and I have an idea of how long I will have to remain here, I will write to you again. And it may be that at that time, if I am settled in living quarters, I can provide the information and address you would need to post a return letter to me. It is distressing to me that you may be worried about me and how I am doing and that until you receive this you will not know that I am well.

Please share the news of my travels and welfare with my family, as I will not be writing to them separately at this time.

Until we are together,

Jan

He carefully addressed the envelope, slipped the letter to Maria inside, and sealed it. After some hesitation, he reached for a fresh sheet of paper and shifted to carefully composing a second letter, this one in German, addressed to Anna. After outlining the progress of his voyage to Buenos Aires as he had done in the letter to Maria, including the information about Chaves and the forthcoming trip to Mendoza, he added more personal thoughts.

*These long days at sea, with some minor adventures along the
way, have passed by much easier because of the pleasant memories
and thoughts I have of you. Your face, if I may say this, shines
bright before me every day and reminds me of the pleasant hours
we shared together in the few days we had with each other. I hope
it is not too forward of me to say those things.*

*An officer on this ship, Mr. Weedfield, will be taking this let-
ter with him on the return voyage to Bremen and will post it to
you. That means it will be some weeks from today before you receive it and much will, I am sure, have changed by then. When my
situation is more fixed I will, if I may, write to you again. And it
may be that at that time I can provide the information and address
you would need to post a return letter to me. Not, of course, that
I would expect you to do that, though I would hope you might.*

*If you think it appropriate, please express my best wishes to
your father and to Anatoly. The kindness your family showed to
me in so many ways is a permanent and pleasant memory in my
life.*

*I find it hard to end this brief letter. I do hope it finds you in
good health, in happy spirits, and with perhaps a small thought
of me.*

Jan

When he was finished, he sat asking himself about the point of
this correspondence with a young woman who he had such confusing feelings for, who might not be interested in hearing from him,
and who, in any event, he was very unlikely to ever see again. He
had no answers to his own questions. After a time he shrugged, addressed the envelope, slipped the letter inside, and sealed it.

It was shortly before eight o'clock Monday morning when Jan

arrived at the gangway, where Dietrich once again had the duty. He nodded to the steward and looked across the dock, where he noticed two figures lounging and talking outside an open set of doors in the warehouse not far from the agent's office. Even at a distance, they were unmistakably DeGroza and Cousins.

Dietrich saw his glance and questioning look. "They apparently thought to get a little morning air on shore. Coincidentally, I'm sure, they also heard — perhaps from the agent or someone else — of the 'rough looks' of these two men you are meeting, and so they seem to have decided to take their morning air in the general area."

"Let's not," Jan replied, noting the approach of Chaves and Karin, "draw the attention of these two to those two."

Dietrich nodded and then, addressing all three, announced, "The men you are going to meet arrived ten minutes ago. They are in the agent's office, probably studying you from that distance as we speak."

Karin took a deep breath. "Jan, will you lead the way? Mr. Chaves, may I hold on to your arm as we walk?"

The two men were standing by the window, waiting for them in the agent's sitting room. The taller of the two bowed as they entered the room. "Mrs. Dischinger, I presume? I am Diego Douala, and this is my associate, Ronaldo Jimenez. And these two men are?"

After Chaves had translated, Karin replied, "I am pleased to meet you both. These men are friends of mine. Mr. Chaves has translated your greeting, and this is Mr. Brozek. I regret that I cannot speak Spanish."

Before Chaves could translate, Douala held up a hand and, in measured but precise German, said, "We both speak some German, as well as some English, so perhaps we can converse without the need of translation, with Mr. Chaves assisting and watching for any difficulties. And please have a seat. We were most saddened to hear of Richard's passing."

The last sentence caught the three friends by surprise. As Karin took a seat and the others followed suit, Douala explained, "We were in a nearby bar yesterday evening and happened to be near some seamen who talked about being on the *Kastledale*. Ronaldo here is not shy, so he rather directly inquired as to whether any of them had met the passenger Richard Dischinger, and they advised us he had been found dead and was buried at sea. Again, you have our condolences."

"That is true, Mr. Douala, and thank you for your concern," Karin replied. "I am afraid that while my late husband had advised me that there would be some men, some business associates, meeting him here, he did not tell me your names or who you were, and I know nothing of the business involved. Perhaps you can tell me about that?"

Watching Douala and Jimenez, Jan thought that both men had visibly relaxed when Karin stated that she had not known their names or anything of her husband's business with them. Jimenez had been sitting with his big, scarred fists clenched, but he began to relax and flex his fingers as Karin spoke.

"Our business was very, well, *speculative* is I think the word," Douala said, looking to Chaves for confirmation. Jan thought that he seemed to be taking care in his choice of words. "He was to bring us some, some ... information. Much of which was probably in his mind but some of which would have been in written... would 'writing' be more correct? Good. I suppose you have looked through any documents he may have left behind?"

"Yes, at least some of them, and I was especially looking for something that might relate to his meeting with you, since I hoped to be able to at least partially fulfill whatever obligation he might have to you and whatever enterprise you had in common."

Douala smiled and looked at her intently. "It is kind of you to be concerned of that, but the obligation is small. Although, in talking of this meeting, did your husband, or perhaps you found such in the documents you have looked at, make any reference to building contracts or papers he might be carrying with him?"

Jan had been looking a bit past the two men as Douala spoke, but at the reference to the building contracts he looked at them more directly.

Karin shook her head. "No, I'm afraid that he said very little about the meeting or its purpose. Also, in what few of his papers I have had a chance to look at, I have not found any contracts and do not recall seeing anything about building projects. What would those be?"

"The specifics are not all that important," Douala said, "and the business involved is not affected by it and need not be of any great concern to you. Will you be staying in Buenos Aires?"

"No. Actually, because of Richard's death, I will be returning to Bremen on that same ship."

"I believe the ship will be here for some few days. Would you, if you have the time before departing, allow us to look through his papers? Or perhaps, if you prefer and if it is not too much trouble, could you do that again yourself? Anything you might find concerning building projects in Argentina or any of your husband's business here would possibly save us some time and a few pesos."

Karen hesitated for a second and, looking directly at Jan, said, "I think I should not allow others to look through Richard's personal papers, particularly since I have not examined them all myself. But I certainly would be willing to look through them again, very thoroughly, now that I know something of what I might be looking for."

Jan silently nodded his agreement.

"That would be acceptable, Mrs. Dischinger," Douala said. "And if you find such papers and could contact us through the agent here, that would be all we can ask. And if it grows late and the ship is leaving, I believe you could leave them with the agent. We can check with him each day, for so long as the ship is here in Buenos Aires."

The previously silent Jimenez now added, in a voice distinguished by its low and hoarse tone, "This is all so trivial that after learning last night of your esteemed husband's death, we first thought to not come this morning. But having said we would be here, we did not wish to cause offense and also wanted to personally express our sorrow to you. We did not learn from the seamen we talked to last night how your husband died. Did he become ill on the journey?"

Karin shook her head. "No, it was an accident. He apparently tumbled into an open hatch one night in the dark and suffered a severe blow to his head, from which he died."

Jimenez raised one eyebrow slightly and nodded slowly. "Tragic. Again, you have our sympathies. And we were looking forward to meeting him. As to the documents Diego has spoken of, they *do* have a certain value to us, and if you find them, well, we will compensate you for that value as we would have compensated Richard. That was our business with him. If the documents are not among his things that is, shall we say, just as well and perhaps to the same result. Diego," he said, standing, "we should go about our business and leave these good people to theirs."

"Yes, yes," Douala agreed, also getting to his feet. "It was extremely pleasant to meet you, Mrs. Dischinger. I suspect your husband was a very lucky man — perhaps luckier than he fully appreciated."

"Thank you," Karin replied. "Can I ask you where you met Richard?"

Douala paused for a second before shrugging his shoulders. "We never actually met, in the sense of being in the same place. We were merely … business associates."

He nodded to Jan, shook Chaves's hand, and followed Jimenez out the door and down the dock. A few seconds later, Cousins and DeGroza sauntered by the window and, seeing that everything seemed to be all right, continued on to the ship.

Chaves looked puzzled. "What do you suppose this is all about?"

Karen shook her head. "I have no idea. Jan, do you?"

He had an idea but quickly decided to keep that to himself, at least for the time being. "Whatever it is, I think, and despite their saying it is all 'trivial,' that it is clear they would very much like to have any papers concerning the building projects and would pay you—I would think a considerable sum—for those papers, just as they apparently would have paid your late husband. But it seems they might be just as happy for those documents, if they once existed, to now be lost or destroyed."

≈≈≈≋≋≋≈≈≈

The boxes and folders of Richard Dischinger's papers that had not been burned in Recife were spread before Jan and Karin on the floor in the third-deck sitting room. They sat cross-legged on the floor across from each other, scanning through the papers, looking closely for any references to building projects, to Douala or Jimenez, or anything else that might be related to the Dischingers' trip to Buenos Aires. It was after 9:00 p.m., and they had the third deck to themselves. Chaves had gone into the city for dinner with local wine merchants and planned to spend the night there. He had assured Jan that he would be back by eight o'clock the following morning, when his wine and cuttings would be unloaded.

When they started, Karin again had asked Jan what he made of the morning's discussion, how Richard might be involved in the building projects, and why it was important to Douala and Jimenez.

"That," he had answered carefully, "is hard to figure out

without knowing the location of those projects and how they are related to the two of them on the one hand and to Richard on the other — assuming that is all that the three of them had in common. They never really said what they were 'business associates' in, although apparently it has something to do with the mysterious building projects. If your late husband had been alive to meet with them this morning, I think they very certainly would have expected him to have the papers they referred to with him — and apparently were going to pay him for those. Be that as it may, all we know for certain is that a meeting had been arranged between three men who had never met before and who, at least to our knowledge, are apparently tied together only by projects that these two were very vague about and which, I'd say, they are not likely to want to discuss with anyone else."

It was now two hours later, and only a small box and a few bulky folders of documents remained to be reviewed. He looked across at Karin, who sat with her head down reading. Next to her she had set aside a small, neat pile of papers that were unrelated to what they were looking for but useful to her for their information on Richard's accounts and other items in Bremen. A bit farther away was a larger, scattered pile of documents that had been reviewed and were to be discarded.

Jan glanced at the five-page document he was holding and quickly discerned it related to some German bank accounts but nothing else, and handed it to Karin for the pile of documents she was keeping. He turned to the remaining box and pulled out a large pack of papers tied together with crossed strips of cloth.

"Oh, those are mine," Karin said. "They are old family letters written by my parents and their parents."

As he handed the tied bundle to her, he saw that remaining in the bottom of the box was a large envelope with *Douala* and another scribbled, illegible word written on the front. The sides of the envelope were pulled out or extended in such a way that it obviously had at some time been full of papers or some object. While the flap had once been sealed, the top of the envelope had been torn open. It was empty except for a small scrap of paper, apparently the top corner of a page that had been ripped off when the envelope was opened. The scrap had printed on it in German *UTMOST CONFIDENTIAL REPORT Page 14 of 14.*

"We seem to have found something, though not much," he said as he passed the scrap and the envelope over to her. "Do you remember where this little box was? Was it in your cabin, or was it one of those you retrieved from the hold?"

"It was in our cabin. Actually, I found it behind the door; though when we boarded in Bremen, Richard had pushed it under the bench, and I don't remember it being moved from there. What is the word after Douala's name?"

"I don't know. It looks like the envelope got wet and that was smeared, perhaps when someone tried to dry it off."

Karin frowned as she turned the scrap over and over in her hands. "This must be — or must have been — part of the set of documents those men were interested in. Where do you suppose the rest of these fourteen pages are? And when was this envelope torn open and the pages removed? It looks to have been done in a hurry."

"I would say so. Another question is, who opened it? If it was your husband's envelope, I would think he would have been more careful in opening it, especially if he was going to be delivering the papers to Douala."

"You would think so. I can also tell you that this envelope was not at the bottom of this box when we started the trip. I put the bundle of letters in the box myself, and there was nothing else in there."

"Is there any chance the papers that were in this envelope are somewhere in your cabin?"

Karin shook her head. "No. There are not many places to hide things in there, and I have looked everywhere, including under the bedding and the bench and even behind a loose board in the wall. And Richard did not have papers like this on his person when he was found." She put the scrap of paper into the envelope. "Do I give this to Mr. Douala and Mr. Jimenez, and tell them that this is all we've found?"

"That is up to you. It is very little, though it may indicate that the papers they were interested in were in Richard's possession. He may have destroyed them—or they may now be in someone else's possession if they were taken from him. Douala and Jimenez might want to know that, even if there is no way of knowing what happened to the papers or where they are or who may have them if they weren't destroyed."

"The question is whether or not I leave the envelope and this small piece of paper with the ship's agent to give to them after I leave," she said, uncrossing her legs and straightening them out in front of her. "There is something disturbing about those two men, the building projects, and this meeting they were to have with Richard. And now, there is this envelope. It also all says something disturbing about Richard and perhaps about his death. And those may be things I do not want to know."

Thinking it was best for her to make this decision herself, Jan busied himself with pulling all the discarded papers into one stack.

Karin sat thoughtfully for a minute. "In some ways, I suppose, it might be best for those men not to know about this envelope and its missing contents. And in any event, what's left is so insignificant that I can't see how it would help them." She paused and watched as he straightened the papers. "Then again, Mr. Douala's name is on it, so you would think it was intended for him. And having said I'd look again, I guess I owe it to him to give him what—as little as it may be—we have found, especially since I have no reason to keep it and would probably just throw it away."

She sighed and put the envelope on top of her pile of saved documents. She hesitated and then turned to look at him inquisitively. "Are you going on with Mr. Chaves to this Marisa or Mendora tomorrow?"

"It's called Mendoza and, yes, we leave tomorrow. I went to the immigration office at the Hotel de Inmigrantes this afternoon. Chaves was kind enough to come with me. All the final processing went easily. I am officially an immigrant to Argentina and am cleared to travel with Gaspar to Mendoza. I also was able to exchange most of my Marks for Pesos." He paused for a moment. "I really don't know if I will stay in Mendoza. I think it more likely that I will return to Buenos Aires and work here until I am able to try again to be an immigrant to America. If I do not find work immediately on my own, the people at the Hotel will help and, if need be, I can live there for some weeks."

"I will miss you." She played with the buttons on her shirt and bowed her head a bit so that he could not see her eyes. "I shall be all alone on this ship, not knowing anyone, on the long trip back to Bremen. I wish," she continued, looking slowly up at him, "that I could stay here in Buenos Aires with you … or you could still sail back with me!"

Jan reached across and touched her hand. "Going back to Bremen is not possible for me, and staying here would not, at least right now, be the best thing for you. I am positive Willows will help you with your affairs in Germany. And as for the return voyage, Dietrich and Ansel will be here, and I believe that Mr. Weedfield will be at your service as well — he asks often about your welfare and needs."

"He does!?" Karin blushed just enough to be noticeable.

"He does." He smiled for a long moment. "Though it is late, I wonder if we might not find your shoes, put these papers in your cabin, and then walk on the deck for a while. The night is warm, and the lights of the city are bright."

She smiled and nodded. After the papers, including the envelope and the small torn scrap, were put away in her cabin, she hooked her arm through his, and they went down and outside to the weather deck, where they remained until well after midnight.

Chapter 15

Mendoza

Mendoza, on Argentina's western fringes near the Chilean border, was a six hundred-mile railway journey from Buenos Aires across, east to west, the widest part of the country. Even though there were relatively few stops along the way, covering that distance required the better part of three days. The stops tended to be long due to the taking on of water and coal to meet the needs of the locomotive, the time it took for passengers to procure food from vendors in the neighborhood of the stations, and the loading and unloading of passengers and freight.

The rails led steadily into the foothills of the Andes Mountains, where spring was not as advanced in its coming as in Buenos Aires. It was early September, and the days were bright and moderately warm, but the nights were cold, resisting the advance of warmer temperatures.

The train was a lifeline through central Argentina and was heavily used. The passenger coaches were almost completely full leaving Buenos Aires, and it seemed that, whatever the number of passengers getting off at any stop, they were replaced by an equal number of new faces headed for destinations farther along the line. The coaches themselves were relatively new but showed the wear and tear of riders who were constantly getting on and off, and who were often loaded down with luggage, boxes, baskets, dogs, and small children. All of those items tended to spill over into the narrow aisles. The padding on most of the benches had mysteriously compacted to a hardness approximating that of their wooden frames. The coaches seemed to fit the tracks "loosely" and they swayed rhythmically from side to side whenever any curve had to be negotiated.

Unlike the rest of the train, the car they rode in contained only a handful of other passengers, almost all of whom had boarded in Buenos Aires and were also bound for the end of the line in Mendoza. Part of the reason for the lack of crowding was that all the seats had been removed in the rear two-thirds of the car. That space was occupied by the crates containing the grape vines Chaves was bringing to the fledgling Portuguese-owned vineyards in the area around Mendoza. The value of the vines was such that Chaves couldn't tolerate the uncertainty of packing them in the boxcars. Instead, he had paid double the freight rate in order to have the crates travel in the passenger car. The crates were carefully secured and stacked just so in order to allow for as much air circulation as possible. And the rule established as soon as he and Jan boarded was that the vines did not travel unescorted: one or the other of them had to be in the car at all times, day and night, whether traveling or stopped.

On the second day out, they talked of wine and the country ahead, with Jan admitting he knew little of wine and less, in fact absolutely nothing, of winemaking and vineyards.

"It is your lucky day!" Chaves exclaimed. "*I* know a great deal, and since we have little else to do on this smoking monster of a train, I will take you beyond knowing absolutely nothing to being one of the foremost Slovak authorities on these subjects!"

For the better part of an hour, Chaves expounded on the wine and wine-growing regions of France, Italy, Portugal, and Spain — which were, in his opinion, the leading European wine-producing nations, and therefore the best in the world.

"In our lifetimes, or shortly thereafter," he declared, "Argentina will, I am convinced, become one of those leading producers. It takes time, much time, to establish vineyards and for those vineyards to mature and to develop to the point where the proper grapes are being grown. The ground and the climate around Mendoza are ideal for that! And there is the exciting possibility that the higher elevation there will add characteristics to the fruit that are rarely obtainable in European vineyards. It will, of course, take time to develop the winemaking art, that which turns grapes into wine, including obtaining the right equipment and polishing the skills to extract the juice and to process, age, store, and bottle the product. All of that will take knowledgeable people. A few of those people are there now, some will come later, and others will be native people who are trained there. And it is even more exciting because this is all developing along four separate lines!"

He paused and stared out the window, apparently absorbed in the passing countryside. After a few moments, Jan realized Chaves was waiting for him to ask the obvious question: "What are those four lines?"

"I knew you would be interested in that! The four lines I refer to show the tremendous potential of the Mendoza vineyards because they involve the interests of four sovereign countries." He paused for a moment, but apparently being unable to wait for Jan to recognize the prompt, he plunged ahead. "One is English and involves the truly great Sir Edmund James Palmer Norton, who was actually, I believe, born in Denmark or Germany or some such place in the north. In any event, he was a famous railway bridge engineer who moved to Mendoza and saw the region's potential for wine cultivation and production. In about 1895, he founded the very first actual winery in the area, south of the Mendoza River in the district of Perdriel, where he planted vines imported from France."

As he spoke, Chaves stood and paced up and down in the

crowded aisle between the rows of seats in the front of the car, oblivious to the annoyed looks of the occupants of those seats.

"Another," he continued, "was Nicola Catena, who came from Italy in 1898 and planted his first Malbec vineyard a few years later, maybe around 1902. Malbec is a purple grape variety used in making red wine, such as Bordeaux. That is named for a region in France, and I would think, though I do not know, that his grapes came from there. A third involves vineyards and a winery known as Trapiche in Godoy Cruz, just outside the city of Mendoza. It was founded by Tiburcio Benegas, who was the grand Governor of the province of Mendoza at the time. It may have been Benegas who introduced the first French grapevines to Argentina, even before Sir Palmer Norton."

Jan was ready for the next pause and prompt: "And the fourth?"

"The fourth and the newest, led by Ronaldo Guterres, are the valiant Portuguese! Our cargo is to go to him to be a part of the impressive vineyard he is developing. Some of these," with a sweep of his arm, Chaves indicated the cargo behind them, "are vine cuttings from France, but most are from Portugal, and they are some of the first Portuguese vines imported to Argentina. It will take some years before these vines become established, create a true vineyard, and begin producing not just grapes but *remarkable* grapes! Fortunately, Guterres has ample financial backing and can use the time not just to tend the growing vines but to build a winery and other facilities. It is a grand and glory-destined project!"

"You mentioned Guterres before," Jan noted. "His brother is a brickmaker in Buenos Aires?"

"Yes. In fact, as it happens, there are bricks in the freight cars of this very train, which I believe were made by the brother in his business and may be destined for Ronaldo. The Guterres brothers come from the city of Braga in northwestern Portugal. It is interesting that Portuguese from certain cities in our home country tend to group together when they come to Brazil or Argentina and also to engage in the same business. An example is that most people from Braga settle in certain areas around Buenos Aires, and many have become brickmakers. The same is true for immigrants from Viana do Castelo, which is another northern Portuguese city. I really don't why that is; except, of course, that by living nearby to each other, it is in many ways much like being back in Braga or Viana do Castelo, even if your neighbor in Buenos Aires from Braga is not someone you knew when you yourself lived in Braga."

"Are there many Portuguese in Argentina?"

Chaves shook his head. "There are not very many for such a big country. I happen to know from some information that was in the Buenos Aires newspaper when I was here two years ago. It said there were fourteen thousand Portuguese in all of Argentina, with most of them around Buenos Aires. Argentina is, of course, very heavily Spanish, with good numbers of English, Italians, Germans, and some others. Brazil, as I'm sure you could tell in Recife, is much more Portuguese."

"Did the paper happen to mention how many Slovaks?"

"Six!" Chaves said, then laughed. "Actually, my friend, you are the only Slovak I know of, and you may well be the only one in Argentina at this time. Think of the responsibility you have to represent an entire people!"

With that, Chaves moved to check the crates behind them, leaving Jan to contemplate his status as the local embodiment of an entire nationality.

〜〜〜〜〜

It was the next morning, as the train was nearing the Mendoza River, when Chaves tugged the sleeve of Jan's shirt and gestured toward the window. "You will remember yesterday that I talked of the winery Sir Edmund James Palmer Norton started in 1895? Well,

I believe those vineyards you see over there are the very ones he planted with vines from France."

Not long thereafter, as they rounded a long bend leading to Mendoza, Jan caught sight of a looming mountain peak west by north of the city. "Near my home of Važec, we have Kriváň, a mountain peak of great height, but that mountain ahead is clearly much higher."

"That," Chaves announced proudly, "is Aconcagua, which is in the Andes Mountains and may, I believe, be the highest mountain in the entire world! It is nearly seven thousand meters high! Because of its stupendous height the summit appears much closer than it is; it is perhaps one hundred twenty kilometers from where we are here. I believe Aconcagua is very close to the neighboring country of Chile, though it clearly belongs to Argentina."

Mendoza was the end of the line for the train they were on. Unlike most European cities of any size, there was no train shed, and as they pulled to a stop in a dusty, open area, the train was engulfed by relatives and friends meeting some of the arriving passengers. As the crowds thinned out, Chaves caught sight of the tall figure of Ronaldo Guterres making his way toward the train with some of his workers. Unloading of the crates of vines was accomplished with care, and their convoy of four horse-drawn wagons was soon headed for the Guterres ranch and vineyards, which were in Godoy Cruz, not far from the Trapiche winery.

Over an outdoor dinner that evening, Guterres described — with Chaves translating for Jan's benefit — how he and his brother, Gualter, had acquired the ranch in 1908 with profits from their brickmaking operation in Buenos Aires and had begun to develop the land into vineyards, using French grapevines. The vines and cuttings Chaves had brought with him would be used to start a new vineyard based on those Portuguese grapevines. Preparation and planting of those vines would begin almost immediately since it was the start of the spring planting season and the vines would have an excellent opportunity to take hold in the next few months.

Guterres listened with interest as Chaves told the story of Jan's travels and his necessary stay in Argentina "until all the pieces fall into place" so that he could continue to America. Guterres indicated that he had the need for additional workers, as might the nearby Trapiche winery. Waving his hand to indicate the gently rolling countryside that surrounded them, he noted that while the work was hard and the hours long, there were, in his view, few more pleasant climates and surroundings in which to work.

Studying Jan for just a moment, he observed that if Jan was interested in settling permanently in Mendoza and learning the business of vineyards and winemaking, he might have an excellent chance of rising to a high position in the Guterres operation. On the other hand, the pay he could offer to start would not be as great as might be available in Buenos Aires — including at the Guterres brickyard — which might be more important to Jan if he was truly committed to going to America as soon as possible. As it happened, his brother had been at the ranch for three days and had traveled with him to Mendoza to meet the same train in order to personally handle the delivery of a large load of bricks destined for use by a new customer, one who might be placing very large future orders. Gualter, who spoke a little German, might be willing to take on a new hard worker, particularly one who was a friend of Gaspar Chaves. Gualter was due back at the Guterres vineyards in two days before returning to Buenos Aires later in the week.

After he had translated Ronaldo's comments about Gaulter's return, Chaves advised Jan, "He already seems to see something in you that might make for a good permanent position here, perhaps eventually as a supervisor, if you learned the language and proved yourself as a worker. That is, if you are at all interested in staying in

Argentina. It is something to think about, but you should also talk with Gualter when he returns."

"I think that is good advice," Jan responded. "Please thank Ronaldo for me. I am truly grateful that, having only just met, he would consider me for a job here. Tell him also that I would like to talk to his brother when he returns so that I can learn more about the brickyard work and see what the possibilities may be. Please be sure to make very clear how much, especially since I am such a complete stranger to him, I appreciate his consideration and interest."

Ronaldo smiled at Chaves's translation, nodded his head, and indicated that they should talk again after Jan had met with Gualter. He and Chaves then turned to settling accounts and business regarding the crates of cuttings while Jan pulled his chair a little to the side, packed and lit his pipe, and watched in some awe as the sun set behind the distant Andes.

<hr/>

The next morning, after helping Chaves regain his flexibility and mobility at 6:15 a.m. after a long night's sleep, Jan pitched-in to help with the unloading and unpacking of the crates. He was impressed with how Ronaldo worked like all the others and with how careful everyone was in handling and preparing the vines, which they would start planting only after allowing some days to pass so that the vines could first become accustomed to the local elevation, humidity, and other variables.

When the unpacking was completed, Jan walked about the vineyards and explored the nearby countryside. Because of the proximity of the Andes, he found much that reminded him of the valley on the side of the High Tatras, though the thick dark soil of the vineyards seemed better and, somehow, the entire country felt fresher and brighter. There was also something he could not define about the place and which seemed to draw him to it. He thought

that if he were truly on his own and without all the other considerations that had been a part of the decision to leave Važec, he might
easily make this area his home. But those considerations were there,
and Maria was paramount—and it would be difficult, if not unfair,
to ask her to pursue their dreams and join him in any place other
than America. However, he concluded, that did not foreclose him
staying and working here until he was ready and able to resume his
journey to the United States. He determined to keep an open mind
until he had talked with Gualter Guterres.

Gualter arrived the next day, and there was no mistaking that
he and Ronaldo were brothers. Their facial resemblance was strong,
and many of their mannerisms were mirror images. They were both
the same height as Jan. However, while Ronaldo was rangy and
wiry, Gualter was heavier and somehow appeared almost stocky
in comparison. Both possessed physical strength acquired through
hard work, dark hair and thick mustaches, rolling baritone voices,
and serious dispositions. Gualter was two years older but had immigrated to Argentina after his younger brother. They seemed to fit
together perfectly as brothers and business partners, though their
personalities were distinctly different and it seemed natural that,
as Chaves put it, "Gualter is somehow bricks, Ronaldo is somehow
wine ... and the reverse would not work."

It developed that Gualter indeed spoke "only a little" German:
in terms of conversation, sentences were slow, short, and carefully
put together. When they met, Chaves was a facilitator and an interpreter, but during their meeting, Jan began to feel that in time
he and Gualter could in some way develop their own combined
language and way of communicating.

The Guterres brickyard was doing well: it had grown each of
the last three years, and Gualter was certain the growth would continue. He had an immediate need for two or three more men at
starting wages that would be half again what the Guterres brothers

paid their vineyard workers — though Ronaldo, who was also present, was quick to point out that if Jan were to decide to stay in Argentina and Mendoza permanently, his pay in working at the vineyard would, within a few years, likely surpass that at the brickyard by a wide margin. He also pointed out that while unmarried workers at the vineyard lived on the property and their lower wages were offset by not having to pay for room and board elsewhere, brickyard workers in Buenos Aires had to provide for their own living quarters and meals in the city.

On another point, Gualter understood Jan's situation but was reluctant to hire someone who might only work for a few weeks; though he admitted that some workers who had been, and always would be, residents of Buenos Aires sometimes came and went on short notice. He seemed satisfied when Jan said that because of things like his eye condition, he now expected it would be at least six months before he could think of leaving for America, with that departure also depending on having saved the funds to do so.

They finished their conversation over lunch. That evening, and though he was wistful about the Guterres ranch and vineyards and the entire surrounding area, Jan decided that, in terms of leaving for America as soon as possible, accepting the job at the brickyard and returning to Buenos Aires with Gualter when he left at the end of the week was the better practical choice.

Chapter 16

The Café Fernão de Magalhães occupied a low, teak and brick building that stretched along the Avenue Briedras across from the main gate and entrance to the Guterres Bricks offices and its vast brickyard. The café's interior was distinctly Portuguese, and in honor of its global circumnavigator namesake it was decorated with paintings and depictions of Captain Ferdinand Magellan; his flagship, the *Trinidad,* and other vessels of his fleet; and the pounding seas and storms of Tierra del Fuego and Cape Horn. The building was set well back from the street and was fronted by a broad cobblestone sidewalk, creating an outdoor piazza with numerous sets of hardwood tables and chairs that were shaded from the sun and protected from the rain by large, brightly colored, heavy canvas umbrellas. The café was in some ways an oasis, set in the midst of a working-class neighborhood of immigrant housing, warehouses, small harbor-related shops, and larger businesses, such as the brickyard, that relied on and were defined by heavy physical labor.

The café was a noted bakery, and the combined aromas of brewing coffee and freshly baked breads and pastries, the setting and its ambiance, and the availability of many copies of the latest Spanish- and Portuguese-language newspapers assured a constant clientele drawn from the surrounding neighborhood, as well as from the shipping and dockyard areas along the waterfront to the south and east.

It was Sunday morning, and the sun was casting shadows across the piazza and across the back of the big Spaniard who sat alone at one of the tables reading the paper. He looked up and pushed some coins across the table to the waiter who had brought him a large cup of coffee and two brioche-like pastries, still hot from the oven and glistening with melting butter. As he had on other mornings, the waiter noticed the man's hands and the scabs of healing cuts on the knuckles, some of which also had signs of having been dislocated or broken in the past. Those, the waiter was sure, were all evidence of someone who was not a stranger to brass knuckles ... and who knew how to use them.

"Not as if the Portuguese need any excuse to celebrate something," the man said, gesturing with the paper, "but it seems they have had a revolt — supported by the military, if the paper is to be believed — including navy warships shelling the royal palace in Lisbon! King Manuel and his family have fled to Great Britain, and some writer has been installed as the head of a government that they're calling the Portuguese Republic. A writer! Can you believe that!?"

The waiter, who was also Spanish, nodded. "Oh yes — I first heard of this yesterday from one who had just come from São Paulo. He said there had been unrest building for some time, and it exploded with a state visit by Brazilian President de Fonseca — though I don't know what de Fonseca could have said or done to start such a revolution. The man from São Paulo said the revolutionaries are also very hostile to the church."

"The church deserves some hostility," the man grunted. He buried his face back in the paper, signaling the end of the conversation.

A few moments after the waiter left, the Spaniard folded the paper and turned his chair so he could better see the Guterres offices across the street. Through the high wrought-iron gate, he could see a man sitting outside the building at a small table, apparently writing reports or letters. He knew the man was there to monitor the fires in the kilns and would be there until nearly noon, and that, in the evening, the same man or some other worker would return to feed and bank the kiln fires so they could easily be brought to full life on Monday morning.

It had been some weeks since, from the comfortable vantage point of the Café Fernão de Magalhães, he had last observed these Sunday procedures at the brickyard; his purpose this Sunday was merely to confirm that the weekend routine and the schedule of the comings and goings of the solitary kiln tenders had not changed. As he sipped the coffee, he realized that the profile of the man writing at the table looked vaguely familiar, though not because he had been at the brickyard on some other Sunday morning. But he couldn't place where he had seen him before.

———≈≈≈≈≈≈———

Jan was alone in the brickyard. More than three weeks had passed since he had returned to Buenos Aires. After checking the kilns, he pulled the small table over into the sunlight and sat down with pen, ink, and paper.

16 October
Dear Maria:

I am in Buenos Aires, but my heart is across the ocean and the land with you. I hope that by now you have received my letters from Bremen and again later from Buenos Aires when I first came to this city. When I first arrived, I traveled to Mendoza with Gaspar Chaves, the Portuguese wine merchant who I met on the sailing from Lisbon to this city. Mendoza is another city located many hundreds of kilometers from Buenos Aires in a wine-growing region near the Andes Mountains, which are mountains of stupendous heights – some it seems are two or three times as tall as Kriváň!

In Mendoza, I met Ronaldo Guterres, owner of a vast farmland and vineyard where grapes are grown to make wine. I met also his older brother, Gualter Guterres, who runs the other family business, which is known as Guterres Bricks. This is a large brickmaking operation in Buenos Aires. I had the fortunate opportunity, thanks to the influence of my friend Gaspar, to have the chance to work either in the winery operation in Mendoza for Ronaldo or in the brickmaking operation in Buenos Aires for Gualter. I chose to return to Buenos Aires with Gualter because the pay is higher, and I can more quickly earn the additional money I will need to complete my journey to America and to provide additional money for your travel.

It will, it pains me to say, take some time to do that. At best, I believe I will have the necessary funds within perhaps five months, but as you know from the letter I wrote from Bremen, I also must overcome the eye condition that would prevent my being allowed to enter the United States. At this point, I believe my eyes are improved, but I am not sure they are well enough to gain entry to America. I will not try to make that journey until that condition has cleared up and been clear for at least 30 days.

Guterres Bricks is in what they call a barrio or part of Buenos Aires known as San Telmo. It is located some short distance from the waterfront and dock areas of the city. San Telmo, as I understand it, is named for a monk who became a saint in the Roman Catholic Church and is the patron or special saint of Portuguese and Spanish sailors. San Telmo is the home of many dockworkers and those who work in the brickyards.

The Guterres Bricks covers much of a large city block, which is an area bounded by four different streets. In size, it is much like the plot of land on which the church and cemetery sits in Važec. Part of this block is both indoors and outdoors, and covers the operation where the bricks are made from clay. Once made, the bricks are cooked in a large kiln or oven, and when cooled are then stored in a huge outdoor yard. The entire complex is surrounded by a high wooden fence, though that does not prevent the theft of bricks, which is a vexing problem at this time.

I am working in the brickmaking operation. We work as much as 12 hours a day 5 days a week and 6 hours on Saturday. The work is hard and can be hot, but we are always busy. I also work, as I am this day while I write this letter, every second Sunday morning since it is necessary that one of us be here to be sure the kilns maintain the temperature we need for the brickmaking when we start on Monday morning.

San Telmo is the home for many Portuguese and for groups of Spanish and Italians. The people in each group tend to socialize together, and the Portuguese are given to much more open behavior than I am used to or which we have in the Slovak homeland. Gaspar thinks I may be the only Slovak in Argentina.

I am living just a few blocks from Guterres Bricks in a home with three of my coworkers, who are Portuguese, and also with two Italians who work in a flower business. I am not sure of what the flower business involves. I share a room with one of the Portuguese, and we also get our meals from the owner of the home. They call that "room and board." (the "board" signifies the food.) The cost of that room and board is deducted from what I am paid and is taken directly to the owner by Guterres Bricks. It is less than it would cost if I arranged my own sleeping accommodations and then had to purchase or cook my meals.

Many of the hours of my day as I work are spent thinking of you and this delay in our plans. I am so sorry about that and hope you will be patient and understand that I wish nothing more than to be in America writing to you to join me. I look forward to the day when I can write that letter to you. In the meantime, I hope your health and that of your family is good. I also hope that you will share this letter and my well-being with my mother, father, and family.

If you should wish to write to me, Gualter Guterres suggests that for safety and to ensure better prospects of the letter being delivered, you address such a letter to me at the brickyard exactly as follows:

Jan Brozek, worker in the
Guterres Bricks Works and Brickyard
063-17 Av. Briedras
Barrio San Telmo
Buenos Aires, Argentina

Since I speak none of the "Latin" languages, as they call them, of Spanish, Portuguese, and Italian, and there are no other Slovaks, most of my life is spent on my work. I am learning to speak a little Portuguese, enough to allow me to communicate at my job with my coworkers as to the things we do there together. It is a hard language for me to learn, more so than was German. Much of my time is spent in silence, and I have not yet become comfortable enough to look about San Telmo and the rest of the city, though in time I am sure I will. If you can write to me, such a letter would be most welcome and would, of course, assure me of your well-being.

I long for nothing more, or as much, as to be with you.
Jan

He read the letter over carefully three or four times before copying, in German and with some needed changes and omissions, the first eight paragraphs on fresh sheets of paper. He then sealed the letter in the envelope he already had addressed to Maria. When the envelope was sealed, he noticed a little bump in its surface and after a moment realized a crumb from the bread he was eating must have dropped inside—and would soon be on its way to Europe. After a few minutes, he turned to the portions of the letter that he had copied and continued that new letter to Anna:

> *You are in my thoughts almost every day, especially when-ever I put one of the Fisherman's Caps on my head and set out for the brickyard each morning. The caps are much admired by those I work with. I also find that there are many things that I encounter each day that, for whatever reason, bring you to mind. Perhaps that is not right, but it is what I experience and feel, and it marks, I am sure, how very much I care about you and your well-being.*
>
> *This is a quiet Sunday morning at the brickyard. The peace and quiet remind me for some reason of the afternoon we spent on the bank of the Vistula, though there is no Anna to lay her head on my shoulder.*

He read again what he had written, added the information about how to address a letter to him at the brickyard, and signed his name. He addressed a new envelope to Anna, checked it for stray crumbs, inserted the letter, and sealed it securely.

〰〰〰

The brickmaking operation at Guterres Bricks revolved around two experienced brick moulders, each of whom was supported by a team of helpers. Jan had been assigned to the team headed by the brick moulder Miguel Alves. With a full team working, Alves would stand at the moulding table for nearly twelve hours and, us-ing beechwood molds that formed six bricks at a time, could on a good day make over one thousand bricks. Alves's skill involved his care in pressing clots of clay, which were prepared by his assistant brick moulders, into the molds in such a way as to fill the mold and pack it to the right density while eliminating air bubbles and controlling the amount of moisture in each brick. Jan was one of three off-bearers on the team. Part of his job was to load four of the six-brick molds, as each was finished by Alves, on a pallet barrow and take them to a drying area where they were placed on a broad bed of sand. After a time, the mold itself was carefully removed and returned to the table to be washed and made ready to receive another group of bricks.

After freshly made bricks had set for a few hours on the sand, they were stacked in a herringbone pattern to continue drying in the air and the sun for two days; they were then turned over and restacked by the off-bearers for another two days to provide uniform drying and prevent warping. In the stacking process, another assistant, called an "edger," would use various tools to assure straight edges and obtain smooth surfaces. After the end of the fourth day of drying in the sun, the bricks were once again restacked, to conserve space, in a tighter herringbone pattern with a finger's width between bricks for further drying, usually under layers of straw or a canvas shade to protect them from rain and harsh sun. If everything went according to schedule, eight or nine days after Alves initially formed the bricks, they were fired and finished in the brickyard's kilns. The highest-quality bricks were used for exterior walls, while those of lower quality, usually because of kiln temperature variances, were used for interior walls.

While constantly going back and forth from the molding table with his barrow, Jan was also involved with the various stacking and restacking operations. And he and the other two off-bearers and the edger on Alves's team also assisted the kiln master in keeping track of the drying time and status of the many stacks of bricks. On any given day, the large outdoor brickyard was covered with chest-high stacks of drying bricks waiting their turn in the kilns.

The fired bricks left the kilns for final cooling and inspection, and usually within a few days were being loaded for delivery. Despite two skilled brick-moulding teams producing a combined total often approaching two thousand bricks each day, the Guterres brickyard was backlogged on orders; a result, according to Gualter, of both the pace of building projects in Buenos Aires and the excellent reputation that Guterres-made bricks carried.

The work was hard, and minor injuries were frequent. Hands took a beating: cuts, jammed and broken fingers, and sprained wrists were commonplace as a result of the loading, unloading, and stacking operations. Flexibility was important because of the potential for back strains and more serious spinal injuries: the Guterres brothers had instituted mandatory stretching sessions at the start of each day's work in a partially successful effort to reduce the number of lost worker days.

For his first two weeks on the job, and despite being in generally good physical condition, Jan had ended each day exhausted, often slept little at night, and usually awakened each morning stiff and sore. Slowly, he fell into a routine, grew accustomed to the physical demands, and joined the others at Guterres Bricks who took quiet pride in their strength and stamina.

Also on Alves's team were the three Mantestrela brothers— Dinis and Jorge, who were, like Jan, off-bearers, and Antonio, who was an edger. All three lived in the same rooming house with Jan; he and Dinis shared a room. For their part, the Mantestrelas shared three things in common: love of wine, love of women, and a frequent lack of love and tolerance for each other. The circumstances of the first two loves would at times combine to exacerbate the occasional lack of mutual tolerance and brotherly affection. At the brickyard, under the iron hand of Miguel Alves, the brothers worked well together as they might have if total strangers.

Outside of work, the brothers were often night owls, particularly on Saturday nights — especially those Saturdays when the Portuguese community got together and closed off one street some blocks away for feasting, music, and dancing. The Mantestrelas participated in all those activities and occasionally enlivened the festivities further with impromptu, no-holds-barred fights between two and sometimes all three of them. They also had various girlfriends, which they were not above smuggling home for the night. Those adventures could lead to unforeseen consequences — such as when Jan became acquainted with one Lidia da Costa one Sunday morning when he awoke to find a very naked Lidia next to him in his bed. She had come home with Dinis, but apparently left his bed in favor of Jan's when Dinis insulted her by falling asleep in the middle of what Lidia managed to make clear to Jan was, at least to her, a very exciting time. She pouted mercilessly when Jan carefully declined the opportunity to fill in for Dinis. Lidia was caught later that morning by the landlady, Mrs. Nobre, as she was exiting the front door, wearing some of her clothes and carrying others. That incident led to a not-to-be-ignored edict from Mrs. Nobre banning women under the age of seventy from her roomers' apartments.

With Jorge, and though he was considered — especially by himself — to be very handsome, the storyline was less women than dogs. Strays on the streets of San Telmo were common, as was their magnetic attraction to Jorge Mantestrela. Few mornings passed without some group of dogs gathering outside Mrs. Nobre's front door, where they would steadfastly ignore everyone else until Jorge came out on his way to the brickyard. They would follow along; though "following" often involved running between Jorge's feet and often being so close in front of him that at times he had difficulty in avoiding being tripped. The scene would be repeated in reverse at the

end of the day, when another group of dogs, often completely different from the morning cadre, would be waiting outside the brickyard. The commotion and difficulty in walking, since the number
of milling dogs could reach a dozen, discouraged his brothers, Jan,
and anyone else from walking to or from the brickyard with Jorge.
Oddly, the dogs never appeared on Saturdays or Sundays, though
occasionally a small handful of strays would discover Jorge at the
street festivals or some other location and instantly latch on to him.
There was no explanation for the behavior since Jorge generally
ignored his canine escort and rarely provided them with any food.

Jorge was, according to a story told by Dinis, at one time recognized or described as the owner of a two-legged dog. This animal
had lost both of her hind legs and spent her days outside the Nobre
house. As such, she was always in the group that met Jorge in the
morning and trailed him to work, propelling herself by thrusting
out her front feet, digging in, and pulling her back end along the
rough sidewalk. She never made it to the brickyard; invariably, after they had reached the first corner, Jorge would pick her up and,
while the other dogs waited for his return, carry her back to Mrs.
Nobre's, where she would settle in for the day. Mrs. Nobre toler-
ated the dog, passersby often fed her, and she had led, according
to Dinis, a reasonably happy life until being horribly and fatally
mauled by rats on the evening of the day of the Feast of Saint Telmo.

Antonio, the oldest brother, had no attraction for the dogs and
seemed single-minded in his devotion to a young lady who lived
across Buenos Aires in a predominately Italian barrio. Antonio was,
Gualter Guterres advised Jan in his pidgin German, saving his money for the day when he could ask for the girl's hand in marriage, with
the idea of then immigrating to America. Antonio was an elected
leader of the Portuguese Mutual Aid Society, which was not only
the center of the migrant community's social activity and festivals
but played a role in assimilating new Portuguese immigrants into

Portuguese society in Buenos Aires. Although his brothers appeared to be the source of occasional rumors that Antonio's evening absences did not involve visits to any Italian sweetheart, but were related to his membership in a gang of cat burglars, that story — given the apparent sources — seemed to be generally ignored, though to many it gave Antonio a certain mysterious, Robin Hood-like image.

Jan found that he enjoyed the Portuguese, including his Mantestrela housemates, their sense of community and coming together, and the often festive partying atmosphere, though much of what he saw and occasionally participated in was very different from anything he had experienced in the more formal and conservative peasant environs of the Habsburg Empire. He was also at times throughout his stay in Buenos Aires very much aware of being different: a lone and sometimes lonely Slovak among what were to him the "wild Portuguese."

———≈≈≈≈≈———

Sunday evening had brought a chill, and the few other café patrons were inside. The only person sitting in the cool shadows on the piazza at the Café Fernão de Magalhães was rubbing a healing lotion into his knuckles. He had left shortly after noon so as not to attract attention by spending the entire day at the café and had occupied the time during the afternoon some blocks away, watching the young Spanish ladies parading on the Avenue Florida in their Sunday finest. A waiter brought him steaming coffee, and as he picked up the cup he watched the movements of two men who were headed in different directions.

One was the worker across the street who, right on a longstanding and unvarying schedule, was closing the heavy wrought-iron gate to the Guterres complex. He watched as the worker tested the gate he had just locked and, pocketing the key, started down the street, apparently toward home.

Watching as the worker moved away, the second man approached the café from the opposite direction, stopping briefly to light the cigar he had been rolling between his fingers as he walked down the street. He puffed quietly while waiting for the worker to move farther away, then continued on to the piazza, pulling up a chair at the table where the big man was putting the cap back on the small bottle of lotion.

As he closed the bottle and examined his knuckles, the big man observed, "They haven't changed their schedules. They are oblivious and stuck in their patterns. Perhaps, Diego, they think that, because nothing has happened these many weeks, the time of disappearing bricks has passed."

Diego Douala signaled the waiter for coffee and, with a scowl, examined the business end of the cigar. "This has something of a stale taste. For the price, you should get better. But then again, isn't it strange to pay any price for something, whether fresh or stale, that you immediately set on fire?"

The big man shrugged and put the bottle of lotion in his pocket.

"Was there," Douala asked after a moment, "anything unusual today?"

"No, not really. As I said, everything was routine, with the exception of this morning's kiln tender. When I first saw him, especially as he was leaving at noon, I thought he looked familiar but perhaps only because I had seen him here before. This afternoon it came to me that I had seen him elsewhere. I am fairly sure he was one of the two men who were with the Dischinger woman when we talked to her on the dock last month."

Douala slowly blew a series of smoke rings. "Why would he be here at this brickyard? Did he see you?"

"No, I was behind the newspaper when he left," Jimenez replied. "As to why he was here, perhaps coincidence. If he is an immigrant, he may have just happened to find this job at this brickyard. Who knows? But in that meeting we never did find out who he was or his relationship to the woman. She introduced both men as friends of hers. This one never spoke, but he appeared to be German like the Dischingers. So perhaps he was some sort of business partner who had traveled with them and knows something of all of this."

Douala studied the smoke rings as they drifted away. "Could he be Dischinger himself?"

They were silent for a moment before Douala shook his head and answered his own question. "That's highly unlikely. Dischinger would have had every reason to complete his transaction with us by himself; there would be nothing for him to gain by doing anything else. Also, we know Mrs. Dischinger left Buenos Aires on that same ship: Tadeu saw her on the rail when the ship left, and the agent's manifest was clear that she departed. Why should she have left and he stayed? And why would she have bothered to leave the envelope and the bits of paper with the agent for us? No, he is not Dischinger. Dischinger is dead."

"I agree with you," Jimenez said. "But this man may know something. He could still be an associate who knows about the investigation and perhaps the contents of that report. And we don't know how Dischinger died. I don't know who else might have wanted the report, but we agree that it was clearly in that envelope at some point and someone took it. Perhaps someone, maybe this man, who pushed Dischinger to his death, took the report and intends to himself sell it to us—"

Douala held up his hand to cut off Jimenez until the waiter who had brought his coffee moved off. "Any of the things you speak of are possibilities, as is the idea that he is a complete stranger who just became acquainted with the Dischingers on the ship, befriended the woman, came to the meeting with us only because she asked, and has now done nothing more than get a job which happens to be at this brickyard. Still, particularly while the whereabouts of that report is unknown, we need to stay alert and keep our minds open. We should have Tadeu watch him for a while, and perhaps find out where he lives, and, shall we say, 'examine' those premises to see what might be found there."

"I will speak to Tadeu. What about the bricks? Does this change the plans?"

"No," Douala said emphatically, waving the cigar. "If, as you say, those across the street are oblivious and have relaxed, nothing changes the plan. There are many thousands of pesos involved for the taking, and the bricks are required in the next week."

"Good," Jimenez said, leaning back in his chair. "That gives us plenty of time to take advantage of their lax approach. Do you have any more of those stale cigars? I'd be happy to burn one up for you."

———※※※———

"How do twenty thousand bricks disappear overnight?"

The kiln master and the two brick moulders had no better answer to Gualter Guterres's question than he had himself.

Miguel Alves broke the Thursday early-morning silence. "They may not have all disappeared last night. Smaller amounts could have been taken over a number of nights, though certainly it was much more noticeable this morning."

The kiln master shook his head. "Even if only half of them were taken last night, how were they taken? Can you imagine how many men it would take to pass them brick by brick over the fence to other men on the outside? And how long would that take? The smaller losses of a few hundred or a thousand bricks in August and September were conceivable; so much as this seems impossible."

Guterres drummed his fingers on the table. He had no answer to those questions. The only gate to the vast property was secure and gave no evidence of having been tampered with. The high fence around the brickyard had been checked and was intact. Almost the entire outside perimeter of the fence was planted with a meter-wide bed of low hedges and plants, and no part of that seemed to have been disturbed. Removing twenty thousand bricks, whether over one night or a number of nights, was a daunting, time-consuming task requiring, he was sure, many men. But regardless, the bricks were gone.

They sat in tense silence for many long minutes. Finally, looking around the table, Guterres sighed heavily. "All right. For now, we do three things. First, we can make up the loss and meet our immediate contracts if we lengthen the work shift by two or three hours a day for the next few weeks. Miguel, when we finish here, gather all the men together in front of the kiln, and I will address them about the extra work needed. Second, I also will be looking to the men to step up for all-night guard duty here in teams of two until we figure out how these thefts have been accomplished. I will talk with the police, but I know they will say they do not have spare men to watch a brickyard. And third, Ronaldo is due here this afternoon, and I believe he and I need to look about the city, visit our customers, and ask questions. Twenty thousand bricks will not be easy to hide. Someone may have seen the activity here or loads of bricks moving in the streets at night."

"Perhaps," the kiln master suggested, "we also can make it easier to identify our bricks. Many of our molds are aging, and we are replacing them next year. Could we not do that sooner—by the end of this year—and see if those new molds can be made with, inside each mold, raised iron letters that would imprint the indented or carved letters GB on the ends of each brick as it is being made? In case of theft, it would make it easier for others to spot our bricks and for us to prove that we made them."

Alves nodded his head in agreement. "Such an imprint on the end of each brick would be difficult and time-consuming for thieves to file off or to fill in. The bricks would always be clearly made by us. And a customer or builder receiving such bricks from anyone but Guterres Bricks would be suspicious."

"Excellent!" Guterres exclaimed. "While the bricks we make are outstanding for their quality, and even now are easily recognizable because of that quality, such a symbol—especially if these thefts continue—will make it easy for anyone to identify bricks made by us. And it would be good advertising and remind men laying those bricks that they are working with Guterres Bricks. It is worth the cost. I will stop at the carpenter's shop this morning and discuss the making of such molds and how quickly they can begin working on them. I am sure that with a blacksmith's help they can do this. Let us get about our tasks. Miguel, remember to get the men together at the kiln."

As the others around the table got up, Gualter wondered about the one thing he had not mentioned: whether anyone at Guterres Bricks was one of the thieves.

Chapter 17

Buenos Aires

In the distance, the bells of one of San Telmo's largest churches could be heard striking midnight, signaling that Friday was giving way to Saturday morning, December 24, 1910. The sky over Guterres Bricks was clear and crowded with the usual array of stars, and despite the hour it was still warm: the outdoor thermometer at the brickyard had displayed over 30 degrees Celsius/86 degrees Fahrenheit when Jan had glanced at it less than four hours ago, and he guessed it had dropped only a few degrees since then. He was sitting outside at the same small table where he had written his letters in mid-October. The table had been repositioned to make it less visible through the wrought-iron main gate, and the lantern on the table was carefully hooded in such a way that its light would not attract the attention of anyone passing by on the street.

He was on night watchman duty with Dinis, who had left a few minutes ago with a smaller, hooded lantern in hand to begin walking a circuit of the interior perimeter of the brickyard fence. Since October, there had been no further thefts at the brickyard. There had also been no progress in discovering how twenty-thousand bricks had been removed or who the thieves might have been. While there was some grumbling from the workers about continuing the all-night guard duty, the Guterres brothers were determined not to let their guard down and invite any repetition of such a costly event, and their caution was spurred by reports of subsequent thefts at two smaller brickyards. Jan had volunteered for the night guard duty for all three nights over the Christmas weekend. In part, that was because of the extra money to be made. It was also in part because, being alone, unlike many of the other brickyard workers, he had no family or others with whom to celebrate the holiday.

As he watched the faint light from Dinis's lantern disappear down the fence line, his eyes drifted to the night sky—and his thoughts drifted to Važec. It would be cold now in the shadow of the mountains. Snow would most likely have blanketed the village. He could imagine it crunching underfoot, especially on Saturday night when families would bundle-up and make their way to midnight services at the church, where the outside of the high steeple would be lit by lanterns placed in various nooks and niches. He remembered last Christmas Eve, when he and Maria had sat together; her family spread out on the bench to her right, his arrayed in the same way to his left. He could almost hear her strong soprano voice rising above everyone else in some of her favorite hymns. This year, as every year, there would be a special Christmas Eve dinner before church, with dishes made from ingredients that his mother had carefully gathered and set aside for weeks in advance. And on Sunday, his family and many others would open their homes to all in the village as part of the old custom of "paying calls" on Christmas Day; after morning church services and until well into the afternoon, the paths and byways of the village would be crowded with families talking, laughing, and stopping at this house and the next to share the peace and joy of the Christian season. He had heard that the Slovak community in Minneapolis, where he had expected to be this Christmas, did much the same thing—often, so the stories went, in weather that was even colder and with deeper snows than in the valley below Kriváň and the adjoining peaks.

Rubbing his left eye brought him back, with a jolt, to Buenos Aires and why he was there this warm December evening. He felt a dryness in his throat and a tightness in his chest, and, looking about the silent brickyard, found it symbolic of how alone he felt. Loneliness was an unpleasant companion; one he had to sometimes fight and sometimes accommodate. He shook himself and stood to step around the table to a point where he could see through the gate to the café across the street. In the low light under the umbrellas, he could see two couples seated at the tables, drinking coffee with their heads bent together in conversation and laughter.

"Jan!"

His head snapped around at the low hissing call from Dinis, whose lantern light was bobbing rapidly toward him. The words tumbled out one after another at high speed, and Jan understood very little until he was able to get him to slow down and take a couple of deep breaths, at which point it became clear that Dinis had discovered something about the fence that he wanted Jan to look at and that it had to do with where the bricks had "left the yard."

Dinis led him around the yard, well past the kiln area and then behind the building that Jan had been sitting in front of, until they reached the far back corner of the property, where extra brick molds, barrows, and other implements were stored. Putting his lantern down and pulling back its hood to provide more light, Dinis grabbed one of the fence posts and easily lifted it part way out of the ground. He then showed Jan how the same could be done with each of the next four posts in line. As they dug around the posts, they discovered that the five posts were not, as with the rest of the fence, anchored in the ground but were merely set in buried metal cylinders. Dinis also pointed to thin, camouflaged braided cords at the top and bottom of some of the posts. Jan saw that those cords were helping to secure the fence sections to the posts in such a way that, when undone, an entire stretch of fence between any two of the five posts might be lifted out. Dinis pointed to the loose end of one of the cords flapping lightly in the evening breeze, which it seemed was what had attracted his attention to the fence.

They examined the ground around the fence, but there was no sign of activity or anything unusual. Jan remembered how, the morning after the theft in October, they had searched the grounds and examined the fence for many meters on either side of the place where the stolen bricks had been stacked after being fired in the kiln. He was sure that a group of men had examined this area, but perhaps not carefully; it was so far from the stacking area that it seemed unlikely that it would be a route someone trying to remove a large, heavy quantity of bricks from the yard would choose to use.

After a few minutes, it occurred to Jan that he should check the area on the street side of the fence. He managed to explain what he was going to do, instructing Dinis to stay behind with his lantern so that he would be guided by its light to the sections of fence they were looking at.

It took some time to walk around the outside perimeter of the fence to the point where he could see the light from Dinis's lantern through the narrow cracks between the wooden slats. He had never been outside the brickyard on this street, which had no lights or signs of life. The opposite side of the street was lined with low, dark workshops and forbidding warehouses. The outside perimeter of the fence on this side of the brickyard was planted with a bed of knee-high hedges and shrubs.

He examined the beds along the length of the four sections of fence without finding any evidence of the plantings having been disturbed. He lifted the lantern to look at the fence and noticed an iron clamp, which seemed to be another device to secure the fence sections to the posts. Stepping into the plantings for a closer look, he caught his boot on something hard that tripped him up and pitched him almost face first into the fence. After catching himself and regaining his balance, he started digging around with the toe of his boot and discovered thin bands of metal, hidden by the dirt and running perpendicular to the fence. He shifted the lantern and saw that what he had tripped over was another band running parallel to the fence.

Stepping back, Jan soon realized what he had found. The entire width of plantings in front of the four sections of fence had been dug up and replanted in a series of metal trays. He was able to find the edges of one of the trays and carefully lifted and pulled it out, exposing narrow wheel tracks in the dirt under the tray. Those tracks had obviously been made by a heavily loaded cart or wagon. He stared at this for a few minutes before pushing the tray back into place, putting the plantings back in order, and heading back around the fence to the gate.

As well as he could, he explained what he had found to Dinis, who, as he began to understand, became very excited. Since it was now well after 1:00 a.m., they agreed that later in the morning, after sunrise, Dinis would go to Gualter Guterres's home and explain what they had found while Jan stayed behind at the brickyard.

Little more than an hour after Dinis had, at the crack of dawn, started off at a trot for the Guterres residence, Jan heard the gate being unlocked and swung open. Gualter hurried through, clapped Jan on the back, and the three of them set out for the far back corner of the property. After examining the cylinders in which the posts rested and the bindings on the fence sections, Gualter listened intently as Jan described in German the trays he had found on the other side of the fence and the tracks underneath the tray he had removed. As Jan talked, Gualter studied the tops of the warehouses across the street.

"I think," he said slowly when Jan had finished, "that I will not go out to look at those trays. We don't know who might be watching that street, and it is now light enough for anyone out there to be observed."

When Dinis asked if they shouldn't call in workers from the brickyard to remove the cylinders and dig new post holes to secure the fence, Gualter shook his head.

"I doubt," he explained to Dinis in Portuguese and then to Jan in German, "if anything is going to happen over the Christmas weekend. In any event, it is enough to now know how the theft was done. We may want to leave things as they are and see if we can't trap the thieves into trying again. I need to think about that. In the meantime, what we now know must stay between the three of us. I will tell Ronaldo when he arrives today, but no one else – including, Dinis, your brothers – is to know of this. The fewer people who know, the less chance there is of someone saying something to someone who talks to somebody else, and then, after a time, the word of the discovery reaches the thieves. We need to proceed, for a while at least, as if everything is the same and nothing has been discovered."

The three of them walked back through the yard. As they approached the gate, Gualter turned to Dinis. "Again, say nothing of this to anyone. But tell your brother Jorge that he need not come for guard duty this evening; someone else will cover that for him, and he can enjoy Christmas Eve with his brothers at the street festival."

As Dinis gathered up his things, Gualter spoke quietly to Jan. "I will substitute for Jorge with you tonight. It will give me a chance, when it is dark, to look at those trays … and perhaps to examine those warehouses located so conveniently across from the fence sections Dinis discovered. For now, I'm sure you and Dinis can use some sleep."

Jan nodded and turned to follow Dinis out of the gate and up the street to Mrs. Nobre's house.

———※———

It was nearing nine o'clock on Christmas Eve. Darkness had again overtaken Buenos Aires, and the surrounding neighborhood was quiet. Even the waterfront some blocks away was subdued. In the brickyard, Jan had just checked the kilns and was returning to the watch post when he caught sight of both of the Guterres brothers coming through the gate.

Ronaldo was carrying a large hamper. "Food fresh from the festival! Your Portuguese Christmas Eve dinner!" he announced as he greeted Jan and set the hamper down. "And also our sustenance through the night."

It developed that the brothers had decided to go to late mass together and that Ronaldo would return to share the night watch with Jan, while Gualter went home to spend the night and Christmas Day with his family. First, however, Gualter took Ronaldo to the back corner of the property to view the posts and fence, and then, hooded lanterns in hand, the brothers went out through the gate to circle the property and examine the trays and plantings outside the fence. They were gone for well over an hour, including a considerable amount of time they spent, with the lanterns doused, walking up and down the opposite side of the street "inspecting," as Gualter put it when they returned, the various warehouses.

They returned the lanterns to Jan's care and headed for the gate, with Ronaldo promising to be back shortly after midnight. They had almost reached the gate when Gualter turned and trotted back, holding an envelope in his hand.

"I almost forgot this," he said, handing the envelope to Jan. "It came in the mail yesterday, and I meant to give it to you then." He hurried back to lock the gate and catch up with Ronaldo.

The envelope was posted in Vienna and decorated by stamps picturing the heavily whiskered Emperor Franz Josef. Although the back of the envelope had apparently become wet at some point in its journey and the ink had run, the name *Ihnacak* was discernible, as was the Baron's seal.

He sat down at the table with the hooded lantern and held the envelope in his hands for a long time. He felt a sense of relief and a desire to prolong a moment that seemed to break some of the chains of loneliness and reestablish ties to people perhaps more lasting in his life than most he had met in his travels over the last seven months.

After a while, he opened the envelope, carefully unfolded the sheets of paper, and began to read.

25 November 10
Dear Jan:

I do not know where to start this letter! Perhaps by telling you that I have received three letters from you, the most recent that of 16 October, which arrived today, containing the address I have longed to have so that I could in turn write to you. I am not troubled by you writing to me! Indeed, I am excited that you think of me in the midst of ALL you have gone through!

The story of your being denied passage to America because of the eye condition, which may have come about because of my kidnapping, filled me with sorrow. I am in part the cause of your troubles, a thought which is painful to me. That you have now arrived in Argentina (it is so far from anywhere and anything) and seem to have met good people and have found work to help you earn your way to America from there seems to me to be a happy ending – no, a passage to a happy ending – to your jour-ney. Please continue to write to me. Please.

If you are interested in my poor life since we parted, we left Krakow not long after you set out for Bremen. We returned to Poprad and stayed there until the first day of September, when we traveled on to Vienna. It was shortly after arriving home that I received your letter of 5 August that was sent from Cardiff. You cannot imagine how excited I was to receive that. I do not receive many such letters, especially from fine young men. (Though there are many notes — all of which I ignore for their complete simplicity and mindlessness — from the dreadfully pompous and eager single young men of court, as well as some who are not single.)

We have early snows here in Vienna, though they are not too bad. The city is, as always, pretty when it has a snow covering. Father says it will be a long winter, and he also tells me to tell you that he has, as promised, put in a word for your brother and expects that he will begin officer training in January of the coming year. Anatoly will finish his schooling this year and will enter officer training. (In June, I think.) I believe he will do well.

I read to Father that part of your first letter in which you wrote of meeting Colonel Strzala in Łódź. He merely nodded that all-knowing nod of his. I think that, as I have, he has forgiven the colonel for his role in what happened, though if the outcome had been different there would have been no forgiveness. Colonel Zakof is now Father's only immediate aide, and Father seems content with that since Zakof is very, very loyal.

In your last letter, or at least the last one I have received, you wrote about things you encounter every day that make you think of me. We share that experience. I cannot think of a day since you left Krakow that I have not thought of you. I too remember the afternoon on the little hill above the Vistula. It is the memory of all memories in my life — I can sense and feel it as if it were yesterday. Sometimes I think of how it would be to join you in Argentina or to travel to America when you are there. But I suppose those thoughts, while wonderful, are childish and the romantic dreams of a foolish Not-A-Princess.

The Holy celebration of Christmas is coming, and I wonder what that will be like for you in Buenos Aires. The candles I light at services Christmas Eve, as well as my prayers, will be for you.

Please write again.

Anna

He read the letter four times. After each reading, letter in hand, he paced between the table and the street gate, hardly noticing when the distant church bells struck midnight. As he read and paced, he tried to reconcile and bring some order to the conflicting feelings and thoughts that swirled within and almost, it seemed, in the air around him. For the most part, the order he sought to find escaped him.

It was nearing one o'clock when Ronaldo came through the gate. As he reached the table, he noticed the letter and the flowing handwriting. "Girlfriend?" he asked absently as he sat down.

Jan raised an eyebrow and slowly shrugged his shoulders with what Ronaldo thought was a look of total bewilderment.

———————

The Café Fernão de Magalhães was closed that night, but at the back table in the piazza, in the darkest corner shadows against the building, the man known only as Tadeu sat silently, carefully shielding his cigar so that its faint glow would not be seen by the two men on watch across the way. In November, he had obtained a job at the brickyard as an assistant to the drivers of the delivery wagons. He worked Tuesdays and Fridays: the days when finished bricks were delivered to building locations in the city and, sometimes, for loading on ships at the docks. His job was to help with the loading and unloading of the wagons. Since the Guterres brothers, after the big theft in October, had grown concerned with the possibility of delivery wagons being hijacked, he often was one of as many as three or four workers, some armed, who now rode along on the deliveries.

From his time working at the brickyard and talking with the men, he had become convinced that the man he now knew was called Jan was nothing more than a peasant immigrant who rarely spoke and who simply had become acquainted with the Dischingers on the English freighter. As, in Jimenez's words, "a prudent precaution," he had quietly entered the Nobre rooming house one morning earlier that week when, with work and Christmas preparations, none of its occupants was at home. Easily locating Jan's shared room, and with a practiced hand conducting a thorough search that left no signs of anything being disturbed, he had found some amateurishly — to his experienced eye — hidden Argentinian Pesos and German Marks, but no documents of the sort Jimenez had described and which might once have been in Richard Dischinger's possession. All in all, Tadeu was sure that Jan's presence and employment at the brickyard was purely a coincidence.

He was less sure about what was happening at the brickyard this Christmas Eve. He had seen the Guterres brothers bring a basket to Jan, assumedly food for his long night of duty at the brickyard. And he had watched the Guterreses leave but then return an hour or more later, stay only briefly, and then leave again, but only after delivering some document to Jan — who had spent a considerable amount of time studying that document and reading it again and again. Now one of the brothers had returned and was obviously planning on staying. It seemed that they were discussing the document. What sort of urgent business, Tadeu wondered, was occupying the brothers on Christmas Eve? One thing was certain, he thought as he stood and quietly worked his way along the edge of the dark piazza to the street, and that was that they were continuing to watch the brickyard around the clock. He would need to tell Douala that if he expected to obtain another twenty thousand bricks from the Guterres brickyard in the early months of the new year, it would be necessary to deal, in one way or another, with the night watchmen on the other side of the wrought-iron gate.

Tadeu reached the street, checked to be sure it was deserted, and then headed off quickly to the south.

Inside the darkened building fronting the piazza, the café's owner turned to the man sitting at the table next to him. "Do you know him?" he asked.

Oh yes," Gualter Guterres responded. He stood and patted the other man on the shoulder. "Thank you, my friend, for giving up this holy night with your family to let me in to watch this man. I did not know who he was when I saw the shadow move as I left the brickyard to go to mass with Ronaldo, but I recognize him now."

"And why was he here?" The owner pulled out his keys as they walked toward the door at the back of the café.

"That, I can't say with certainty. But it was clear that he was watching the brickyard and watching Ronaldo and the other man I have there tonight. And that," Gualter concluded as they stepped outside, "is probably not a good thing."

Chapter 18

Buenos Aires

When he first moved into Mrs. Nobre's and the room he shared with Dinis Mantestrela, Jan had divided and hid his remaining savings in two separate places that he felt were safe and secure.

One was a small space he had found when fixing a slightly warped, squeaking floorboard. The causes were a broken, rusted nail and a small split in the wood. When he pulled the board up, he discovered that two supporting timbers did not quite meet under the flooring, creating a rectangular pocket of sorts. He wrapped the majority of the money in a soft cloth, making a package that fit snugly in the pocket under the board. The squeak was eliminated by a couple of new nails, and he further secured the hiding place by moving his bed a short distance away from the wall so as to place one of the bed's heavy legs on top of the repaired floorboard and the shining heads of the nails. The other hiding place was in an old, broken cup behind some books on the high and dusty top shelf of the wooden cabinet where he hung his clothes. He kept the Pesos he earned and a few German Marks in the cup, adding to that stash as he was paid and occasionally taking out a few pesos to cover miscellaneous expenses.

When he had arrived in Buenos Aires, there had been a flurry of such expenses for sturdy gloves, clothing suitable for work in the brickyard in the hot weather, and other items. The costs of those purchases, when combined with that portion of his wages that were allotted to Mrs. Nobre for his room and board, meant that his first months of work at Guterres Bricks yielded little that he could add to his savings. But since late November, he had begun to have a little each week that was extra. The weekly growth in savings was slow, but as the end of the year approached, he was heartened by the funds accumulating in the cup. While that involved an increase in money saved, in his mind, each saved peso also shortened the time remaining before he could resume his journey. There would be great satisfaction, as the coming months passed and from time to time as the cup filled and refilled, in removing some of the pesos and adding them to the package under the floorboard.

It was two days before New Year's when, standing on a small bench next to the cabinet, he retrieved the cup from its place behind the books. As soon as he lifted it, he knew it was lighter than it should have been. While the Marks remained, the pesos were gone. He quickly moved the bed and counted the money under the floorboard, breathing a sigh of relief when that turned out to be unchanged and undisturbed.

Replacing the floorboard, he sat heavily on the bed with the cup in his hands. He trusted the Mantestrela brothers completely: there was no chance of thievery there. The Italian borders were clearly innocent; they had left for Brazil ten days before Christmas, and he had taken the cup down shortly after their departure without there being any money missing. The only other occupant of the house was Mrs. Nobre, who was above reproach. Someone from the outside had to be the thief, and if that was the case, it was possible that others in the house had been robbed as well. He returned the cup to its place in the cabinet and started off to alert Mrs. Nobre to the break-in.

As he went down the stairs, he thought of his loss in terms of both money and time: as to his savings, and unless the thief could be found and the missing pesos recovered, he was in very much the same position he had been in when he started working at Guterres Bricks in early October. Anger at the theft and the unknown thief quickly gave way to frustration: it took but a few minutes to calculate that it would take at least a month, perhaps a week or two more, to make up the loss in savings and, essentially, to get back to where he should have been that evening.

〰〰〰〰

Mid-January brought the height of the summer heat: while gremlins in the outdoor thermometer at the brickyard refused to allow it to register more than 30° Celsius, on most days the mercury in the Fahrenheit side of the instrument climbed steadily to dance well above 90°. The days were still and sweltering: no breeze was able to penetrate the enclosed brickyard, and the heat seemed trapped within the walls of the surrounding fence. By mid-morning those laboring in making, curing, and firing bricks were streaming sweat. Tempers were at times short, water breaks many, and absences caused solely by fatigue frequent. Contributing to the discomfort, and providing both good news and bad news, Guterres Bricks was swamped with new contracts and short deadlines. The workload led to longer hours and uncertain quitting times, which were usually achieved when Gualter began to sense that his men were spent.

The saving grace throughout the city was the ocean breeze that arose shortly before midnight each evening, dissipating much of the preceding day's heat to make room for that of the next and allowing most people to get a reasonable night's sleep. At the Nobre boardinghouse the upper windows were never closed, and though some feared the nameless mysteries of the "night air," sleep came to most shortly after the wind picked up, blowing through the house and playing a lullaby in the rustling leaves of the nearby trees.

It was a Tuesday morning, and the breeze was still strong short-ly after 5:00 a.m. when Jan left the house and stepped into the quiet street. He set out for the Hotel de Inmigrantes, where he needed to make a personal report about his employment, including turn-ing in a certificate that Gualter had signed for him on Monday. He hoped — despite the fact that Gualter had waved off any concern about him being late for work — that if he reached the immigration complex when it opened at 5:30 a.m. the lines would be short, and he could do his business quickly and be at the brickyard on time with the others.

When he arrived at the Hotel he found a place as the second in line, and within fifteen minutes he was out the door on the opposite side of the building. Deciding to take a different route back to Mrs. Nobre's, he began to skirt the still-active immigration complex con-struction site, which turned out to adjoin another extensive build-ing project. There were few workers around, and he quickly found that the construction area was a confusing maze. He was beginning to think he should retrace his steps and go back the way he had come when he saw a small group of men talking under a canopy of bright lights.

He stopped for a moment and watched as the group broke up, leaving two men behind. They looked familiar, and as their profiles registered with him, Jan stepped back into the darker shadows out of sight of those he now recognized as Diego Douala and the man known to him only as Tadeu.

While taking care not to be seen, he thought back to the meet-ing with Douala and Jimenez when the *Kastledale* arrived in Buenos Aires. Though Douala had referred to their relationship with Richard Dischinger as that of business associates, that association had never been clarified, and he couldn't recall that Douala or Jimenez had said what business they themselves were in. It could well be construc-tion: the other men who had been in the group seemed to have been listening to Douala—perhaps they were getting work orders for the day—and they were now moving off into the vast building site.

After a few minutes, Douala and Tadeu began walking slowly in the direction taken by the larger group of men. As they moved away, Jan began backtracking the route he had taken from the Hotel de Inmigrantes and was soon retracing his steps toward Mrs. Nobre's. It occurred to him that since Tadeu worked but two days a week at the brickyard, he might well be working the rest of the week for Douala: certainly, on a two-day schedule, pay at the brickyard was not enough to support a man, much less—if Tadeu were married—a family. It seemed to all make sense, though as he walked through the awakening streets, Jan thought that he might ask Gualter whether he knew or had ever heard of Diego Douala.

—————

The following Friday morning, before the day's efforts began in earnest, the entire workforce gathered in the morning shade around the moulding tables to hear about the brickmaking processes that were to be instituted the following week.

The plan to make new molds containing raised iron characters that would indent the letters *GB* on the ends of each brick as it was made had proven both possible and unworkable. While the molds were made easily enough, many days of trial and error had proven that the bricks could not be removed from the molds at any point in the curing process without obliterating or smearing the letters. The idea had been abandoned until early one evening, after almost everyone had left for the day, when the carpenters hurried through the gate to demonstrate to Gualter a new device that easily accomplished the intended result.

It was, Gualter explained as he held one up for all the gathered men to see, a simple beechwood board of the same dimensions as a six-brick mold.

"You see that on this side, and properly spaced so that when the board is placed on top of the mold they center exactly on each brick, we have six sets of glazed iron *GB* letters. The two handles here on the top side allow one man—it will be the off-bearers and edgers who will do this—to easily place the board in proper alignment, like this, on top of the mold and with the slightest quick pressure imprint *GB* in the top of each brick."

Gualter lifted the board he had just used and tipped the mold so that everyone could see the perfect imprints it had made on each brick.

"These letters," he continued, "are but a few millimeters in depth. They do not affect the strength of the brick and, of course, once the brick is used and laid, mortar will fill in the letters. The depth of the letters is enough that we have found it requires twenty or thirty minutes to file down a single brick to make the letters unrecognizable. That is a lot of time and work. And the filing itself marks and defaces the brick so that any builder will become suspicious of what has been done to it."

As the men looked at the result, one of the edgers asked, "When will this be done? As soon as the brick moulder has finished making the bricks?"

Gualter shook his head. "The best result, such as I just made here, is after the bricks have set in the mold for perhaps thirty minutes. The clay is then just firm enough to take and keep a clear impression such as this. After the impressions are made and the bricks have set as always, the molds will be removed as before, rinsed, and returned to the moulding table. This will add some time to the process, though not too much. To make up for that, we will require more molds to keep up the rate and pace of making bricks. And those additional molds are being delivered here today. Also, we have more than a dozen of these boards to make the impressions, so while some are being quickly rinsed after use, others will be fresh and ready for the next batch of bricks."

"Even with more molds, this will slow us down a bit," Gualter concluded after a slight pause. "I believe it will mean that we might make perhaps as many as two or three hundred fewer bricks in a day. But it is worth it. It will make our bricks distinctive, and we believe builders who already prefer our bricks for their quality will want them even more and will market the added prestige of *GB*-stamped bricks to their customers. And it will help prevent thefts: our bricks will stand out and be clearly identifiable. We will spend today practicing the new methods and will start this new process on all bricks we make beginning next Monday. We have bricks in storage, curing, and at the kiln right now, but within two weeks at most, those all will be gone, and from then on, we will have only our stamped *GB* bricks."

The men all nodded their understanding and agreement and, as the meeting ended, the two brick moulders began organizing their teams to discuss how they would implement the new processes. As he moved off with the others on the Alves team, Jan noticed Tadeu examining the newly stamped bricks—and that reminded him to remember to ask Gualter about Diego Douala.

⟫⟫⟫⟫⟪⟪⟪⟪

His memory failed him until the following Monday. The first day of production of bricks with the new *GB* embossing started slowly, but by early evening the new steps and processes were smoothing out; it was clear that within a few days, the molding teams would hit their stride and the new way would quickly become the routine.

It was nearing eight o'clock in the evening, and Jan was walking out the main gate with three others, all shielding their eyes and squinting into the low, setting sun, when Antonio Mantestrela caught up to him with the message that, "Mr. Guterres wants to see you in his office."

As he stepped onto the low porch and turned toward the open office door, he heard the low clicking of the ceiling fan an instant before he felt the cool breeze. Guterres looked up from the papers strewn in front of him, smiled, and gestured to two envelopes lying on the corner of his desk.

"Those came for you today. You are quite a popular fellow!"

Jan nodded self-consciously as he picked up the envelopes; the thickness of one indicated many pages, and the careful block printing of his name and address quickly identified Maria as the sender. He glanced at the other, which had English postage and a smudged, unreadable return address.

"Thank you again for agreeing to allow my mail to come here," he said.

Guterres shrugged his shoulders and, thinking the German words through as he spoke them, said, "It is nothing. Since they seem to move so often, many of the other workers also have such little mail as they may get sent here to the brickyard." He looked at Jan and, seeing what he took to be a look of hesitancy, asked, "Is there a problem?"

"No, no ... no problem. But I wonder if I might trouble you to ask if you know of a man named Diego Douala?"

Guterres shuffled some of the papers on the desk. "I do. But why do you ask? How do *you* know of Douala?"

"I met him the day I arrived in Buenos Aires. I went with a friend, a fellow passenger from my ship, to a meeting he had requested. The passenger—a single lady, a widow—had never met him before; Douala was a business associate of her husband, who died during our voyage from Europe. I don't believe we ever learned what the business with her husband was or what business Douala himself is engaged in. I happened to see him last week near the Hotel de Inmigrantes and thought that since that is a construction site he might be someone you know or have heard of in terms of his business."

Guterres leaned forward in his chair, folding his hands and resting his forearms on the desk in front of him. He chewed on his lower lip.

"Douala is ... well, he has a big construction business, here and in Uruguay, in Montevideo. Actually, he is a co-owner of the business with another. Most of their work seems to involve government projects or projects paid for with English or other foreign money. Sometimes the projects are ones that seem beyond their capabilities, at least so it appears from what I know of their resources and number of workmen. But they get the business and do the work, so ..." he shrugged his shoulders. "Some, perhaps out of jealousy, have criticized the quality of their work, but they seem to do well and certainly appear prosperous. We used to supply bricks, not a lot but some, to Douala, but sometime last year—perhaps it was in April or May, I forget which—they stopped ordering from us. Said they had new suppliers in Uruguay, though I don't know that I've ever heard who those suppliers are. They do still buy bricks and materials from other businesses here in Buenos Aires." Guterres paused for a moment. "I regretted losing the business, though we have mostly made it up with others. I did not necessarily regret no longer doing business with Douala. Let us just say he and I are cut of somewhat different cloth, if you understand my meaning."

Jan nodded. "I think I do. And thank you for that. It satisfies my curiosity about him."

"Did your friend, the wife of Douala's late business associate, stay in Argentina?"

"No. She was German and, not being able to help Douala with regard to papers he thought her late husband might have had with him on the ship, and knowing no one here herself, she returned to Germany on that same ship."

"Life takes strange twists," Guterres observed as he began to organize the papers in front of him. He gestured at the letters Jan held in his hand. "If that thick one is from your lady in Slovakia, I would guess it is long, full of news, and something you are anxious to read. Have a good evening."

Jan nodded and stuffed the letters into his rucksack. As he was turning to leave, he added, "There is one other thing. When I saw Douala last week near to the Hotel de Inmigrantes, he was talking with a man that I am fairly certain was Tadeu. It may be that Tadeu works for him as well."

He turned, clattered down the porch steps into the heat, and soon was headed out the gate.

He sat back in the bed, his back against the wall in a position that gave him the best exposure to the breeze coming through the window. He had the room to himself. Dinis had broken his left wrist and three fingers on the same hand in an accident at the kiln shortly after Christmas. Since he was confined in a rough, full-forearm cast and couldn't handle the molds with one hand, he had drawn regular night watchman duty at the brickyard. Their status as roommates at Mrs. Nobre's had changed; they now saw each other only in passing twice a day, as one went to work and the other came home.

Maria's long letter was dated December 5 and was full of news of both of their families, gossip about various happenings in the village, the first signs of winter weather in the mountains, and preparations for the holy season. She wrote also of receiving his letters, her distress upon reading of his eye condition and the rejection by the authorities in Bremen, and of her confidence that he would persevere. His spirits lifted as he read her expressions of understanding and her promise to be ready to leave to join him as soon, whenever it might be, as he wrote to say that he was in America and that she was to begin the journey that would reunite them.

Twice as the evening grew late he had started to write back to her, but had finally decided to wait a few days to collect his thoughts. Looking again at the sheets he held in his hand, he realized just how much seeing the Slovak words on the paper, and thinking of the effort and thought Maria had put into choosing those words and expressing herself, meant to him.

He folded the letter carefully, returned it to its envelope, and was about to put out the dim light when he thought of the second letter. Rummaging in his rucksack, he pulled it out, studied the handwriting for a moment, and then slit the envelope open. The letter was in German, with very small writing in closely packed lines on a single odd-size sheet. Looking immediately to the bottom of the page, he found the signature of Gareth Willows.

13th December 1910, Llandaff, Wales
My friend Jan:

>*I hope this letter reaches you. Thomas Weedfield, who accompanied Karin Dischinger when she returned to Cardiff and sought me out on your recommendation, was, through the Kastle Shipping Lines, somehow able to acquire information about your employment with Guterres Bricks and your address in Buenos Aires. I am pleased to advise you that, in part through my poor services, Mrs. Dischinger should soon attain control of her affairs and her husband's considerable estate.*

>*My deepest thanks again for your assistance and comfort in our travels and as I brought Elizabeth home to Llandaff. She rests in peace on a sweeping promontory at the cemetery; no doubt waiting the time when I will join her, which is an event I look forward to as each day passes.*

>*Mrs. Dischinger related to me the unfortunate circumstance of her husband's demise at sea and the assistance you rendered to her in meeting with his alleged business associates in Argentina.*

The man Douala was, if memory serves, one of those prominently mentioned in the documents that, you will recall, I told you of as not having been accounted for after the fire that claimed my Elizabeth and, for all intents and purposes, my life. Those documents, if not destroyed in the fire, may now well have been recovered, though if so by who that may be is at this time unknown to me.

I will, early in the new year, travel to Bremen to meet with Mrs. Dischinger and conclude the closing of her husband's estate, which should assure her financial security for life. How he acquired an estate of the size that is now hers is irrelevant, but there are no other claims upon it. I intend also to advise her to leave Germany within the year; in my opinion, that country makes ready for war.

Let me repeat my thanks for your friendship and companionship during our short acquaintance on the voyage of the Kastledale. It may seem little to you but it was significant to me in that time of sorrow.

My best wishes for your safety.

Gareth Willows, Esquire

He put out the light and lay quietly in the dark as the evening breeze arose, thinking about the vague way in which Willows had alluded to the possible "recovery" of the once-lost documents by some unknown person. If, he wondered, Richard Dischinger was the thief and had the documents with him on the *Kastledale*, perhaps in the torn envelope he and Karin had discovered, what had happened to them? If Richard was the victim of foul play, it seemed that part of the murderer's mission would have been to retrieve the documents. And if that killer was Clysters, acting for Willows, wouldn't he have by now conveyed the documents to Willows? As to the documents and the "prominent" mention in them of Diego

Douala, he remembered a shipboard conversation where Willows noted that those documents involved corruption in building projects in South America. He fell asleep trying to focus on that discussion with Willows, exactly what it was that Gualter had said that afternoon about Douala … and why Willows's letter had closed with best wishes for Jan's safety.

———≈≈≈≈≈———

Gualter had telephoned the brickyard well before sunrise to advise Dinis and the other night watchman that he would be there much earlier than usual. When he arrived, they met him at the gate. As they walked away, headed home for breakfast and sleep, Gualter noticed Jan coming across the street from the Café Fernão de Magalhães, a large mug of coffee in hand.

It was now nearly an hour later, and they sat in the office with the fan turning and the door closed. He had listened closely, interrupting frequently to clarify unfamiliar German words and expressions, as Jan unwound his tale of Willows and the fire in Germany; the missing documents relating to corruption in South American building contracts; the disappearance and death of Richard Dischinger and the note found in his pocket; the disappearance of Clysters; details of the dockside meeting with Douala and Jimenez, and their interest in any documents Richard's widow might have found; their discovery of the torn envelope with Douala's name scribbled on the front; and other incidents and details culminating with the letter from Willows that Jan had just handed him to read.

"Perhaps," Gualter mused, "if Dischinger was murdered, it was not this Clysters person who did it. Or, if it was, perhaps he was not acting on behalf of your Mr. Willows. He may have been acting for others—perhaps even while Willows thought he was acting on his behalf—who either wanted the documents themselves or wanted to be sure they were destroyed and never reached South America."

Jan nodded. "I suppose that is possible. As I said, I am not sure what it all means, but I thought that I should tell you this because of what you said about Douala yesterday."

Gualter handed the letter back. "Willows's closing is unusual, unless he always ends his letters that way. If not, do you know why he is concerned about your safety?"

"I don't know. His letter is unclear or strange in a number of ways."

Looking out the window at the men rapidly coming into work and the wagons being lined up and readied for loading for the Tuesday deliveries, Gualter said, "I need to think about some of these things. For now, there is a good deal of work to do. We will talk some more of this again, perhaps later today."

As he watched Jan leave the office, Gualter leaned on the desk in front of him, thinking of the previous afternoon and Jan's report about seeing Douala and Tadeu together at the Hotel de Inmigrantes construction site. He thought also of Christmas Eve and Tadeu's mysterious midnight presence on the dark plaza of the Café Fernão de Magalhães. And he thought about Richard Dischinger, Douala's government contracts ... and twenty thousand stolen bricks.

⟨⟨⟨⟩⟩⟩

It was nearing ten o'clock that same morning when word spread that normal operations would cease at noon, the kiln fires would be banked until the next day, and that the remainder of the day, as well as whatever additional time it took Wednesday morning, would be devoted to maintenance and clean-up activities in the brickyard. Since this sort of thing normally took place every few months, no one thought twice about it, though a few remarked that they couldn't recall any previous time when it had been on such short notice or in the middle of the week.

The first sign of there being something different afoot was when sacks of cement and sand were pulled out of the storage buildings, along with shovels, mauls, and rakes. When Gualter appeared in the yard, the men almost automatically gathered around him in a circle, some still chewing on the last bread and fruit from their lunches. They listened quietly as he explained the situation with the four sections of fence and the uprooted and replanted bushes and flowers on the street side of the brickyard, facing the warehouse. Pausing to look around at the silent group before him, Gualter continued:

"I decided to let that work of thieves remain undisturbed for a time and to continue the system of night watchmen on the chance that the thieves would strike again and be caught in the act. Some things, which I cannot explain to you now, have happened which provide another means of preventing future thefts. And so, it is time for us to repair the damage, to re-anchor and repair the fence, and to restore the plantings to the true earth and not to dirt in trays. By doing this openly and in daylight, we will not only ensure that we do the job correctly, but will send a message to the thieves and such spies as they may have in the neighborhood that we are aware of their crimes and the means used, and will not again be victimized."

"We must secure the fence first and will break up into two teams; I will lead one team on this side of the fence, while Alves will take a second group to work at the problem from the street side. Once the fence is secured as it should be, we will turn to the plantings on the street."

After a few more instructions and directions, the work groups formed and moved off quickly, first clearing the stored materials away from the area of the four fence sections and then, working from both sides, separating the four sections and setting them aside, pulling out the cylinders that had held the fence posts, and preparing the holes to be filled with the concrete that others were beginning to mix. It was late afternoon when, just as the delivery wagons were returning from their rounds, the fence posts were lifted, placed in their holes, and braced in place as the fresh concrete was poured in to secure them.

The wagon team crews joined in the work, but as Jan was helping to maneuver one of the last fence sections, he noticed Gualter beckon Tadeu to come with him, and he watched them disappear into the office. A half hour later, as additional braces were being placed to support the fence posts while the concrete set, he and others saw the two men walk to the main gate, which Gualter relocked once Tadeu had exited and hurried down the street.

After checking the bracing on the inside of the fence, Gualter called a halt and, while the men waited, he left to walk around the outside perimeter to join the group working on the street side.

"We have," he said when he reached that group, and nodding at some men lounging across the street in front of the warehouses, "an audience. That," he continued, raising his voice so that he could clearly be heard on both sides of the fence and by the onlookers, "is a good thing. Among that group may be the thieves or their agents, and they can see we are not fooled and are on to their game."

Some of the onlookers looked around at each other; a few shuffled their feet and studied the ground intently.

By the time twilight had turned to darkness, the last of the fence sections was set securely in place, and the cement, sand, and tools had been cleaned up. Alves took command and instructed everyone to be back early Wednesday morning, when they would turn to the outside plantings, test the strength of the fence, and return the yard to order. Instead of the usual two night watchmen, a double shift of four was set — with instructions to also patrol the outside of the fence and the warehouse-lined street.

As clean-up continued and men broke off in small groups to go home, Jan joined Guterres in carrying extra cement sacks back into the storage building. When they were alone inside, stacking the last of the sacks, Gualter said, "Your story was a big help to me this morning. Together with some things I know, it began to explain many things, including the thefts. And that is why we have finally fixed the fence."

"It is not my concern," Jan said hesitantly, "but Tadeu ....?"

"Tadeu has been dismissed. He denied having anything to do with the thefts. He did not deny being with Douala last week — I told him it was I who saw them, and I did not mention you — though he claimed he does not work for Douala. I, however, have other information about Tadeu's doings that point some additional fingers in his direction."

"Will you," Jan asked, "report all of these things to the police, the authorities?"

"No. There are a number of problems with that, two of which are chief. One is that it is hard to know, in the corruption situation in your friend Willows's documents, who it is that is corrupt. It may include the very people to whom a criminal report about the brick thefts should be made. They might well protect Douala and take, shall we say, an 'opposite' stance regarding the person making the report; such a thing is not unheard of in Buenos Aires. Second, the evidence, while substantial, is indirect. There is, at this point — unless someone such as Tadeu were to confess — no direct proof that it was Douala, or for that matter any other specific person, who stole our bricks: though clearly someone did."

"So even with the fence fixed, might there not be other theft attempts?"

"I don't think so. Stealing our new *GB* bricks would not be a smart thing; sooner or later, someone would raise a question, and the bricks would be traced. Also, since Tadeu admitted knowing Douala, I gave him a sealed note to take to him. The note tells Douala that I am aware of the contents of certain documents he once expected to receive from a source in Europe and that those documents are not favorable to him … and that I'd be more than happy to tell my story to the proper authorities if necessary. He may doubt that I would do that, for the exact same reasons I just explained to you. But he cannot be one hundred percent certain. I think that, if he is responsible for the thefts, he will leave us alone, though he may find other places to obtain bricks in one way or another without paying for them."

"I understand," Jan nodded. "I have had a similar situation where I knew many things, but disclosing them to others who might be interested would correct nothing and accomplish no more — other than raising suspicions and perhaps damaging innocent people — than saying nothing at all."

"Will you tell the lady who you accompanied to meet Douala what you now know about him?"

"No, I don't think so," Jan said slowly. "First of all, I am not sure how to contact her, though I might be able to find out how to do that. But it would accomplish nothing positive. And it would also reveal some things about her husband that would only trouble her and not in any way be something she needs to know or that would help her in her life. For all I know, it might unnecessarily compromise her in some ways."

Gualter looked around the storage area. "I think we are done here. Please keep everything I have told you about Tadeu and Douala, as well as what else you may know about this business, to yourself. There is here, as in the case of your lady friend, nothing, save for gossip, to be accomplished by others knowing the details, which might then get back to Douala in unconstructive ways. I would rather have him worrying about who knows what and about what he himself doesn't know, than having him act on what he hears as gossip or conjecture."

"You have my word."

As they left the storage building and stepped into the rapidly darkening yard, they saw that everyone else had left, except for the four men on night watchman duty.

"Jan, I will let you out and lock the gate. Then I need to come back and talk to these watchmen."

Out on the street, Jan began to make his way home just as an early-evening breeze began to pick up.

Chapter 19

Buenos Aires

It was an early Sunday morning in May, and Jan was having coffee and pastries at the Café Fernão de Magalhães. It was a simple indulgence that he had begun to allow himself every other Sunday, though on each occasion he felt a small twinge of guilt at the expense, modest though it was. As usual, he had settled in at one of the smaller tables on the edge of the piazza. He was glad to be alone, for it was a troubling morning. In front of him were the latest letters, both of which had arrived the previous week, from Anna and Maria.

Maria's letter contained the terrible news that her mother, who was only forty-six years old, had taken ill in January and, within a few days, passed away. The entire family, she wrote, had been shocked and devastated. She herself had felt lost and confused for weeks, and it was only after more than two months had passed that she had found the strength to write to him about her mother's death. Although not exactly saying so in as many words, it was clear that she had become discouraged by the delay in Jan reaching America and seemed to view the delays and her mother's passing as bad omens. Unlike the letter she had written in December, she was now apprehensive about the turn of events and less certain about traveling to America. And then there was the issue of her father. Jan picked up the letter and read the final paragraphs again.

I must grieve with and for my father. It was one thing for him to accept his son and oldest daughter leaving some day for America when he could look to a future life and growing old here with my mother. And my brother Daniel continues to assure me he will travel with me to America when the time comes for me to join you. But if that comes about, my father will be left without his wife and without his oldest children. He would have only my sister Andrea and my younger brothers. He still says I should join you, but I know there is great loneliness in his heart. He looks at me sadly. I do not know if it is possible for me, his daughter, to leave him. I do not know what those in the village would think of such a daughter. And I worry for Andrea as well. My father is not so old, and she could be tied to looking after him for years to come.

Things are not as they were when we planned our future or when you left last May. I care no less for you than before and my entire heart remains yours, but I wonder whether, with these events and the long delay in your reaching America, it really is our destiny to share our lives together there. I cry to say that. I so very much wish you were here to help me think things through and decide that which is right. I lay awake at night thinking of you and wondering what, if you were still here, our plans would be now and whether we would still be thinking of America.

Pray for me, Jan. I so want to make the right decisions, and I so do miss you.

Maria

He had felt depressed and uncertain since first reading Maria's letter on Friday, much the way he had felt that morning at the emigration center in Bremen and in the days that followed. He couldn't help but think about his last night in Važec and his mother's admonition that Maria was "not to be disappointed." Disappointment was exactly what the delays in his travel had now helped create, and those delays had, as yet unknown to her, been compounded and lengthened by the theft of his money in December.

He also thought about the time that had passed since, late in March, she had written this letter. What, he worried, had transpired since then, and how did she feel now — how would she be viewing things today, and what decisions might she already have made or would she make by the time, five weeks or more from now, when any letter he wrote this morning might finally reach her? Would what he might have said to her on the day she wrote the letter, or what he might write today, be the right thing to be saying to her in June or July when she received and read his letter? And what was he to do with his — their — plans?

Then there was Anna's letter. It had also been written in late March and was full of light stories of minor adventures, the acquisition of a new and wonderful horse, thoughts about books she had been reading, and news of her father and brother. Some of the thoughts she expressed were of a sort that he was sure she would not easily share with others, yet clearly felt she could confide in him. And near the end, there was a simple, forthright paragraph:

> I think often of what you have written and shared with me about the wine country and Mendoza. It assuredly is a wonderful place where, no matter their backgrounds and the difficulties, a fine man and someone who is truly not a princess could feel happy. I wonder if I could travel there — and if you would want me to?

Were these just the flights of fancy of a young and perhaps lonely girl, just something to write about in a flirting way? Or was there something more? And how was he to respond to her?

The answers to his own questions continued to escape him, as they had since the two letters had arrived. He sighed heavily, set the letters aside, picked up his coffee, and looked across the street to Guterres Bricks.

Though silent on this day, the brickyard had been incredibly busy. With moderate early-autumn weather, elimination of the night watch duty, and working days that were made shorter by earlier sunsets, mood and morale were high. The embossing of the bricks and the identity they created in the construction and building trades was a source of pride to all. That was fortified when the Guterres brothers determined to publicize and strengthen their new brand with signage on the brickyard and the delivery wagons prominently featuring GB in bright green and gold.

The impact of the brickyard's identity was most noticeably felt in the first week of April when Ronaldo Jimenez had arranged a meeting with Gualter Guterres to discuss a large, multiple-structure building contract for city schools that Douala Construction was negotiating—and which was subject to the city's specification that only GB bricks be used. Gualter had insisted that Diego Douala himself be involved in the meeting and had taken advantage of Douala's clear need for GB bricks to negotiate a premium but fair price that allowed Douala to close the larger contract.

After announcing the new business in an early-morning gathering in the brickyard, Gualter had winked at Jan. And later in the day, he had simply and privately said to him, "I'm not sure if it has occurred to Douala, but the premium in this contract represents the cost of a large share of the twenty thousand bricks that were stolen. He really had no choice and knows that. And he also knows that if his business is to continue to succeed, he will probably have to use us on other contracts. I'm sure that galls him, as does the uncertainty about the existence of those documents concerning his past business and what I might know about that."

Soon, by early August, nearly half of the brickyard's production of its very best bricks would be destined for Douala's construction company and the school buildings.

Looking away from the brickyard, Jan set his half-empty coffee cup down and turned his attention back to the papers on the table. Near the letters were a few sheets of paper on which, over the last few weeks, he had done and then redone some calculations.

He had obtained what seemed to be accurate information on the costs of passage of various types from Buenos Aires to New York. For safety's sake, he used a high figure, and to that added the estimates he had made more than a year ago for expenses in New York, as well as transit from there to Chicago and, eventually, to his ultimate destination, Minneapolis. He had also determined that upon arrival in Chicago he would immediately write to Maria to join him, and would also send her additional funds to supplement those they had saved and which she had in hand. Originally, they had planned that he would earn those additional funds from the work he hoped to find in Minneapolis, but that plan had been based on his arrival in that city in the fall of 1910. He was seriously behind that schedule, and was now unwilling—if not afraid—to run the risk of more delays in Maria's travel while he looked for work in Minneapolis and tried to set aside funds to send to her at some unknown date in the future. He was determined to somehow save and have all the money that was needed before he left Buenos Aires.

The savings he had accumulated were now all in Argentinean pesos, and earlier that week, at the immigration complex at the Hotel de Inmigrantes, he had obtained information on the local exchange rate for pesos to American dollars. The official who had provided that information cautioned him that the exchange might be slightly different in New York. The calculations on the sheets in front of him totaled all of the anticipated costs, plus the funds he would send to Maria. The sum was appreciably greater than what he had saved. He now looked at the difference and divided that by the amount of his weekly earnings, after the deductions for his room and board, which he could continue to set aside in savings. Even before he completed the division and entered the number, he knew that at best it would be November, if not December or even later, before the amount in the savings column equaled the amount at the bottom of the column of all the funds needed.

The result wasn't surprising, and he knew of no way to earn more. Nor could he save more of his earnings. His existence in Buenos Aires was frugal, if not monastic. To save money, he did and enjoyed very little outside of work. Social opportunities were limited; invitations by the Mantestrelas and others to join in the fiestas, feasts, and other Portuguese community activities were things he generally and politely declined because of the costs (even though small) of his fair share, the language barrier, and his feeling of being an outsider of sorts. For many of the same reasons — and though he got along well, seemed to fit in, and had "friends" at work — those friendships rarely extended outside the workplace. He most often kept his own company and sought entertainment in reading, long walks in the city and on the waterfront, and in small pleasures like his occasional Sunday mornings at the Café Fernão de Magalhães. He had learned to accept the situation and could continue to do so.

As he put his pen down, he saw that a corner of his page of calculations had fallen across Maria's letter. How would he, especially in light of her letter and her concerns and hesitancy, tell her that it would be at least another six months, perhaps more, before he could leave Argentina, much less arrive in Chicago to send for her? What would that do to their dreams – dreams of a life together that somehow, no matter what, he had to make come true?

His calculation sheet reminded him of another task he had set for himself that morning. Rearranging the papers in front of him, he found the wrinkled slip of paper he had carried with him from the start of his journey bearing the name and address of Andrew Jurua, a Slovak contact in Chicago who worked with other Slovaks in New York in providing new immigrants with help in settling in the American Midwest. Before receiving Maria's letter, he had planned to write to Jurua about his situation and his questions on what he would need to do upon arriving in Chicago, including how to send additional money to Maria for her trip. He knew he should still write to Jurua along those lines, even though there was now a seed of doubt.

Three difficult letters to write, and he knew the first should be to Maria. Somehow, he thought, I need to be understanding, sympathetic, encouraging, and unselfish in what I say—and I need to figure out what her situation will be and how she will feel one day some weeks from now when she receives this letter, so that I say the right things for that day, not this day. And in writing to Anna, he concluded, it was perhaps best, at least at this time, to not respond directly to her thoughts about coming to Argentina.

He reached for his pen and sheets of clean writing paper just as the young waiter passed by his table. As he refilled Jan's cup, the waiter couldn't help but notice how pale, drawn, and worried this solitary customer looked.

—————

The following week, normal brickyard operations were interrupted one afternoon so that coverings of canvas and wood could be erected over the outdoor areas where bricks were curing prior to being fired in the kilns. The protection was less against the cold than the possibility of steady rains, which could compromise exposed newly-made bricks in the early days of their natural setting and curing. With the various temporary roofings shielding as yet unfired bricks, the brickyard quickly began to take on the appearance of a temporary camp, with the rough log posts that supported the coverings creating obstacles to movement in the yard.

The value of the coverings was apparent in early June with the onset of a prolonged period of daily morning fog, invariably followed by afternoon drizzle and light showers. The air and the workers were perpetually damp. On most days, the lights scattered about the yard were on all day, and the rate of production slowed as extra steps were taken to protect the bricks from the moment they left the molding table.

The morning of the second Friday in June started out much the same as every day that week, with heavy, wet morning fog. As the molding tables and kilns geared up for the day, a small but unusually intense and deepening low-pressure system was boiling up from the Straits of Magellan, rapidly picking up moisture from the warmer waters off the Patagonian Coast. At the same time, a broad Andes Mountains-generated cold front was riding seventy-mile-an-hour downslope winds on a south by southeast course toward the Atlantic. The systems collided shortly before 4:00 p.m. on a line that cut across San Telmo and the southern suburbs of Buenos Aires.

In the midst of what had been a light drizzle, the wind picked up rapidly, the rain intensified, and the temperature began to drop so noticeably that Jan and others who happened to be near the large outdoor thermometer were startled to be able to track the fall of the temperature from 50° Fahrenheit to below freezing in little more than two or three minutes. As the temperature dropped, the rain turned first to pea-sized hail and, as the men began to run for cover, to irregular, jagged pieces of ice and balls of rough-surfaced hail the size of oranges that were hurled violently at the ground. The onslaught was so thick that it was difficult to see anything more than an arm's length away, and the noise of ice chunks hitting one another, buildings, trees, and the ground, combined with the breaking of windows in the warehouse across the street and the ripping of canvas in the yard, was deafening. In the few seconds it took the men to reach cover in one building or another, all had been pummeled and stunned, and many had blood running down their faces.

Jan and some of the others had scrambled up the stairs and crossed the porch to the safety of the office, where they turned to look back on a yard blanketed in an accumulation of hail that was already shin deep. The three large trees in the yard had been instantly stripped of their leaves. Despite the howling wind, the leaves were not able to blow away but had been pummeled into the accumulating ice. The scene was also littered with the carcasses of seagulls, ravens, and smaller birds that had been knocked from flight or plucked from the haven they had sought in the trees. Those that hadn't been killed instantly were being pounded to death by the hail. Across the street, it could be seen that the tougher canvas of the umbrellas at the café was acting as a trampoline and descending ice was chaotically bouncing off in all directions.

"Jorge!"

The cry that rang out almost simultaneously from the two Mantestrelas in the office directed everyone's attention to the stumbling figure of their brother as he collapsed at the base of the porch stairs in a bloody mess. Dinis and Antonio scrambled down and were in the process of each grabbing an arm to drag Jorge up the stairs when all three were engulfed by a large piece of canvas that had torn loose and come billowing across the yard. Somehow they pulled Jorge up onto the porch, where others managed to disengage the canvas and throw it aside. It was immediately clear that Jorge's many wounds needed medical attention, especially an eye that was grossly swollen and was a running pool of blood. Both of his brothers had sustained additional blows and cuts in the few seconds it had taken to pull him up the stairs, but while bloody, none of their wounds appeared serious.

Almost as suddenly as it had begun, the gigantic hail stopped as the front quickly moved on and the wind diminished, though still occasionally giving way to brief, sweeping gusts. A steady freezing mist, almost a heavy fog in its smothering texture and thickness, began to settle in. The entire ordeal had lasted little more than ten or twelve minutes. An eerie silence prevailed, punctuated by an occasional, rattling gust of cold wind; the last death cries of some of the birds; and the muted, terrified howl of a dog, apparently somewhere outside the main gate. Many of the soaked men were gasping for breath from a combination of exertion, shock, and the rapid swings of the barometer. Those that had taken shelter in the kiln building or one or another of the storage buildings, picked and pushed their way through the littered, ice-choked yard to join those gathered on the porch and in the office.

There was an immediate need to get medical attention for Jorge and two other seriously wounded men, but the telephone lines were down and it was clear that the men would have to be taken to the hospital. Getting there was another question, given the almost knee-deep depth and slipperiness of the ice in the yard and, they assumed, throughout the neighborhood, if not the entire city. Gualter set those whose injuries were minor to work in cleaning and binding the wounds of the more seriously injured while he sought some way of transporting them to the hospital. He was beginning to give orders for the building of a rudimentary sled when the crack of a rifle shot at the front gate froze everyone.

Coming through the gate was the Friday delivery wagon team, making their way on foot through the ice after one of the men had relieved the battered dog of its misery. They had been returning to the yard and had stopped not more than three blocks away when they saw and heard the storm ahead of them. The giant hail had not reached them and apparently had not affected any point in the city north of where they had stopped and left the wagons. They were certain that if the seriously injured men could be moved the few blocks to the wagons, it would be no problem to reach the hospital from there.

Gualter quickly organized three teams of four men each to gather up the largest pieces of the remaining canvas covers to serve as slings for the three seriously wounded men. When that was accomplished and the injured men were wrapped in the canvas, the teams hoisted the slings and began carefully picking their way across the yard, out the gate, and down the street to the wagons. Before leaving, Gualter put Alves in charge of assessing damage and securing the brickyard. With the accumulated ice, the approaching darkness, and the fact that power and phone lines were down, it seemed that little could be done until the next day. Men with families were told they could leave to try and reach their homes; those without families were given the choice of spending the night in the office building or trying to make their way home.

Some of the men who left and worked their way out of the yard returned in under a half hour to report that the storm had cut a relatively narrow path through the city: streets and neighborhoods beginning two blocks to the northeast and perhaps six blocks to the southwest were only slightly affected, with small amounts of hail on the ground and no sign of having taken the beating the brickyard and its surrounding area had suffered. Alves secured the yard, posted an overnight guard, and directed everyone who was physically able to work to return Saturday at 7:00 a.m.

When Jan reached Mrs. Nobre's, he found the house had been unaffected by the storm, though she herself had been out walking and had seen the hail coming. She told him, "I walked another block and was out of it before the big ones started to fall. I pulled up my skirts, sat down on the curb, and watched it pass. Oh, and I also hoped all of you were uninjured!"

During the night, Dinis returned from the hospital to say that

Jorge might lose the sight of his eye and had suffered a concussion. Antonio, while appearing uninjured, had for some reason collapsed at the hospital, but seemed to be fine and likely would be home sometime Saturday. Another of the seriously injured men, Abres Gonzalez, had become unconscious on the way to the hospital and was still unresponsive when Dinis had left for home.

Though he slept fitfully, Jan was one of those who reported to the brickyard Saturday morning. The ice had largely melted into an ankle-deep slush, littered with leaves, small branches, shards of shingles and bricks, torn canvas, mangled bird carcasses, and other debris that created a cold, unpleasant soup. Though many of the canvas coverings over the curing bricks had been blown off or shredded, they had held out long enough to ward off the brunt of the hail. Nonetheless, the top layers of all the stacks of bricks, even those that had been fired in the kiln and were awaiting delivery, had been destroyed or so damaged as to be useless. Alves was of the view that more than two thousand bricks were now scrap. One of the storage buildings roofs had caved in, and many of the plantings around the outside of the yard wall had been shredded and severely damaged. Fortunately for future production, the covered molding tables, molds, kilns, and the warehoused clay supplies were unaffected.

Clean-up activities were interrupted at noon when Dinis arrived at the yard to report that Antonio was fine and at home, but that Jorge would lose the sight in his right eye. And that Abres Gonzalez had died early that morning.

A deep silence engulfed the yard. The men worked silently in the cold wind. Jan was bagging dead bird carcasses when he stopped to look at the three denuded trees: now without a single leaf among them and with oddly broken branches that resulted in grotesque shapes, especially in the lingering fog. They stood as mute, constant reminders of the storm ... and of Abres Gonzalez.

It took close to two weeks to restore the brickyard to something fairly resembling what it had been before the storm. The grotesque trees were trimmed, and one was cut down. The roof of the storage building was replaced. Just as work on restoring the yard wound to a conclusion, a spell of dry, parching weather accelerated construction work throughout the city, and bricks flowed from the yard to job sites to meet the increased demand.

Jorge Mantestrela returned to work, but as a changed man, depressed and clearly having difficulty coping with the loss of his eye. Inexplicably, the pack of dogs had ceased to gather in the mornings to wait for him outside Mrs. Nobre's — a development that he saw as an evil omen and which contributed to his gloom.

July faded seamlessly into August. The aberrant weather gave way to more typical winter conditions. Ronaldo Guterres had arrived in town with a number cases of wine from the Guterres's vineyard, and late in the afternoon on a cool, pleasant Friday, large planks were laid across waist-high stacks of GB bricks, the planks were covered with checked tablecloths, and soon the makeshift tables were loaded with wine bottles and glasses, cheeses and meats, and baskets of baguettes from the Café Fernão de Magalhães. Ronaldo and then Gualter began moving through the yard calling a halt to work for the day. And as the molding tables shut down and the kiln fires were banked, one of the delivery wagons returned from its rounds, having first made a stop at Gualter's residence to pick up his wife and several large trays heaped with freshly baked and grilled hot Portuguese dishes. Such a thing had never been heard of — and as the astonished workmen gathered around, Gualter raised a glass of wine and said simply, "To the success of Guterres Bricks and to us, for all that we have been through together!"

With a glass of wine and a plate full of Portuguese food he

couldn't identify but was sure would be delicious, Jan had just found a seat on the steps of the porch when he heard the office door open behind him and realized that whoever had come out had stopped next to him. He looked up into the grizzled, smiling face of Gaspar Chaves.

"Wine and cheese in the afternoon! My Slovak has become a Portuguese!" he exclaimed.

Before Jan could answer, Chaves made a beeline for the tables. In what seemed to be less than a minute, he returned with a full plate, a glass, and two of the bottles of wine.

Gesturing at the bottles as he set them on the step, Chaves humbly allowed that "Of course, we will share these with anyone else who sits nearby," though he thereafter managed to look off anyone else who seemed to have intentions of sitting somewhere that by any definition would be "nearby."

It developed that Chaves had arrived in Buenos Aires on Monday and had been doing "overwhelming" business with Argentinean wine wholesalers and restaurants. Modestly, he confided that "The family business will continue to be secure for decades as a result of my humble efforts this week!" That morning, he had met with Ronaldo, and, he said with a shrug of his shoulders, "After I had shamelessly groveled and whined for less than three minutes, he invited me to this grand party!"

They sat and talked for nearly an hour about the events in their lives during the past year. When Jan asked about his family, Chaves shrugged and sorrowfully responded, "All are well, though my oldest daughter, and as you can surely imagine much against my wishes, ran off with some less-than-worthy, grotesque Basque caballero."

The description was clearly not complimentary, and as Jan was ruminating on its exact meaning, Chaves plowed on. "But that does remind me that I traveled this trip on another Kastle Lines ship, the *Kastlemoor*, and encountered Dietrich, formerly the steward on the *Kastledale*. He sends his regards, by the way. In any event, he imparted to me that Weedfield — the splendid navigator and doctor of sorts, as you'll recall — has asked for Mrs. Dischinger's hand in marriage!"

Chaves paused to hold his wineglass up to the last rays of the sun. "Really splendid! The wine, that is, though she is as well."

Long used to Chaves's conversational techniques, Jan waited a moment before asking, "And did she accept the proposal?"

"The answer was 'pending' when the *Kastlemoor* and Dietrich sailed from Liverpool. Though that is Weedfield's home and the former Mrs. Dischinger has, according to that shameless gossip Dietrich, moved there, so I would wager a hundred bottles of this wine that she has by now accepted. They have," he added slyly, "been living together, 'in sin,' as the English would call it! Whatever! It is a good match for both, don't you agree?"

"I would think so —" Jan began, but his answer remained unfinished as Chaves literally leaped to his feet, clapped him on the shoulder, and started down the stairs, sloshing wine as he went.

"The time! I must hurry across the city for dinner with a customer. I need to thank the Guterres brothers for their hospitality! Did I mention I am going to Mendoza tomorrow with Ronaldo? I am thinking of buying some land there! Will you go with me? No? Of course, that is probably best. I will be back here in a couple of weeks before leaving for Portugal. I will stop to see you then!"

And with that, Gaspar Chaves took leave of Jan and the Guterres brothers, and soon seemed to fly through the brickyard gate and out into the street.

Chapter 20

Buenos Aires

The last time he could recall waking up and having to rub his eyes to break and clear encrusted mucous was near the end of August. Within a short time thereafter, he had finally begun to see definite, slow improvement in both eyes: the right eye was soon consistently clear, and the signs of inflammation in the left eye, while persistent, were definitely fading.

Now, as he stood before the mirror in the bright light of a Saturday afternoon in early October, there was only the slightest tinge of pink in the inside corner of the left eye. He was sure that spot of pink had receded from what it had been just a few days ago. In August, he had begun to chart the long-awaited progress of each eye and to develop more than just a hope that by sometime in December, when his savings should be sufficient, his charts would have a record of over a month of no signs of mucous, irritation, or discoloring. He marked his chart and took another quick glance at the mirror—and stopped to study the face looking back at him.

For months, his focus in mirrors had been almost solely on his eyes or, when shaving, on the razor and the care required in scraping that sharp instrument across his face. He realized that it had been a long time since he had really looked at himself, and this afternoon it struck him that the face in the mirror was not the same person who had left home over seventeen months ago in May 1910. Physically, he was harder, more weathered, and perhaps sterner of expression. "I have," he mused to himself, "aged, and perhaps grown, more than I would have had I been in Važec all this time."

It wasn't just physical. He knew he had—almost forcibly, and with little choice in the matter—grown into a different person with a different outlook and base in life than would have been the case if he had stayed in the valley below Kriváň's snowy peak. Or, for that matter, he thought, if he had not been detoured in his journey to America. The question that crossed his mind was whether the person behind the face in the mirror was not just a different man but a better one.

"That," he thought as he eyed himself seriously and carefully, "is yet to be determined."

<hr/>

The letter came the following week in an envelope bearing the name of Schwiddle, Nation & Tidwell, a law firm with an address on LaSalle Street in Chicago.

September 4, 1911
Dear Mr. Brozek:

My apologies for the delay in responding to your letter of May the 27th. In part that has been due to the letter having been misplaced by a secretary in this office, a woman who is now no longer with the firm. In part it is also due to my investigating how you might best reach Chicago from South America.

I have been pleased to assist others from the Slovak homelands who, like my father, have immigrated to America. I believe I can help make your arrival and relocation here proceed smoothly. And certainly when you arrive we can, through a bank here in Chicago, make arrangements for the secure transfer of funds to

Maria Kresiak for her travel to join you in the United States.

Since you are now in Argentina, I would earnestly suggest that instead of journeying to New York and Ellis Island, you consider entering the country through the city of New Orleans. There are a number of reasons for this, including a shorter distance at certainly no greater cost and the fact that New Orleans is far less busy as a port of entry and immigration. There is also a reasonably priced overnight train from New Orleans to Chicago that would bring your journey to a very quick conclusion. In New Orleans, a man named Lech Rusnacko is often used by the immigration authorities there to assist and translate in the processing of Polish-, Czech-, and Slovak-speaking immigrants. Lech can also help you procure lodging in New Orleans, exchange money, and purchase train tickets for Chicago. I am taking the liberty of writing to him today to let him know that you may be arriving in New Orleans sometime in the next two to six months. Enclosed is a letter in English that you can give to the immigration authorities in New Orleans, and which requests that they contact Mr. Rusnacko to assist in your entry. They are familiar with him, and he lives near the immigration center on the harbor.

In the event you prefer to travel through Ellis Island, I will, of course, be happy to help in similar arrangements there, though my best advice to you, as noted above, is to immigrate through New Orleans. Whichever you choose, can you write to me at least three weeks before departing Buenos Aires to let me know whether you will enter through New York or New Orleans? That will help me to ensure that someone will help you. upon your arrival, with your immigration processing and with your continued journey to Chicago.

I have reviewed the list of documents in your letter, and they are the ones you will need to enter the United States. One additional item that you will need, since you will now be an immigrant

from both Austria-Hungary and Argentina, and have been resid-
ing in Argentina for more than six months, are proper emigration
documents from the Argentine authorities. That should be a very
simple form that provides the date of your entry to Argentina,
your current legal status in that country, and a few other details.
It is a standard form that they surely process routinely.

It is my pleasure to be of assistance to you. There is no charge
or cost for that assistance. It is but a small way I have of helping
others as those who came before my father helped him.

Please be sure to write me at least three weeks before leaving
Buenos Aires as to your final plans and destination (New York or
New Orleans) in the United States.

Sincerely,

Andrew S. Jurua

Attorney at Law

At first, just the idea of another change in plans was upsetting; at times he felt as if there were no real plans and that he was simply blown about by unexpected and changing winds of various sorts. But then he reasoned that what Jurua suggested was an option and a choice, and that he should learn something of New Orleans and how he might travel there from Buenos Aires.

He started with the map of the Atlantic and the Americas he had purchased in Bremerhaven, noting the location of New Orleans and the relationship of the city to both Buenos Aires and Chicago. He weighed Jurua's advice, coming as it did from someone who was knowledgeable about the United States and experienced in help-ing immigrants. He considered the benefit of the presence and as-sistance of someone like Lech Rusnacko, whom he could converse with in a familiar language and who it seemed might be of help there in much the same way Gaspar Chaves had helped him in his early days in Argentina.

At the Argentine immigration center, he talked to the contacts he had made over the past year and made certain of the documentation he would need from them in advance of leaving Buenos Aires. He went to the Kastle Lines office on the Puerto Madero waterfront, still manned by the agent who had assisted in the meeting with Douala and Jimenez when the *Kastledale* had arrived many months ago. The agent remembered him and was happy to investigate shipping to New Orleans. Within a few days, he provided Jan with information on sailings in the next three months. There was little in the way of departures for New Orleans from Buenos Aires, but there were a number of coffee traders operating out of the Brazilian ports of Recife and Santos who had frequent sailings to New Orleans. The agent also advised him that the *Kastleheath*, another of the *Kastledale*'s sister ships, would be arriving in Buenos Aires in February. While in port, the ship's refrigerated holds would be loaded with meat and its forward holds with hides, and she would then return to England via Recife.

"I could," the agent offered, "arrange passage for you on the *Kastleheath* to Recife, and perhaps find a ship that would take you from there to New Orleans."

It was not easy for Jan to contemplate a delay of yet another three months, but he could use the extra money he would earn in those months to augment his savings. After a couple of days of thought, he returned to the agent's office and asked him to book passage on the *Kastleheath* and to look into whatever arrangements he could make for travel from Recife to New Orleans.

That night he fretted over what he hoped was an appropriately written and business-like letter to Andrew Jurua outlining his travel plans. He also wrote warmly and at length to Maria. She had yet to respond to the letter he had written in May, and he worried every day over the lack of a response and what that might indicate. He also worried, of all letters that might be lost, whether she had actually received that letter and, if it had gone astray, what additional doubts might be in her mind as she wondered why he hadn't written. He decided to assume that the May letter had reached her and merely mentioned it in passing, filling most of the space with positive information about the latest change in plans and his anticipated arrival in Chicago in March. He also wrote to her about Andrew Jurua, including Jurua's mailing address in Chicago.

And finally, he wrote a shorter note to Anna, who also had yet to respond to the letter he had posted to her in May. He updated her on his plans, concluding with the promise to write again when he was safely at the end of his long journey to America.

It was late on a pleasant spring afternoon two weeks later, as work was winding down, when Antonio Mantestrela shyly announced that he and Lucia Rizzuto, the mysterious and by-now-legendary Italian girlfriend, would be married in June and that they would be immigrating to New York—where she had many relatives—soon after the wedding. Gualter promptly broke out a half dozen bottles of wine and led the toasts to Antonio's good fortune and to the future of the bridal-couple-to-be.

As, glass in hand, Jan joined in congratulating Antonio, he noticed the groom-to-be's brother, Jorge, had edged away from the crowd and was sitting alone, off to the side on a low stack of bricks. Jorge's shoulders were slumped and rolled a bit forward. His head followed the shoulders so that his face was only partially visible, and he seemed to be looking at the ground. It was, Jan thought, a posture that had become familiar; even when standing and talking to someone, Jorge had adopted a way of partially hiding his face and averting his gaze.

It was but one of many changes in Jorge following the hailstorm and the loss of his eye. Almost immediately after the injury, which had left a disfigured and discolored scar where the eye had been, he had begun wearing a black eye patch, though he seemed almost as self-conscious about that as he did about the wound it was covering. He grew a thick, though not particularly long, full beard that came in jet black, matching the eye patch. And he often wore, indoors and out, a matching black slouch hat with a brim that seemed to rest on his eyebrows. Combined with the tendency to tip his head forward, Jorge's face was often a hidden mask. In conversation, Jan reflected, you usually felt as if you were talking to Jorge's hat.

The changes in appearance were matched by changes in disposition. He worked hard, often volunteering for extra hours, but rarely initiated conversation, either at the brickyard or outside of work. He no longer attended the Portuguese festivals and spent many of his off hours alone in his room at Mrs. Nobre's. Antonio said that most of that time was spent sketching or writing; filling a number of composition books, though what he was writing about was not a subject he shared with anyone. He was often visibly depressed and seemed to have lost confidence in himself. Dinis was convinced that Jorge equated the loss of his eye with the loss of some of his manhood; a point the two brothers had argued about — though, as Dinis put it, "I argue and try to persuade; he sits silent and just shakes his head." In a rare moment of self-revelation, Jorge had matter-of-factly said to Jan that he expected "to be a sort of hermit and always have to live my life alone." While Dinis and Antonio, in a demonstration of brotherly concern that hadn't previously been apparent among the three, worked hard, as did Jan and others, to reach out to Jorge, no one seemed to be able to achieve anything but small successes.

Looking from Jorge to Antonio, Jan wondered whether Antonio's announcement, the congratulations, and all the attention weren't, at least in part, a source of anxiety for someone who didn't see such a day or that sort of happiness in his future.

And as he watched Antonio, Jan also couldn't help but wonder whether such a day was in his future, much less Jorge's. The lack of any letter from Maria had become a daily and growing cause of worry and concern. He was lost in that thought, and also feeling sad for Jorge, when he became aware that Gualter was standing at his elbow, talking to him.

"Are you all right?" Gualter looked at him quizzically.

"Yes," Jan nodded. "I'm sorry, I was thinking of something. I didn't mean to be rude."

Gualter shrugged and then smiled. "You were not rude, but you do seem a little lost or preoccupied. I was saying that this letter came for you today. And it seems to be in a lady's handwriting, one I've seen before. Perhaps this will cheer you up." He handed Jan the envelope, clapped him on the shoulder, and turned to pour Antonio some more wine.

It was Anna's handwriting. Jan put his glass down, walked across the yard, and sat down on the steps of the office porch. He looked at the familiar stamps and opened the letter. It was but two pages.

25th August 1911

Dear Jan:

I have your wonderful letter of 27th May. It arrived a week ago, and that ended a month in which I pestered my father almost every day as to whether anything had come for me. The mails are so shamefully slow when they have to travel such distances as there are between us! I have resolved to write more, perhaps monthly, and not to wait for your responses to my letters. If we both keep writing only when we have received a letter from the other, we will over a year's time exchange only three or four letters!

It was, of course, interesting to read that you expect now to be in Argentina until at least November. That will mean it will be a year and a half since you left Štrbské Pleso, and it is now also more than a year since we last saw each other in Krakow. If only we could have spent all of that time together and not so far apart as life has dictated.

I went with Anatoly this morning to visit our mother's grave. Have I ever told you of her? Although she passed away from this earth almost five years ago, her memory is strong. I miss her now as I did when she died. She was a wonderful mother, and she and my father had known each other all their lives. She was not of a wealthy or a positioned family. Her family actually worked in my grandfather's household, on his estate near Budapest. Her father was, I believe, in charge of the stables, and her mother was the chief housekeeper. Despite their different stations in life, my father and mother grew up together as children and fell in love. It was unheard of and scandalous to some, but even as a young man my father trusted his own heart and judgment, and overcame all the obstacles to their relationship and marriage. She was a very polished young woman, became widely read, and as her life with Father progressed she grew to be a leader among the ladies of the nobility in Budapest and then in Vienna. Few of those ladies, I am sure, had any idea of her parents' station in life.

She was an amazing person. I am constantly told that I am cast in her image and resemble her strongly. That is a source of great pride to me, but I have far to go in terms of the skills she possessed, the breadth of her knowledge, and the great caring for others in her heart. Much of that came from within her, and much was the result of my father's devotion to her and his encouragement in all she did. He says I grow more like her every day, which inspires me greatly – though to live up to her model and his faith, I probably also need what she had, someone like my father, the true hero in her life.

Father himself is well. I told him I was writing to you today, and he insisted I send you his regards.

Please do write to me more often. Please let me know where you are and where you are traveling. Please be sure I always have a mailing address to reach you. And please think of me often and fondly.

Yours,

Anna

She was, he thought, a very pleasing person. Folding the letter, he held it for a moment as he looked out across the brickyard. It would be hard not to answer her simple requests. He would write to her that evening and, as she had asked, more often.

He gathered his things and headed toward the gate and the walk home. When he reached the empty street, he suddenly felt the return of the loneliness that visited him from time to time — perhaps, he thought, something like what Jorge felt. But as he walked, he found himself smiling, and the lonely feeling slipping away, as he begin to imagine what it would be like, when all was said and done, to be going toward a home where Maria would be waiting for him.

Chapter 21

Buenos Aires

O ctober gave way to November. Jan's chart recording the condition of his eyes took on a welcome monotony of simple daily check marks to indicate no redness, no mucous, and no irritation. The mounting row of check marks was encouraging, though he still felt apprehensive and held his breath when he looked in the mirror each morning—he imagined that feeling would not go away until he had passed through American immigration in New Orleans.

Another letter from Anna, dated September 29, was full of news of Anatoly's progress in the Royal Officer's School. He responded to that, and a week later sent her a second letter, describing a colorful Portuguese festival and parade in the city, including descriptions of the brightly-colored dresses the young ladies wore in the parade.

As pleasant as that correspondence was to receive and send, he grew increasingly frustrated and worried by the lack of any word from Maria. The thought struck him more than once that perhaps the issue wasn't lost mail but that something terrible had happened to her and that neither her father nor anyone else knew how to reach him. At other times, he grew disconsolate over the possibility that perhaps she was fine, but had decided not to join him in America and wasn't sure, after all they had planned and all that had transpired, how to tell him. He wondered what he would do if she did write such a letter and, as part of that, begged him to return to Važec. And in particularly dark moments, he imagined that in his long absence she had been attracted to someone else and didn't know how to tell him. With all those thoughts floating in the background, he continued to plan for immigrating through New Orleans, though not without wondering what he would do if, for whatever reason, that journey and his life ahead was destined to be something other than what he had so long planned.

<hr />

As the hours of summer sunlight lengthened, so did the work-day at the brickyard. The demand for *GB* bricks remained steady, and operations now often extended well past sunset under the glow of the yard lights. At the end of the day, Mrs. Nobre's board-ers walked home in the dark, ate the large dinner she knew they would need, and retired early in anticipation of rising before the sun the following morning. As night set in, the Nobre house tended to be dark and silent well before its neighbors, save for the low light in the first-floor sitting room where Mrs. Nobre sat with her sewing until the wee hours of the morning.

December's arrival brought warm and windy weather. At the brickyard, a brief lull in the workload gave way to a special "family order": custom-glazed finishing bricks for new construction that was underway at the Guterres Vineyards and Winery in Mendoza. On the evening of the Tuesday before Christmas, many palettes of those bricks were loaded onto trucks and wagons for transport to the railroad station's freighting area, so they would be ready for loading on the northbound train the following morning. At 4:00 a.m. the next day, Jan was part of a crew of six that, under Gualter's supervision, carefully transferred the bricks to the freight cars. They used sturdy square timbers to space the stacks and to serve as anchors for lashing the palettes tightly together to prevent them from tipping or sliding during the journey.

Loading of the bricks was completed shortly before 7:00 a.m., and within a few minutes the train, which also carried Gualter and his family to spend Christmas with Ronaldo, pulled out of the station. As the men headed for the day's work at the brickyard, Jan couldn't help but think what his life the last year would have been like, and what turns it might have taken, had he stayed in Mendoza instead of returning to Buenos Aires.

Guterres Bricks was closed on Sunday, December 24. As the day passed, Mrs. Nobre's house emptied out as first the always inscrutable and mysterious Italians, and, later, the Mantestrela brothers, left to spend Christmas with friends in the Italian and Portuguese communities. Well after 10:00 p.m. that evening, Jan, wearing the gray Fisherman's Cap that he saved for special occasions and his best trousers, shirt, vest, and boots, accompanied Mrs. Nobre to midnight mass at her church some nine blocks away.

He had not been in a church of any kind since leaving Važec. The sanctuary was impressive and full of people from the working community. He was not familiar with the Catholic liturgy and could not follow the Latin service. He took his cues from Mrs. Nobre, who held his arm and was clearly happy that he had come with her. And it did not matter that he could not understand the priest's words: he found his own peace in the service and in the atmosphere, and was sorry when it ended. They left the church to a cacophony of ringing bells, among them, he knew, the same bells he had heard early on Christmas Eve Day a year before when he and Dinis had made their discoveries at the brickyard.

With Mrs. Nobre on his arm they headed home, falling in with a large, happy group of parishioners who, as they moved through the streets, sang traditional Christmas hymns. The group would stop whenever someone's home was reached, and at Mrs. Nobre's they were both engulfed in good-night hugs and wishes before the group moved on, their voices already rising in the warm night air with the next hymn.

———≋≋≋≋≋———

1912 was only five hours old as Jan dressed by the dim light of one low lamp. He was not surprised to see that Dinis's bed across the room was empty and clearly had not been slept in.

New Year's Eve in the immediate neighborhood had been quiet. The Italian boarders had vanished the day before, while the Mantestrela brothers left early in the evening for a big party sponsored by the Portuguese Mutual Aid Society. Midnight had been marked by the sound of pistols and rifles being shot into the air some distance away, prolonged blasts of the horns on a few ships in the harbor, and a brief symphony played by Mrs. Nobre and other women on the block—each sitting on her front steps, happily banging away with wooden spoons on large, upturned kitchen pots.

While Dinis was unaccounted for, the distinctly different tones of two people snoring in the room across the hall indicated that Jorge and Antonio had made their way home sometime in the wee hours of the morning. Downstairs all was quiet, and he spotted his landlady sleeping peacefully in her favorite chair. The orange-and-white cat that was curled up in her lap opened narrow, sleepy eyes to scrutinize Jan briefly and critically as he tiptoed across the room toward the front door.

As he carefully closed the door behind him and turned to go down the steps, he almost tripped over the body propped against the baluster, facing the street. It was Dinis, comfortably and deeply asleep with his legs extended out in front of him, his hands folded in his lap, and his head tipped back, resting against his rolled-up jacket. Leaning against the step next to him was a sign, scrawled in Portuguese by an unsteady hand.

Shaking Dinis by the shoulder brought no response whatsoever, but it seemed clear that he was all right and contentedly sleeping-off the effects of his New Year's revelry … and had probably been placed in this position by his somewhat more sober brothers. After watching him for a few minutes, Jan propped him up a little more securely, and with a wry smile and a shake of his head, moved off down the dark street.

His destination was the brickyard and the Café Fernão de Magalhães. After checking the kilns, adding a few shovels of coal, and banking the fires, he locked the gate, crossed the street, bought a half dozen assorted baguettes and pastries—the first out of the ovens that first morning of the New Year—and headed home by a long, circuitous route that took him around past the warehouses behind the brickyard and then down the narrow streets and alleys leading to the waterfront.

The streets and the docks were empty, except for a few sleeping seamen who had not made it back to their bunks that morning and, wrapped in their coats, had found comfort propped against a piling or curled up on a bench. The ships in port were brightly lit, but showed few signs of life. The only sounds were the cries of a few seagulls, the lonely slapping of water against the piers, and muted bells signaling the change of the watch on one nearby freighter.

He worked his way back from the docks and was less than two blocks from Mrs. Nobre's when he saw the dog. It was small and black, with matted hair and a hungry, emaciated look. At Jan's approach, the dog backed off, cowering toward some bushes that masked a high rock wall.

As he began to walk past, the dog paused and then, whimpering all the while, crawled through the dirt and grass toward him. He stopped, bent over, and held out his hand. The dog began to come forward, but then glanced back at the bushes and made to turn that way, looking over its shoulder in Jan's direction. He took one of the baguettes from the bag, broke it in half, and held it out. Whining and hopping forward and backward, the dog was obviously hungry, but every step toward Jan was accompanied by a look back at the bushes and a move to go in that direction. He drew even with the dog and in three more steps could see through the tangle and the branches.

The girl was perhaps twenty. She was leaning against the rock wall, sitting on a torn blanket that had probably served as a bed during the night. Her face was smudged. Her clothes were wrinkled and tattered. She had unbuttoned the top of her dress, and a small baby was pulling hard at one of her breasts.

At the sight of Jan, the girl looked up wide-eyed and frightened, but made no move to cover herself or to stop nursing. The area around her right eye was faintly discolored, clearly the lingering sign of a black eye. The rest of her face was drawn and pale, with scratches that might have come from crawling through the bushes where she had spent the night.

She was staring at the baguette in his hand, and when he held it out, she quickly grabbed it and forced half of it into her mouth. She chewed hard in silence, swallowed much of what was in her mouth, and then carefully removed a wad of small, chewed bread that she broke into tiny pieces and fed to the baby. For ten minutes, he kneeled next to her as another of the baguettes went the way of the first, with most of a third one devoured by the dog.

As the girl chewed, she began to cry and reached out to lay her hand on Jan's arm. She said something softly in Spanish. He could only shake his head and indicate he didn't understand. The girl was not only alone, but clearly exhausted and weak; she had difficulty pulling the baby back to the breast and holding it there. He stood, smiled in what he hoped was a reassuring way, and nodded to her as he held up one finger, praying she would understand that he meant for her to stay and that he would be back shortly.

Even with the progress he had made in conversing in Portuguese, it took ten minutes to explain the situation to Mrs. Nobre, who then sprang into action—quickly gathering up a large bottle of water, cloths and towels, and a small blanket before pushing Jan out the door ahead of her. She stopped briefly at the house next door and had a quick conversation with Mrs. Bastella, one of her fellow midnight musicians from the evening before, and then hurried down the street after Jan.

The girl was still where Jan had left her. After a quick, low conversation with her, Mrs. Nobre took charge: washing the faces of mother and baby, carefully wrapping the infant in the blanket she had brought along, instructing Jan to carry the girl, and setting them all hurrying back toward the house, with the dog trotting gamely along behind. They maneuvered their way up the steps and past the still-slumbering Dinis and into the house, where Mrs. Bastella and another neighbor, Mrs. Rodriguez, were waiting. The Italians' empty bedroom was commandeered, and once Jan had carefully placed the girl on one of the beds he was summarily dismissed, with Mrs. Bastella confiscating the remaining pastries and bread.

In the kitchen, he found coffee and, with a mug in hand, he went outside and sat on one of the porch chairs, where he eyed the snoring and immobile Dinis. He sipped the coffee and watched the sky grow lighter with the first sunrise of the New Year.

After nearly an hour, Mrs. Nobre came out of the house with Mrs. Rodriguez, who was soon moving down the street for home.

Mrs. Nobre sat down next to Jan and patted him on the knee. "Her name is Emilia, the baby is Isadora, and while only the mother can speak, they both thank you for stopping and bringing help."

"Anyone walking by would have done that. Are they all right?"

She nodded. She spoke slowly and carefully, watching Jan to see that he understood her words. "They are weak, neglected, and penniless, and for now, have nothing more in life than what you saw with them in the bushes. With rest and food and baths, which they have had, they will be fine. They came here—I know not how — from Necochea, which is a town on the ocean coast, some long distance south of here. The baby is only a few, maybe five, months old. There is, shall we say, no father."

"Emilia," Mrs. Nobre continued, "came here on her way to find her only relatives. Those are an uncle and aunt who live in a village north of Buenos Aires. As it turns out, with great good luck, Mrs. Bastella actually knows the aunt. The aunt once, years ago, lived somewhere in this neighborhood, though I can't recall her myself. Mrs. Bastella says the aunt is a good person. We should be able to help Emilia find them, and in the meantime they can stay here. The Italians are gone for some days yet, so their room can serve for our two new guests."

"How," Jan asked, "did she, Emilia come to be in those bushes in, well, such condition?"

"Let us just say," Mrs. Nobre said, looking out at the street, "that all men are not kind, and leave it at that. I think that while she shared some of her story with me, it is not for me to share that with others. Perhaps she will tell you herself."

"And her dog?"

"I think the dog is fine. He is also asleep. And he is not her dog. He apparently appeared during the night. She had never seen him until she awoke to find him lying in the grass outside the bushes, as if on guard. It is strange, and now he will not leave her side. We washed him up too, and he is sound asleep on a blanket, next to her in the bed."

She stood and turned toward the door. "I have some cooking to do, but first, I will get you some more coffee. And," she said, glancing at Dinis, "you might want to wake him up and get him up to bed."

"What does his sign say?"

"It says, 'Good People! Behold the Sad Remnant of 1911!'"

———≈≈≈≈≈———

Over the next week, Emilia, Isadora, and the newly named dog "Savior," all flourished in the Nobre household. Simple but new clothes appeared as the result of a shopping trip financed by contributions from neighbors, Jan, and the Mantestrela brothers. To the surprise and silent amusement of Dinis and Antonio, Jorge became particularly attentive to the new guests: hurrying home from the brickyard each day, silently rocking Isadora to sleep every evening, and constantly checking on Emilia's needs.

On Friday evening, Mrs. Bastella brought the news that Emilia's uncle had sent word and that arrangements were to be made for mother, daughter, and dog to travel as soon as possible to live with him and his family. Late in the evening, after Emilia had gone to bed, there was discussion about the cost of train tickets and other details, and Jan was about to speak and suggest another collection when Mrs. Nobre, apparently reading his mind, caught his eye and shook her index finger slightly, while also inclining her head in Jorge's direction.

After a moment, Jorge cleared his throat and quietly said that he would like to pay for the tickets and, with Emilia's permission, would be pleased to accompany the party on the trip. "Solely," he added, "to assist Emilia in managing Isadora and the dog, and to be sure that there are no complications in reaching the safety of her uncle's home."

And so, the following Sunday afternoon, the entire household found itself at the railroad station, bidding goodbye to the little group that was soon headed off on the short trip north.

———≈≈≈≈≈———

Jorge caught the Monday afternoon train back to Buenos Aires. He stopped at the brickyard in the evening after most of the workers had left for the day, and when he reached Mrs. Nobre's, he brought Jan a letter that had been delivered late that afternoon after Jan had gone home. As he thanked him for playing mailman, Jan thought that, in a way he couldn't quite describe, Jorge seemed somehow different.

The letter had been written and dated in October. However, from a hasty Christmas wish added at the end and the earliest postal markings that had been stamped on it as it began its long journey, it seemed to have been mailed some weeks later, perhaps in mid-November. In any event, Maria clearly had not yet received his October letter and was not then aware of the decision he had reached to further delay his departure and to enter America through New Orleans and not New York.

The letter was short and, to him, far from clear as to her state of mind. While more positive than in her last letter, and speaking of some of the plans they had made for her travels, Maria again expressed concerns for her father and the "expected duties of an eldest daughter." But at the end, he took heart from her simple statement that, "I so look forward to the time, I hope soon, when we will again be together."

Later that evening, he sat in the small parlor with Mrs. Nobre. As she sewed, he wrote a long letter, recounting his Christmas Eve church attendance and telling Maria the story of Emilia and Isadora. He also repeated much of the detail of the new plans outlined in his October letter, including his contact with Andrew Jurua. He had put his pen down, folded the pages, and was preparing to slide the letter into its envelope when Mrs. Nobre cleared her throat and quietly asked, "Did you tell her you love her?"

A bit self-consciously, he nodded, picked up the pen, and added another paragraph before sealing and addressing the envelope.

PART FOUR
To America

Chapter 22

February inched by at the same snail's pace that had characterized January; it seemed to Jan that something was clearly wrong with the rate of speed at which time passed in 1912. He was increasingly anxious about the timely arrival of the *Kastleheath* in Buenos Aires, since that arrival would heavily influence the ship's departure date and, in turn, its arrival in Recife on its homeward trip. And he needed to be in Recife by the sixth of March: he held a ticket on the *William Whitehead*, which would depart from that port for New Orleans by way of Havana, on the seventh.

The ship's agent had consistently targeted February 21 or February 22 as the *Kastleheath*'s likely arrival date. So it was that on Wednesday, the twenty-first, Jan left the brickyard at the end of a long day and hurried through the fading light of evening to the waterfront. His anxiety was instantly relieved when he sighted the mirror image of the *Kastledale* tied up at the wharf. While the agent had left for the day, the sailing list on the outside wall of his office contained a fresh entry showing the *Kastleheath* would depart at dawn on February 28.

On Thursday, he spoke with Gualter and reconfirmed that he would leave the employ of Guterres Bricks at the end of the day on Monday, the twenty-sixth. On Friday morning, he went to the immigration center, where he picked up the departure documents he would need to board the *Kastleheath* and to verify his residence in Argentina for the American Immigration Service in New Orleans.

He knew he would need new clothes to replace the shirts, trousers, and other articles he had worn, and worn out, in the last year, and it took little effort to persuade Dinis to come along after work on Saturday afternoon to serve as interpreter and critic on a shopping trip. It had occurred to him that the style of dress among the working class in America might be different, and he didn't want to be embarrassed by standing out as an ill-dressed foreigner, so he was determined to be careful in his purchases and to save some money for buying clothing in America.

Dinis had consulted with his brother Antonio and was prepared with a list of shops to visit. At the third one, Upmann & Larranaga Mercantile, they found two pairs of trousers, three shirts, and a few other items that Jan was comfortable with. and Dinis proved his mettle by bargaining adroitly with the shopkeeper on all the items, except for a pair of boots that the shopkeeper refused to bargain over and which Jan reluctantly decided were too expensive.

Early the next morning, he dressed; collected all of his personal, German, and Argentinean documents; and set out for a last Sunday of coffee and baguettes at the Café Fernão de Magalhães. When he opened the front door to step outside, he was surprised to find Jorge sitting on the stoop, taking the first rays of the morning sun. The street was otherwise quiet and deserted, except for two dogs lounging on the sidewalk some distance away, near Mrs. Bastella's house.

Since early January, Jorge had become a regular weekend railway traveler—journeying to visit Emilia and Isadora in their new home to the north. He also showed signs of becoming a changed man: he was more careful in his appearance, had straightened his posture, no longer hid behind the slouch hat, and only rarely exhibited any signs of the depression that had been his hallmark since losing his eye to the hailstorm. And he had developed a new interest in shopping; looking, he explained, for "a few nice things for Isadora." To that, Dinis had dryly observed that "Jorge will soon be both broke and completely domesticated. I will lose him, as I am losing Antonio."

This weekend, however, Jorge was in Buenos Aires, and it took only a passing mention of baguettes at the café to get him to come along. When they reached the corner, Jan glanced behind them, tapped Jorge on the shoulder, and pointed to the two dogs that had left Mrs. Bastella's and were following cautiously. When Jorge looked at them, the dogs immediately, as if on cue, sat down. He shrugged, but Jan could see a tear in his eye and the beginnings of a smile at the corners of his mouth.

The dogs followed along at a careful and wary distance, and at the café, they quickly dozed-off in the sun at the edge of the piazza while Jorge read the newspaper and Jan reviewed and arranged his documents. When he finished, he was satisfied that he had everything he had been told he would need to enter the United States.

Over their coffee, Jorge quizzed Jan about the time he had spent in Mendoza when he first arrived in Argentina, the work at the Guterres Vineyards and Winery, where and how people lived, and what the city and countryside were like. It was, Jan surmised with a quiet smile, not just idle curiosity. Around ten o'clock, Jorge finished his third baguette and fourth cup of coffee, thanked Jan for the pleasant morning, tucked the newspaper under his arm, and headed back "to wake up my worthless brothers." As he left, the dogs bestirred themselves and fell in line some little distance behind him.

Jan watched Jorge and the dogs as they moved off down the street, and then turned to look across the way to the Guterres brick-yard. Someone, he wasn't sure who, was moving around in the kiln area, stoking and banking the fires as he himself had done on so many Sunday mornings. He thought of Miguel Alves and the Mantestrela brothers and all the others he had worked with, and of the Guterres brothers who had both been so kind to him. And, as he pushed his chair back and prepared to leave, he thought of Jorge—who might, with Emilia, Isadora, and Savior, perhaps live the life in Mendoza that he had once considered and that Anna had fantasized for them.

—————————————

Monday at Guterres Bricks passed as most workdays until five o'clock, when Gualter called a halt, brought everyone together to say goodbye, and led the group in three cheers for good luck for Jan. After the cheers, Gualterhe announced that they also had a going-away present, which turned out to be the Upmann & Larranaga boots. When Jan glanced at Dinis, he shrugged his shoulders as if he knew nothing about it.

He spent Tuesday walking about Buenos Aires, taking a last look at the city he had called home for a year and a half. The ship's agent had sent word that, because of the *Kastleheath*'s first-light departure on Wednesday morning, passengers could board as soon as 5:00 p.m. on Tuesday. He made his way home, finished packing, and, shortly after four o'clock, brought his duffel bag and rucksacks downstairs. He had barely set those items on the floor when he was enveloped in a long farewell hug from Mrs. Nobre, who also stuffed the remaining spaces in his bags with meats and breads wrapped in old newspapers. As he walked down the steps and turned up the street, he experienced some of the same feelings he had felt when first setting out from Važec for America nearly two years before.

—————————————

"The steward at the top of the gangway is an English lad named Rory," the agent said as he checked Jan's papers and filled out the form in front of him. "He speaks only the King's English, though apparently the king in question had a limited vocabulary. Give this to him when you get up there. Since you traveled on the *Kastledale*, you won't need a tour here. It's the same. The form tells him to skip the tour and take you to your cabin. As to that, any particular cabin you'd prefer? You can pretty much have any cabin you want. There are only four of you traveling as passengers to Recife, although she'll fill up there and all spaces will be taken for the rest of the voyage."

"If cabin number five is available, that would be fine," Jan replied.

"It is and it's yours. I'll put that on the form. You've paid for a shared cabin but, as I said, there are only four of you, so you'll have cabin number five all to yourself." The agent handed him the form, smiled, and extended his hand. "Good luck to you in America!"

He was just starting up the gangway when he heard someone shouting his name. Turning, he saw Dinis Mantestrela far down the dock, running in his direction. He put his bags down at the foot of the gangway and watched as Dinis, seeing he had Jan's attention, slowed to a walk to catch his breath.

"Mr. Guterres wanted me to try to catch you. This letter," he said, handing Jan one envelope, "came for you this afternoon. This other envelope is from Mr. Guterres himself."

Jan glanced at the first envelope and smiled when he saw the postage and the picture of the Emperor Franz Joseph. It was thin, while the second envelope, with only his name written on it, was much thicker. He pushed both into one of the rucksacks.

They talked for a few minutes, shook hands, and said goodbye yet again. Jan watched as Dinis walked slowly away, turning at one point to wave. He waved back and, with a heavy sigh, picked up his bags and made his way up the gangway.

Rory was young, pimply-faced, and eager to help. He read the information on the form and from a box at his feet selected two sheets of paper, which were printed in German, and handed those and a red armband to Jan. He grabbed the heaviest of Jan's bags and led the way up the stairs.

As the agent had indicated, the ship was a near carbon copy of the *Kastledale*, differing only in the color of the paint in certain areas and that, instead of a long bench, the wall of cabin number five opposite the beds was occupied by a narrow table with a straight-back chair at either end. The chairs were upholstered in black leather, which was worn and faded on the seats.

As Rory left, Jan tossed the rucksacks on the upper bunk, placed the duffel bag on the table, and looked at the papers Rory had given him. They were headed "Ship's Information" and provided many of the details that had been covered on the *Kastledale* during Captain Cameron's meeting with the passengers before departing Bremerhaven. He noted that the *Kastleheath* was under the command of Captain Trevor Wycliffe, and its First Mate was Sean Wanderman. There was information about smoking areas, when passengers could walk the weather deck, and many other things he had learned on the *Kastledale*. Passenger meals would be at 8:00 a.m. and 6:00 p.m., beginning that very evening.

The fare at the evening meal was similar to that on the *Kastledale*. His fellow passengers were all present. They included an English couple named Thomas — he being a member of the British consulate staff in Buenos Aires who was being furloughed home to the UK for a new assignment, much to the distress of his wife, who clearly wished they could stay in Argentina. They both spoke some Spanish, as did the fourth passenger, an elderly but lively Portuguese lady from Recife who had been in Buenos Aires for a month visiting her "much younger" sisters. Her name was Rosa, and she was ninety years old; her sisters turned out to be eighty-six and eighty-four.

She delighted in serving as translator for the others, including having wonderful patience with Jan's broken Portuguese and being "exactly" sure of his comments before conveying them in careful, simple Spanish to the English couple.

After dinner, he went out to the aft weather deck, where he leaned against the railing, smoked his pipe, and watched the sun set over the city that would soon fade from his life.

It was after nine o'clock when he returned to his cabin. He glanced at the rucksacks he had stored on the upper bunk and thought of the meats and breads Mrs. Nobre had tucked into them. He pulled one of the sacks down and pawed through it. Though he had just eaten a few hours before, a pastry with a dusting of honeyed white flour was too tempting, and he put it out on the table while packing the rest away; the meats and breads would make for some meals on the way to Recife.

As he closed the sack and returned it to the upper berth, he remembered the letters Dinis had delivered. He found them in the second rucksack, placed them on the table near the pastry, and then thought to go down to the Mess to see if he could get coffee from the cooks.

Minutes later, he returned with a steaming mug, sat down at the table, and opened the envelope from Gualter Guterres. It contained a one-page note, written in precise, simple German and wrapped around a small stack of American money. The note explained that Gualter had accumulated this money over the years, was sure he would neither use it nor bother to exchange it, and, running across it in his desk that afternoon, thought it might be of help to Jan.

He put the note down, dusted the remains of the pastry off his fingers, and studied the pictures and designs on the bills. He counted out forty six United States dollars in one-, five-, and ten-dollar bills. That, applying the exchange rate in Buenos Aires, was the equivalent of over one hundred and eight pesos. It was a significant sum. He thought of how lucky he had been to know the Guterres brothers and work for them, and as he examined his first American money, it made him feel somehow closer to the end of his journey and to life in his soon-to-be new home.

The second envelope had the familiar Austrian postage. He did not notice the handwriting until he began to read the brief letter.

Fourth January 1912
Jan:

I hope this letter finds you well. Beyond that, it is a struggle as to how to say what must be said, as terrible as it is to be the messenger of the news I bear. We have lost our Anna – she died late on the twenty-fourth December of head injuries suffered in a throw from her horse while out on a Christmas Eve ride.

His hands shook, and his fingers seemed to lose their strength; the letter sagged to the table. His stomach turned over as when he was seasick, while in his chest he felt a crushing weight. His mind seemed to go blank, and then raced with images and thoughts of Anna. The small room was a blur. He became aware of the tears running down his face and dropping on the letter. Pushing the letter aside, he leaned back in the chair, closed his eyes, and found himself lost in the weight and depths of a sorrow he could never have imagined. It was much later, when the coffee in the mug had grown cold, that he slowly and hesitantly picked the letter up again.

She suffered very little. From the time the blow was received until the time she passed was less than two hours, and she was unconscious almost the entire time. There was nothing anyone could do.

I had been home on leave but a few days when the accident happened and have been granted extended leave time. As you can know, this was a tremendous blow to Father, but I believe he is recovering from the loss, though in his face the grief still shows and probably always will. He seems suddenly old. We laid Anna to rest next to Mother in the family plot. It was but a small service, at Father's request. The day after the burial, His Grace, the Emperor, called and with his eyes brimming with tears personally, with his own hands, placed a bouquet of flowers on the grave – a singular honor for the family and Anna's memory.

As you know, Anna and I were very close. She had shared some of her letters to you with me before posting them. Despite the short acquaintance you had, you were always her ideal for your kindness and your unselfishness and probably for many other things that she kept to herself in her heart. She often spoke of what she quietly called her "fairy-tale imaginings" of her hero and his Not-A-Princess.

I have read your last letter to Anna, of November of last year, and know that you will soon be leaving Argentina for America. It has been a long journey for you. I wish you, and Father does as well, the success I know that Anna prayed you would have, and I hope this reaches you before you depart and we perhaps lose track of you.

I am, Jan, so terribly distressed to have to write this letter and bring you this news.

Cmdr. Anatoly Ihnacak

He read the letter a second time and then a third — trying to will the words to be different. He needed fresh air: after donning his vest and his cap, he went out to the weather deck.

Before starting up the deck, he turned to climb the stairs to the bridge. The First Mate was alone at the wheel. He looked up and beckoned as Jan tapped on the door. First in German, and then in slow, simple Portuguese, Jan tried to explain what he wished to do—Wanderman understood neither language. Both men were pondering their next step when the night lookout reported for duty. He proved to know enough Portuguese to understand the request and relayed it to Wanderman, who after a moment nodded his assent, with the caution that Jan report to the lookout when he finished and before returning to his cabin.

He walked forward and found the tool chest bolted to the weather deck near the crane closest to the bow. As on the *Kastledale*, the chest made a bench of sorts, with the side of the steel vertical ventilation shaft serving as a back rest. He sat down heavily and leaned back, gazing out over the quiet docks to the city lights.

They had spent perhaps forty or fifty hours of their lives together, and in his mind it seemed he could call up images of every minute. He alternately smiled and shed silent tears as he thought of the accident at the rack railway; feeding the deer in the meadow at Štrbské Pleso; shopping in the Market Square in Krakow; sitting together, with her head on his shoulder, on the banks of the Vistula. It would have been impossiblde, with the realities of life and his love for Maria, for the "fairy-tale imaginings" of a young woman's heart to come true. Still, he vowed silently to never forget her, while at the same time realizing such a vow was unnecessary—she would be a part of his life, for life.

He took off his Fisherman's Cap. Since the brown one had been lost in the hurricane at sea, the black one had been his everyday hat. It was faded to uneven color from the summer sun; was stained in some places by sweat and dirt; had protected his head against the summer hailstorm, suffering small punctures in the process; and had become something Dinis and others had identified with him. The gold thread on the inside band had stained as well, but the letters were still clear, even in the low glow of the ship's night lights.

As long as he had the hats, black and gray, Anna—with her bright eyes, her soft touch, and laughing voice, and the barely spoken but deep mutual affection they had shared—would be with him.

It was nearly 2:00 a.m. when he walked back down the weather deck, exchanged waves with the lookout up above, and returned to his cabin. He pulled the gray Fisherman's Cap from his rucksack. It had been rarely worn and was as if new: the gold thread bright and clear. Carefully he flattened it and wrapped it in the newspaper that had held Mrs. Nobre's baked goods. Dumping the contents of the duffel bag on the floor, he placed the package at the bottom and then repacked the contents on top of it. After cleaning up the table area, hanging up his vest, and undressing, he doused the light and climbed into bed—for sleep he knew would not come, that night or for many, many nights.

〰〰〰〰

The *Kastleheath* plowed north under sunny skies but against strong winds that made for choppy seas. Jan quickly found his sea legs and spent hours on deck, where the crisp wind in his face seemed to blow away some of the shock and sadness. He was thankful for the hours alone and the time they gave for the haunting memories that crowded his mind. Initially, the memories brought on only sadness and tears for what had been lost; but, as the days passed, he learned to treasure the images and happiness of those times and the simple, true affection two people had shared—perhaps the only such love in Anna's all-too-short life.

The third day out, he spent hours at the table in his cabin, quickly writing a letter of thanks to Gualter and then working most of the afternoon in writing, correcting, rewriting, and finally making clean copies of what he hoped were appropriate letters of sympathy and condolences to the Baron and to Anatoly. And every evening, alone and long after dinner, he returned to the tool chest near the bow to smoke his pipe, to think and remember, and to watch the night sky until well into the early morning.

At dinner on the evening of March fifth, Captain Wycliffe stopped to inform his few passengers that they were sharing their last meal together: the *Kastleheath* would arrive in Recife during the early-morning hours and would dock shortly after sunrise. If the *William Whitehead* was on schedule to depart on the seventh, Jan thought he should be able to board her sometime on the sixth and avoid having to find lodging in Recife for the night.

The next morning, shortly before eleven o'clock, he helped Rosa down the gangway. She cleared immigration and customs quickly, waved a jaunty goodbye, and was soon off in a waiting carriage. In another fifteen minutes, Jan was cleared and in possession of a temporary pass, authorizing him to stay in the dock area, but not enter the city, until the *Whitehead* was ready for boarding. He located the ship's agent, who examined and processed his papers and ticket, recommended a dockside café, and directed him to a berth some distance away where the *Whitehead* was tied up.

He found the ship easily. From bow to stern, the *William Whitehead* was not as long as the *Kastleheath*, though appearing to be considerably broader of beam. She sported a black hull with a white, seven-deck superstructure midships; one funnel; and two masts. He would later learn that the *Whitehead* was a single-screw vessel with a speed of fourteen knots. The seven superstructure decks and additional space below decks originally provided accommodations for one hundred and forty-two passengers: seventy in first class, twenty-four in second class, and forty-eight in third class. For some years, the ship had been used on its owner's New York — Recife — Buenos Aires service, but had proved to have too much passenger capacity for that trade and had been shifted to its current Recife — Havana — New Orleans route. After a time, the former third-class space had been reconfigured and given over to crew quarters and secure, locked storage for particularly valuable cargo.

It was an unusual ship since, though still possessing a fairly significant passenger capacity, it was a true cargo liner that, on its northbound route, carried large quantities of both Brazilian coffee and Cuban sugar to the United States. It was also, he would learn, viewed as having some of the most comfortable passenger accommodations of any ship in the Caribbean.

When he first sighted the ship shortly before noon, she was taking on hundreds, if not thousands, of sacks of coffee beans, which were carried up the gangway and on board on the shoulders of a long line of shirtless men. The line of men trudging up the gangway with the heavy sacks was passed by a similar line headed down for another load. After buying coffee at the café the agent had recommended, he found a comfortable bench where he could watch the loading while sipping his drink and downing the last of Mrs. Nobre's breads. For some time, he was distracted with watching another incoming vessel tie up nearby; when he turned his attention back to the *Whitehead*, he noticed that two queues of what were obviously passengers had begun to gather at a second gangway that had been let down to the dock, and he scrambled to his feet to join them. A crew member at the gangway took a quick look at his ticket and directed him to the much shorter, second class boarding line.

It developed that, while first class was full, there were only seventeen passengers for the eight second-class cabins that normally held three persons each. He was assigned with one other man to a starboard, three-bed cabin with two portholes and large individual trunks that were bolted to the floor and were intended to be used like closets for storing personal clothing and other possessions. Each trunk had a large padlock and a single key.

His roommate was Arthur Cornelius Kansay: a small, quiet – if not sullen – man with a hoarse voice and pince-nez reading glasses perched on a nose that clearly had been broken a number of times, causing the glasses to be perpetually askew. He had long, dark hair that was gathered together in a horse's tail in the back and tied with an orange ribbon. Kansay was dressed in a starched, brilliantly white shirt with a multicolored cravat, seaman's trousers, and a pair of low-cut black boots. One of the boots was missing its heel, giving him an odd, tipping gait.

Kansay was headed back to America after some apparently unhappy experiences in Brazil. He spoke a rough, understandable pidgin Portuguese and was civil enough when the need required, but seemed to be of a mind and demeanor that meant such "required" times were likely to be few and far between. He arrived in the cabin dragging one large piece of luggage and was closely followed by a sweating steward maneuvering two other pieces, one of which was an oversize trunk and the other a medium-size cask.

On arriving, he gave Jan a quick glance while asking what sounded like a question, though it was more of a statement, "I would be using two of those trunks if they're not of your need."

"That's fine," Jan replied. "One will do for me."

He finished unpacking, storing a number of items in his trunk, and was exiting the cabin to look about the ship when Kansay croaked, "So you'll not lock your trunk? I might would if I were you."

Jan eyed Kansay for a moment before nodding and locking the trunk. Pocketing the trunk and room keys, he took a quick look back at Kansay — who was staring intently at Jan's now-locked trunk — and headed out for the weather deck.

Chapter 23

The Caribbean

The *William Whitehead* left Recife, rounded the northeast shoulder of South America at Ponta do Calcanhar, and set a northwesterly course for the Caribbean Sea, paralleling the Brazilian coast.

Crossing the equator was an event that went largely unnoticed by those in second class, but provided the occasion for a noisy, champagne-bloated afternoon in the first-class lounge. That party ended suddenly when one of the celebrants suffered a series of violent seizures. The ship's doctor struggled to bring those seizures under control; eventually, they subsided, though more because of running their course than due to the doctor's ministrations. The patient, a later-than-middle-aged man, seemed to have recovered by the following morning, but in midafternoon suffered another series of seizures and fell unconscious for a brief period, the victim of what was now diagnosed by the doctor as a series of strokes, or "brain infarctions." When a third, though milder, bout of seizures occurred late in the evening, Captain Wycliffe responded to the urgings of the doctor, as well as the two young women accompanying the man, and determined to make port in Georgetown the following day, with the aim and sole purpose of transferring the man to the Dutch hospital in that city.

At the Georgetown harbor entrance the next afternoon, they were met by a pilot boat and advised that no berth at the wharfs for a ship of the *William Whitehead's* size would be available for at least another day. However, the boat's captain agreed to provide transportation to the docks and to arrange for the party to be taken from there to the hospital.

It was a sunny but windy afternoon, with occasional high gusts. In addition to the stricken man, the two women and their luggage were to be lowered to the pilot boat, utilizing a canvas sling that was rigged by long lines to one of the ship's cranes. Jan was among those who gathered at the railing to watch the operation. The man, a Mr. Trodden, appeared alert enough, though unsteady and a bit disoriented. The women were gaily overdressed, with flowing skirts, white gloves, and broad-brimmed straw hats. Trodden was lifted carefully into the canvas and, with the crane maneuvering so as to keep the sling close to the side of the ship and out of the wind, he was eased down to the deck of the boat, which had tied up alongside the *William Whitehead*. The first of the two women followed, scrambling into the sling and soon joining Trodden on the boat below. Many of those on the rail began to drift away as the sling slowly made its way back to pick up the second woman. She tumbled into the sling, clutching her billowing skirts with one hand and holding her straw hat in place with the other. When she seemed settled, the sling began to rise and swing out over the deck railing at the end of the crane's arm.

All seemed to be going well until a strong gust of wind sweeping across the deck caught the sling and whipped it out and up over the water, where it paused in midair before swinging rapidly down and back toward the ship, with the woman's straw hat spinning off its perch and out into the sea. Those still at the railing barely managed to duck down in time as the sling and its now screaming passenger hurtled back over the deck. Reaching the top of its arc, the sling started another outward-bound swing.

In an attempt to stop the swinging, two men at the railing grabbed the canvas as it passed overhead — only to find themselves lifted off the deck and dangling from the sling as it once again swung out over the water. The weight of the two men hanging on to the sling pulled it down and threatened to spill the woman out into the ocean. However, their weight also provided some stability that counteracted the wind and slowed the sling's wild swinging; it slowly drifted and swayed back toward the railing, stopping at a point out over the water some ten feet from the side of the ship. And there the sling hung for some minutes as those on the ship argued over whether to lower them all to the pilot boat or to try to pull the sling back on deck.

While the argument continued, the crane operator followed his own instincts and lowered the sling, though at a speed which deposited its cargo on the deck of the pilot boat in a heavy, confused heap of canvas, bodies, skirts, and ship's lines. Once it was determined that no one was injured, the sling was untangled and put in order to lift the two shaken men back to the deck of the *William Whitehead*.

Watching the men being lifted back to the deck, Jan became aware that Arthur Cornelius Kansay was standing just down the rail from him. As Kansay turned to leave, he paused long enough to shake his head and growl, "What a comedy of errors! As to our recently departed fellow passenger, at that age, well, two pretty young things such as those are bound to cause an old man's brain to infarct. Though," he added, "it could be worth it, I suppose."

⋙⋘

The weather remained favorable after they cleared Georgetown, with blue skies and light winds. The South American continent receded astern, and they steered a course to pass through the southern islands of the Lesser Antilles and into the Caribbean. Jan welcomed the languid weather and pace of life on the ship. He spent much of his time outdoors, leaning on the railing or sitting on the deck with his back against the wall, lost in his thoughts of both Anna and Maria. He also found out a little more about his reclusive cabinmate.

Kansay spent much of his non-sleeping, non-eating time wandering about the ship, a sheaf of loosely organized papers, some of which always seemed to be in danger of slipping away, tucked under his arm. He also carried a variety of writing instruments, most of which poked out from the ink-stained breast pockets of his shirts. Early each morning he would, after some searching, find a spot — sometimes indoors, sometimes outside — with a table or other flat surface, where he would sit down to write. The writing, Jan observed as he watched from a distance, was sporadic. Sometimes it seemed Kansay would scribble away madly for thirty or forty minutes without pause, filling sheet after sheet. Other times, he would contemplate the passing seas for hours without putting pen to paper, and then break into a sudden, brief frenzy; committing, it seemed certain, no more than a few dozen words to paper before resuming another lengthy stint of contemplation. Whichever mode he was in, he somehow exuded a silent but definite message that anyone thinking of intruding would quickly regret any effort to carry the thought into action.

The paper Kansay used, and of which he seemed to have a large supply, was of an odd-size and a distinctive grayish color. As Jan came down the stairway to the second-class deck one morning and looked down the hall, he noticed that two of those sheets of paper were pinched in the door to the water closet. He opened the door, checked to see that the room was empty, and extracted the papers. One sheet was blank, while the other had four short groupings of English words, two in sets of four lines and two in sets of six lines. He recognized a couple of common words, but the rest was meaningless.

The papers were in his hand when he opened the door to their cabin, expecting to find Kansay; but like the water closet, that room too was empty. Turning to leave, he saw that the cask that the steward had dragged in when Kansay boarded in Recife, and which had sat in a corner for days, had been pulled out, and its lid was ajar. When he lifted the lid, he found that the cask was full of what at first looked to be children's dolls, but proved to be dozens of small stuffed toy monkeys and bears. After a moment of fruitless thought about the purpose or meaning of a barrelful of bears and monkeys, he secured the lid, then thought to open it a bit so it was ajar in much the way he had found it. From the shelf by his bed, he retrieved his pipe and tobacco, folded the papers and put them in his back trouser pocket, locked the cabin, and went in search of his cabinmate.

He found Kansay in the modestly furnished room that served as a lounge for the second-class passengers. He was seated at a three-person table with, as usual, papers carelessly scattered in front of him. There were three cups of hot tea arranged on the table, but both of the other chairs were empty. Kansay was chewing on the end of one of his pens. The few days they had spent together had amply demonstrated that while they both spoke a pidgin Portuguese, they were apparently different dialects, so Jan rarely spoke to Kansay in other than simple sentences and without first rehearsing them in his mind.

"I found these in the water closet," he said, unfolding the papers and holding them out.

Kansay studied the papers and Jan's hand for a long moment before putting down the pen and taking the two sheets. He nodded, which Jan took for a sign of thanks.

"May I ask why it is written that way, in such short lines?"

Kansay stared at him. Finally, with a look of resignation, he said, "It is called, how to say it ... pottery."

"Pottery?"

"No! No!" Kansay fumbled. He paused to think and then continued carefully, "Po-et-ry. I am a po-et."

"What does a po-et do?'

"A po-et writes po-et-ry."

"I am not familiar with that."

Kansay reddened and exasperation flashed on his face, but then he sighed and gestured at the sheet Jan had just given him with the groupings of English words. "*That* is po-et-ry. It is a po-em, which is the expression of emotion. Do you know what emotion is? Good. A po-et expresses emotion through the sound and the meaning and the rhythm of words." He studied Jan carefully to see if he was being understood.

"Must you do it in such short lines?"

"It is part of what makes po-et-ry. The sound of words together and how they sound alike or rhyme."

"What does this po-et-ry say?" Jan gestured at the sheet. "I do not read English."

Kansay gave Jan a penetrating, questioning look, as if deciding whether it was worthwhile or necessary to continue the conversation. At length, he shifted his weight and gestured to one of the unoccupied chairs.

Jan hesitated. "Your companions ... I don't want to take one's place."

"There are no companions. I arrange it thus to discourage idle interruptions by the riff-raff of the world. Sit. Have the tea, if you choose." He looked at the sheet in front of him, picked up his pen, and spent some minutes chewing on it before scribbling Portuguese words above the English ones in the first grouping. At length, he circled that grouping and tapped it with the pen.

"These lines are a verse," he said slowly. From the twisted expression on his face, he seemed to be choosing and weighing

what words to speak. "A po-em has many verses, though no certain number. In a good po-em, each verse brings its own message,
and is also part of the message of the total po-em. This is a verse I
will fit into a larger po-em," he gestured at the other sheets on the
table, "that I am writing." After a moment's hesitation, he read
the verse:

Blue-green water everywhere
Cloud-speckled sky above,
The ship eases through the sea
At peace, much like a dove.

"The po-em is about this journey. I may or may not use that
verse. At this moment, I don't know. It is missing something. I don't
know. Whatever. Thoughts sometimes come to po-ets, and you
have to write them down as they come. Often you discard them."

"I hear the rhyme," Jan mused, "and can see the picture the
words paint. Are all these sheets and the many others you have
part of this po-em?"

"No, no." Kansay shook his head. "There are many po-ems here.
Some I have been working on for many months. They are about my
travels and places I have been and people I have met. It will take
many more months to finish them and select the best."

"And then?"

"And then I hope they will be published in a book of po-et-ry,
such as this one." From a bag at his feet, Kansay pulled out a book
and pointed at the cover. "This is a book of my po-et-ry. The po-
ems in this are about a young boy growing up."

Jan paged through the book. "You have a great talent. I have
never before met anyone who has written a book. I wish I could
read the words you have written."

"Keep the book. It is a triumph to have introduced someone to
po-et-ry. Someday, you will learn English and can read the book.
Now, you can stay here and keep company if you wish, but please

do not speak — I have a number of po-et-ic thoughts I need to write down while they are fresh in my mind."

Jan turned his chair to look out at what he now viewed as a cloud-speckled sky. He decided that any questions about the barrel of monkeys and bears could wait for another day.

———≈≋≋≋≈———

In the following days, which were sun-drenched but frequently featuring strong, warm winds, the *William Whitehead* moved through the Caribbean on a course that would carry her off the western shore of Jamaica, making steam toward the passage between the Yucatán Channel and Cuba. Almost every day, around midmorning, Jan would find Kansay wherever he happened to have settled in. They would have tea and share a few minutes of conversation, plus Kansay's translation and reading of one or two poems from the book he had given Jan. Afterward, Kansay would write, and Jan would reflect upon some line or verse that had been read and that had caught his mind's eye. He wasn't sure whether Kansay was a good poet, but he enjoyed the idea of poetry, especially the thought and imagination needed to capture emotions and thoughts in the few words of a verse.

They reached the western tip of Cuba early one particularly humid and sticky morning, swung to the northeast into the Gulf of Mexico, and arrived outside Havana in the late afternoon. Most of the ship's passengers were gathered at the rails as they passed through the harbor's long, narrow entrance, guarded by the three ancient Spanish fortresses that Kansay pointed out and identified as El Morro, San Carlos de la Cabaña, and San Salvador de la Punta. By sunset, the *William Whitehead* was tied up at the Marimelena docks across the harbor from the main portion of the city.

At 5:00 a.m. the following morning, dockside cranes and dozens of workers began loading hundreds of bags of raw sugar destined for the sugar refineries in and around New Orleans. Later in the morning, Jan left the ship along with many other passengers to walk down the long docks. A quarter of an hour into his walk, he encountered Kansay coming back from a stationer's, where he had purchased pens, ink, and other writing supplies. As they wandered about together, they passed a cobbler's stand, and Jan suggested they stop to have the missing heel on Kansay's boot replaced.

Kansay shook his head. "No. And it is not missing. I removed it."

They walked some distance in silence before Kansay said, "I imagine you wonder why."

"What is it that I should be wondering why about?"

"The heel. If you can possibly remember to a few seconds ago, we were just talking about that. You wonder why I removed it."

"I assume you have good reason, perhaps an injury to your foot."

"No, my foot itself is fine."

"Well, I would think that if you keep walking in this unnatural way, you might injure it and it will not be fine."

"I had a dear friend in Brazil," Kansay said slowly after they walked a bit farther. "Actually, it was in the city of São Paulo, some ways south of Recife. He was an artist, a painter of pictures, especially multicolored birds with huge red penises. He had difficulty selling those. Whatever. He and I were out late one night. We had had a great deal to drink. We accosted many very pretty girls, though to little avail.

"We were walking down the street—in the middle of the street, on the trolley tracks—singing, talking, pushing, and pretending to fight, all those stupid things you do when your head is unbalanced and you are very happy. A trolley came along, one we wanted to catch. As it approached, I stumbled into him. He tripped onto the rail, and the trolley wheel ran over his foot. The doctors sewed him up, and in some ways he was lucky, but part of the heel of his foot was somehow crushed and could not be saved." Kansay stopped walking and looked out over the harbor. "It was an accident, but in my heart, it was — it still is — my fault."

They watched as two seagulls fought over some scrap of food in the oily water near the dock. Kansay shrugged his shoulders. "I thought I should do something as penance. You know, to punish myself and to earn forgiveness for my actions. So, I removed the heel on the boot of my right foot... so that I walk much as he is forced to walk. I have grown used to it, though it strains my knee and makes a bloody callous on my heel. I could cure my pain easily; my friend cannot cure the pain I inflicted on him by my drunkenness."

"It was, as you say, an accident," Jan observed.

"It was. But one must be responsible for his actions, of whatever sort." Kansay stirred himself and started walking. "Come, we should return to the ship. I have new ink and paper and thoughts for a new po-em."

By that evening, the loading had finished, and some minor repairs on the ship had been accomplished. The weather was clear, and with all the business in Havana completed, the crew began preparing for a late-evening departure.

⸻

Jan was on deck near the bow at 11:15 p.m. when a rusted, floating vessel that passed for a tugboat and belched clouds of thick black smoke helped push the *William Whitehead* away from the dock. He stayed on deck as the ship moved through the harbor, which was ablaze with lights on all sides, and out through the narrow entrance to the open sea and the Straits of Florida. The *Whitehead* gained speed, pushing the white waves it created to either side as it headed north. Ahead, the ocean was dark, with the lights of another ship barely visible off to port.

He lit his pipe and thought of the many nights he had now spent at sea. And he thought of America, now only some forty-odd hours away. After so many months, his dream was close at hand, but he felt little satisfaction or excitement: the dream meant little if he was to live it alone and lonely.

Chapter 24

New Orleans

By 10:00 a.m. on Friday morning, when the American immigration officials boarded the ship, the *William Whitehead's* eighty-four passengers were all gathered on the weather deck, each standing next to or sitting on their baggage.

Jan had spent a restless night and wasn't sure if he had slept at all. He finally had abandoned the idea of sleep, rolled out of his bunk at half past four, and quietly made his way out of the cabin. Before going down the stairs, he stopped at the water closet to peer into the mirror and smiled faintly at the clear, bright eyes that looked back at him.

Once on deck, he watched from the portside rail as the *Whitehead* moved slowly up the Mississippi River Delta. Despite the early hour, the muddy river was already alive with large ships, barges, and smaller vessels; many of the latter were under sail, and others were being rowed by anywhere from two to six men. The traffic upriver seemed equal to that headed out to sea. As the sky grew brighter and they reached the broad harbor area of the city, he thought the activity and bustle at and along the docks far exceeded that of any other port he had been in during his long journey.

The passengers were organized into three groups. One, and by far the largest, was composed of US citizens such as Kansay, who were returning to the country from business or pleasure beyond its borders. Another group involved those from South America who had journeyed to New Orleans for business reasons and were not intending to stay in the country beyond thirty days. The final group—five married couples and Jan—were immigrants, largely from Brazil, hoping to enter the country for permanent residence. Once organized, each of the groups received brief instructions, and then fell into lines to follow one or another of the officials down the gangway and to the immigration and customs building. Kansay's group left the ship first. Walking past, he stopped to wish Jan an awkward "Good Luck." As Kansay toppled away, he was trailed by a steward pulling a cart that contained his luggage, including the mysterious cask of stuffed bears and monkeys.

Jan moved down the gangway and walked along with his group. It was March 22, 1912, and he was at last on American soil, even if it was more accurately the worn and rough American wood of the dock and wharf area. He took a deep breath and filled his lungs with the sea- and fish-scented waterfront air of his new homeland.

It was a short walk to the immigration and customs building. They were ushered into a cavernous, wooden-floored hall that was brightly lit by sunlight streaming in from large windows high up on the south wall. As he waited in line with his fellow passengers from the *Whitehead*, he carefully arranged his documents, with Andrew Jurua's letter referencing Lech Rusnacko on top. Looking around the room, he noticed a number of men seated in a row against the wall below the high windows. That group included three in uniform, one of whom seemed to be making notes based on whispered exchanges with the others. He could see Kansay in one of the other two lines, both of which were moving much faster than the line of immigrants he was in.

When his turn finally came, he handed the documents to the inspector, who glanced at Jurua's letter and, looking over at the row of men below the high windows, motioned to one of them who was lounging with his chair tipped back against the wall. Slowly that man tipped his chair forward, stood, and made his way toward them. He was stocky and solidly built, with a broad, flat face. That face was deeply creased by the lines of a nearly perpetual smile and was distinguished by a large black handlebar mustache that melded into equally black, thick sideburns. He wore a flat, black cap, a black leather vest over an off-white shirt, and gray trousers.

Extending his hand as he approached, he said simply, in the first Slovak speech Jan had heard in months, "I am Lech Rusnacko, and I am delighted to welcome you to America! My guess was that you would be arriving this morning, so I came down to wait for you."

The inspector forestalled further conversation by pointing to the two chairs in front of his desk and, when they were seated, raised an eyebrow in Rusnacko's direction.

Lech turned and, putting a hand on Jan's shoulder, explained, "He is going to ask a number of questions — twenty-nine, actually — which I will translate for you and then translate your answers for him. He will fill out the form. It will take no little time, but most of the questions are easy, and he already has some information from your ship's passenger list."

The questions were routine and simple, but with two translations, it took some time. The inspector seemed uninterested in most of Jan's documents, except for the church record verifying his birth date and the emigration documents from the authorities in Bremerhaven and Buenos Aires, which he kept and attached to the form. One of the last questions related to the amount of money Jan carried.

"They want," Rusnacko explained, "to be sure you can support yourself for some time and have money to get started, and that includes having the money to get to Chicago, as you indicated were your travel plans from here. He needs to see the amount of money you have."

Jan pulled out his accumulated savings in Argentinean pesos and the forty-six U.S. dollars he had received from Gualter Guterres. The inspector looked at the money, spoke .at length to Rusnacko, and then turned to writing on the form.

"He says you have more than enough to satisfy the requirement. He also reminded me to tell you that your wisest course is to exchange your pesos here, actually at the bank across the street, where you will get a fair rate. I can vouch for that since these inspectors refer most people to that bank, and they will be honest and charge only a small fee for the exchange. We will go there when we are done here."

The inspector returned the money, completed the form, and handed it to Rusnacko, who read the answers he had recorded, asked the inspector one question, and then gave the form to Jan. "I believe he has recorded your answers correctly. Please note that he has filled in your name here at the top as *J-O-H-N*, which is how it was spelled on the ship's manifest. It is the English version of Jan, pronounced the same way. He will issue your entry card in that name, so that is how you need to sign it on the form, and it is the spelling of the name you will probably need to use in America."

Jan — now John — signed the form and the stiff blue card that the inspector gave him. The inspector smiled, handed his remaining documents back to him, and pointed the two of them to another station behind a screen.

As Rusnacko rose, he said, "Now a quick stop at the doctor, and we will be on our way."

Behind the screen, seated at a small table, were two of the uniformed men who had been seated along the wall.

"Army doctors," Rusnacko whispered. John felt himself grow tense.

One of the doctors looked up at him briefly, pushed his chair back, and came around the table. He used a tongue depressor to check John's mouth and teeth, examined his hands and twisted his arms, glanced quickly at his eyes and ears, had him stand first on one foot and then the other, and ran his hand slowly up the length of John's spine. He said something to Rusnacko, who answered without translating and consulting with John. The doctor nodded, stepped back, and looked at John for a few long seconds before turning and speaking to the second doctor—who promptly signed the blue card and gave it back to John.

"We are done! You are admitted to the United States of America!" Rusnacko explained with a smile. "Come, we have places to go."

Once they were outside, John stopped to catch his breath—feeling at once relieved, fulfilled, ecstatic, and, in a way, vindicated. Years later he would recall this moment as one of the greatest in his life, for many reaons. Rusnacko stood patiently to one side, finally reaching out to shake John's hand and offer congratulations.

"Thank you for your help," John said and then, thinking of the years when the condition of his eyes and the prospect of another inevitable, and possibly life-defining, examination had weighed on his mind, he added, "I expected the doctor's examination to be longer."

"It was longer than you think: they were watching all of you from the ship as you walked in and stood in line. They are well-trained to find the things they are looking for and that cause problems. They can easily spot the lame and ill, as well as the deranged, and are also alert to those who are more nervous than they should be or who sweat even though it is cold.

"That, across the street, is the bank," he continued. "I will explain later, but I think you should exchange only some of your pesos here."

At the bank, he counted his money and, on Lech's advice, presented eighty pesos, less than half of what he had, for exchange.

After they had walked some distance from the bank, Rusnacko noted, "We are on Bourbon Street in what is called the Vieux Carré, or French Quarter, an old part of town. It is an interesting area, and you will often hear the French language spoken here, although somewhat different, I believe, than the French you would hear spoken in France itself. That restaurant right across the street, the white one with the green gas lamps, is called Jean Bart. Both Marta — she is my wife — and I work there: she during the day for the lunch trade, and I start at four o'clock for the dinner meal. Often I am there until after midnight, but it gives me days like this free. We live not too far from here on a street called the Rue Toulouse. You are to stay with us as our guest while you are here."

A few blocks past the restaurant, they reached the Rue Toulouse and were soon climbing the worn stairs of a three-story building to the Rusnackos' three-room apartment on the top floor. In the small, simply furnished kitchen, they found the table set for two, including fresh bread. On the stove were two covered pots.

Lech lifted the cover of the larger pot, releasing a small cloud of steam. "This, my friend, is a soup called gumbo. It can be of many types, but this is shrimp gumbo. It has a strong stock, celery, onions, peppers, and a thickener, which Marta makes from flour and fat. And in this other pot is a little jambalaya, another local dish made of chicken, sausage, rice, tomatoes, and spices. The jambalaya is actually from Jean Bart; it was left over at the end of the day two nights ago, and I brought it home. We had it last night but saved some for you to try. It is all very much local food to New Orleans. I don't think you would find this in other parts of America."

To John, the two dishes bore some similarities to the Portuguese food he had experienced in Buenos Aires, but in other ways it differed, especially in what Lech insisted was a "mild" spiciness.

"Tomorrow morning," Lech said as they ate, "we need to go to the train station and buy your ticket for Chicago. There is an overnight train that leaves at eleven o'clock Sunday morning and arrives in Chicago Monday afternoon. It is about twenty-six hours total but may take somewhat longer. It makes a number of stops. Mr. Jurua will meet you at the station in Chicago or have someone else there who will meet you. They do not run that train with a departure on Saturday, but that's just as well. You can spend the extra day with us. Is Chicago your final destination?"

"No, I intend to go to Minneapolis to join the Slovak community there. I believe there are trains from Chicago to Minneapolis."

"I imagine so, but I do not know. I am sure Mr. Jurua does, and he will help make the arrangements for you. You may be able to leave for Minneapolis shortly after you arrive in Chicago. I don't know; it depends on the schedules."

"Do you know what the ticket will cost? To Chicago, that is."

"I believe it will be at most eight dollars, perhaps not that much. The train has a dining car, but we will also pack food for you here." Rusnacko paused with his soup spoon in the air. "This reminds me that you will want to exchange the rest of your money, the pesos, for U.S. dollars in Chicago. I did not want you to do that here because one thing you will need to look out for — and it is not a big thing, really, if you know to watch out — are men who are sometimes on the trains and who might easily recognize you as an immigrant or a 'foreigner,' as they say. You do not want to be taken advantage of, and in the worst case, having money such as that from Argentina, foreign currency that they would not be interested in, is a good thing. We can talk about that more tomorrow."

"What do you know of Mr. Jurua?" John asked.

"Little. He is trained in the law, a successful lawyer; very educated and I believe quite well- to-do, perhaps even rich. His father was an early immigrant who came, perhaps forty years ago, from

a village in Bohemia near Prague and did well in the United States
with help from others. Mr. Jurua apparently feels a debt there:
helping others as his father was helped. I believe the father is quite
old. He was, I've heard, once the proprietor of a number of food
markets in Chicago. You are perhaps the fifth person I have been
involved in helping with Mr. Jurua, though I know there are others
who he assists when they come to Chicago from Ellis Island – that,
as you probably know, is in New York and the point where most of
us enter this country."

"Yes, I know. I too had planned to go through Ellis Island,"
John said. For the next hour, he told the story of the long, circuitous
journey that had brought him to New Orleans. Rusnacko listened
quietly and with great interest, especially when John pulled out his
worn map and traced his route from Važec to New Orleans.

When John had finished, Lech observed, "I am glad I did not
have to deal with such a trip when Marta and I came here six years
ago, but I think the things you have had to overcome will help you
in facing life and different types of people, and in being successful
here. And I suppose it has been something of an adventure; you
have seen much of the world."

They ate and talked until midafternoon, when Lech began to
dress for work and suggested that John walk with him to Jean Bart:
"Marta waits until I get there before she leaves, so you can walk
back with her."

They made their way back down Bourbon Street, which was
crowded with people, horse-drawn wagons, and a number of small
motor cars – all of them black, some bearing the name Ford, others
that of Renault. The shops and stores seemed to be mostly restaurants and public houses or bars, with a few of the other businesses
apparently selling the favors of the pale-skinned, long-haired, red-
lipped women who peered outside from behind thin curtains or
leaned over the railings of second-floor balconies. The air smelled

of cooking food; the fishy, oily nearby waterfront; and standing garbage waiting to be collected.

Marta was taller than her husband, slim but full-figured with dark hair, enormous brown eyes with long lashes, flashing white teeth, and a mischievous look. She had two large rolled-up cloth shopping bags and took him on a detour that brought them to the sprawling market near the river.

"This French Market," she confided, "does most of its trade in the early morning, but late in the afternoon, especially on a Friday like this, and before what will be a busy Saturday, things are cheaper, sometimes free — if you bargain just so."

The French Market was as large as any outdoor market John had seen in Europe or in Argentina. There were many large stands under the cover of long, open-sided sheds. Large produce carts, which had probably been overflowing earlier in the day but were now only partially stocked, stood on the street. Smaller two-wheeled carts were everywhere; men were using those to carry goods and produce from one place in the market to another. As he tagged along, he discovered that Marta's bargaining "just so" involved a lot of laughter, a certain amount of flirting, and a willingness to allow a stray hand to rest on her hip or touch her bare arm. As they went home, with him carrying both bulging shopping bags, he asked how much such a large quantity of food had cost.

"For me, less than three dollars. But for you doing the shopping, it might have been five or even six dollars," she said, laughing. "Though there was some additional cost of sorts that only a woman can pay. When you have a wife, and if she is pretty, remember that she should do the shopping in markets like this!"

He slept soundly on a pile of blankets on the floor in the sitting room, waking only briefly sometime after 1:00 a.m. when Lech came home from work. He fell back asleep to the music of Marta's giggles from the next room.

At about nine o'clock the next morning, as the dishes from a late breakfast were being washed, John was drawn to the open windows fronting the street by the sound of loud music, largely from trumpets and other horns he was not familiar with. The street below was full of what seemed to be dancers in a parade, many of the women in bright, colorful dresses and most of the men in black suits and white shirts; some of both sexes were twirling small parasols or umbrellas. All of those in the parade were of black skin. Lech came up behind him with a cup of coffee and stood on his toes to peer over John's shoulder.

"What are they celebrating?" John asked.

"Well, it is actually a funeral procession—see the casket coming up, back there?"

Listening to the music and noting the people on the sidewalk clapping their hands, John was incredulous. "If not for the coffin, you would not know it is a funeral procession. It seems like a festival or carnival!"

"A bit of both, I guess. The Negroes—the black people—love music, and they put that together with the dancing to celebrate the passage of the dead to what is surely a better life."

"There seem to be many of these Negroes here in New Orleans," John observed. "I would guess many more than there are in Buenos Aires. And they are darker. Are they as populous throughout the country as here?"

"No, I think not. They are much more prevalent in the southern states, such as Louisiana, where we are now. They are descendants of true slaves who were terribly treated, worse than serfs in Europe, not more than forty or fifty years ago and in some ways even today." Gesturing at the street, Lech continued, "When this person died, the sorrow was indescribable: the wailing and the moaning undoubtedly loud and heartfelt, and the tears a river of loss. Now, they celebrate release and the passage of the deceased to his heavenly Father. I think, myself, that it is better than our old customs of crying for days and shrouding ourselves in black for weeks or months — which does not bring back the dead and merely depresses the living."

Later that morning they walked the mile or so to the two-story brick Union Station on South Rampart Street. The building was fronted by a broad lawn with many palm trees and low garden areas. The station was relatively quiet, and they purchased a one-way ticket on Sunday's *Panama Limited* for Chicago, train number three on the Illinois Central Railroad line.

Anticipating John's question, Lech explained, "The train is named in honor of the Panama Canal, which is being built by America across the Isthmus — which is a fancy name for a large marsh or swamp — of the country of Panama. It is an enormous building project covering many, many miles and employing thousands of men. Only a country such as the United States could build something like this, and, even so, many say it would not have happened but for the will of President Roosevelt. The French, so I have heard, tried for years and failed. When the canal is done, probably in 1914 or 1915, it will bring ships from the Pacific Ocean here instead of going around the tip of South America and then to Florida and New York. When it opens, shipping in and out of this city will, at least so they say, grow tremendously."

As they walked around the station, Lech pointed out the Pullman cars parked on various tracks. "The *Panama Limited* has nothing but Pullman cars: dining cars, lounges, and sleeping cars. The sleeping cars have beds for, well, for sleeping during the night travel of the train. Your ticket is for an open-section accommodation, which gives you a seat during the day that converts to a bed at night, should, of course, you wish to sleep. You will see how it works when you are on the train."

From the Union Station they walked back toward the French Quarter, passing down Saint Louis Street to Decatur Street and then over to Jackson Square and the towering Saint Louis Cathedral. They went inside the church, walked about the Square, watched street artists at work, and bought ices from vendors on the sidewalk. They stopped now and then to admire the artists' efforts, were both fascinated by a few new motor cars parked along the street, and perched for some time on a wrought-iron fence to watch slow-moving games of chess and fast-paced games of checkers in progress. Small groups of two or three musicians played on some street corners, collecting coins tossed by passersby into old broad-brimmed hats set on the sidewalk. Mid-afternoon they wound their way back up the Rue Toulouse so Lech could prepare for work that evening.

John and Marta had dinner together, after which she turned to sewing while from the sitting room window he watched the sun set, the skies grow dark, and the streetlights begin to glow. He was drawn to the people passing on the street below: groups of loud and laughing men, silent workers going to or coming from work, couples wending their way in one direction or another, and pairs of policemen walking their beats. In the background, there was the constant low hum of music coming from somewhere up the street. Across the way, two small Negro boys – they seemed to be perhaps seven or eight years old – had set up boxes and would occasionally convince one of the passing men to have their shoes shined for a few pennies. He hadn't realized how late it was until Marta whispered a "good night" as she closed the bedroom door behind her. He lay down on his pile of blankets and was soon sound asleep.

They were up before 6:00 a.m. Sunday morning and were soon walking down Decatur Street to The Morning Call Coffee Stand, where they found a table near the street.

"We come here almost every Sunday morning," Marta said with a laugh, "though usually not quite this early. Sunday mornings at this place is our sinful extravagance, or at least one of them!"

She then proceeded to deftly order three café au laits and a large platter of beignets.

As the waiter left, she turned to John and explained, "Café au lait is thick chicory coffee, such as you have never, ever had anywhere, I am sure. The coffee is mixed with an equal amount of near-boiling milk. It is deliciously frothy! You will see ... and I guarantee one will not be enough."

"The beignets are donuts," Lech added.

"No, not hardly!" Marta corrected. "Beignets are square pieces of special hand-rolled dough that are plunged into hot oil and fried. Then they are folded and dusted in heavenly powdered sugar. The platter we ordered will have twelve beignets. Perhaps enough; but then again, perhaps not!"

The beignets proved to be as advertised by Marta, and it wasn't long before another round of café au laits was in order. All three soon sported traces of white powder on chins and blouses.

As they ate, John asked, "I can't help but notice that you both speak English very well. Was it hard to learn? How long did it take you? I was in Argentina for well over a year, almost two, and was never able to really learn and be comfortable with Portuguese."

"Perhaps that was because you knew you were not staying there permanently," Marta observed.

"That could be," Lech said, "or perhaps it is just a difficult language? English also is not very easy: some people from the old country struggle with it for years. We were in New York for over a year and lived with some who could help teach us. We also had each other to practice with, which we did for hours every night. We made up our own lists of Czech and Slovak words, and some Polish, and what each word was in English. There were many hundreds of words in our dictionary. And, after a while, we would write each other letters in English and leave them for the other to read. That was a good test and a good way to learn."

"And sometimes funny when we used the wrong words," Marta added.

"She did that frequently—on purpose, I think," Lech said, laughing. "It was good that we learned as much as we did because, when we came here, we never could have worked at Jean Bart as a waiter and a waitress without being able to understand and speak to our customers."

"And our jobs," Marta said, "force us to learn more all the time. But it really is not an easy language to learn. We both should get even better at it, and we will." She sipped her coffee thoughtfully. "What you will do for a living in America will have an effect, but I think it would be hard to get by in any country for a length of time if one does not speak that country's language."

The Morning Call was not particularly busy that morning, and they sat for some time talking about the Rusnackos' life in New York, their travels to Louisiana, and their hopes of someday having the money to open their own business—Lech giving some detailed descriptions of his vision for a "Rusnacko's Books, Music & Tobacco" shop in the French Quarter.

"We have the big American dream," Lech confessed, almost shyly.

"It will be more than a dream," Marta said firmly, and somehow John felt that her purpose was so strong that the dream could not help but come true.

From The Morning Call they wandered through the crowds in front of the Saint Louis Cathedral: people dressed in their Sunday finest, with the women in fashionable long dresses and colorful large-brimmed hats. As the morning lengthened, they walked down a much quieter Bourbon Street and then returned to the

Rusnackos' apartment, where Marta immediately began cooking and then packing a small box that she filled full of crawfish, jambalaya, breads, and other foods.

As soon as Marta had finished, Lech tapped his watch and said, "We should be leaving for the station—the train does not wait for the tardy."

John hoisted his duffel bag, and Lech shouldered the rucksack.

At the door, Marta stood on tiptoes, pressed her body closely to John's, tipped back his cap, held his face in her hands, and gave him a long kiss. "I wish you luck, John," she whispered. "You are to be a success and a fine husband for your Maria. Do you understand?"

He nodded—somehow, he felt, one had to do what Marta Rusnacko demanded; though mention of Maria's name brought the uncertainty of that situation back to the forefront of his thoughts.

He boarded the train at 10:45 a.m. after standing by while Lech had a long conversation with a tall, uniformed black porter he seemed to know. "His name is Ike," Lech said. "He worked at the restaurant, at Jean Bart, when I first started there. This is a far better job. I told him to look out for you a bit. He will."

They shook hands as he boarded. "Remember what Marta told you," Lech laughed. "I can tell you that there can be hell to pay for not following her instructions!"

As he arranged his bags and settled into the seat Ike directed him to in one of the coaches, John saw Lech loitering near a pillar some short distance away on the platform. The train began to move promptly at 11:00 a.m. Lech stepped away from the post, waved goodbye, and gave John a thumbs-up signal with both hands.

Chapter 25

Chicago

Ike directed John to a seat on the right side of the Pullman car, facing forward as the train headed north. The seat was paired with another that faced backward; identical pairs of seats stretched the length of the car on both sides of the aisle. Although in some cases both seats were occupied, John was one of many who had a pair to themselves with no one sitting in the facing seat.

The train was much more comfortable than those he had ridden on in Europe and Argentina: the seats were cushioned and showed little wear, the aisle was carpeted, there were shades on the windows, and small glass chandeliers were set in the ceiling above the aisle. And as soon as they had cleared the edge of the city and began to accelerate, it became clear that the *Panama Limited* would travel at a faster speed than any other train he had ridden. Glancing at the man sitting across from him, he saw that he had put his bags on and under the facing seat, so he did the same.

He was quickly absorbed in the passing scenery. The land immediately north of the city was covered with low scrub brush, open water in some places, and marshes in others. As the train rolled on into the early afternoon, the marshland gave way to forested countryside interspersed with cultivated fields stretching far into the distance. It was early in the season and many of the fields were freshly plowed: some crops had just been sown and since only the smallest green shoots had poked through the dirt, it was hard to tell what crops had been planted. The fields seemed to be immense, with no signs of being divided among many farmers—how much, he wondered, belonged to one man or one family? Would it be possible for an immigrant to have such a farm?

His gaze rarely left the window, taking in everything: solitary farmers working fields with horse-drawn plows, farmhouses and cluttered yards that stood near the roads that the tracks crossed, small towns that the train passed through. In some fields, large groups of workers were bent to the tasks of planting and weeding. The train slowed down noticeably but did not stop at a number of the smaller stations: after a while he realized the reduced speed was for the purpose of picking up mail bags that were either tossed into the open doors of the mail car at the rear of the train as it went by or which, in some cases, were hanging on poles near the track and were caught or snatched by hooks attached to the mail car.

The afternoon was brilliantly sunny. He became aware of the passage of time only when he saw the lengthening shadow of the train on the ground outside and noticed the people seated on the other side of the aisle pulling the window shades down against the sun, which was lowering in the western sky. He was surprised when he looked at his watch and saw that it was almost 4:00 p.m.

As early evening set in, passengers from adjoining cars began to walk through on their way to the dining car. A few of those in John's car also headed that way. He saw that they took no particular precautions about their bags and seemed secure in leaving them behind, which was a relief to him in light of Rusnacko's cautions about other people on the train. He also noted that some of those who remained had food items in their bags as he did, making him comfortable in taking out Marta's carefully packed jambalaya, rolls, and water.

As he ate, he continued to watch the passing countryside, though his mind drifted back to scene after scene from his long journey: Maria on the evening before he left Važec; Anna on the cog railway tracks below Štrbské Pleso; the Polish Brozeks in Poronin; staying at Baron Ihnacak's in Krakow and shopping in the Market; gypsies and Cossacks in Russian territory; Colonel Strzala at Mother Panas's pensione in Łódź; the doctor at the emigration building in Bremerhaven; Gareth Willows and Cardiff; the disappearance and death of Richard Dischinger; the "Jolly Rodgers", DeGroza and Cousins, at Cuellar's bar in Lisbon; Gaspar Chavez; Douala and Jimenez; the Guterres brothers and all those at the brickyard; leaving Buenos Aires; … and the letter from Anatoly Ihnacak. At that memory, he stopped, his eyes lingering on the Fisherman's Cap resting on the seat across from him. He had, he realized, much to be thankful for in the people he had met and who had helped, encouraged, influenced, and perhaps changed him as a man along the way – and maybe none more so, in her own way, than Anna.

The man across the aisle had returned from dinner, pulling a cigar from his coat pocket as he walked by and headed toward the back of the train. John thought for a second, then found his pipe and tobacco in his rucksack, closed his bags up, and followed along.

The smoking car had comfortable single seats and was relatively empty: three men, including the man he had followed, were smoking cigars or pipes and either reading the paper or looking out the window at the darkening scenery. He found a seat at a small table, packed his pipe, and was digging in his pocket for a match when a waiter in a long white apron appeared at his elbow, struck a match for him, and asked, "Coffee, sir?" John nodded and soon was sipping strong black coffee and thinking about being in an atmosphere and a place that he never could have imagined.

When he returned to his seat, Ike had already set up the sleeping berths for many of the passengers, who were now hidden behind maroon curtains. When he spotted John, he raised his eyebrows and gave him a questioning look that was easy to understand. On a nod from John, Ike put the duffel bag and rucksack in the aisle, folded the two facing seats over to make a berth, and unhooked the upper berth from the ceiling. From the upper berth, Ike removed a folded sheet—which he spread out and tucked in on the lower berth—a blanket, and a pillow. With a practiced hand, he pulled down the lower berth's curtain, which was attached to the upper berth, and then placed John's bags on the empty upper berth. It all took less than five minutes, and, with a tip of his cap, he moved down the aisle to set up the next berth.

John removed his boots and slid through the curtains. He pulled the chain to turn on the small light on the wall next to the window. After removing his vest and shirt, he folded them and set them aside. While the berth was not long, he found he could stretch out comfortably enough. Once he was under the blanket, he turned out the light. He decided to leave the window shade up and for a long time lay awake in the dim light, watching the night speed by, before finally drifting off to sleep.

It was still dark shortly before dawn when he awoke. They were slowing down and soon pulled into and then slightly past a station with a number of signs that read "Carbondale." After putting on his shirt and vest, he looked out through the curtain and found no other signs of life. Once he had his boots on, he checked his bags and found they had not been disturbed.

Ike was standing at the end of the car. He smiled a good morning and indicated John could get off the train but made it clear he needed to stay nearby. Stepping down from the car to the ground, he saw that they had stopped on a spur track some little distance past the station. Their caboose had been detached and left back beyond the point where another track met the spur. He stretched his legs walking back to the platform and into the station, which was almost deserted at that hour. From inside, he could see another engine coming into the station from the opposite direction, pulling two Pullman cars much like the one in which he had been riding. When it passed the connecting track leading to the spur, railway workers who were standing-by threw large switches, and the tracks moved so that the engine could back the two cars through the connecting track and onto the spur. As he started walking back, it became clear that the two cars were being added to the *Panama Limited*.

When he returned to his seat, he found that the upper berth had been pushed up and secured to the ceiling, the lower berth had been returned to its paired-seating configuration, and a metal tray with a newspaper, coffee, china cups, and buttered biscuits was centered on the seat across from him. The train lurched slightly, spilling a little of his coffee, as first the two additional cars and then the caboose were connected. Just as the sun came up over the horizon, the train resumed its run, leaving the spur and picking up speed as it returned to the main northbound track.

The morning passed quickly as they headed north through Illinois. Vast patches of lingering winter snow began to appear in the fields, and the sun slowly gave way to overcast skies and a light, cold rain. Shortly after noon, they began to slow down as they entered the edges of what was obviously a great city. From the Pullman window, the city seemed to extend forever. The train passed through livestock yards, manufacturing areas, railroad yards, residential areas with block after block of tall side-by-side houses, and areas of stores and businesses. And soon they began to enter the long sheds of Chicago's Central Station.

As he gathered his bags and left the train, he had no idea how he would recognize Andrew Jurua and worried what he would do if Jurua was not there to greet him. He glanced around the platform and then followed the crowds into the busy terminal, where many were greeted by waiting relatives and friends. Deciding that he shouldn't stray too far from the doors where the passengers from the *Panama Limited* had entered the waiting room, he stopped near a bench and stood beside his bags as the crowds began to thin out.

"Jan?"

The voice was deep and behind him, and when he turned around he saw that it belonged to a tall, serious-looking man in a black overcoat and matching top hat. His distinguishing features were large dark eyes, thick black eyebrows, and a perfectly trimmed black mustache. Both the eyebrows and the mustache were flecked with premature gray. Walking with him was another man dressed less formally and carrying his cap in his hand.

The tall man smiled, doffed his hat, and extended his right hand. "I am Andrew Jurua," he said in precise Slovak, "and this is Michael Onchek, but he will be insulted if you do not call him Mike. We are pleased to welcome you to Chicago. Are these all of your bags?"

"Yes, they are," John replied.

"Good. Mike will take the duffel bag. We have a motorcar waiting outside to take us to my office, where we can talk and tend to such business as is needed and which will help get you on your way."

"If I may ask, how did you know who I was? How did you recognize me?"

"That was easy," Jurua said, laughing. "After you purchased your train ticket in New Orleans on Saturday, Rusnacko sent me a telegram telling me you would be on the Monday *Panama Limited* and describing you in a few words. He mentioned the blue-and-brown duffel bag you would be carrying and that you would be wearing a black cap."

The car parked in front of the train station on Michigan Avenue proved to be a new two-seat Ford Model T. Jurua and John climbed into the back, with the bags on the passenger side of the front seat. Mike expertly turned the hand crank no more than half a turn before the engine started, and he quickly stepped into the driver's seat.

John's first ride in an automobile involved a slow drive through the busy city to Jurua's law firm on LaSalle Street. The streets were crowded with horse-drawn wagons and carriages, but automobiles also seemed to be everywhere. When John expressed surprise at the number of vehicles, Jurua shrugged and said, "They say there are almost a million cars on the roads in this country, and we seem to have more than our share; probably because we are close to the city of Detroit, where most of them are made by Mr. Ford."

John quickly concluded that Krakow, Berlin, Bremen, Buenos Aires, and all the other cities he had been in were nothing compared to Chicago. As they rode through the city with Jurua pointing out various sites and occasionally waving to people on the street, he also concluded that this was a man of substance and someone he could trust. And he was impressed that the son of an immigrant could have achieved such success in America.

At Jurua's office, they quickly got down to business. "It seems to me," Jurua began, "that we have three or four things to accomplish for you here, and I have taken the liberty of beginning some of those things, though obviously the decisions are yours to make. And if there are other things that concern you and that I can help with here, we will do those as well. Let us talk first about your further travels to Minneapolis."

John nodded. "Yes, I am anxious to get there. Chicago is, I can tell, a wonderful place that I would like to see more of, but perhaps that is for some day in the future. I would like to leave for Minneapolis as soon as possible."

"I thought as much. There are a number of trains that travel between the two cities. The Chicago, Milwaukee, St. Paul and Pacific Railroad — which most people just call the Milwaukee Road — has overnight train service, similar to what you were just on from New Orleans, that leaves late every afternoon from the Union Depot, which is another railroad station located just a few blocks from here. We could get you a ticket on that train leaving as soon as tomorrow if you like."

"If you believe that is the best way for me to travel, then I should do that. Where do I purchase a ticket?"

"Mike will be up here shortly after he parks and secures the car. He can walk to the ticket booth and purchase that while we are talking. Do you have U.S. dollars? I am not sure of the exact ticket price, but he can buy the ticket and then you can repay him."

"I also have some Argentinean pesos that Rusnacko advised me I should exchange for American money when I arrived in Chicago. Where is the best place for me to do that? Or should I wait until I reach Minneapolis?"

"We can do that here. There is a bank in the building that handles this law firm's banking and also does foreign exchange." Jurua glanced at his pocketwatch. "They are open still. It will take just a few minutes, and we can do that now."

They went down a flight of stairs to the bank, where John's remaining ninety-five pesos were quickly exchanged for U.S. dollars. Since the exchange rate was nearly the same as in New Orleans, he felt that he had been treated fairly in both banks. When they returned to the office, they found Mike sitting in the lobby, and Jurua dispatched him to the Union Depot to purchase a ticket on the late Tuesday train to Minneapolis.

After Mike had left, they returned to Jurua's office where he began rummaging about in the papers on his desk. Looking up at John, he said "I have a couple of things I need to find here before … ah, here's one of them, a letter you wrote to me in October." Glancing at the letter, he continued, "You wrote here about your Maria — my six-year-old daughter also is named Maria — following you to America and about sending her some of your money to help pay her way. You certainly have enough to do that, but it may also be possible to just buy her steamship ticket and send that to her, particularly if you know when she would be leaving Bremen — I'm assuming she would depart from Bremen as you did. It might be safer than just sending her a lot of extra money that she would have to carry on her travels."

"I am afraid that I am not at all sure when she would be leaving," John said slowly. "She is waiting to hear from me that I have arrived in Minneapolis before she sets out from Važec. And there are some other considerations involved, including the death of her mother not too long ago. Can a ticket be sent to her? What do you think best? How long will it take to send something to her?"

"It depends. Wait here a moment while I make a telephone call."

Jurua left his office and was gone for about ten minutes. When he returned, he was followed by a secretary carrying a tray with a teapot and two cups.

"The tea is not exactly the best," Jurua said after the secretary had left, "but it is hot. I just talked to Mr. Misalko at the Skala Bank, named for its founder, Frank Skala. It is a private bank and steamship ticket office that often works with Czech, Slovak, and other immigrants with regard to bringing relatives to the United States. He will be here at ten o'clock tomorrow morning and we can talk to him about what is best in Maria's case. He assures me that once we decide that, they can begin the process right away, before you leave tomorrow evening."

"Thank you very much, that is an enormous relief to me," John said. After a moment's hesitation, he decided to speak frankly about his correspondence with Maria and the uncertainty that had crept into their plans and her travel to join him.

Jurua listened attentively and patiently, stirring milk into his tea until it turned a light mud color and occasionally asking a question. When John finished, Jurua sipped his tea slowly before putting the cup down.

"I would guess such hesitancy after such a long period of time is something to be expected. And certainly her family situation has introduced concerns that, I am sure, neither one of you had thought of or imagined before you left Važec. I would suggest that we — you — go ahead along the lines you had originally planned. A good amount of time, almost a year it seems, has passed since her mother died. In addition, the news that you are actually here may relieve many of her doubts."

"I think," Jurua continued, "that it would be best for you to write to her from here so that we can post such a letter before you leave tomorrow. I say that because in that letter, and after we meet with Misalko, you will want to let her know about what is going to happen. I suggest that perhaps this evening you might write to her about, well, all those things you may want to write to her about, and leave space at the end so that after we talk with Misalko you can then add instructions to her about tickets or money or whatever, depending on what you decide. You need, I believe, to relieve some of her concerns and give her a definite plan she can act on."

"That is what I have been thinking," John said, "and it is a comfort to hear you reach that same conclusion. I will write such a letter. Also, I need to find a place to stay tonight, if you have any suggestions."

"Ah! That is the other thing on my list. Onchek, Mike, has an apartment across the river, maybe six or seven blocks from here. An easy walk, even — " Jurua gestured at the gray skies outside the window. " — in this rain. He lives alone but has an extra bed and is happy to have you spend the night there. And while I have appointments tomorrow afternoon and will not be able to go to the train station with you, Mike will—just to be sure you get off well and to help if there are any last-minute changes."

"If Mike will have me as a guest, that would be wonderful, and I would be grateful."

"He will: it was his idea. And" Jurua said as there was a light knocking on the office door, "I suspect that is him, and you can thank him yourself."

Mike had John's ticket on the Tuesday *Pioneer Limited* for Minneapolis, and the two of them were soon off walking through a drizzling rain to Mike's apartment. Their walk took them under the noisy tracks of the trains that ran through the city.

"They call the trains 'the L' because they're elevated," Mike observed with a grin. "Without them, there would be even more carriages and cars on the street, and you couldn't get anywhere."

"There seem," John said as they came up to a large crowd waiting on a corner for the traffic to pass, "to be just thousands and thousands of people here."

Mike grinned again. "That used to be true. Now there are over two *million* people in this city, and it certainly isn't through growing."

They had an inexpensive dinner at a small neighborhood restaurant that John insisted on paying for with his new American dollars. After they returned to Mike's apartment, he sat up late by the kitchen table writing a five-page letter to Maria, carefully leaving most of the last page for the material he would add in the morning.

<hr />

Mr. Misalko arrived at Jurua's office at the stroke of ten o'clock the following morning and outlined the options John had with regard to Maria.

"If you want my advice," he concluded, "and since you don't know either exactly how much money Maria will have to start her journey or exactly when she will be in Bremerhaven to depart for the United States, I suggest two things. Send her a small but useful amount of money with your letter. At the same time, purchase an open ticket on the Norddeutscher-Lloyd Lines for either second- or third-class passage, whichever you prefer, from Bremerhaven to New York; such a ticket can be used for any available sailing for a year after it is issued. I can issue such a ticket through our bank and provide you with a receipt that you can send to her and that she can present to the Norddeutscher-Lloyd agent in Bremen or Bremerhaven. They will then give her a ticket on their first available sailing. We have done this many times and do it through the Norddeutscher-Lloyd office in New York so there are no mistakes. I can also help you in writing what you need to include in your letter to her."

John looked over at Jurua, who nodded and said, "I believe that is good advice and the safest way to do this. Just sending a large amount of money can be risky."

"All right," John agreed. "How long will it take to do this?"

"Not long at all," Misalko replied as he opened his briefcase. "I thought you might choose this route, so I have brought all the paperwork with me, including that which will be needed by Norddeutscher-Lloyd."

It took less than an hour. John paid for the ticket, and then sat for some time adding the information Misalko gave him to the letter. He wrote carefully, being sure in his own mind that all would be clear to Maria. He enclosed the money and the receipt, sealed the envelope, and checked the address for the third time. At Misalko's suggestion, he used Jurua and his law firm as the return address.

"If you like, I will see that your letter is posted with our firm mail when it goes out today," Jurua said after Misalko had left. "I would also offer two other bits of advice. One is that, in let us say a week, you should write to Maria again, alerting her to the letter you wrote today. That should reach her after the time when this letter should arrive. In that second letter, you tell her to write to you immediately if she has not yet received this first letter. Give her an address in Minneapolis where she can write to you to confirm she has received the receipt and instructions or to let you know they have not arrived. If, by the way, she writes to say the receipt, money, and instructions have not arrived, then you should contact me immediately … and you also should contact me immediately if, heaven forbid, she writes to say she has decided not to join you here. My second piece of advice relates to the money you still have. It is, for a recent immigrant, a fair amount of money. I would not tell anyone, including those others you know in Minneapolis, exactly how much."

"I will write that second letter to Maria … and I understand what you mean about the money. I guess I am fortunate to have what I do at this time."

"You are," Jurua said, "and I am sure you will do fine in your new country. Do you have some specific people, one or two, who you know in Minneapolis that would meet you at the train? If so, I can telegraph those I know in Minneapolis and have them carry the message to your friends about the train and its arrival time."

"There are some who live in what is called the Bohemian Flats area of the city, particularly Michal Busova and Samuel Pavel."

"The telegram," Jurua said as he made notes on a small pad, "will go in an hour and should be delivered to them today."

They talked for a while—about Jurua's father and John's time in Argentina—before Mike Onchek came to the office. To John's thanks as they parted, Jurua shrugged and said, "My thanks will come when you write to tell me that Maria has arrived and you have been married and are starting your new life together."

Later that afternoon, after a small lunch at Mike's apartment, they walked to the Union Depot, where John found himself saying goodbye to yet another person who had helped him along the way.

The *Pioneer Limited* left the station a few minutes late, headed north into a rainbow at the end of an afternoon of drizzle and showers. It was yet another, though the last, of many trains Jan had ridden on his long journey … a journey that, improbable as it had seemed at times during the last two years, was rushing, literally on track, toward its intended end.

The Pullman car seats were comfortable, and again he had a pair to himself. He was at the window on the left side, facing forward with the late-afternoon sun in the distance to his left. As the train traveled through the low rolling hills of northern Illinois and into southern Wisconsin, he had on his lap a map that Mike had given him covering the two states, and with a pencil he marked each town on the map as the train passed through.

He enjoyed the sound and slight sway of the train and the long blasts of the whistle as it approached crossings with country roads. He found he was thinking along a totally different line than he had on Sunday while heading north from New Orleans. Then, he had focused on scenes and memories from his long journey. Now the thoughts were a mixture of worry and anticipation: making contact and fitting in with the Slovak community in Minneapolis, what sort of work he could find there, how long he could reasonably live with others before finding a place to live on his own and what sort of place that might be, writing the second letter to Maria; the wait there would be before she arrived — and what he would do if now, for whatever reason, she wouldn't come. Looking out the window and to what lay ahead tomorrow, he knew that while his ultimate destination was just hours away, there was no answer to the question of whether his real dream would be realized.

Chapter 26

Chicago

To the north, the *Pioneer Limited* was slowing down as it approached the station in Kenosha, Wisconsin. Back in Chicago, Andrew Jurua said good night to his secretary as she left for the day, loosened his tie, unbuttoned his vest, and turned to the stack of mail on his desk.

He appreciated the gentlemanly pace of the practice of commercial and business law. Exchanges with clients, as well as those with opposing counsel on less than urgent matters, even in the early stages of potential litigation, were typically conducted by mail. As a result, much of the progress and pace of Chicago's legal business was dictated by the speed of the postal service. It was fairly normal within the central business district, and except for Special Delivery items, for delivery of standard mail to take two, sometimes three days. Courtesy required allowing the busy recipient at least three or four days—more in complicated matters where research was necessary—to formulate and compose an appropriate, reasoned response. And another couple of days would be required and expected for the mailing and delivery of that response. So it was not unusual, unless one was expecting something of an especially urgent nature, to turn to the incoming mail only at the end of the day or even to let it accumulate for a day or two.

It was his usual practice to just work through a stack of mail from top to bottom, but for some reason this afternoon, he thumbed through the stack until he reached a thick, faded-yellow envelope with postage stamps featuring the unmistakable visage of the Habsburg Emperor Franz Josef. The two letters inside were written in Slovak on crinkled, slightly stiff vellum. He carefully unfolded the sheets, laid them on his desk, and smoothed them flat with the palm of his hand. The ink was a light blue and the writing precise. The first letter was addressed to him.

27 January
Mr. Jurua:

My name is Maria Kresiak, and I am intended to be married to Jan Brozek, an immigrant to America who is presently in Buenos Aires, Argentina, and who has given me your name and address as a person through whom he may be contacted in the United States of America.

To my knowledge, Jan will soon be leaving Argentina to travel to Chicago through the American seaport of New Orleans. I have written a letter to him and sent it to his address in Buenos Aires but am uncertain of the exact date when he will be leaving that city and whether it will reach him before he departs on his journey to Chicago. I have, because of that, made a second copy of that letter and enclose it in this same envelope. I would humbly presume to ask you to give this letter to Jan when he arrives in your city. It is a major favor, which I hesitate to ask of you, but I believe this letter will be of interest and importance to him, and I know of no other address in America to which I can send this. I would beg your assistance in the safekeeping of this letter and delivery of it to Jan when he arrives in your city.

God bless you for your help.
Maria Kresiak

Jurua glanced at the second, much longer letter. It was not addressed to him and was obviously personal correspondence, though it was not separately sealed. If John were still en route from New Orleans, he would set the letter aside unread and give it to him when he arrived. But John had arrived, passed through, and was now well on his way to Minneapolis. And because he had passed through, the circumstances had changed. They had had a frank conversation the previous afternoon in which John had confided in him about the uncertain situation involving Maria, which included more than a shred of doubt — if not fear — about whether she would be traveling, soon or ever, to join him. He had sought, and taken, Jurua's advice as to what to do next.

As a result of that conversation and the lack of any recent word from Maria, they had worked out a plan, a large part of which included the letter, ticket receipt, and money that were sitting in the firm's outbound mailbox. Whether that plan was still appropriate, and whether John's letter should have been differently worded, might be significantly affected by this letter from Maria — a letter that was simply too long not to shed some light on the uncertainties and might clear them up completely.

He looked up at the Regulator clock ticking quietly on the opposite wall: the firm mail would punctually, as it was every day, be taken to the post office in a half hour. The time element certainly wasn't determinative of what was proper in the case of this letter, but it did have a bearing.

Of greater import, he concluded as he picked the letter up, was the fact that though there was no retainer and certainly no fee, John was his client, and he could not ignore his client's best interests when something affecting those interests and the advice he had given his client was right in front of him.

27 January

Dear Jan:

It was so very wonderful to receive your letter of October and the news of your decision to travel to Chicago by way of New Orleans. I wonder at your patience with all the changes in our plans and with all you have gone through. And your patience with me is no less a wonder.

Much has happened since I wrote to you in October – and I believe you had not received that letter when you wrote to me in the same month. Some sad news you may not be aware of involves the death of your friend Johan Schmidt. He died after a short illness in early October of this past year, though it was some few weeks before anyone here in Važec knew of the death. It became generally known only when his wife Katrina came to visit your father and bring him a collection of pipes that Johan had wished her to give to your father and to you.

My father was at your parents' house visiting after church services on the Sunday afternoon when Katrina arrived. She stayed throughout the day and the evening meal, and left to walk back to Východná as it was getting dark. My father would not hear of her walking home alone. He took a lantern and walked with her to Východná and then turned around and walked back home alone that night. It was very, very long after midnight when he returned home. It was but the first of many walks my father would make to Východná. He said he needed the exercise. Your father scoffed and thought otherwise. He proved correct.

The holy season here, as was the entire month of December, was marked by such heavy snow! It was difficult to move about the village at times and the snow and freezing damaged a number of homes, but Christmas Eve and Christmas Day were still exceptional times for many reasons. One of those was that Katrina came to stay for Christmas – and on Christmas Day, my father announced to myself and my brothers and sister that he and Katrina would be married in March! We were all so happy. He has changed from what he was after mother's death when he seemed lost and at times alone in his thoughts, far away from us. Katrina has made his life alive again in ways it is hard to describe, and she is such a wonderful and talented woman. Your own mother laughs and says, "Michal Kresiak does not deserve to have two wonderful wives in his life!" But I can see that she too is very happy for them.

I was determined, despite my concerns for my father and because of my love for you, to proceed with our plans for me to join you in America, no matter how long, or how many years it took for that to come about, but it is now so much easier to do that knowing that father has Katrina and that my sister Andrea will have more free choices in her life. I was very concerned for both of them, but much has changed.

Daniel and I continue our plans to travel to America as soon as you have arrived and written to me. There is no wavering in that, and Daniel in fact says that if I were not to go he would, as you did, journey by himself. Though he would not go to Argentina! And we have found traveling companions in Samuel and Margret Slovaska. They live in Strba, and you will remember Margret as the sister of Karol Bohus. They were visiting Karol at Štrbské Pleso and began talking about their plans to travel to America. Karol knew, of course, of my plans to follow you, and soon Samuel and Margret came to Važec to talk to Daniel and me about our journey. They are ready to travel as soon as September, and though that may be later than Daniel and I might be ready, once we have word from you to travel, we think it would be better and safer for the four of us to go together. We all wait word from you about your safe arrival in Chicago.

I am somewhat concerned about the costs of the trip, though

that concern will not lessen my resolve. The events here have forced me to use some small portion of the money you and I had saved for my ship's passage on other things following mother's death, and Daniel has little extra in his savings. Also, Samuel thinks the amount of money needed for each person may be more than you and I had estimated. I hope you will be able to send some small additional funds to help. Also, since we are likely not to leave until at least September, and now that Katrina is here to care for father, I will work for Karol at the resort this summer and, by living with Samuel and Margret, should be able to save much of my earnings.

Your mother and your family ask me to wish you well. They are writing a long letter to you which they will send to Michal Busova in Minneapolis to hold for your arrival. There is much good news in your family, and all of them are well.

I myself am very well. Influenza has been present and has taken lives in many of the villages here but less so in Važec. The cold winter weather has kept many inside, and visiting has been less than normal. Perhaps that has kept the ill at home and prevented them from spreading the influenza to others. The winter freezes have damaged the church and the homes of some, and if the bitter cold continues, many will run out of firewood for cooking and heating. We hope it will not come to that and are all looking forward to warmer weather and with hope for the early arrival of spring.

I cannot believe how much time has passed since we have seen each other. My heart remains full of its caring for you. And I will be watching the mails every day for the news from you about your arrival in the great country that will be our future home.

I pray your travels are safe and that they will soon, at long last, end.

Maria

Reading the letter had, Jurua concluded with a slight smile, been the right thing to do. He looked again at the clock, though he was no longer concerned about the mail that was about to go out. He reached for a sheet of firm stationery, wrote a short note to John, and carefully enclosed it together with Maria's letter in an envelope that he sealed and addressed simply to "John Brozek, Minneapolis."

Envelope in hand, he walked out through the reception area to Mike Onchek's small windowless office, where he found Mike issuing instructions to one of the firm's messenger boys. As the messenger hurried off, Jurua asked, "Have any of my esteemed partners scheduled you for anything particular or demanding over the next couple of days? Anything that couldn't be changed?"

"No," Mike said as he turned the pages of a small calendar that was open in front of him. "Nothing other than routine business that, with proper instruction, any one of the boys could do. Is there something special you need?"

"Yes, there is. As I recall, Great Northern has a morning train to Minneapolis, and I need you to be on it tomorrow in order to personally deliver this envelope to our friend Brozek as soon as possible. You should find him in the Bohemian Flats area of that city. I will telegraph ahead to have someone meet your train."

"By the way," — Jurua paused as he turned toward the door — "You are to be the bearer of good news. The envelope contains a letter just received from his Maria that will, I'm sure, make young Brozek's day — and his life."

Chapter 27

May 1913 – Minneapolis

The house on the low west bank of the Mississippi River, below the high steel structure of the Washington Avenue Bridge, had been John Brozek's home since he had arrived in Minneapolis. The bachelor Kissell brothers, Wasyl and Frank, were happy to take him in as but the latest of a number of new immigrants to temporarily occupy the extra bedroom in the four-room wood-frame house they had built eight years ago. As with the homes of most of their neighbors, the Kissells' house sat on land that they rented from someone who owned much of the riverfront property that had come to be known as the Bohemian Flats.

The Kissells also had helped him in finding employment at one of the flour mills that faced the river a mile or so north of the bridge. The brothers themselves had worked at the same mill for years. A ten-hour day, five days a week job paid two dollars a day. The mere six dollars a month rent that he paid the Kissells, combined with his own frugality, allowed him to save more money than he had dreamed possible. And two months ago, he had begun adding to that income by becoming the community barber: as he sat at the table in the front room this early Saturday morning, he knew that with more than a hundred men living on the Flats, a half dozen or more would soon—as was now the case every Saturday—start showing up at the front door, ready to pay four bits each for a haircut.

And the house was now his. After saving their money for years, the Kissells had found and bought a seventy-five-acre farm some sixty miles west of Minneapolis. John had agreed to buy the house for $100 cash and small monthly payments to the brothers for the next two years. He also had assumed the ongoing obligation for the annual land rental payments.

His attention this morning was, however, focused on the open book lying on the table in front of him. It was the Brozek family Bible. His parents had insisted that Maria take it with her when she had left on her own journey—which took only a little more than a month—to join him in America. They had been married in late March, but he had only now turned to that blank page in the Bible where he could make a record of their marriage.

As he picked up his pen and opened the ink bottle, Maria, singing softly as she so often did in the mornings, came in the front door carrying the broom she had used to sweep off the porch and the boardwalk that ran from the house to the gravel-covered street. Despite all the things that hadn't gone exactly according to the plans he had when he first set out from Važec almost exactly three years ago, the one that mattered the most, by far, had.